# Lessons

# Lessons

## Kim Pritekel

P.D. Publishing, Inc.
Clayton, North Carolina

ISBN-13: 978-1-933720-08-1
ISBN-10: 1-933720-08-5



9 8 7 6 5 4 3 2 1


Cover art and design by Stephanie Solomon Lopez
Edited by Day Petersen/Penelope Warren


Published by:

P.D. Publishing, Inc.
P.O. Box 70
Clayton, NC 27528



http://www.pdpublishing.com

Acknowledgements:

Thanks to Alexa Hoffman for Chase's wonderful original songs. Much appreciated.

## DEDICATION

To Cindy.
Thank you for being my life friend.

# Prologue

## July — Tucson, Arizona

*"I can't, Dag. I just can't," I cried, hanging on to the side of the pool with everything I had in me. The overhead sun was hot, and it made me sweat underneath the orange floats around my biceps.*

*"Of course you can, Chase. Come on. Swim to me."*

*I wanted to cry but didn't dare, not in front of my fourteen-year-old babysitter. She was new this summer, our first year together, and already Dagny was everything to me — my friend, my hero. She was so pretty and fun. I didn't want her to think I was a baby.*

*"Please, can we just get out now?" I clung a little more tightly to the side, glancing at the ladder just five feet away. I could try for it. Dagny might get mad, though. I didn't want her mad at me.*

*"We'll get out soon, hon. You said you wanted to learn to swim. What happened to that?"*

*She stood in the middle of the pool in her green bathing suit, short blonde hair slicked back from her face, green eyes looking concerned. I looked at the part of her that was out of the water. Would I ever look like that? My mom said Dagny was going to be short when she grew up, but I didn't see what difference that made. I thought she was perfect. She knew a lot about everything, and knew so many games and fun things to do. My best friend Carrie wished she had Dagny as a babysitter, too.*

*"I do." I pouted. I did want to swim and didn't want to disappoint her or make her mad at me. I didn't know what to do. "But I can't, Dagny. I just can't."*

*Dagny swam over to me, stood right in front of me, and bent down to look me in the eye. She brushed some hair off my face. She said once that my hair was the darkest hair she had ever seen. That made me happy.*

*"Honey, you never fail if you quit. But then you never win, either." She smiled at me. She had such a nice smile.*

*"Okay."*

*Her smile grew bigger as she backed away from me again. I could do this, I had to. My mommy got mad at me all the time because she said I didn't try for her. I never wanted to let Dagny down.*

*I turned so I was facing the rest of the pool, and took a deep breath. I let go of the side with one hand but wasn't ready to let go with both hands yet. Dagny's smile widened encouragingly.*

"Come on, Chase.  You can do it; I know you can."

I nodded, not feeling at all as confident in my own ability as my babysitter did.  I let go with the other hand and felt my body drop into the water, the water clear up to my chin.

"Oh, no!  Dagny!" I panicked as I felt one of the floaties on my arm sliding down, my body lowering with it.  "Help!"  Water was going up my nose, filling my mouth and eyes.  I started to cry, and my eyes stung with tears and water.  I felt strong arms wrap around me, drawing me up to the surface and back to the wall.

"Shh, it's okay.  I've got you."

I cried, burying my head against her chest, so angry with myself, so worried she wouldn't like me anymore and would stop being my babysitter. I didn't know how to express that to Dagny.

"I'm sorry.  I didn't mean to, honest."

"I know, Chase.  It's okay.  We'll try again another time."

# Chapter One

"Yes, Mom, my room is fine. ... No, I haven't met my roommate yet. Don't really want to, either. Why couldn't I just get a single? ... I know, I know. ... Yeah, see you guys next weekend. ... I love you too. Bye." I pushed END on the phone and plopped down on the narrow mattress.

I had been in my dorm room at the University of Arizona for an hour, and already my mom was trickling into my college life. She had called me on the cell phone nearly every five minutes on the drive here, which wouldn't be bad except that it's only a little more than a half hour drive from home. Personally, I thought she kept calling to make sure I was actually going to the university and not pulling off on some side road to join the local circus.

I'd thought about going to school out of state but didn't really want to register in the first place and didn't want to waste any more of my parents' money than I had to. I was lucky enough, as it was, to have folks in a position where they could help me.

I was a bit of a black sheep in my family. My older sister, Carla, the apple of my father's eye, was going to the University of California at Berkley to follow in his footsteps and get her medical degree. My father was a pediatrician and my mother, an administrator at my old high school. The Marins were quite educated, and happy to be so. But not me. Chase Marin was known as the "lacking" one in the family. I loved my family, don't get me wrong. I just didn't like the way they felt a need to push me in directions I really didn't want to go.

Hell, I'd made them happy by agreeing to go to college.

I grabbed the larger of my two suitcases and tossed it onto the bed. Looking around, I saw that each of us, my roommate and I, had one dresser and a tiny closet at the foot of our beds. Good thing I'd packed light. As I refolded a shirt, the cell phone ring tone played Beethoven's *Ode to Joy*. My mother had bought the phone for me, which I had been happy about at the time, but at the moment it was feeling like an electronic leash more than a device for added freedom.

"Hello?"

"Hey, babe. What's up?"

"Hey, Mike. I'm just unpacking." I tossed the shirt at the suitcase and sat on the bed, a small smile coming to my face. Mike and I had been dating semi-seriously for nearly a year, and my parents thought he was the greatest thing since Swiss cheese. He was already a student at UA, and they figured he'd be a good influence

on me. If only they had known he was flirting with academic probation, they might not have been so happy.

"Hey, want to go out for something to eat?" he asked. "I've
arranged a party later tonight to celebrate."

"Sure. Celebrate what?"

"Whatever."

"Great. Sure, count me in."

"So, who did you get as a roomie?"

I could hear the smile in his voice and imagined the smirk on
his face. "Hell if I know. She hasn't showed up yet. She can stay
lost, for all I care." I flopped back, staring up at the ceiling and the
dirty marks around the walls where posters used to hang, idly wondering what they had depicted. "God, I so don't want to be here."

"I know. But your folks are happy and won't give you shit, so
suck it up."

"Yeah, thanks. You're no help whatsoever."

"I do my best. I gotta run; just wanted to see if you got here
okay, since you never called or anything."

I rolled my eyes at his patronizing tone. "Sorry. I forgot."

"Later."

"See ya." I ended the call and turned off the phone. I didn't
want anyone else to reach out and touch me, just wanted to crawl
into bed and sulk all alone. As I set the phone at the foot of the bed,
I spotted my guitar case standing against the wall. I forgot about
my sulk and got up and snagged it. My trusty acoustic Melo in
hand, I sat on the floor, positioned my fingers, and began to play,
softly humming along.

As night fell, I finished putting away the last of my clothes,
slamming the dresser drawer closed with my hip and heading to the
mirror that hung on the back of the door. Mike would be here soon,
so I figured I should start getting ready to go out. My hair — which
I had let grow out since chopping it last summer, thereby completely freaking out my parents — now hung just below my shoulders. I gathered it up and tied it back into a ponytail. I stared at
the face that was reflected back at me. Mike loved my eyes; he said
they were an awesome shade of blue. I didn't mind them. I was the
only one in my family to have such light eyes; everyone else had
hazel or brown. I swear my mom and the milkman have some serious explaining to do. She says no, but who knows.

I decided to change out of my grubby, comfy jeans and put on a
pair of cargo shorts and a tank. It was still ridiculously hot out, and
I was anxiously waiting for fall and winter to take away some of the
heat. Slipping my tennis shoes on, I was ready to go.

I reached for the doorknob, only to have my hand nearly
whacked off as the door opened into me. Stunned, I took a step
back, cradling my injured hand against my chest. A head appeared

around the door, eyes wide as saucers.

"Oh my goodness! Did I hurt you?"

"Well, I guess everything still works." Just to be sure, I wiggled my fingers and rotated my hand around, testing the wrist. "Who the hell are you?"

"Oh..." The girl stepped into the room, her hand to her mouth. "You mustn't say things like that."

I put my hands on my hips, ready to pounce. "Like what?"

"Hell is a place, not a word to be thrown around lightly."

"You've got to be kidding me."

The girl pushed the door all the way open, revealing a large duffel bag and two suitcases. She wore a dress, sleeveless, which hung on her stick-thin body and ended just above her ankles. A large silver cross hung from a chain just above her breasts. "Hello." She smiled warmly. "My name is Natalie."

"Um, hi, Natalie. Chase." I extended my left hand, not wanting to chance her doing any more damage to the right.

"Oh, you're a southpaw, just like me." Her brown eyes twinkled.

I looked down at my hand, wondering what the hell she was talking about. She wiggled her left hand in clarification and I chuckled. "Uh, sure." So was Hitler. "Look, I gotta get going. My stuff's all unpacked, so any space left is yours for the taking."

"Okay. Thank you, Chase. That's very nice of you." She smiled again, the biggest damn smile I'd ever seen. What was this girl on?

"Later."

* ~ * ~ * ~ * ~ * ~ *

I closed my eyes to the satisfying taste of the Mich as it slid down my throat. "Ahhh. Oh, that's good." I smiled at the bottle in my hand, having been denied for nearly two weeks. My parents had taken me on a short vacation just before school, and they'd spent the entire time watching my every move and consumption.

So far, about ten people had shown up at the apartment that Mike shared with his friend Mario. They had a party every semester to get things going, and it was just a matter of time before everyone else showed up. That's how we met. Even though I was still in high school, I had come to the party last year with my friend, Carrie. She knew a friend of a friend of a friend of Mike's and had introduced us. This year, she and I were both legitimate freshman. And not *only* was the beer flowing, but I would have free reign of the Mike's pool table to kick some serious ass. It got even more funny as everyone got drunk or high.

Carrie sat next to me, her eyes closed as she exhaled, a puff of white smoke escaping her mouth. She smiled and looked at me, extending her hand. I accepted the small white roach and took a drag, cringing as the harsh smoke burned my lungs and throat, coughing slightly. I rarely did pot, but felt the need tonight. I handed the joint to Mike and leaned back in my chair.

"How do you feel?" Carrie asked, running her fingers through the hair of the girl sitting beside her.

"Okay, I guess. That shit tastes funny tonight, though." I glanced at Mario, who had just taken a drag. "They better not have put anything in it."

Carrie shrugged, her short red hair falling into her face. "Who knows? Right now I don't really give a fuck." She reached over and grabbed the girl and drew her into a kiss, large and sloppy.

I had promised myself I would try to reduce my partying to a manageable level, having nearly gotten kicked out of high school during my senior year for going to school drunk too many times. I had been so ashamed at the look of disappointment on my mom's face. She had handled it fairly well, taking me to my Saturday detention class every time, not letting the lectures get too out of hand. They had done so much for me my entire life, the least I could do was keep my promise.

"Here."

Mike was handing me the joint. I took it, stared at it a moment, then shook my head, handing it to Carrie as she finished her impromptu make out session. She happily took the small joint from my fingers.

More people began to show up, the party swinging into high gear. I downed the rest of my beer, reached for another, and began to mingle.

At the end of the night, I was awfully glad Mike lived within walking distance of campus. There was no way in hell he could have driven me home and had us make it alive. As I walked home, I grinned like a drunken idiot; my mom would have been so proud. Why is it that parents feel the need to tell their children about all the dangers in the world — sickos, zits, periods, how to clean out the fish tank — but they never tell you about hangovers? I stumbled up the last set of stairs to my dorm room, my hand sliding along every wall to help steady myself. I dug in my pocket for the key to the room, figuring that Natalie was more than likely asleep at...I glanced at my watch, then glanced again. Couldn't read it. Hell, who knew what time it was?

After the third try, I managed to get the key in the lock and turn it, falling inside with the opening door. The room was dark, smelling of fresh soap and shampoo. I glanced in my roommate's direction, only to see her on the floor, kneeling beside her bed.

"Amen."

She stood, climbed under the sheet, her long nightgown looking terribly warm to sleep in. Within a few moments she was asleep, and I stumbled to my own bed, realizing I hadn't bothered to put any sheets on it before I had left. *Shit.* Deciding sleep was more important than bedclothes, I plopped down face first and was out.

* ~ * ~ * ~ * ~ * ~ *

Classes started, and as I rushed around campus to find my first one, I realized this wasn't the auspicious beginning to my year that I'd hoped for. I settled my backpack a bit higher on my shoulders as I ran.

Breathless, I leaned against the doorway of Dr. Bordeux's Advanced French class. I had taken French during my entire academic career thus far, having fallen in love with the language as a young child. This course was one of the few that I was really looking forward to at UA. Everyone was already settled in, some talking to the professor. I tried to sneak in, to no avail.

"*Excusez-moi, manque. Est-ce que je puis vous aider?*" He looked at me expectantly. His hair, once dark, was beginning to gray, his shirt pressed and starched, slacks impeccable along with newly shined Wingtips.

"Yeah. I'm enrolled in this class—"

"*En français, s'il vous plait.*" He put a hand on his hip, looking at me with disdain.

"Oh, sorry. Of course in French." I cleared my throat, taking a step toward his desk to explain that I did belong in his class and was sorry I was late.

"*Je vous laisserai cette fois, mais pas encore.* Learn to show up on time."

"I'm sorry, Dr. Bordeux. It won't happen again."

"It better not. Get in here."

I took a seat near the back of the room, my usual location, and looked around to see who I would be stuck with for the next few months. We had a pretty good mixture of your bookworms, outcasts, etc. I wondered if I'd make any sort of connection with any of these folks. I always did that, no matter where I was. I wondered what went on inside their heads, what they were thinking and why. What made them tick? Would they like me? Why or why not? Why were they here, for what purpose—

"Listen! *Vous devez écouter et cesser de parler.*" He looked at me. He and I were not going to connect. I just had a feeling.

As the class continued, I realized that Bordeux knew his stuff and took no crap. As long as I paid attention and did my work, we'd be fine. Part of me couldn't keep the slight grin off my face. It felt good to be a part of something again. For so long I had been disjointed, not caring, or rather, caring, but about the wrong things.

And the wrong people.

The faces of my three friends flashed into my mind, their never-to-be-forgotten names on my tongue. I'd never forget that night, either, the night that really woke me up as to where I was headed.

Brian, Toni and Heather were driving home from Rick's party. I was supposed to go, but had come down with the flu. I have never in my life been so happy to be sick, nor will I ever feel so guilty, either. Brian was driving his Range Rover down the highway at a speed of sixty-two miles per hour, he and the other two drunk and high, a water tanker coming the opposite way. The truck driver couldn't react fast enough to the SUV that had drifted over to his side of the road. The heavy tanker, like a tank, wasn't real maneuverable. There was nothing the trucker could do.

I found out about it that same night, my mom waking me up to tell me the tragic news — not one of them has survived. I was devastated, having grown up with all three, going to preschool together, and then on to elementary, middle, and finally high school. Heather was supposed to follow me and Carrie to UA. Not to be. It took me a long time to get over the loss...and the realization that I would have been in that car with them.

By the time I returned my attention to Dr. Bordeux, the abbreviated first class was over. With my next class not starting until noon, I made my way to a campus cafeteria. Carrie was supposed to meet me, and I hoped she could find the place. There were times she couldn't find her way out of a paper bag.

"Hey, you."

I turned, glad to see a familiar face. "Hey. I was just wondering if you were going to show up."

"Ha ha. Yes, I found it, and yes, I'm late. So sue me." Carrie sat in the chair opposite mine, dropping her bag on the table with a thud. "So how are your classes going so far?"

"Well, I've only had one, and so far so good, I guess. It's going to be a long year. Two hours of Dr. Bordeux at a time; I may just have to kill myself. You?"

She shrugged, the long earrings in her double piercing making little *tink, tink* sounds against each other as she moved. "Okay, I guess. I've got some asshole for Bio. But I guess that's what happens when you're a freshman. God, I hope I get through the year without fucking killing anyone. Hey, you gonna go to the party tonight?"

I shrugged and sat back in my chair. "I was just thinking about Brian and Heather and Toni. Sad, you know? Me and Heather were supposed to be roomies. Instead, I got Mother Theresa. Not happy about this."

"Yeah, it's sad. If you're going to be stupid, though..."

"Come on, Car." I sat up in my chair, leaning my elbows on the table as I looked deep into my friend's blue eyes. "Do you really think they thought that party would be their last? I don't know." I sat back with a thud. "I just wonder about all of us sometimes — the things we're doing, whether they're right."

"Your mother would absolutely have an orgasm to hear you talking like this, you know."

"Yeah, I know."

"Come on, Chase baby. Don't wimp out on me now that we finally have some fucking freedom."

She looked at me for a long time. I wasn't sure what she was expecting me to say, so I just shrugged. "Come on. Let's get something to eat."

We found a place in the cafeteria that sold pizza and got in line. I leaned against the railing that separated the lines, my hands dangling as I looked around.

"So ,who was the chick at the party?"

Carrie shrugged. "Hell if I know. I don't even remember her name. I think it starts with a D or something. Darla? Doreen? Fuck it. I don't know."

I grinned. "Is she your newest squeeze?"

"Hell no! She was just fun for that night, and not even all that fun." She pulled a small mirror out of her bag and looked at her face. "Fucking Arizona heat; my make-up is melting." She pulled out a Kleenex and wiped off the heavy eye shadow before it streamed down her face, then quickly applied new color.

I shook my head in wonder. "My God, you're obsessed."

"Yeah, and?" She put her menagerie of make-up away and looked at me with a dark red smile.

"How much do you spend a month on that shit?" I moved forward as the line moved, taking my same stance when we stopped.

She shrugged. "Too much."

"So, what is it this week, Car? Gay, straight? You confuse the crap out of me."

"Yeah. Adam asked the same thing last night. I don't know. I guess it's just whoever I see, whatever gets me going, you know?"

"I guess."

We finished our lunches, and Carrie had to hurry to her next class. With nearly an hour remaining, I hung out, pulling out a piece of paper, deciding to write a little. No one had ever read any of my poetry or heard any of my songs. I liked to tell myself that I had yet to meet someone that I thought was worthy of that honor. Actually, I was just chicken. I didn't think anything I did was any good and couldn't bear to hear criticism about something that had come from the heart.

I hummed out the music as I re-read the lyrics I had written, words about how alone I felt, about how I wondered where I was drifting to, about how life can make you feel like you're being swallowed up and spat out whole. Don't get me wrong. I wasn't one of those depressed, let's-go-jump-from-a-bridge-to-make-a-point kind of teens. Nope. Just confused about life.

I glanced at my watch. "Shit." Well, two teachers would be getting the wrong impression of me right off the bat. I hurriedly jammed my notebook and pen into my bag and ran out of the cafeteria, headed for Psych 101.

By the grace of God I managed to make it in the door at exactly 12:00. I might have been out of breath and wanting to faint, but I was there. I found a seat in the back row, glancing around at the handful of students that were already there. It appeared that being on time to this class was a rarity.

I took out my notebook and continued to work on my song, staring off into space as I listened to the tune in my head. I could play this one on piano or guitar. I was sure they had a piano somewhere on campus. Or maybe I could coerce my folks into bringing up my keyboard when they came up for Parent Weekend in a few days. It was pretty large and I wondered if Natalie would mind.

"Hello, everyone. I want you all to close your eyes."

My eyes shot up at the sound of the voice. At the front of the room stood a surprisingly young woman. I remembered that I had heard a grad student TA taught this section of Psych.

"Come on, don't just look at me like I'm crazy."

That got a couple of chuckles, but everyone closed their eyes. I kept one slightly open. Did I know her from somewhere?

"Now I want you to imagine that there are no mental hospitals. I want you to conjure up a picture in your mind: imagine that the person you're sitting next to is absolutely crazy, I mean a real loon." Arms behind her back, rocking slightly on her heels, she looked around at all of us.

I lowered my chin to the desk so I could get a better look at her without her seeing me. She had blonde hair, cut just below her ears but all one length. One side was tucked behind an ear revealing a simple gold hoop earring. She wore a light green sleeveless top, exposing tan skin and arms that looked well toned. Her white slacks were fitted without being tight. She looked comfortable.

"Okay, now open your eyes, but don't tell me what you saw or thought of. I want you to think of it as I take roll. Oh, since we're on the subject of names, I'm Dagny Robertson. You can call me Miss R or Miss Robertson, up to you. I'm a grad student here, getting a Ph.D. in psychology. Okay..." She picked up a list off the podium and began to call out names.

I listened for a second before her voice faded out in my mind and I began to try to figure out the feeling of familiarity. I knew I had heard that name before, but for the life of me couldn't remember where.

"Hello? Chase Marin? Earth to Chase?"

My head shot up as did my arm. "Here."

She smiled. "Good to know." She looked at me, her eyes narrowing for a second, cocking her head slightly. It almost looked as if she were in the middle of a thought before she shrugged and went on to the next name on the list. Finished with attendance, she moved out from behind the podium and began to walk the aisles, looking at various people and asking them questions about what they'd thought of and why. I was amused at some of the responses, including one guy who said that if that were the case, and everyone was crazy, then what he' thought all along was true, and his brother really *was* insane. Another girl felt she could learn a lot from someone who was crazy, as she felt they saw the world for what it was, instead of having to live behind the protective walls of propriety.

"Okay. You all have come up with some pretty good thoughts about the world of the insane. What you probably don't know is that about a third of our walking population would be considered mentally ill to some degree." She looked around to see what we thought about that. There were murmurs and quiet chuckles throughout the room. "Pretty amazing, isn't it?"

The girl next to me raised her hand.

"Yes?" She walked toward us.

"So how many of us in here could be considered crazy?"

Miss Robertson brought a finger up to her chin, tapping as she lost herself in calculation. Suddenly, she lurched at the girl — hands out wide, eyes open, and screaming.

"Jesus!" the girl yelped.

"Nope. Just crazy." The TA laughed as she patted the girl's shoulder. "It could be any of us, really."

I watched her, listened to her talk. I could not shake the feeling of déjà vu. It was creepy. As Miss Robertson continued, the feeling intensified. What she had to say was very interesting; she obviously knew her stuff. She was amusing and intelligent, and I couldn't shake the thought that I'd met her before. She had the slightest bit of an accent, one that I had heard before. Was it Texas? More Southern?

Finally the class was over and everyone got their things together, me included. I stood, slung my backpack over my shoulder, and headed down the aisle toward the door. The TA stood by the podium talking with students as they passed. I got closer and closer, looking at her without trying to make it obvious. She was talking with another student, but her eyes fixed on me, and she gave me the slightest bit of a nod as I exited. Confused, I headed to my next class.

*~*~*~*~*~*

Mike sat across from me, his half-devoured hamburger in hand as he chewed some fries. "What's her name?" he mumbled around the food.

"Robertson. Dagny." I absently played with the straw in my Coke.

"So what's the deal?" He swallowed, wiped his mouth with the napkin, then took another massive bite from the burger.

I watched in amazed disgust. "God, that's gross. Your mouth isn't even big enough for that."

He grinned, mashed food seeping out between his top and bottom teeth.

"Yeah, I'm impressed, you pig." I sipped from my drink, my mind still indexing through people I'd known and seen. "Just can't figure it out."

"Why don't you ask her?"

I shrugged. "I don't know. Don't want to look stupid, I guess." I sighed. I had been accused of being a dweller, and my current fixation was proving that the assessment was right on. Finally deciding it didn't matter, I finished my dinner.

Mike wiped his mouth and threw the napkin on his empty plate. "By the way, I talked to Doug today, and he wants to hear you sing."

My head shot up, my eyes accusing. "Mike! You promised."

"Come on, Chase. You're so good. Please?" He gave me his puppy dog eyes, which would gain him nothing, as he should have known by now.

I sighed. "Shit."

"You know you want to do it, so why don't you? I'll be there, too." I lowered my eyes, and he lowered his head to try and capture them. "It'll be just me and Doug, honest."

I looked at him, sizing up his sincerity. "Fine. But only one song."

"Yes!" He stood, quickly pumping his fist in the air.

"You're embarrassing the shit out of me, Mike," I mumbled, looking at everyone looking at him. He resumed his seat, a childish smile on his face. He ran a hand through his dark hair, making the normally unruly look even more unruly. "Get a hair cut," I added.

*~*~*~*~*~*

The garage was small and stuffy, the air hot and heavy. Mike sat with the bassist in their band, Casually In Debt, or CID as it was affectionately known. I stood with the mic in front of me, Melo in my hand, millions of songs running through my head, trying to figure out what the hell I wanted to sing. God, why was I doing this?

"Okay, Chase, any time you're ready." Doug smiled at me, gathering his mid-back length hair into a ponytail at the crown of his head, the hair underneath shaved. Sighing heavily, I took a step toward the mic, closed my eyes, and let the song flow out.

"Hey, Jude..." As the song went on, I felt myself become lighter and lighter, my eyes never opening. I had never sung for people before, but as the song took hold, my hands strumming along, my nervousness died at the tip of my tongue, lost in the words and their meaning. I dragged out the last chord, slowly opening my eyes.

Doug and Mike sat riveted in their seats, neither moving or saying a word. Finally Doug cleared his throat. "Wow. Sign on the dotted line."

I grinned, my shyness coming back tenfold. "'Kay."

He stood and walked over to me. "How do you feel about being our new lead singer?"

I looked at him, eyes wide in surprise. "Wait, I thought I was just coming to audition for back-up." I glanced at Mike accusingly.

"Well, initially you were. There's no way I can let you go, though. Shit, no way." Doug stroked his goatee. A huge smile plastered on his face, the guitarist turned to my boyfriend. I smiled too, not sure what to say.

* ~ * ~ * ~ * ~ * ~ *

The dorm was quiet, everyone wanting to start the year with good study habits and decent bedtimes. I knew it was a matter of time before that changed, but for now it worked. I put my key into the lock and opened the door. It was only near midnight so Natalie was still awake, studying at her desk. She turned to me with a smile.

"Hello, Chase. Thank goodness you're okay. I was beginning to worry."

"Nope. I'm fine. Just had an audition to go to." I smiled as I changed for bed.

When she realized I was taking my shirt off, my roommate quickly looked away and buried her nose in her textbook. "Oh? An audition for what?" Hearing me slip into bed, she turned to look at me again. I lay on top of the sheet in a tank and pair of boxers.

"For a band. I guess I'm their new singer," I said, bringing my hands up behind my head. I stared at the one single poster I had hung up, a poster I had gotten at a Melissa Etheridge concert last summer. That had been so much fun, my first taste of the great one.

"Really? You sing?" Natalie turned her chair around to face me fully, her hands clasped in her lap, silver cross catching the light from her desk lamp. "I saw your guitar the other day. You play?"

"Yup."

"Oh, thank you, Lord." She smiled up at the ceiling. I looked up to see what she was looking at. Only water stained tile. I looked back at her. "Our Bible study group meets every Tuesday night to worship, and we're talking about...see I'm the president of our little group...we're talking about bringing in musical guests to entertain us."

Oh, Lord, indeed! I saw where this was headed and steeled myself for the question.

"Would you? I mean, could you sing and play for us, Chase? Please?" She brought up her clasped hands as she begged.

"Well, I'm not that good, really," I stuttered.

"Oh, I beg to differ. If you made lead singer for a band, I bet you're a wonderful singer. And to have your very own musical instrument, that is a gift from God, Chase. Please share it."

I looked at her, her big doe eyes begging me. How could I possibly say no to that? "Okay. You get me music ahead of time so I can learn some, and I'll do it."

"Oh!" Natalie jumped up from her chair and ran over to the bed, nearly throwing herself on me as she gave me a massive hug. "Thank you, thank you, thank you. Bless you, Chase. That is so nice of you." She finally stepped away from the bed, smiling down on me as if I was a saint myself. "I must go to bed now. Early class." She switched off the desk light and I scooted down on my bed, fully expecting quiet as we both went to sleep. Not to be.

Natalie took two towels from her little closet, folded them both into perfect padded little squares, placed them just so on the floor, then knelt down, a knee on each towel. She clasped her hands together, closed her eyes, and began to mumble her prayers. I watched her in absolutely amazement. I thought I heard my name spoken, then she turned to look over her shoulder at me, that huge smile firmly in place, before turning back to her bed, elbows resting on her mattress. She mumbled on for a few more minutes before startling me with a loud, "Amen." She climbed into bed and not another sound was heard out of her.

* ~ * ~ * ~ * ~ * ~ *

I refolded the wash cloth and stuck it on my forehead again. The closer we got to fall, the hotter the weather seemed to be getting. I didn't understand that for a second.

"Does it need to be sprayed down again?" Carrie asked, water bottle in hand just in case. She had just finished spraying herself down though we sat under a tree, the only immediate shade we could find. It was way too hot, the day's temperatures reaching the one hundred mark, and the dry desert air didn't help.

"Why did my parents feel the need to live in an oven?" I wondered aloud, lying back on the grass, the wet terrycloth cooling my head. We had our usual break for lunch between classes and had decided to have a picnic.

"So, tell me about this TA of yours again. What's the deal with her?" Carrie asked, taking a bite from her taco.

"I don't know. She just really looks familiar. Can't place it. Don't you hate that?"

She nodded, wiping some cheese from her lip. "She cute? I mean you said she's young, right?" She took a drink of her Sprite, then wiped her mouth again. "I've never had sex with a teacher-type." She stared out over campus, the wheels in her mind smoking away.

I pushed her shoulder. "That is so wrong."

She shrugged. "Hey, if she's cute."

"She is." I readjusted the towel to accommodate a sip of my Gatorade.

"Hey, I heard about you and CID. Congrats." My friend flashed one of her huge grins. "I'm so happy for you, Chase. You're so good; it's about time you did something with your talent." She crumpled the trash from her lunch and tossed it into a nearby trash-can before reclining next to me, arms above her head.

"Yeah, well, I'm not so sure what I think about it." I sat up, pulling my knees to my chest, wiping my forehead with the cloth that was quickly drying.

"You're going to do fine; you know it. There is absolutely nothing that can go wrong. You have to believe. When is the first gig?" Carrie pulled a pack of cigarettes out of her bag and lit one. I watched, hating when she lit up but really unable to say anything. That was one habit I was forever grateful I hadn't picked up.

"We have a show at some bar called Gotfry's on Friday night." I leaned back against the tree behind me, closing my eyes. The heat was giving me such a headache.

"Wow. That soon. Good for you."

"Yeah."

Carrie left for class, and I stayed where I was, staring up into the sky. I'd been at UA for just under a week, and so far was enjoying my stay. Part of me felt as if I were in a prison of sorts. My father had given me a stern lecture the night before I left, making it crystal clear that he expected to have two professional daughters. Since the almighty Carla was already headed for her M.D., that meant I could either follow that path, or go into law, or pick some other thing I had no interest in. I hated the pressure of successful parents. It wasn't fair. What if I wanted to be a ditch digger, or just a bum on the street? Neither of these was true, mind you, but what if? I felt I should have that right.

A glance at my watch told me it was time to head to Psych.

This group seemed to have figured out where they were supposed to be at noon on Monday, Wednesday and Friday. The class was a bit smaller than it had been Monday, which was fine, as it was a large class. I sat in my same seat, way in the back, notebook already out alongside my psych book.

The song I had started the other day was there waiting for me. I hadn't had a chance to work on it since. I looked over the lines, closing my eyes as I sang in the dark cave that was my mind, tapping my fingers on my desk in time. Suddenly I felt someone's presence very near me. Slowly opening my eyes, I looked up at Miss Robertson. She was staring at me, her head slightly cocked to the side, and she opened her mouth, about to speak.

"Miss R? Can you come here for a moment?"

Her head shot up in the direction of someone sitting near the front and she smiled at me before walking away. I watched her go, wondering what she had stopped to talk to me about. I couldn't imagine I had already gotten myself in trouble. After speaking with the other student for a moment, she took her place in front of the podium. Miss R looked good in a skirt that reached to just below her knees, a dark gray color, with a satin maroon top, sleeveless yet again.

"Greetings, everyone. I have some bad news for you all. Today we have a pop quiz."

This was followed by the obligatory grumbling and sounds of notebooks and pens and books being taken out of bags or put on the floor. I watched with half-hearted interest.

"This quiz will be on what I assigned you to read on Monday. Hopefully, you all did." She smiled wickedly and walked to the first row of desks with a stack of papers in her hand. "Put this face down on your desk and don't start until I tell you, please."

I moved everything from my desk to the floor except for my pen, watching as the TA gave the front person in our row enough tests to pass back for all of us. She licked her thumb as she tried to separate the pages, then glanced briefly at me before moving on. Within five minutes, everyone had a quiz and was waiting for the word to start.

"Okay, you may begin."

I flipped the page over, afraid of what I'd find, since I hadn't bothered to read the assigned pages. My brows drew together as I read the questions and chewed on the cap of my Bic. It wasn't that bad. I quickly read through the questions, marking answers as I went, stopping to think about one before I circled "A" and moved on, whizzing through the material, getting lost in it until I reached the end of the sheet. I'd had no idea I had gotten through the entire 50-question quiz already. I leaned back in my chair, looking at my handiwork, then looked around to see heads bowed as my fellow classmates continued working. I set my pen down and began to chew on my lip.

The door near the TA's desk opened, and a man entered. He walked over to Miss Robertson and sat on the edge of the desk, apparently in an attempt to look suave. He was an older man, probably in his mid- to late fifties, hair graying around the temples, skin tan, probably from hours of golf. He looked like one of those types. His white dress shirt was unbuttoned just enough to show off the gold chain he wore around his neck, the shirt tucked into khakis.

I was amused to see this man flirting with our teacher. He didn't even try to hide it. I watched Miss R to see what her reaction would be. She was polite, but did not rise to the bait. For some reason, I was proud she handled herself so well as the guy made an ass out of himself.

"Okay, time's up." The TA stood from the desk, turning her back on the man who now wore a stunned expression, and walking toward the head of the first row.

"Please pass your papers up to the front. Thank you." She collected them down the line, smiling at the person who handed her the stack. "Everyone, this is Dr. Sauder. He is the head of the psychology department." She indicated the man who had risen from her desk. He smiled at everyone.

"Hello, and welcome to Psych 101," Sauder said. "You are very lucky to have Dagny as your teacher. She's wonderful." He smiled at her.

*Yeah, I bet she is.* I rolled my eyes. Finally, the old man left and our TA stood in front of the class.

"Okay, folks, since this is our first quiz, I want to go over these with you. These aren't for a grade." A sigh of relief came from somewhere behind me. I grinned. "Yes, I heard that, so don't panic just yet. I just want to see where you all are. So, shall we?" She smiled at the class again, such a great smile, and looked at a piece of paper she had in her hand. "Let's begin."

The TA went over every question, asking different people what they thought the answer should be, or why they chose what they did. I watched her, watched her mannerisms, the way she looked and talked to people. I knew her; I knew the way she worked. But how? It was almost as if she came from a dream, a person I'd conjured up long ago but couldn't quite figure out where I'd left her. I had the distinct feeling that Dagny had played some sort of role in my life. *Dammit, who are you?*

"Okay, now hang on a second. Don't get frustrated just yet." I looked up to see the TA talking with a girl not far from me. "It's actually less complicated than you're making it out to be... I'm sorry; I haven't memorized names yet."

"Kelly."

"Kelly. Think about it for a second. What type of thought process would it be considered if someone were to go into a sudden rage?" Miss R's voice was calm and even, almost comforting.

"This is driving me crazy. I read the text, Miss Robertson, I promise."

Miss R smiled reassuringly. "I believe you."

The girl was quiet for a moment. You could almost see the wheels turning in her head as she concentrated. "I can't do this." The girl surprised us all by starting to get really angry at herself. "I'm going to flunk out of this class. I can't. I can't fail, Miss Robertson."

The TA bent down over the girl's desk, hands on either side. "Kelly, you never fail if you quit. But then you never win, either."

I stared, those words reverberating over and over in my head. I saw the water, the pool in our backyard, the orange floats on my arms...

*"...but I can't, Dagny. I just can't." Dagny swam over to me, standing right in front of me and bending down to look me in the eye. She brushed some hair off my face...*

*"Honey, you never fail if you quit. But then you never win, either." She smiled at me. She had such a nice smile.*

"Dag," I muttered, looking at my former babysitter as she moved away from Kelly's desk to talk to another student. Holy shit! How could I have forgotten her? How could I not have recognized her? She had been such a profound influence on me, even for the short time she was in my life.

As I looked at her now, I could see it all over again, and was shocked that I hadn't picked up on it the moment I saw her. I remembered when she had come by my parents' house to tell me she couldn't babysit me anymore, that her parents were moving.

*"Want to go for a walk, Chase?" she asked, standing just inside the front door of my house.*

*"Sure!" I was so excited. Just me and Dag, even on a day when my parents were home. She had come especially to see me.*

*Dagny took my hand and led me toward the park that was just across the street and down a bit. She took me to the swings and started to push me.*

*"I'm afraid I won't be your babysitter anymore, Chase," she said, her voice sad.*

*I craned my neck around to look at her, dragging the toes of my tennis shoes in the dirt to stop my momentum. "What? Why not?" Fully stopped, I jumped out of the rubber seat.*

*"Well, my dad got a new job. We have to go back home to Texas for a little while."*

*She sat in the dirt, not caring if her shorts got dirty. I loved that. I sat with her as we both made patterns with a stick. "So if it's only for a while, you'll be back, right?" I was filled with so much hope. Maybe I could have her as my babysitter again next summer.*

*"Well, hon, I just don't know." She ran a hand through my hair, combing it with her fingers.*

*"I don't want another babysitter!" I jumped up, throwing myself at her, her arms wrapping around my small body. I couldn't keep the tears inside. Dagny rubbed my back, whispering quiet words of comfort into my ear.*

"Are you okay?"

I jerked in my seat, startled, and looked up into the green eyes of my memory. She smiled as she sat in the empty desk in front of me. I looked around to see that the other people in the class were beginning to filter out, then looked back at my teacher.

"Yeah. I'm fine." I felt really stupid. How long had I been drifting in my own thoughts?

"I wondered where you had disappeared to there for a while." She smiled again. "It's been a long time, Chase. How have you been?"

I stared at her, shocked. "You remember me?"

"Of course. How could I forget Chase Marin?" She put her hand on my arm for a second. "So, did you ever learn how to swim?" She smiled again.

I shook my head sheepishly. "No. Never tried again."

She leaned back from my desk, hand on her chest. "After all the time and effort that we put into it that year? Tsk, tsk." She smiled and stood. "Well, I must say I'm shocked and utterly pleased to have you in the class, Chase. It's wonderful to see you again, all grown up."

Suddenly I felt very shy. "Thanks. You, too." With a small chuckle, she walked to her desk.

# Chapter 2

I sat on my bed with my back against the wall, knees up, with a book resting on my thighs. I decided that perhaps I should actually read the text for Psych. The more I read, the more interested I became. Why hadn't I ever taken any psychology in high school? Then my mind drifted to my teacher. *Hot damn. Dag.* I couldn't believe it, nor could I stop the smile that spread across my face. My mind raced back to the perceptions of an eight-year-old girl who had a serious case of hero worship.

*I was not happy. I did not want a new babysitter, I liked the one I'd had last summer and the summer before that, and the summer before that, just fine. I couldn't keep the frown off my face. It wasn't fair! Carla got to go to camp, and I had to stay home with a stupid babysitter.*

*"You'll like her, I promise," my mom said, sitting in the living room with the newspaper as I paced back and forth in front of her, my shoes thudding noisily on the wood floor as my lower lip popped out, the ultimate pouting position. "You might want to tuck that in, Chase. You'll trip over it," my mom said from behind her USA Today. I stomped to the foyer. She was supposed to be there any time. With that thought, the doorbell rang.*

*"Would you get that, Chase?"*

*"Yes," I muttered, already opening the heavy front door. On the step stood a young girl with short blonde hair, sparkling green eyes, and a smile.*

*"Hi." She knelt down to my level. "Are you Chase?" I nodded. "Well, it certainly is a pleasure to meet you. I'm Dagny." She held her hand out to me and I stared at it, then back at her. "Don't you want to shake?" I shook my head, the lip coming out again. "That's okay. We'll try that one again later." My new babysitter stood, looking over my head. I looked back to see my mom standing behind me, then my eyes went right back to this strange girl.*

*"Hello, Dagny. So nice to see you again. I'm so glad you could do this for us."*

*"Thank you for asking, Mrs. Marin. I was hoping to find a job this summer." Dagny looked down at me. My eyes had never left her, even as she talked with my mother. "This little one doesn't seem so excited, though." She smiled. I glared.*

*"Well, Chase doesn't like change," my mother explained as she ran her hands through my hair. "We had another babysitter for the past few years that she'd gotten to know and like, but unfortu-*

*nately, Mary had to quit to have a baby."*

*"Oh. That's too bad." She smiled at me again. I didn't under-stand it. My glare didn't seem to do a thing. That only made me more angry. "That's okay, Chase. We'll have fun."*

I set the textbook aside, realizing that reading was a lost cause for the time being. I smiled as I thought of myself back then. Quite the little shit. No wonder my parents did everything they could to stay out of the house. My father had worked nonstop, but my mother had the summers off since she worked for a school district. I often used to wonder why she didn't stay home with me. She played on golf leagues, went shopping with the girls, and was a tire-less photographer. I used to dream about going on a shoot with her. I imagined us in our Jeep Cherokee, driving along the highway, headed to the Grand Canyon. My mother had an entire portfolio of just that trip alone. But she never took me.

I shook my head to clear it, picking up the text to try again. I had begun the chapter on sleep when someone knocked at my door. With a growl, I tossed the book aside. "Dammit, what?"

"It's Carrie."

I got up off the bed and opened the door with a nice glare.

"Shit, what did I do?" she asked, taking a step back.

"You knocked," I grumbled, moving back into the room, my best friend following.

"Hey, I could have just walked in." I glared over my shoulder; she smiled unrepentantly. "So, what's up?" She plopped down on the bed next to me, the bed bouncing me slightly.

I shrugged. "Attempting to read my psych book." I grabbed it for the third time.

"Oh. How's that going?"

"It *was* going fine."

"Oh. Oops. Sorry. You didn't meet me by the cafeteria, so I got worried. You okay?"

"Aw, shit." I closed my eyes, slamming my fist into the com-forter. "I'm sorry, Car." I looked at my friend. I had been so stunned after Psych, I had forgotten all about it. "Yeah, I'm fine. Just spaced it."

She looked at me with accusing eyes. "Chase, we've met there every day after class."

"I said I was sorry. Damn."

Her dark red brows drew together. "Hey, come on. What's wrong? Everything okay with you and Mike? Your folks? Mother Theresa?" She waved in the general direction of the bed across the room.

I grinned and nodded. "You'll never guess who my TA is in Psych." I looked at her, wondering if she'd even remember Dagny.

She shrugged. "How many guesses do I get out of four billion people on the planet?"

"Dagny," I said, waiting for the proverbial light bulb to go off. It didn't. "The ultimate babysitter?"

"You have a former babysitter for your Psych teacher? God, your mom really is trying to keep tabs on you."

I smacked her with a pillow. "Don't you remember? She took us swimming when we were eight, and I almost drowned? The summer your brother went off to the Army?" Ding. There it was.

"Oh my God! What is she doing here?"

"She's a grad student."

"But I thought she had moved with her family to Texas or something." She leaned back against the wall. "Is she still hot? She was even then."

"Eww." I looked at her. "You're lusting after a fourteen-year-old."

"Yeah, but at the time I was eight, so it's okay." She smiled. "You know how I love those older women."

"God you're horrible." I glanced out the window. The sun was setting.

"I want to see her."

I looked at her to see if she was serious. Yep. Should have figured. I shook my head. "No way. I must protect Dag from you, you living hormone."

"Fuck off. You're just jealous."

"Bite me."

* ~ * ~ * ~ * ~ * ~ *

The rest of the week flew by until it was finally Friday night, time for Casually In Debt to make its debut at Gotfry's. I wanted to cry, pee my pants, and laugh, all at the same time. I would never forgive Mike for dragging me into this, and I told him so.

"Nah, you'll thank me for this one day, Chase. Just wait. When you're a big star out there, you'll remember when." He smiled and kissed me softly.

"You're probably right, but I still hate you." He ruffled my hair, then smacked me soundly on the ass.

The place was the local hangout for college kids. Having 18 and older nights three times a week gave the underclassmen a chance to have some fun, too. This, however, was not one of those nights, and I was glad. The last thing I needed was to have all of my classmates see me make an ass out of myself and my boyfriend's band.

Doug and Mike had come in early to set everything up. The other band members were steadily trickling in. During our rehearsals over the week I had met them all — a great group of guys, me the sole woman.

I tapped Mike on the back to get his attention as he worked on the sound system. "I'll be right back." He nodded, not looking at me. Pale and shaky, I headed to the ladies room.

It was empty, and I was forever grateful. I went into a stall, closing the door as I sat on the closed toilet seat, my head in my hands. *God, I'm so nervous. Would I be hunted down if I split right now?*

I heard the door to the bathroom open, and then someone was at the sink, washing their hands. With a sigh, I decided to go out and face the music. I grinned at my own joke, stopping short when I saw the back of short blonde hair. My eyes traveled to the mirror to see my Psych teacher's reflection looking at me. A smile spread across her face for just a moment before it slid off to be replaced with accusation.

"Okay, Chase, now I know for a fact that you are not old enough to be here."

I smiled, nodding as I stepped up to the sink next to hers and wet a paper towel. "Yeah, well, when you're the entertainment you can get in at any age." I pressed the wetness to my face, trying to cool myself off.

"Are you with the band?"

I nodded. Dagny pulled her own paper towel from the dispenser, dried her hands. I glanced down at them. "Do you always wash your hands *before* you go to the bathroom?"

She smiled. "Ha ha. No, someone decided to spill a drink on me out there."

"That wasn't very nice." I suppressed a smile and concentrated on washing my own hands.

She looked at me, shaking her head. "I can't believe you're standing here in front of me, all grown up. I know I keep saying that; it's just amazing."

I grinned. "Tell me about it. Imagine my shock."

She looked at me from my boots up to my jeans and tank, and finally, my face. "I can't believe how tall you've gotten. The last time I saw you, I could use the top of your head for an armrest."

I smiled, proud for some reason. I looked down at her. "I bet I could try that trick now."

She glared, then smiled. "I'd better go. My friends are going to wonder if I fell in. Good luck out there. A little birdy told me you guys are quite good." With one last smile, she walked out the door.

I walked up the stairs to the stage, looking out at the dark bar. With the lights aimed at the stage, it was hard to see much of anything except for the smoke swirling in the beams of light. We hadn't been introduced yet, so I had a few seconds. I just prayed I'd remember the words to the songs.

"Hello, everyone, and welcome to Gotfry's. We've got a special treat for you. Casually In Debt, a local band, will be rocking you tonight." The crowd in the bar cheered; high pitched whistles came at me from everywhere. "Okay, okay, hold it down. Save it for the lady." The announcer/bartender Greg smiled and winked at me. "Here's CID, with their lead singer debuting with us tonight, Chase Marin." That was my cue. I stepped up to the mic, Melo in hand. The whistles started all over again. "It's all yours. Good luck, guys." Greg turned to all the guys behind me and smiled as he headed off the stage.

I looked out, shading my eyes with my hand, which was probably a mistake. When I cut the light, I could see everyone staring at me expectantly. Gulp.

"Um, hi." *Real slick, Chase.* "This is my first time performing, so give me a break, huh?" More whistling.

"Come on! Sing already," someone yelled from the back, followed by a, "Shut up, man. Leave her alone."

I turned to the band, counted to three, and they began to play. We started off with a classic, Janis Joplin's *Piece of My Heart.* It only took me a few bars before I lost myself in the music, forgetting completely about the audience. My toe tapped along as the music consumed me. My fingers raced over my guitar with an almost desperate need to get the song out.

The song came to an end and my eyes opened. The crowd erupted. I looked around, nearly startled to hear the applause and yells, and, of course, whistles. The grin on my face spread faster than a wildfire. I reached for the glass of water that had been left for me on a stool, sipping from it as I glanced back at Mike. He was smiling ear to ear, nodding at me. I smiled back, wiping my hand across my forehead to indicate my relief. He nodded again.

I turned back to the mic and began to strum my guitar, the only sound in the place, the guys waiting for their cue. I began Eric Clapton's rocker, *Layla.* The bar quieted down, someone coughing now and then, but I had everyone's attention and it felt damn good.

After a few more songs, it was time to take a break. Mike and I headed to the bar. I had finished my water about three songs earlier and was dying for some more. Greg came over to us immediately.

"You guys rock." He grinned, sliding a beer mug of ice water to me, half of which I downed in one drink. "You want to come back next week? We can fit you in every Friday night. Prime time," he added to sweeten the deal, looking from each of us to the other.

I indicated Mike with my head. "He's the deal man. Talk to him."

I turned away from the bar as the boys talked, looking out into the crowd that had gone back to drinking and laughing. People came up to me to tell me what they thought of the performance or to make requests. It felt strange. I'd never had fans before.

"You were fantastic, Chase." I turned to see Dagny standing next to me, a beer in her hand. "I had no idea you could sing. When did that happen?"

I grinned, shyly poking at the barstool behind me with the heel of my boot. "I've always loved to sing, just never really shared it before."

"I bet your mom and dad are proud as hell. Are they here?" She looked around the place.

"Um, they kind of don't know."

She turned to me. "What? Why?"

"Great job," a guy said as he passed.

I saluted him with my mug, turning back to the TA. "They wouldn't approve. It's just a hobby, anyway. Nothing to tell them about." I sipped from my water.

"I don't know about that. I have to tell you," she leaned in close, "people like you who have natural talent like this make me sick." She smiled; I blushed.

"Thanks."

"Babe, we gotta go. We're on."

I turned to see Mike standing next to me, looking Dagny up and down. "Mike, this is my Psych TA. Dagny, my boyfriend, Mike."

"Hello." Dagny smiled; so did Mike.

"Hi. Come on, Chase." He grabbed my hand, started to yank me.

"Thanks, Dag," I yelled over my shoulder as I was pulled toward the stage. I set my water down and took my guitar in my hand, ready for round two.

I was dead on my feet as I entered my dorm, once again balancing myself against the wall as I stumbled to my room. I'd thought that pathetic sort of display was only for drunk people. Who would have thought singing could be so exhausting? CID was only scheduled to play for one session, which was only just over an hour or so. We ended up there for nearly six.

I smiled like an idiot when I saw my door and managed to get the key into the lock. To my surprise, Natalie was already asleep, prayers long finished, I assumed. Also the telltale folded towels were on the floor.

I leaned Melo against her place on the wall next to the closet and stripped out of my smoke-covered clothing before I fell into bed.

"How did it go?"

I nearly jumped out of my skin as I squeaked. Natalie was holding herself up on an elbow looking at me, smile firmly in place. "It went fine; thanks for asking. Goodnight."

* ~ * ~ * ~ * ~ * ~ *

I smacked my lips, a smile on my face as my sleeping mind conjured the most wonderful images, hugging my pillow a little tighter.
Abruptly, I rolled over as I bolted up, thinking the world was coming to an end. My head shot to the left as I heard someone pounding
on the door again. *What the...*

"Crap!" I jumped out of bed, a bit taken aback to see that I
wasn't wearing a stitch of clothing. I looked around, confused when
I saw the pile of clothes I'd left on the floor. I looked to Natalie's
made bed, wondering if she'd had to get saved all over again this
morning when she'd seen me naked. I grabbed the closest thing to
me, which was a robe that barely reached mid-thigh. With a deep
sigh, I ran my hand through my hair and pasted a smile on my face
as I opened the door. "Hi."

"Hi, honey." My mom's smile faltered just a bit at my appearance. "You forgot, didn't you?" She looked past me into the room.

"Well, I had kind of a late night last night, so..."

"Studying?" my father asked, disapproval clearly etched on his
face.

"Well, yeah." I smiled. "How was the trip?" I asked cheerily,
trying to change the subject.

"It was fine. Why does it smell like a truck stop in here?" My
mother walked past me, turning in a circle to look at everything.
"Do you smoke, Chase Nichole Marin?" My mother, hand firmly on
her hip, looked at me, the lines around her mouth deepening.

"No." *Shit, shit, shit. What do I say?*

"Then why does it smell like you do?"

I knew I couldn't tell them about Gotfry's. They would never
approve in a million years. God, why couldn't Natalie be their
daughter? "Carrie was in here last night." As self-castigation, I bit
the inside of my cheek until it hurt. They knew Carrie smoked, but
still... My mother stayed as she was, sizing me up to see if I was
telling her the truth. My father joined her. *God, they're already
ganging up on me!*

"Look, if you guys want to take a walk around the campus, I can
meet you at the library." I looked down at myself. "I kind of need to
take a shower." My parents looked at each other, that strange silent
communication that I never understood.

"We'll meet you there in one hour," my father said sternly,
holding up the obligatory finger to show me just what the number
one meant.

I nodded like a good daughter. "One hour."

I closed my eyes and rested my head against the tiled shower as
the cool water ran over my heated skin. I really didn't need this; I
didn't need their criticism right now. I finally felt good about some-

thing. Last night had been the greatest rush of my life, and I couldn't share it with my family, not even my sister. I sighed heavily and finished my shower. They were waiting.

The weather outside was turning cooler, finally. I really was not a fan of summertime and hot weather. I always said I should get a summer home in Montana, or better yet, Antarctica. I pulled on a pair of clean jeans and a button-up shirt over a tank, the sleeves rolled halfway up my arms. I brushed out my hair and drew it back into a braid. When it was wet, as it was now, it looked almost black. I looked good, I guess. I stared at myself one more time, really not wanting to do this. But sometimes in life we must do what we really can't stand.

Sure enough, there they were, looking like the perfect couple. My father was a very good looking man, his dark hair cut perfectly, graying just a bit around the temples, his tan giving him a rugged look. He wore slacks, carefully ironed. His polo was blue to match his eyes, the same color as mine. I had never seen a man so picky about his appearance. Sometimes he was more vain than my mother. She was also the picture of health and beauty. She was nearly a head shorter than me, with medium brown hair, thick and beautiful. She had bright blue eyes, and a very trim, athletic body for a woman who was in her mid-fifties. She also wore a polo, slacks, and a sweater tied around her shoulders. Bill and Judith Marin — quite the couple.

"Ah, there she is." My father wrapped long arms around me in a tight hug.

"Hey, Dad." I looked around, feeling stupid. He stepped away, giving my mother her turn.

"You look so beautiful, honey." She looked at me as if I were under a microscope. "How are you doing here? Are you enjoying yourself?" She put an arm around my shoulders, my father walking on the other side of me as we headed toward the cafeteria where a buffet table had been set up for breakfast.

"It's going well. It's not too bad."

"It shouldn't be bad at all," my father chimed in. "Why, college was the best time of my life." He smiled as he looked around the campus, nodding at passersby. "Yale was some of the greatest years of my life. I must say, Chase, I was a bit disappointed when you decided against my alma mater. I had hoped that my children would go to fine schools. I was so proud when Carla decided on Berkeley. Wonderful school, and a great town, too."

"This is a good school, Dad," I said, suddenly feeling like I should defend my chosen institution of higher learning.

He patted my arm with a smile. "Of course it is."

Have you ever felt like you were being put on display? As we entered the cafeteria, my parents both had a firm hold on me, smiling at everyone as if they hoped that their pearly whites would bring attention to their daughter. I tried to smile, too, but ended up avoiding the eyes of everyone we passed.

We found a table and, thank God, I spotted Carrie and her family as they arrived. Her mother and father, as well as her younger brother and older sister, came to our table and sat down. Our parents had been great friends throughout our lives. They laughed and nudged each other and congratulated themselves on having such wonderful children. Carrie rolled her eyes, and I smiled.

"So, I hear you were quite the little rocker last night," she whispered, leaning in to me.

I shrugged, butterflies fluttering in my stomach as the sensations and memories from the previous night came flooding back. "It was great. I loved it," I whispered back.

"Loved what, hon?"

I looked up to see my mother looking expectantly at me, a half smile on her painted lips. "Oh, um, a class I have. Psychology. In fact, you won't guess who's teaching it." *Good save.* I heard Carrie chuckling quietly next to me. I smacked her leg under the table. "Dagny Robertson."

My mother drew her delicate brows together as she tried to bring the name to mind. Then it hit her. "Your former babysitter?" I nodded. "How wonderful! So she became a teacher, then?"

"Well, she's actually a grad student. She's getting her doctorate in psychology."

"Oh, that's absolutely wonderful! I'd love to see her. She was always such a lovely girl." My mother clasped her hands together in delight.

*Why can't you get that excited about something* I'm *doing?* Though I was also proud of Dagny, I couldn't help but feel bitter.

During breakfast, everyone talked as they ate, catching up. Carrie's parents had a ton of questions for me; mine narrowed in on Carrie. I just prayed that they wouldn't bring up the smoking part. She'd kill me. I looked around the room, hoping for some sort of escape, but there was none to be had.

* ~ * ~ * ~ * ~ * ~ *

It felt strange being in the psychology building when it was nearly empty. A few students and their families were walking around, but it was nothing like it was at noon on a weekday. We rounded the corner, and I could already hear Dagny's laugh. An involuntary smile rose to my lips. Carrie had wanted to come with us, determined to see Dagny, but had to go off with her own parents to meet her professors.

We walked into the room to see Dagny talking with the father of one of the students in my Psych class. They were laughing, the TA gracious and friendly. She looked great in a pair of khakis and a sleeveless top, again, the color of her eyes. She absently reached up to tuck some hair behind her ear.

"Well, Sam certainly is a pleasure to have in my class." She smiled at her student, then at his father.

"Thank you, Miss Robertson. It was a pleasure meeting you." The man shook Dagny's hand.

"The pleasure was all mine." She patted Sam on the arm as they turned to leave.

"Chase. Hello." I was greeted with a huge smile, then green eyes looked behind me to my parents. "What a treat. Mr. and Mrs. Marin." She extended her hand, but my mother walked up to her to gather her into a gentle hug.

"How are you, hon?" She pulled away, holding Dagny by the arms, looking at her. "You're so beautiful."

Dagny smiled. "Thank you. Imagine my surprise when I found that I had Chase here in my class." She gently pulled away from my mom and put her arm around my shoulders. "She is such a good student, studious and smart as a whip."

I stood there too stunned to do anything. My parents looked from one of us to the other.

"How wonderful, honey. Why didn't you say anything?" My mom caressed my arm, looking like she'd just given birth again.

I shrugged. I didn't know myself.

"So, we hear you're going after your doctorate?" my father chimed in.

"Yes, I am." Dagny patted my back. "Chase scored the highest on a pop quiz I gave out this week. She's quite the sponge."

"Well, when she was little I used to work with her on flash cards, helped to increase her memory." My father smiled.

"Well, come on now, Mr. Marin," Dagny smiled charmingly. "She's not a computer. It's just natural for her. She has wonderful retention, from what I've seen."

"That's wonderful, sweetie. We're so proud of you."

My mom subjected me to a bone-crushing hug. I looked at Dagny for help. She was trying to hide a smile.

"Are your parents here, Dagny?" my father asked.

"I'm afraid they couldn't make it." She shrugged with a small smile. "My mom couldn't get away from school, and my father is overseas right now. He's been a busy man since September 11th," she said sadly.

"Oh, well, I'm sure. He's a Marine, right?" Dagny nodded. "I'm sure he's incredibly busy. He must be pretty high up in rank by now."

"He's a lieutenant colonel."

"Good for him."

"Well, it was so nice to see you both again." She smiled warmly at my parents. I could almost see both of them falling in love. I shook my head.

"You, too, honey. Oh, we have reservations for dinner tonight. You must come." My mother clasped her hands together as she gave the TA an adult version of puppy dog eyes.

"Well..." Dagny looked at me, trying to gauge my reaction. I shrugged. "Sure. I'd love to."

"Perfect!"

We had made dinner reservations with the Rodman family. I was thrilled that Carrie would be there to help balance out the weirdness of having dinner with my parents and Dagny. I didn't have a clue how I was supposed to act around my teacher. Was this like a social occasion, or should I treat her just as I did in the classroom? I wasn't looking forward to dinner.

Dagny had to visit with other students and their parents, so she made plans to meet us at the restaurant at seven. Carrie and I went back to our dorms to change into something a bit more appropriate for, a classy seafood place. That would be interesting, since I couldn't stand seafood.

I changed into a pair of well fitting black slacks and a blue knit shirt that was on the tightish side but nothing too risqué; black boots completed the outfit. I looked into the mirror on the back of the door, trying to decide what to do with my hair. *Leave it down, put it up, ponytail. So many choices, so little time.* Deciding to keep it simple, I grabbed my brush and turned my hair into silk, leaving it free to brush my shoulders.

Carrie met me downstairs, and we headed for the lobby, where our parents were waiting.

Sea's the Day was a quaint little out-of-sight place that served excellent food with not so excellent prices. As we were led to our table, I kept looking around to see if I could spot Dagny. She hadn't arrived yet, and I didn't want to miss her.

"Your waiter will be with you shortly." The hostess smiled, put menus in front of each of us, and walked away. Carrie was seated to my right, for which I was grateful. The other members of our families were randomly seated at the two square tables they had scooted together to accommodate all of us. The chair across from me was empty, which meant one thing: I'd be looking at Dagny the entire night.

I was sipping from a goblet of water when I felt a hand on my shoulder. I looked up and back to see Dagny smiling at us. I glanced at my watch — seven on the nose. I couldn't help but feel special; her hand dragged along my shoulder as she walked past me to her own seat. I felt strangely disappointed when she did the same to my mother as she passed her. Shaking off the childish feeling, I smiled at her as she settled in across from me. I looked at Carrie, whose eyes were transfixed on my Psych teacher. I nudged her with my knee. She looked at me with drawn brows.

"Stop it," I hissed. She cleared her throat and stared at the folded cloth napkin in front of her. I could see her eyes were still anxious to roam back to Dagny. *This will be a long dinner.* I wanted to apologize to Dagny in advance.

"Mark, Gloria, do you remember Dagny? She used to babysit for Chase years ago."

Carrie's parents looked at the TA, her father oblivious, her mother's eyes showing recognition. "Oh, yes. You used to take the girls swimming," Gloria Rodman said. She smiled. "How are you? What a coincidence that you're teaching at the same school as our girls here."

"Well, actually I'm a grad student," Dagny explained. "I'm a TA."

"Oh. How nice. Do you enjoy it?" Mark asked, selecting a carrot from the appetizer platter.

"I do. It's a lot of work, but I have some fantastic students that make it worthwhile." She winked at me. I smiled down at the table.

The conversation swirled, unabated by the arrival of our food. I didn't say much, certainly didn't start any conversation. I watched as my parents and Carrie's family laughed and talked, my mother good naturedly tossing half a bread roll at my father when he made some outrageous comment. I smiled. My parents had always been very playful with each other. I had always hoped for that someday in my own relationship. Carrie and Dagny talked quite a bit, catching up on what Carrie was taking in school, what she had been doing for the last ten years, what she had done the previous summer. I could tell Carrie was quite taken by the teacher. The whole evening was amusing.

It was getting late, and everyone was getting tired. The bill was paid, and we all headed outside to our respective cars. I had already given Mr. and Mrs. Rodman a farewell hug. They were going home first thing in the morning.

I followed behind my parents, tired from the late night at Gotfry's and the little sleep I'd gotten. Glancing at my watch I realized it wasn't quite eleven, far too early for me to be tired. I was getting old. Suddenly I felt someone walking beside me. I turned to see Dagny.

"Hey." She smiled.

"Hi. I'm sorry you had to sit through that."

"Nah. I think it's great that you guys' parents care enough to come at all." She yawned. "I'm really glad you're in my class. I always wondered what had happened to that feisty little girl I used to know." She smiled at me again. "Just really glad to see you."

I smiled too, but inside I was absolutely beaming. "Me, too."

"Well, look, I have to get going. This old lady is tired." She winked at me, gently patting my shoulder. "See you around."

"Yeah." I watched as she headed toward her car, a little blue Honda. She turned to smile at me one last time, then got in and drove away.

I hugged my mom and she kissed my cheek. "We're proud of you, honey. I'm so glad Dagny is here with you. If you have any problems, you know she can help you."

She smiled; I just nodded. *I'm sure you are, Mom.* How is it that some people can intertwine a compliment with a slap in the face, all in one sentence? "Thanks."

"Chase." My father hugged me, kissing the top of my head. My parents loaded themselves into the car, and I watched them drive away, my hand still in the air, waving.

Freedom!

It felt nice to be alone again, but at the same time my heart felt heavy. I put my hand where I hurt and walked slowly back to my dorm.

\* ~ \* ~ \* ~ \* ~ \* ~ \*

I gripped the steering wheel of my car, knuckles nearly white. I was filled with a strange kind of...energy. I didn't understand it, nor had I ever felt it before. After my parents left, I studied, or at least tried to. My mind kept drifting to different things, so I gave up on the books and brought out my notebook to work on my song. I felt the need to express feelings and emotions that I didn't quite get. They were at the tip of my brain, but I couldn't reach them.

After an hour of trying to write, I slammed the pen down in frustration. I checked my watch; I had forty minutes until we were to meet at Mike's for rehearsal and it only took me five to get there.

There was only Mike's motorcycle in the driveway of the apartment building, which was good. He was alone. I slammed my car door and hurried up the stairs, not even bothering to knock. Mike stood in front of the TV, hair still wet, a towel wrapped around his waist.

"Holy shit, Chase. You scared the crap out of me."

Without a word, I wrapped my hand around the back of his head and forced his face down to mine. A short time later, as I pulled my shirt on, I suddenly felt very shy. My back hurt from the carpet burns, and my body was sore. I sat up with a groan. Mike lay on the floor, as naked as the day he was born. He grinned at me.

"What the hell got into you? Not that I'm complaining."

He rubbed my back, and I closed my eyes, suddenly not wanting to be touched anymore. I decided to start talking to avoid his question. "Remember the whole deal with my Psych teacher?" I asked, scooting away from him and turning to face him, pulling my knees up to my chest.

He nodded. "Did you finally figure out the mystery?"

"Yup. She was my babysitter when I was eight."

"No shit. That's too funny." Mike sat up and leaned against the couch. I wished he would put some clothes on.

"God, she was so fantastic, Mike. I had the absolute worst case of hero worship you've ever seen." I smiled at the memory. "She was everything to me back then — my best friend, my playmate, my confidante." I sighed, thinking of her. "And now, God, she's smart, she's beautiful. She blows me away, makes me feel, I don't know... Can't explain it."

I reached for my jeans and yanked them on, following them with my shoes. I looked at my boyfriend, hoping maybe he'd have the answers that I sought. He just stared down at the ground. "Dagny is everything I wish I could be. She makes me kind of feel like I have the power to do stuff."

He looked up at me. "Sounds like you've still got a serious case of hero worship."

"Oh, I don't think so." I laughed nervously.

"Listen to yourself, Chase."

"What? It's true. She's fantastic. God, to be so driven and so centered. I can't imagine."

He sighed. "Well, I guess it's a good thing you've got her as a TA now, huh?" He stood and went into the bedroom to dress.

I stayed where I was, but lay back on the carpet, hands behind my head. Staring up at the ceiling, I began to wonder about things. Where was I? I didn't understand it.

\* ~ \* ~ \* ~ \* ~ \* ~ \*

I got home at a reasonable hour so I could get up the next day and get to class on time. Natalie sat at her desk, typing away on a laptop. She smiled as I walked in.

"Hello, Chase." I gave her a small wave and plopped down on the bed. She turned to look at me, brows drawn. "Are you okay? I know you're not drunk, otherwise I'd smell it on you."

I smiled, shook my head. "Nope. Not drunk."

"Want to talk about it?" Her voice lowered, and she looked truly concerned.

I looked up at her with tired eyes, desperate to understand where my restlessness was coming from. I was just starting something new. Shouldn't that at least keep me content for a while?

"Have you ever felt lost, Natalie?" I pushed myself back on the bed until I leaned against the wall, expelling a weary sigh.

"Of course I have, Chase." She moved from the chair to sit on the edge of my bed, hands in her lap. "I think everyone experiences this, really. We're at an awkward stage in our lives." She looked out the window above the desk, sighed, then looked back at me. "Everyone has something that works for them. For me, it was the love of God. The Lord showed me where I was straying to and helped me get back on the right path."

She smiled the most peaceful smile I'd ever seen. I opened my mouth to protest, but she covered my hand with hers. "Chase, that may not be the antidote for you; I understand that. Basically what it comes down to is, you have to be comfortable in your own skin." She smiled understanding to me and patted my hand. Without warning, I felt overwhelmed. I grabbed Natalie and pulled her to me. I needed human contact, and a hug from Mother Theresa was as good as any.

"There you go. That's all it takes," she said softly, giving me a good squeeze.

Natalie slowly pulled away, pushed some stray hair from my face, and stood, sat back at the desk and continued to type. I watched her for a little while before I laid back, faced the wall and fell asleep.

* ~ * ~ * ~ * ~ * ~ *

Monday came, and with it the second week of school. Dr. Bordeux was there in his usual militant style clothing, starched and sharply creased. He sat at his desk, going over papers from the quiz we had taken at the end of last week. He looked up as I entered.

"*Bonjour, Chasse. Vous êtes à l'heure aujourd'hui.*"

I grinned, looking down at my watch. "*Bien, j'ai obtenu réellement d'enfoncer à un temps décent.*"

The professor laughed. "Yes, it certainly does help to get enough sleep. Have a seat."

I went to my seat in the back and pulled my notebook out to work on my song. I thought about what Natalie had said the night before. My chin resting on my hand, I looked out the window beside my desk. It was just before eight in the morning, and people were walking around, talking, holding hands, laughing, running — any number of things.

"Chase?" I turned to see Dr. Bordeux looking at me. He beckoned me over. "On the quiz we took last week, you did very well. I think you really know what you're doing. How would you feel about tutoring?" I stared at him, dumbstruck. He smiled. "If you're not comfortable with that, I do understand, but I think you'd be very good at it."

I nodded, wondering why. "Okay. I think I can handle that."

He smiled, patting my hand. "I figured as much." He smiled again. *"Maintenant, allez s'asseyent."*

"Yeah, yeah." I grinned as I headed back to my desk. I almost felt myself standing a little taller, my shoulders out proud. *Wow. Who would have thought?*

The other students began to trickle in, making varying attempts to rouse themselves. I felt strange at having been the first one there, and certainly the most awake of the bunch. I had to grin.

At lunch, I appropriated the table that Carrie and I had started to claim as our own, having to glare and growl at a skinny guy who was already sitting there. With wide eyes, he quickly packed up his stuff and scampered off.

I pulled my notebook out of my backpack. Something was still missing from the song, but I couldn't put my finger on it. I stared at it, hummed it out loud, but nothing seemed to catch. With a frustrated sigh, I put it away.

"Hey, girl. How's it going?"

I looked up to see Carrie dropping her bag on the floor, flopping down in the chair across from me, and I shrugged. "I've been recruited as the newest tutor in French."

Taken aback, she looked at me with wide eyes. "And you're gonna do it?" I nodded. "That's great, girl." She smiled. "Congrats. You're so damn good at it, I don't really know why I'm surprised. But I thought you hated that guy? Boredom, or whatever the hell his name is."

"Bordeux. I don't hate him. He's just a tough teacher."

"Well then, I'm happy for ya." She looked toward the food lines. "God, they're already piling up. Come on. I'm starving." Carrie took my hand and pulled me toward the Mexican food place. "I've been craving tacos all day," she explained at my look of startlement. "You don't mind, do you?" She flashed me one of her charming smiles. I shook my head, glare firmly in place. "You know, I was thinking about Dagny Robertson last night."

Here it comes.

"Damn, she is hot!"

"Thinking or dreaming?" I asked dryly.

She glared. "Ha ha. But since you asked..."

"Ew, Car!"

She laughed evilly, then relented. "No, but seriously, she seems like a really nice person." We moved up in line, just two people away from the counter.

"She is." I looked down at the floor, my boots shuffling across the tile as I contemplated my shoes. I had Dagny's class in just under two hours, and part of me felt nervous. I think it had a lot to do with the fact that I had seen her in a social aspect over the weekend, and was worried what she thought about me. Social and academic are two very different settings. *Does she think my family is as strange as I do? Did she mind my best friend looking her over like a ripe tomato?*

All these things scuttled around in my mind as Carrie talked on and on about her classes and the cute guys and girls in them. My thoughts shifted to Mike. My parents had asked a few questions about him when they had visited on Parents' Day, but to my surprise, and relief, they hadn't asked to meet him. Mike had let his hair grow long, and the unshaven look he had recently adopted would have flipped them out. I didn't need to deal with that, especially since I didn't see any real future with him. He was a fun guy, but I felt alone, even when we were together. I sighed.

"You okay?"

I looked up to see Carrie looking at me, her open wallet in her hand as she paid the guy at the counter. I nodded with a smile. *I really need to stop falling into introspection in the middle of socializing.*

*~*~*~*~*~*

The classroom had a few people in it, but the majority had not yet arrived. Dagny sat at her desk reading. It looked like she was studying. I quietly took my seat, setting everything up for class. I glanced up from my textbook, my eyes automatically moving to the TA. She tucked a lock of hair behind her ear, then rested her cheek against her hand. I noted the way the fluorescent lights made her hair shine, clean and healthy. She licked her lips as she turned the page, concentrating on something she saw there. Suddenly green eyes shot up, met mine. I felt stupid, as if I'd been caught doing something bad, but I couldn't look away. She smiled. I smiled back.

I wondered if she would come over and talk; I knew that I wouldn't be able to stand up to go to her. I felt glued to my chair, nailed to the floor. Why? Why was my stomach feeling as if I had a rope inside that was being turned and turned, tighter and tighter? It made no sense to me. All that I did know was that part of me wanted her to come over, and part of me didn't. I felt the need to keep distance between her and me. At the same time, I admired Dagny enormously. Maybe Mike was right, and my hero worship hadn't quite died out.

Dagny scooted her chair back, as if she were about to stand, but then Dr. Sauder strutted into the room, and she turned to him with a smile. I released the breath that somehow seemed to have gotten trapped in my lungs.

Class finally started, and I made a conscious effort to give the instruction my entire attention. I don't know how successful I was, but I didn't end up in la la land again, so I guess I was improving.

"So, that's the theory behind the mind. Any questions?" Dagny looked around the class, making sure she had everyone's attention. "I must warn you, we'll be having our first test three weeks from today, so be prepared." At the word "test" she certainly had my interest. "Between now and then, we'll be going over chapters four through fourteen. That's what the test will cover. We'll be doing some group activities next week, so be ready for that. I'll assign groups Friday before class is dismissed." She continued to look for questions. When her eyes reached me, she gave me a slight nod and a smile. I smiled back. "Okay, folks, I'm done, put a fork in me." Some students chuckled as they gathered their stuff and headed out.

Dagny remained at her desk, stuffing papers and books into her bag. "Chase, where're you headed?"

Surprised at hearing my name, my head snapped up "Calc."

"Oh, I'm so sorry." She winced then grinned. "If you don't mind, I'll walk out with you. I'm headed toward the math building."

"Um, sure." I smiled. Well, tried to anyway. *God, why does she make me so damn nervous?*

We walked out of the psych building, side by side — me with my backpack on one shoulder, her with her bag's strap across her chest, a couple books held in her arms — neither of us saying much. Finally she smiled as she turned to me.

"How is it that your mom doesn't age?"

I looked down at the ground with a shrug. "I think her secret is that she found the Fountain of Youth somewhere and is now hiding it in her closet."

Dagny laughed. "I think you're right. They're nice. They were always good to me when I was younger."

"Yeah. I know they both really liked you. My mom used to brag you up to the neighbors all the time."

"Really?" She laughed again. "Never would have imagined that one." She gave me a sidelong glance. "So, what do you think of college thus far?"

I shrugged as I looked around, people milling about around us as we made our way to our respective destinations. "It's okay, I guess. I wasn't expecting much, so I guess it meets those expectations."

She nodded in understanding. "I remember when I started here. I was so excited; I'd always wanted to go to college. My mom used to say I came out of the womb saying university. She swears that was my first word, but I don't know that I believe that." She smiled at the memory. "With my mom in education herself, it was really pretty much expected. But then, I'm sure you understand that."

I nodded vigorously. "Oh, yeah. You can bet your butt on that one."

She grinned. "Well, here I am. I'll see you around." She smiled one last time and walked toward the building where her next class was. For a few moments, I watched her walk away, sighing as my shoulders slumped.

# Chapter 3

I stood near the side of the building, feeling like a voyeur as I watched Dagny sitting on the bench, a stack of papers on her lap. I knew she had been grading our tests and I was wondering how I had done. But at the moment, some guy was standing there talking with her, and I didn't want to interrupt.

As I waited, I thought about the night before, and it made me grin. I had gone to Natalie's Bible study for the first time to play my guitar. Even though we'd been playing at Gotfry's for the last three weekends, I still wasn't so sure I would sing, especially with the choices of music she had given me. A Gospel singer I'm not.

I arrived at the place, the YWCA, and set up my guitar and sheet music. There were about a dozen people there. Never having set foot in a church-type setting in my life, I wasn't sure what to wear, so I decided on conservative — jeans, sweatshirt, and tennis shoes. It seemed to work out great. Natalie was beside herself when I showed up, so proud that she had a "local celebrity singer" as a roommate. It took everything I had not to roll my eyes. I tried to smile graciously, just wanting to get the hell out of there.

I hated to admit it, but I had been really charmed by the way everyone interacted, so kind and considerate. I didn't understand it. They had me sing first, then someone read some scriptures, then I sang a song that went along with the message, or something. This morning when Natalie and I had gotten up for class, she smiled at me like I had performed life-saving surgery on her mother overnight.

The guy walked away and Dagny went back to grading. *Oh, here's my chance.* I pushed away from the wall, tugging my backpack up a little higher, trying to determine the best angle of approach. I could check on my grade, or how she thought the test went. I could ask what she thought of our show Friday night. I had seen her there with the same group she was always with.

I sucked in my bottom lip and chewed on it. She looked great in a knit skirt that reached to just above her knees, sandals, and a sweater. She looked really good in skirts. I shook my head, feeling ridiculous, then took my courage firmly in hand and walked out into the late September sun, the air a little chilly. Our overly warm summer was turning into a slightly cooler fall.

"Hey." I stood beside, and slightly behind the TA. She looked up at me, squinting into the sun. I realized I was standing directly in its glare and moved to the side. She smiled when she saw it was me.

"Hi." She straightened a bit, putting down her pen. "You have impeccable timing. I just graded your test." She indicated the papers on her lap. I looked down at the papers. "I must tell you, Chase, you're kicking some serious ass in my class."

My smile turned into a grin that spread from ear to ear. "Really?"

She nodded. "Yes, ma'am. Sit." She patted the bench next to her. I sat, putting my backpack on the ground at my feet. "You did very well on this." She looked at me with pride shining in her eyes. "You seem to grasp psychological concepts very well. Have you ever thought about going into psychology?"

"I haven't really thought about going into anything at all, yet," I said with a sheepish grin.

She patted my knee. "You'll figure it out. So, Friday...you guys were terrific. Your rendition of Melissa Etheridge's *Keep It Precious* was fantastic."

"You a fan?"

"Of course! Who wouldn't be?" She sounded genuinely insulted, and I laughed. "How's Mike?"

I looked at her, shocked right out of words. *Quite the change of subject.* "Uh, he's fine. Doing great."

"Good." Dagny went on to tell me about Darrel, her boyfriend of four years that she had broken up with over the summer. They had met at UA, gotten serious, but then after graduation he had gotten a job in California, and she had wanted to stay in Arizona to finish school. Not interested in anything long distance, she had broken it off.

"That must have been hard," I sympathized.

She shrugged, staring off into space. "The sad thing is it hasn't been as hard as I figured it would be." She looked at me. "Sometimes I think I must be pretty cold and heartless. Darrel put so much of himself into our relationship, really trying to make it work, but in the end, there wasn't enough of me in there to keep it going. Does that make sense?"

"More than you think."

"How long have you and Mike been together? How did you meet?"

Dagny put the test papers into her bag and turned so she was facing me, her arm running along the back of the bench, her fingers near the middle of my neck. I swallowed and cleared my throat. "We met last year, August, at a party he was having at his place. He rents an apartment off campus with a friend. My friend Carrie knew someone, some friend of his, and there you go."

"Is it serious?"

I shook my head. "No. I know that much. He's really a good guy, and someday he'll get himself together. Right now I think he's a little too invested in having a good time." I looked at Dagny to see if she understood. She was slowly nodding.

"It's a danger of dating in college. Sudden freedom from parental restraints, and partying becomes the group activity. I see it every day."

"I think I could easily get sucked up into that again." I looked out into the grassy area in front of us.

"Again?" She cocked her head to the side and rested her cheek on her hand.

I nodded, looking at her shyly. "I nearly got kicked out of high school because of it. Got mixed up in the wrong crowd. Carrie and I, together we'd get into so much trouble. Still do." I smiled, and so did she.

"But you're learning, right? I mean, life is nothing but a series of lessons. What we choose to learn and take from it is up to us." She began to play with the hair near her temple. "I remember when I was in high school when we'd already moved to Texas. I had a friend there named Kathy. Oh, did we get into trouble." She grinned wickedly at me. "Her father had at least two or three business trips a month. Since her mother didn't work, she'd go with him. Well, we started throwing parties, kept them pretty low key for the most part, but one time it got out of hand and Kathy's house was nearly set on fire. It was terrible, and I felt so bad." She shook her head with a wry smile. "I think about Kathy now and then. Wonder where she ended up." She looked off into the distance, into the past.

"Why? When did you see her last?"

"The night of that last party. When her parents got back, they yanked her out of our school. I heard she was put into a rehab center for teenagers. I don't know if that's true, though. Kathy had a problem with drugs, and I thank God I never got caught up in that mess." She sighed. "Who knows?"

"Sounds like my friend, Carrie. I think she's heading for trouble if she's not more careful." Dagny nodded. We continued to talk — about school, parents, my sister Carla. Dagny was an only child.

I listened to her talk, mesmerized by what she had to say and how she saw things. It was fascinating. She was only about five or six years older than me, but I couldn't stop looking up to her. I felt safe around her, as if I could do anything. She was what I wanted to be. I wanted to make my parents proud, see me like they saw my older sister. I wanted them to *see* me.

"Um, Chase? Do you have somewhere you're supposed to be?" Dagny asked after a glance at her watch.

I glanced at mine. *Shit.* I looked sheepishly at the teacher. "I had Ethnic Lit. forty-five minutes ago."

Dagny groaned. "Oh, no. I'm sorry I kept you so long."

"Hey, I stayed. You have nothing to apologize for. Besides, I'm the one who interrupted you."

"Well, I guess we'd both better get going." She shouldered her bag and smiled at me as she stood. "I really need to finish grading these tests."

I stood also, my hands buried in the back pockets of my jeans.

"So, see you Wednesday?"

I nodded. "Yeah. See you in class."

She touched my arm as she walked by me. I watched her go. I didn't want my time with her to end, and I sure as hell didn't want to have to wait until the day after tomorrow to see or talk to her again. I sighed, turned and set my feet on a nearby path. I wasn't sure where I was walking to, but I needed to think.

In the five weeks that I had been in school, and the month that I had known who Dagny was and had begun to get to know her again, I was feeling the confusion of life crashing down on me more and more often. Something in my life was off kilter, but I didn't know what it was or how to start to put it to rights.

In class the Friday before, we had started to learn about word association. Afterwards, as the assignment dictated, I snagged my notebook, flopped down on the bed on my stomach, and began to write. I had nothing in mind, just began to jot a bunch of words on the paper, then looked them over to see out if I could find something in there that was map-like. At first it was difficult, nothing would come, but then I realized I was trying to make it make sense. That was not allowed. I cleared my mind and let my heart speak.

In an hour I had finished two full pages and wanted to keep going. Instead I stopped, curious to see what my subconscious had come up with. I sat up, my back against the wall and began to read. At first it made no sense, just random words like baseball, orange, and Play-Doh. But eventually I worked out the connection — everything I'd written made me think of Dagny. I saw her everywhere on the page. Words like strength, green, beautiful, friend, lost and found. I ripped the pages out, crumpled them up and tossed them across the room. "Screw it."

Moving to idea number two, I grabbed Melo, sat on the floor, and began to play. I closed my eyes and all I saw was a pair of green eyes staring at me. Closing them tighter, I continued playing until finally the image of Dagny disappeared, and my mind was clear.

I played anything and everything that I had ever known — fast songs, folk songs, slow songs. My fingers raced across the neck of the guitar, pushing out the notes for all I was worth. I got lost in it, my entire being surrounded by music, lyrics, chords. My body rocked with the rhythm, my eyes still closed, head bobbing with each beat. The volume soared in my head, echoing through me until I was on a stage, thousands of people before me, listening, cheering for me. For *me*.

I cried out when I jammed my finger into the chord and sliced open the skin on my index finger. It bled pretty badly. Setting Melo aside, I reached for the first aid kit from my closet and dressed my wound, almost shocked to be back in my reality. Night was falling quickly. I decided to watch TV until bedtime.

* ~ * ~ * ~ * ~ * ~ *

The semester flew by, my classes wrapping up. I was excited and proud to be nearly through my first semester of college. In one piece, no less. I had decided that the confusion I was experiencing and all the resultant questions were just not doing me any good, only holding me back. I tried to push it all to the back of my mind. I tried.

Carrie and I walked across campus, both heading for classes, trying to stay warm in the November cool down. She went on and on about the little tryst she'd gotten herself into after the party over the weekend. We didn't see much of each other anymore. She was getting sucked further and further into the party life. She and Mike, both. It worried me

"God, Carrie, please try and be careful?"

"Hey, ladies. I can't believe you're up and actually have your eyes open."

I looked for the speaker and saw Dagny standing with someone. She was smiling at me.

"Ha, ha. Aren't you just the funny one this morning?" I noticed the Styrofoam cup she was holding. "Besides, you're cheating." I pointed to the coffee. She looked down at it, then grinned sheepishly.

"All right, you busted me. See you in class. Hey, Carrie." She gave my friend a charming smile and Carrie nearly swooned. Dagny chuckled as she turned back to her companion.

"Oh, my God." Carrie closed her eyes for a second. "Fuck me; she is so hot. I can't believe she said hi to me." She looked back over her shoulder at the TA. "She's looking at me, Chase. Check it out." She smiled and turned back to the front. "I wonder if she'd be interested in dinner or something." As Carrie rambled on I was shocked to feel a pang in my stomach, almost making me feel sick. "What do you think?"

"I don't think she swings that way, Car."

"Hmm. Yeah."

Only a few of us were in French class. As the year had gone on, some of the students had dropped it, so there was only a handful of us remaining. My tutoring sessions were going well, though I was getting sick of French four times a week. As usual, Dr. Bordeux sat at his desk. I feverishly scribbled in my notebook. The chance meeting with Dagny that morning, and the way Carrie had carried on about Dagny being gay and giving her a chance, had brought back so many feelings I had tried to bury over the last few months. I had been pretty successful, but now all the hard work crashed into ruins at my feet.

"Chase?" My head snapped up to see the dapper French teacher staring down at me, his hands behind his back. "Are you okay? You look so down today." He perched himself on the desk beside mine. "I'm not saying that you're usually the picture of sunlight, but you look disturbed." He crossed his arms over his barrel chest.

I grinned at his comment. "I'm okay, Dr. Bordeux."

"As you wish, but if you need to talk, I'm here, okay?"

I nodded my thanks. As he walked away, I brought out the old notebook again and read the couple of lines I had managed to write the other day.

> *Lessons learned, as days go by,*
> *I test my wings, learn I can fly.*
> *I test my heart, find I can soar,*
> *Every day you believe in me,*
> *I can do more.*

I sighed. *Something's got to give. This can't go on.*

When I reached Psych class, no one else was in the classroom yet, so I hurried to my seat in the back and buried my nose in the novel I had brought.

"Long time no see."

I raised my head to see concern-filled green eyes looking at me from the desk in front of mine. I didn't know what to say to Dagny, or how to explain if she decided to ask if anything was wrong. I had only seen her during class, and that was it. I didn't usually come in early anymore, and as soon as class was over, I bolted for the door. Being around Dagny was confusing me too much. If I just avoided her, maybe my confusion would go away. I didn't even know if she was part of the problem, but I'd decided it had started once I figured out who she was. Dagny broke the silence. "How's it going?"

I grinned and felt the tension inside melt. "It's going okay. Just been kind of busy with mid-terms coming up and everything."

"Yeah, I understand all about those mid-terms. Not looking forward to those. Not only do I have to deal with my own classes, I have to grade all of yours, too." She smiled; I smiled back with a nod.

"I can imagine."

She folded her fingers together, leaning on my desk. She stared down at her hands, then back up at me. I knew something was going through her mind. I could see a question on the tip of her tongue, but she seemed to decide against asking it.

"Listen, Chase, if you need to talk about anything, or are having any problems, you can talk to me, okay?"

She looked into my eyes, trying to convey her concern. I nodded. "Thanks." I smiled, hoping it was believable. *Yes, Dagny, I have something wrong! I'm confused. I don't know what's wrong with me. Why does my world seem to be falling off its axis? Why does your name come up when I think of my problems?*

"Okay." She patted my arm and rose to take her place at the front of the room as students began to arrive.

* ~ * ~ * ~ * ~ * ~ *

I stood on the stage, the lights going down in the bar. We had worked out a heavy mix of classic rock and modern music. Mike began, clicking his drumsticks together to the count of three, and the band joined in. We made our way through music from Led Zeppelin, Skid Row, Barenaked Ladies, even a Cyndi Lauper song. The audience, mostly made up of twenty- and thirty-somethings, appreciated the selections, both age groups able to relate. In short, we had the place rockin'.

We had been performing at the bar for most of the semester, and I had finally gotten to the point where I nearly felt at home up there. As word about our band spread through the community and campus, the crowds were getting bigger and bigger. Tonight before we went on, Greg had asked if we'd be interested in playing on Wednesday nights when it was eighteen and older night. I told him I'd think about it. I was the only one in the band who really halfway gave a shit about school. Mike was edging closer and closer to academic suspension every day, and he was quickly getting to the point where he didn't really care. I knew it was just a matter of time before he dropped out all together.

I finished the song with one last yell of grievance in Skid Row's *Eighteen and Life*. My sorrowful last note echoed out through the bar and the place erupted. I stepped back from the mic, a mile-wide smile plastered on my face. "Thank you! Be back in five."

We had started out as openers for better-known local bands, but now *we* were the main event. It felt damn good. Not to mention the extra money was great. I skipped down the stairs and headed to the bar, craving a huge glass of ice water. Greg was anticipatory and had one waiting for me, along with a grin.

"You guys have, like, tripled my business." He leaned his elbow on the bar as he looked out at the establishment he'd bought from the original owner, Larry Gotfry, the year before. He smiled at me again. "You know, there's a few talent shows in the city every summer. I bet you guys could do pretty damn well." He sipped from his own mug of water.

I shrugged. "I don't know. I kind of like what we're doing now." He nodded and went to wait on a customer.

"Hey. You did great."

I turned to Mike who had come up behind me. Things between us had become difficult. I felt like I was distancing myself from him, and I knew he didn't understand. He was a good guy, but I just didn't feel like I was getting what I needed from him. Had I ever?

"Thanks. You, too. You had a killer solo there." I leaned back against the bar and stared out at the customers. People waved and smiled at us; I waved back. Part of me wished someone would come up and talk to us so I could get out of this uncomfortable position. Lately I'd had the distinct feeling that if Mike and I were alone, he'd ask me questions that I just didn't want to answer. Then I saw her — the distraction I needed. I smiled as she approached, and I could hear Mike cursing under his breath.

"Hey, guys, you were fantastic."

"Thanks, Dagny. Great crowd, great place — you know. All that stuff helps."

The TA smacked me lightly on the arm. "Yeah, right. It helps when the talent kicks ass all on their own." She turned to my boyfriend, who was pretending to study his watch. "You're pretty great on those things." She indicated the drums on the stage behind us.

"Thanks. Excuse me." He hurried between us, heading up to the stage.

Dagny's gaze followed him, then turned back to me, her eyes filled with a question. How could I possibly tell her that she was part of the problem? Mike did not like Dagny and I really didn't know why. Did he see her as a threat? I didn't understand it.

"He's been having some problems lately," I explained, but my voice was weak and the excuse sounded lame to my own ears. "So, did you enjoy the set?" I leaned back against the bar and sipped from my glass.

Dagny nodded vigorously. "You guys have gotten so good. I mean, don't get me wrong, you were good from the start, but I have to tell you, Chase, you are superb. The rest of the guys are good, and they know what they're doing, but you really reach into here." She put her hand on her chest. "You really have a gift, Chase."

I looked down so she wouldn't see the color of my face, running my hand down the front of my tank. I finally smiled up at her. "Thanks."

"Aw, are you embarrassed? That is too cute." She patted my arm. Her hand was warm against my already heated skin. Her comments made me that much redder. "Well, hey, I'll let you go before you turn into a tomato, okay?" She laughed. I nodded, feeling like an idiot. Dagny rubbed my forearm then went back to her friends. I took a deep breath, my hand, of its own accord, going to my arm, still able to feel the touch of Dagny's fingers.

* ~ * ~ * ~ * ~ * ~ *

I decided I needed to talk about how I was feeling; I needed some feedback to understand what was happening. That meant Carrie. I called her up to make sure she was in the dorm and told her I'd be there after I took a take-home quiz for Ethnic Lit.

The door was already open, the music of Pink pulsing out into the hallway. I rolled my eyes, hoping she'd be sober and lucid enough to talk to me. I heard laughing mingling with the music, male laughter. I sighed. *Shit.* I peeked in. Carrie and some guy were lying on her bed on their sides, facing each other. The guy seemed to be trying to tickle her. I looked around the room — empty and not so empty bottles of liquor everywhere.

"Okay, nooooo."

Back on the bed, the guy was trying to run his fingers up under Carrie's shirt. I think that he would have had a problem, even if she'd been co-operating. That shirt was so tight, nothing could fit underneath. Hell, her own breasts barely did. Leaning against the doorframe, I cleared my throat.

Carrie looked at me and pushed the guy away, nearly off the bed. She smiled big, her red lipstick spread over her teeth and smudged all around her mouth. "You gotta go now, Robby. My friend Chase needs to talk."

My best friend rose from the bed on wobbly legs, straightening her clothes as she did. I saw Robby wince as he stood, which drew my attention to the bulge in his pants. *Oh, he's going to be hurting.* It took all the control I had not to laugh at the moron. He glared at me as he left.

"Come here." Carrie sat on the bed, patting it next to her in invitation. She grinned. "What's up, girl?"

"You look like a clown." I tugged a couple of the baby wipes she kept on her desk for just such a purpose, free from the container and wiped her mouth. "Stop," I warned as she squirmed against me. I felt like I was wiping the mouth of a two year old. Finally she pushed me away, running the back of her hand across her mouth.

"So, talk to me."

I sat next to her. *Talk? What to say?* "I don't know. I need to talk about Dagny."

Carrie put her hand to her chest. "Oh, yes. Please. That woman makes me cream my pants." She shifted on the bed to reinforce her point.

I glared at her. "That's gross, Car."

She laughed wildly. "Okay. Sorry. Continue."

*How pathetic.* Feeling sick to my stomach, I shook my head

and stood. "I'll talk to you later, when you're sober."

Carrie grabbed my arm, looking up at me with desperate eyes. "No, please stay, Chase. I'm sorry. Please? We just had a few; we'd already planned it. I'm sorry."

I looked at her, trying to decide what to do. I did need to talk. I sat, and Carrie clung to me.

"Talk. But," she put up a finger, "first I want to run an idea by you." I looked at her, baffled, but nodded. "Well, I can't get that old babysitter of yours outta my mind, so I'm thinking I'll ask her out to lunch, or maybe dinner. What do ya think? There's no con-fic-confle-conflict of interest 'cause she's not my teacher."

I swallowed back the tears in my throat. This was a lost cause, the alcohol she'd drunk had taken control. And how could I talk about Dagny with someone who it seemed really didn't want to hear about it?

"Think she'd go?" Carrie slurred out.

My stomach clenched. I suddenly had a picture in my mind of Carrie sitting across the table from Dagny, talking with her, smiling and flirting. I felt angry, really angry, and really jealous. I sat up abruptly, shocked at the realization. I looked at my friend who was looking at me, confused, and trying to stay awake. I was jealous — not of Dagny, but of Carrie. I didn't like the possibility of Carrie spending time with Dagny outside of class when I didn't. Stunned, I wanted to get out, be alone, chew on this newest bit of information. I stood and headed for the door.

"Chase? Where ya goin'?" Carrie tried to stand, but fell back onto the bed. "Don' leave."

"Sober up, Carrie. You're really starting to fuck up your life," I said with entirely too much venom but couldn't stop myself. I slammed her door shut and dug my hands into my pockets.

As I walked in the cool night back to my building, the stars hidden by the lights of Tucson, I began to think, wondering about life in general and the life I knew. I had had crushes before, small cutesy little things on people that you wish to be like, look like, or want to be friends with. I had had a crush on Dagny when I was eight, I recognized that now. So, what was this? It felt different.

I sighed, filled with so much sadness. Who was there to talk to about this? My family was out; Mike was out for sure. Carrie had hurt me tonight. I needed her, and she let me down. Again. I loved her dearly, and she had been my best friend for almost my whole life, but what was she doing with her life? I had a bad feeling in my stomach when it came to her. I'd never turn my back on her, and I hoped she knew that, but I did need some space. I needed to get my life and future in order.

*~*~*~*~*~*

I couldn't keep the smile from my face as I strummed the guitar, the group of kids sitting on the floor around me smiling and clapping along. Natalie stood next to me, reading the words from the scripture in time with the music, almost a biblical rap song. The kids at this Bible study were anywhere from nine to thirteen. Natalie and her fellow theologians had gotten the idea to start a kid study on Thursdays, and she had asked me to supply the music. Shocked by my agreement, I did it.

The song came to an end, and the kids clapped in appreciation. I rested my hands on Melo as I answered questions about music, guitars, and singing. Some of the questions were actually pretty good, very insightful and well thought out. I laughed with the kids, amused and amazed at their depth, and charmed to no end.

"Okay, my young friends, I'm sorry, but I have to go." A chorus of "no" rang out, and I nodded sadly. "I have to go study."

"Are you going to go study your Bible?" a young girl asked, her big blue eyes expressive and curious.

I smiled. "Um, well not exactly. I have to go study for a psychology test."

I left the YWCA feeling good, good enough that I whistled as I made my way to my car. I put my guitar in the back and whistled my way to the driver's seat. I slid in behind the wheel, grinning out into the night like an idiot as I drove back toward campus.

Early the next morning, I was walking to my French class, lost in my thoughts, when out of the fog I heard my name. I turned to see Carrie running over to me. She finally caught up, out of breath.

"Hey," she said, bending over, hands on her knees.

"Hi."

Finally getting herself together, she stood, but could not look me in the eye. "Listen, um, I'm really sorry about the other night. You needed to talk, and I wasn't there for you." She paused, finally looking at me when I said nothing. "To be honest, I really don't remember anything, what was said or anything, but um, well, I'd like to have another chance."

I looked at her, listened to her entire speech. I realized about halfway through I could smell alcohol on her. It was before eight in the morning, and she had already been drinking.

"Carrie, you have a real problem," I said, crossing my arms over my chest. "How did you get so gone so fast?" She looked at me in confusion. I leaned toward her, looking her in the eye. "I can smell Jack Daniels on you." She took a step back, her eyes drifting again. "You're headed for shit, Car. What are you doing?"

Her chin lifted, her eyes defiant. "And to think I came over here to apologize to you and offer my friendship." She looked me up and down, then stomped away.

My heart in my stomach, I watched her go. I didn't know what else to do. My shoulders slumped as I headed to class. I walked through the door, glad to see that the room was empty except for Dr. Bordeux, sitting at his desk in his usual crisp attire. He smiled at me. *"Bonjour, Chasse."*

*"Bonjour,"* I muttered as I walked to my seat. I was setting my bag down on my desk when I heard the door to the classroom close. I looked over my shoulder to see my professor walking toward me, a determined look on his face. He sat on top of the desk in front of mine.

"Talk to me, Chase. What's been getting you so down lately?" He folded his hands together and waited patiently.

At first I just stared at him, not wanting to talk to him about something so personal. Seeing the expectant look in his eyes, I decided that it might be better to talk to someone who was not involved; that might be the least biased way to go. With a sigh, I looked out the window.

"I'm so confused, Dr. Bordeux. Nothing in my life makes sense anymore. My best friend and I are at a crossroads; I don't have a major or any idea what I want to do, and my parents have put the weight of the world on my shoulders." I glanced up at him. "How's that?"

He leaned back a bit on the desk. "Life can certainly be rough sometimes, Chase; this is true. Especially at your age." He rubbed his chin, studying me. "Sometimes what you need to do is sit back and observe what you have. Find your passions in life, Chase. If you live your passions, you will be a much happier person in the long run. As for not having a major yet, that isn't really uncommon. Many, many freshmen come to school with no inkling of what they'd like to do. See what your loves in life are. I hear you play a mean guitar at Gotfry's on Friday nights." He winked at me; I grinned. "If that's where your passions lie, then go with it. If you find you love math and can't get enough of calculus, go down that path." He put a hand on my shoulder. "Life is full of paths, and each one can teach us a different lesson. It's up to us to use them for our good."

I smiled at my teacher, impressed that he'd taken the time to notice something was wrong with me. I nodded.

"As for your friend. When people come to college, it's generally their first time away from home for any extended length of time. Granted, I don't know what's happened there, but each person deals with that freedom in his or her own way. Time will pass, and it will also tell if you grow together or apart."

"Thank you, Dr. Bordeux. I'll do my best."

"I know you will. I have every faith in you." He scooted off the desk, opened the door, then sat back in his chair, looking almost as if he had never spoken a word to me.

\* ~ \* ~ \* ~ \* ~ \* ~ \*

As I sat in Psych class, my realization from the night before came crashing back to me. I looked at Dagny, who sat at her desk grading papers, and I felt myself blush. It was almost like when you have a sex dream about someone you know, then the next time you see them it all comes back to you and you feel guilty, even though you did nothing wrong.

After a deep breath and a lot of swallowing, I walked down the aisle to her desk. When she heard my approach, she lifted her head. As soon as she saw me, she smiled.

"Howdy."

"Hi." I looked down at the stack of papers that made a neat pile right in the center of the desk, and the smaller pile of finished papers to the side. "More grading, huh? You know, if you'd stop assigning stuff, you wouldn't have near as much work to do."

She grinned at me, cocking her head to the side. "Ha ha. Yeah, that'll happen."

"Just a thought." I smiled, not feeling any of the confidence behind that smile.

"So, what's up?"

She put down her pen and ran a hand through her hair, tucking it behind her ear. She looked beautiful in a mint-green dress with cap sleeves, and a skirt that reached to just above her knees. She re-crossed her legs as I stumbled through the options springing into my mind in answer to that question.

"Well, um, my class tonight after this one has been canceled, so I was wondering if, um, well, if you'd like to get a Coke or something?"

She looked at me, sizing me up. "Are you okay?"

*God, is it that apparent? I really need to learn to hide my distress better.* "Well, Carrie and I are having problems. I'd kind of like to talk. You know."

"Yeah, I do. Sure. That sounds good. I didn't get a chance to eat lunch today, so do you mind if I grab something?"

"Oh." I couldn't have eaten just then if my life depended on it. "Sure." I smiled, feeling like little Ralphie from *A Christmas Story* when he gave his teacher the fruit basket to try and get a good grade on his Christmas essay.

"Great." She smiled. "Let's do it."

The café was bustling, people coming and going in large numbers. Dagny dug into her cheeseburger with an appetite that scared me. God forbid anyone get their fingers in the way. I sipped my Dr Pepper with amusement.

"So, what's the problem? You talk, I'll eat." She drowned a French fry in her ketchup-mayonnaise mixture and popped it into her mouth.

I shrugged, playing with my straw. "She's going to ruin her life," I blurted. "The other night I went to her dorm to talk about something, and she was loaded and had some strange guy in her room."

Dagny wiped her mouth, shaking her head sadly. "So, I'm guessing you didn't really get to talk?"

"No," I said quietly, then it hit me what I had gone to talk to Carrie about.

"Anything I can help you with?"

I nearly choked on the drink I'd just taken. I coughed, beating my chest to help clear my windpipe.

"You okay?" She reached across the small table and pounded my back.

I nodded, red faced and watery eyed. "I'm okay."

"You sure?"

I nodded again. "And it's just something I need to work out myself. No big deal." I tried to smile but wasn't very successful. Dagny seemed to take the weakness for choking, for which I was glad. I really didn't need questions. I was emotionally exhausted. I was also very sad. "I guess when I talk about it and dig a little further into the past, I realize that Carrie's had a problem for a while." I shook my head, running my hand through my hair.

Dagny nodded, sipping from her chocolate milkshake. "Hindsight. We don't see what we don't want to; people are famous for it. What would you like to see happen with Carrie?"

"I'm not sure, to be honest. I just want her to be happy."

"How do you know she's not?" Dagny raised an eyebrow. "I hate to play devil's advocate, but has she said anything about being unhappy? I mean, sure she's not doing what she, quote end quote, should be doing, but it seems to be what's her bag right now."

I sat back in my chair, not sure what to think or do. I knew that Dagny was right, and Carrie certainly had to live her own life, but how could I just watch her fall into the void?

Eventually we moved from the subject of Carrie to that of Mike. I told her how he was letting it all slip away, just like Carrie. "When he started college, he was an A student, excelling in the sciences and dreaming of becoming a renowned scientist, the first to discover a cure for cancer."

"Sounds like me. When I first started with psychology, I had visions of becoming the first psychologist to find the key to treating the terminally psychotic." She chuckled. "You have to love the young and idealistic. As for Mike, he may get back on track, Chase. If you care enough, stick with him."

I sighed, setting my fork down, the last bite of my pie still on the plate. I looked at it, trying to decide if I wanted it or not.

"That's part of the problem, Dag. I just don't know if it is worth it to me. I feel like I'm going in such a different direction from my friends."

"It sounds to me like you're growing. That's important, Chase. You have to grow, or you become stagnant."

I studied her face as she sipped the last of her shake. "How do you know when you're done?"

"Growing? Oh, you never will be. You never stop growing, Chase. You never stop learning. It's a life-long thing. One of the great things about life, actually. I mean, would you really want to get to a point where you stop? Stop learning, stop understanding?"

I shook my head. "It's funny. Where I'm at right now, part of me just wishes I were already seventy years old. By that time I would know what I had done with my life, which paths I had chosen, and I'd know who I was. Now, I feel like such a child."

She smiled. "I understand, Chase. Really I do."

I looked at her, my head cocked to the side. She was so together, so with her life. "Can I be you when I grow up?"

She grinned, looking at me like I'd just eaten a bug. "Why on Earth would you want to subject yourself to that?" She took the straw from her shake container and began to chew on it. I laughed.

* ~ * ~ * ~ * ~ * ~ *

Mike was quiet on the drive to Doug's house. His motorcycle had broken down again, and I had picked him up. He sat in the passenger seat, his hands in his lap as he stared out the side window. I occasionally glanced over at him, wondering what was going on. I knew he had bailed on school for good the day before. His grades so far in the tank, too hard to bring back up, he had just quit. I wondered if he was bothered by that, or if it was something else.

I pulled into the driveway and turned off the engine. Without a word or a look, Mike got out. I watched him through the windshield as he walked up to the open garage door, shook hands with Doug and patted his back. With a sigh, I got out too.

Rehearsal went well, some new songs being thrown into the mix. I did not sing well, my mind on too many things, none of which involved music.

"Whoa, whoa." Doug looked at me with narrowed eyes. "Chase, where the hell were you? You missed your cue."

"I'm sorry, guys. My mind just left me." I put up my hand to wave off my efforts on the last song. "Let's try that one again." Albert on keyboard started the intro to *The Rose*. I closed my eyes as I heard my cue coming, then softly began to sing. I kept my eyes closed, wanting to see the song in my mind, then my mind's eyes became filled with pictures of Dagny. I saw her sitting across from me — eating, laughing, talking. All the things she did when we went to lunch last Monday. I couldn't shake her from my mind.

Finally rehearsal was over, and for the first time, I was glad. I didn't want to be around people, especially not Mike. I pulled up to his apartment building, but he just sat there, staring out into the night as a slight rain fell.

"You okay?" I asked, really just wanting to go home.

"Are you seeing someone?" he asked, not looking at me.

*Where the hell did that come from?* I was completely taken aback, not having expected to be accused of that. "No. Why do you ask?"

He shrugged. "You're just so, I don't know, distant, I guess." There was pain in his eyes. "What's happened to us, Chase?"

I sighed and shrugged. "I don't know, Mike. I really don't."

"We used to have so much fun together. I swear, since you've met up with that psychology bitch, our relationship has turned to shit."

"Stop right there." My voice lowered to a dangerous tone. "Dagny is my friend. She has nothing to do with us."

"No? Then why do I have to hear her fucking name every fucking time we're together? Why is she always at the bar on Friday nights?"

"A lot of college kids are at the bar on Friday nights, so don't even try that shit with me."

"I'm tired of her!" He slammed his fist against the dashboard. "I don't want that bitch around you anymore, you got it?" He pointed a warning finger at me.

I looked down at it, then up into his eyes, my blood turning cold. "Don't you dare try to tell me what I can or can't do, Michael. You don't have a prayer of making any of it stick." I almost smiled, thinking how proud Natalie would have been. "You're not my father, nor are you my keeper."

"Don't you see, Chase? Since you've met her we've begun to fall apart."

"Have you thought to look at yourself?"

He looked stunned, and I felt bad as soon as the words were out of my mouth. Mike really didn't have a whole lot to do with it. It was me, the one who decided to have a mid-life crisis in the middle of my freshman year of college.

"I'm sorry, Mike. That was uncalled for. It's not you." I looked down at my hands as they played with the steering wheel.

"Are you, ah, are you saying you want to break up?" He wouldn't look at me, instead hiding his face from me as he looked away.

"I don't know," I said quietly, not really sure. "Is that what you want?" When he turned to me, the tears in his eyes surprised me.

"Don't put this on me, Chase. It's your baby. Either you do or you don't. Pretty simple."

I stared at him, seeing the pain in his eyes, the rejection in his body language. Slowly I nodded. "Yeah, I guess so."

Mike nodded, pressing his lips together. He took a deep breath and a small sob escaped him, ripping at my chest.

"Mike." I placed a hand on his shoulder.

"Don't touch me." He fumbled for the handle to the door, finally finding it, pushing the door open. He hurried out of the car...and out of my heart.

# Chapter 4

I sat at my desk, my heartbeat finally starting to slow as Dagny collected the last of the papers. *That was just not nice.* My second finals experience, and it was a so-so event. It could go either way. I relaxed for the first time in nearly four hours. I felt faint, but in general just damn glad it was over.

I looked around to see everyone else either looking around, too, or burying their faces in their hands. But as everyone did their own thing, there was almost a communal sigh of relief, a quiet that was equal parts worry, happiness, and exhaustion.

I looked to the front of the room where Dagny was getting all the tests in order, stacking them neatly as she looked out at all of us. She found my eyes on her, smiled with a slight nod, and wiped her hand across her forehead with a smile. I nodded and smiled in return.

The class was over, and students were trickling out, some talking with Dagny, shaking her hand, thanking her for a great class. I stayed where I was, trying to get my bearings. My mind felt like mush.

"You still breathing?" I looked up to see a very amused Dagny looking down at me, arms crossed over her chest. I nodded, mouth slightly open. She laughed. "Come on. You look like you could use a drink. Coke okay?"

We found a small restaurant off campus and sat in a booth near the back. I hadn't eaten in two days, so worried about finals and too busy studying for the first time in my life. I'd had Bordeux's yesterday, and it had been just as mind boggling as Dagny's.

"So what do you think of college now?" She grinned as she accessorized her cheeseburger.

I glared. "It sucks. Why did you make that test so damn hard?" I put some salsa on my taco salad.

She laughed again, shaking her head. "Ain't them just the breaks?"

I shrugged. "All in all, I have to say that it wasn't all that hard, really." I looked at her, fork poised to my mouth. "It was actually quite interesting. I'm thinking I really like this psychology stuff." I looked at her from under my bangs. She was smiling like a kid at Christmas.

"Really?" She put both hands flat on the table and leaned forward slightly. "I'm so glad."

I smiled at her enthusiasm. "Me, too." I wondered what she'd do if I told her I was thinking of going into psychology. I mean, hell, I thought it was interesting and I seemed to be good at it. We'd see how my final turned out. "So, what are your plans for Christmas?" I asked, wiping some cheese from my lip then taking another bite.

Dagny looked down at her lunch, dipping a French fry in her special sauce. "Since my father is still overseas, my mom is going over to be with him." She looked up at me with a small smile and popped the fried potato into her mouth.

"Oh. So, you get to have a foreign holiday?" I put my taco down and wiped my hands.

She shrugged. "No. It's really not worth it to me to fly all that way for just a few weeks, anyway. Probably just hang out here. That's what I did last year." She smiled. "I bought this beautiful little tree; it's about three feet tall. Decorated the little guy and stuck him in the corner of my apartment." She sipped her Coke. "I go all out."

"But you're alone," I objected, incredulous.

"What can you do? I just make the best of it. And I'll have you know, I make a mean turkey."

I looked down at the remains of my taco mess and, without much thought, and certainly without talking with the folks, I blurted, "Why don't you come home with me?" I swallowed as the realization of what I'd just done smashed into my brain.

"Oh, I couldn't intrude on your family like that."

I shrugged, all nonchalant. "It wouldn't be an intrusion at all. We usually just end up fighting with each other anyway. I mean, at least then I'd have someone in my corner."

She cocked her head to the side as she studied me. I just stared, not wanting to lower my eyes because I didn't want her to think I'd changed my mind or hadn't meant the invitation. She smiled, then covered my hand with hers. "You've got yourself a dinner guest."

\* ~ \* ~ \* ~ \* ~ \* ~ \*

I sat on my bed, phone to my ear, watching Natalie as she knelt by the side of her bed on the folded towels, hands pressed together. She had been that way for nearly thirty minutes. *What did she do? Shoot someone?* I leaned back against the wall as I listened to the ringing of the phone. Ring number three, number four. I was about ready to hang up when my mother's voice was suddenly there.

"Hey."

"Hello, honey. How did finals go?"

I rolled my eyes, my fingers playing with the phone cord. "Fine. I have one more to go, but the others weren't so bad." I wiggled my toes, watching them for something to keep my mind busy so

I wouldn't tell my mom what I really thought as I listened to her babble on and on about Carla, and the special mentions of her in the newspaper in Berkley. "That's great. And I'm glad you mentioned her coming home for Christmas, because that's why I'm calling."

"Why's that?"

Her voice had hardened a little. I think she was afraid I was going to tell her I was indeed running away with that circus, or worse, dropping out of school to move back home.

"I've invited a friend to come with me." The line grew silent for a moment though I could hear her breathing.

"Who?"

"Dagny."

Like the sun bursting through the clouds, my mother's voice lightened. "Really? How nice." I could hear the smile. "Why? Isn't she going to her own family?"

"They'll be out of the country."

"Oh, what a shame. You bring her along, and I just can't wait! She's such a nice girl, so polite, and so ambitious."

I closed my eyes. Somehow, to my amazement, I was not jealous of the fact that Dagny could provoke such excitement. Perhaps because I understood. I could just imagine Dag in the middle of my family. The large table that my mom would put leaves in to extend it to its full length, large enough to accommodate twelve people.

"Your grandparents will be here, and Carla is bringing Todd, of course."

I grimaced at the thought of my sister's boyfriend. He was about as interesting as a field post.

After another half hour of listening to my mom run on and on about her plans for the holidays, I said that I had to study and hung up, running my hands through my hair. I turned to see my roommate had finished her prayers and was lying in bed, hands behind her head. She was staring up at the ceiling. My brows drew together, a realization suddenly striking me.

"Natalie?" She looked at me, eyebrows raised in question. "What is your major?"

"Biology."

I looked at her, surprised.

"I know what you're thinking. It definitely goes against my beliefs." She shrugged. "I love it."

I shook my head with a smile as I flipped off my desk lamp to get some sleep.

* ~ * ~ * ~ * ~ * ~ *

The scenery whooshed by as I drove along the highway toward home. I glanced to my right where Dagny was looking out her window, arm resting along the door, window open to allow in the breeze from the unusually warm seventy-five degree December day. The wind was blowing through her hair, blowing it away from her face, her sunglasses mirroring the sun high above us.

"Such a beautiful day," she said, turning to smile at me.

I nodded. "Too hot, though. I want snow. Never had a white Christmas in my entire life. Hell, I've barely even *seen* snow."

She looked at me, pulling her shades down to peer at me over the rims. "You're kidding me."

I shook my head.

"Well, we'll have to take care of that." She put the glasses back in place and turned up the radio.

I couldn't keep the smile from my face at her energy and exuberance. She was such a different person away from school, away from all the stress and responsibilities.

All classes and the semester had officially ended Monday, so I was also like a kid in a candy store, all smiles and laughter. I hadn't expected to be so excited to go home for Christmas, but then I wasn't expecting to be bringing home my psychology teacher, either.

There was only one car in the driveway, and it belonged to my father. I wasn't sure whether my folks were home or not. Dagny took off her glasses and put them on top of her head.

My dad had already put up the Christmas lights all around the place; the little plastic Santa with the light inside was set next to the front door, his hand up to wave at all the kids. Eight plastic reindeer followed by Santa and his sleigh were positioned on the roof.

"Looks just like it always did." She stared out at the adobe-style house to which I had been brought home from the hospital and raised. "It was always such a beautiful place. I love the decorations."

I tried to look at it through the eyes of someone who hadn't seen the house for ten years, and I realized that it was a nice home. I had just taken it for granted for so long that I only saw the cage, not the shelter.

We took our bags from the car and went inside. It was nice and cool, a lot of the house furnished in hardwood flooring and Mexican tile as opposed to carpet, to keep things comfortable. Rugs were scattered here and there, especially in the bedrooms.

"Hello?" I called out.

No answer. The house was apparently empty. I figured they were probably out in the pool or hot tub.

"Well, come on." I led Dagny upstairs to the room she'd be using. It was small, but had a nice big bed, an armchair in the corner, and a dresser, as well as its own bathroom.

Dagny dropped her bag on the bed, then turned in a slow circle to take in the entire room. "Do you remember that weekend I stayed with you when your parents went skiing in Colorado?"

I thought for a moment, then my smile matched hers. I nodded. "Yeah. I've never eaten so many s'mores in all my life. And, I'll have you know, I haven't touched them since."

Dagny threw her head back and laughed, then put her arm around my shoulder. "Come on, Chase. Let's go find some trouble."

We hurried down the stairs, giggling like schoolchildren. I was thrown back in time to an eight year old who liked her babysitter better than her own parents.

*The weekend my parents went on their getaway, I was upset with them, at first, for not taking me, afraid I would be stuck staying with my grandma Carol. She always took me to the nursing home when she took care of her mother, and wanted to show me off to all my great grandmother's friends. It was boring.*

*I stomped my foot on the floor, my arms crossed over my chest as I pouted. "I wanna go with you." I didn't want to cry, but I could feel the sting behind my eyes, trying to blink it away, which was the wrong thing to do. When I blinked, it forced a tear out of my left eye. Impatiently, I wiped it away.*

*"Now stop that, Chase," my father said, his finger in my face. "Your mother and I are going, and you're not. That's final." He went outside to load the car.*

*My mother came down the stairs, heavy coats folded over her arm. She looked at me. "Honey, you'll have fun." She kissed me on the forehead.*

*"I won't! Grandma will make me go to the nursing home." I stomped again.*

*My mom smiled, running her hand through my hair. "You're not going to Grandma Carol's, honey. Dagny is coming to stay with you."*

*I stared up at her, ready for her to tell me she was only joking and Grandma would be there in a few minutes. She held her smile, understanding in her eyes. "Really?" I squeaked out weakly. She nodded and kissed my forehead again. I was thrilled but didn't want them to see that, so I continued to pout. Maybe if I acted sad long enough, they would take me and Dagny both with them. It hadn't ever worked, but it didn't hurt to keep trying.*

*My mom leaned down to my ear. "I don't blame you, honey. I wouldn't want to go with Grandma Carol, either."*

*She stood, smiling down at me; I looked up at her, incredulous. She'd say something like that? I grinned. She put her finger to her lips for me to keep it quiet. I nodded. Our little secret. I liked it when Mom trusted me with little secrets.*

*An hour later Dagny rode up on her bike, a smile on her face.*

*She had a grocery bag on her handlebars, and brought it in with her to show me after my parents left.*

*"Do you know what s'more's are, Chase?" I shook my head. "Well, this weekend you're going to find out."*

*That night we set everything out on the back patio: a jar of marshmallow creme, a small stack of Hershey bars, and a box of Graham crackers.*

*"Okay, this is what you do."*

*She began to build the treat, my eyes open wide as I watched her intently. A smile spread across my face at the completed creation; I couldn't wait to get that thing in my mouth.*

*"Here you go."*

*I took the s'more from her most willingly, took my first bite, my eyes closing as the different tastes mixed together in my mouth. Oh, yeah. I could definitely handle a weekend of this.*

Later, after she was settled in and my parents reappeared, Dagney went out with my father to put more Christmas lights up on the roof, while my mother and I worked on the dinner. It was Christmas Eve, and I was excited. Tonight, as was always our custom, we'd have a simple dinner and cookies, everyone opening one gift each, the rest to wait for Christmas morning.

"So, how is school going?" my mom asked as she took the innards out of the turkey.

I watched in warped fascination. "It's going good. I'm starting to like it more, I think."

"You'd better." She looked at me over her shoulder. "College isn't cheap, Chase." She turned back to the bird in the sink.

"Yeah, I know." I started chopping vegetables for the salad for dinner.

"Have you given any thought to a career?" My mom filled a bag with discarded turkey goodies that the dogs would find most yummy.

"Well, um, actually I'm thinking about psychology."

Her hands stopped, pulling out of the bird to rest on the edge of the sink. She looked at me. "What can you possibly do with that?" She continued with the turkey.

I shrugged, at a loss for an answer. I had been excited and feeling better since I'd found something that had caught my interest. I hadn't necessarily been excited to tell my parents about it, maybe because I expected just such a reaction.

"Well, there's a few things. I plan to go talk with my advisor after break." I shoved my tomato slices to the side and started on another. I could feel my blood beginning to boil, but held it down as much as possible.

"I don't know, Chase. Your father and I were hoping you'd find something that could be lucrative for you in the future, something that would *have* a future."

She looked at me again, but I couldn't return the look. My chopping slowed down to almost nothing as I tried to rein in my emotions. I felt my purpose crumbling around my feet. "Aunt Shelly is a counselor," I said, my voice quiet.

"Yes, and Aunt Shelly is crazy. Of course she'd go into something like that; she understands those people. You, Chase, are not crazy."

I looked up at her. *You people* make *me crazy!* In my mind I yelled it, yelled it loud, then ran from the room. In actuality, I nodded and continued to cut up vegetables.

When dinner preparations were finished, I wandered off to find a book. I kept thinking about what my mom had said, her rejection of my idea. I felt my confidence in my decision slipping. Was it the right thing to do? I hated law, had no interest in cutting people up. I could barely balance my own checkbook, let alone run a business or do someone else's checkbook. I sighed. I just did not know.

* ~ * ~ * ~ * ~ * ~ *

"Hey."

I looked up from Stephen King's *The Talisman* to see Dagny walking into the room.

"I've been looking for you." She sat down on the couch next to me. "And here you are in the living room, all snuggled up with a book." She looked over at the bookshelves that lined the entire wall, got up and walked over to it. "My mom was an avid reader, still is, actually." She picked out a book and flipped through its pages. "This book right here?" She showed me Ayn Rand's *Atlas Shrugged*. "This is where I got my name." She opened up to a page and showed me. "This character right here." She tapped it with her finger.

"Dagny Taggart?" I looked at her, she nodded.

"Yup. My mom's favorite character. You should have seen how I was teased for that when I was a kid." She shook her head with a small smile. "So, how are you?" She plopped down beside me.

I shrugged. "I'm okay." I stared down at the book in my hands. I wanted to talk to her about my conversation with my mom, but didn't know how. I had never been very good at opening up to people. Would she laugh at me, tell me I was being childish? Overly sensitive?

"You sure? You look down." She tilted her head down to see my face. I smiled, glancing at her.

"Yeah." *Maybe I'll talk about it later.*

* ~ * ~ * ~ * ~ * ~ *

My sister Carla stood at the sink in the main bathroom in the hall near our bedrooms. She was removing her make-up with some sort of white cream. She saw me pass by in the mirror.

"Chase?"

I stopped, backtracked to lean in the doorway. "Huh?"

She smiled at me, patting the toilet lid. "I haven't seen you in so long."

I looked at my sister. She really was a beautiful girl — her long, flowing hair, chestnut like my mom's, and her gray/blue eyes. She was not as tall as I was, but taller than our mother. Good height.

I sat on the seat, my legs spread, elbow on each so I could split at any sign of trouble. We weren't the closest of sisters.

"So how have you been? How is everything?"

She continued with her before-bed regimen, face mask to unclog the pores, followed by an abrasive cleanser that was left on for an additional ten minutes. Right now as she looked at me, she looked like Casper the Friendly Ghost, her hair pulled back into a ponytail to keep it off her mask-white face.

"I'm okay. Just glad to have a firm foothold now that the first semester is over." I picked up a tube of her gunk and read the back.

"I'm sure. It's not fun to start."

"Yeah." I put the tube back, grabbed another one.

"I'm proud of you, Chase. I think it's fantastic that you're going and doing it. Mom and Dad haven't always been easy on you." She brushed some hair off my forehead.

I was stunned. *Who is this person, and where's the pod she came out of?* "Thanks."

"You'll do fine, Chase. You're a good egg."

She ran her hand from my bangs to the top of my head, messing up my hair like I was a four year old. I giggled as I slapped her hand away. "Thanks, Carla." I stood, smiled, and walked out.

* ~ * ~ * ~ * ~ * ~ *

The Christmas tree stood in the corner of the living room, the star nearly reaching the ten foot ceiling. Lights were wrapped around it in abundance. Tinsel, little silver and gold balls, bells and lights adorned it, making the tree glow in the dark room. Presents were piled underneath, obliterating the bottom length of the trunk and spreading out into the room. My mom told me they had gone out and gotten Dagny something, which shocked me to no end, but it was a very nice gesture. It made me feel like crap since I had nothing for her.

Christmas Eve we sat around the tree drinking eggnog and

laughing. I have to say, it was the most fun I'd had with my family in a long time, and I knew it was because of Dagny. She was funny, interesting, and everyone in the room just fell in love with her.

I watched her — the way she interacted with my parents and could match Carla point for point on just about any subject. Even the stiff Todd actually participated as they discussed the pros and cons of cloning. I looked at my parents, wondering if my father would jump in, but he just sat back, arm on the back of the couch around my mom's shoulders, ankle crossed over his knee. A smile on his face, he looked proud. My mother looked at me and smiled. I sighed, a feeling of satisfied peace washing over me.

"You have the most wonderful family."

I looked at Dagny as we walked up to bed. I grinned, shook my head. "You can have them."

She laughed, rubbing my shoulder. "Be glad you're all together, Chase."

* ~ * ~ * ~ * ~ * ~ *

I lay in bed, the night dragging on as sleep still eluded me. I glanced out the window at the moon that was high and bright. Perfect night for Santa. I smiled, remembering when I was a kid, nearly having to tape my eyes shut for me to get any sleep. Christmas had always been a huge deal in my family. My mother's parents were long gone, so it had just been my father's folks, my folks, and Carla. My mom's sister, Shelly, had been the black sheep of their family for so many years, I couldn't even remember what she had done that was such a sin. I shook my head. It didn't matter.

Dagny was in the room next to mine; we shared a wall at our heads. I wondered if she was asleep. If so, was she dreaming? What about? She was so different here, away from school. So relaxed, almost like a kid. She was fun and interesting at UA, but nothing like now. Today she had wadded up some wrapping paper and thrown it at me, which ended up in an all out paper war, most of the make-shift snowballs being recycled as ammo. Even my parents had gotten into the action.

I was startled by a knock on the wall just above my head. My brows drew together, then I smiled. I brought my hand up and quickly knocked five times. Within a few seconds, the appropriate two knocks were returned. I chuckled to myself, knocked again, which was quickly followed by matching disembodied knocks. I felt like a little kid, giggling as our game continued, careful not to knock too loud and wake the rest of the house. The knocking stopped and I was disappointed, then I faintly heard my name being called. I repositioned myself so I could put my ear to the wall.

"Chase? Can you hear me?"

"Yes." I pushed my ear as close to the wall as I could without pushing my head through it. "Barely, but yeah."

"Merry Christmas."

I looked at my alarm clock: 12:04 a.m. I smiled. "Merry Christmas."

"Good night."

I was a bit bummed, but I knew we both needed sleep. "Night."

I rolled over, a smile on my face as I closed my eyes and let sleep take me.

\* ~ \* ~ \* ~ \* ~ \* ~ \*

Light was streaming in the window, right into my eyes, no less. I squeezed them shut as I rolled over to give the sun my back. Too late. I was awake. I groaned as I pushed myself out of bed and pulled on a pair of boxers and a tank to wear downstairs.

Everything was quiet as I crept down the stairs, feeling like I was nine again, not sure if I should be up. I made my way to the kitchen to put on the coffee, knowing it would be The Grinch Who Stole Christmas if I didn't. Every year my mom bought some exotic blend of coffee from a specialty store, and this year was no different. I saw the brown bag folded and taped shut next to the brewer, and I picked it up. Chocolate Burst. *Sounds good.*

Coffee percolating, I turned toward the living room, sucking in a breath as I nearly ran smack into Dagny. I put my hand to my chest. "God, you scared the crap out of me." I looked at her grinning face and saw that her hair was wet. My eyes drifted down to her bathing suit and the towel wrapped loosely around her shoulders. I was confused.

"Sorry." She put a hand on my shoulder. "Your mom said I could use the pool. I go for a swim every morning."

"You still go out there and put your life in Poseidon's hands, huh?"

She grinned. "Yup. Every chance I get." She turned, sniffing the air. "Is that coffee brewing?"

"Yup. Chocolate Burst. You're amongst drinkers here, my friend." I turned back into the kitchen, followed closely by Dagny.

"And that's bad because why again?"

I stood at the counter in front of the maker, waiting for it to perk its last perk so I could pour two cups. She stood next to me, leaning over me slightly.

"Oh, that smells good." She took a step back from me. "I'm going to go get dried off and changed, then you can warm me up with a cup of that stuff." With a smile, she was gone.

I watched her, watched everything about her — the way the towel clung to her body, the material wet from her wet suit and skin.

Her calves, muscular from years of swimming. The way her hair stuck up just a little in the back where it was starting to dry, and how it turned a dark blonde with random streaks of darker color. She was beautiful.

Eventually, after everyone managed to get their butts out of bed and make themselves somewhat presentable, we gathered in the living room. The laughter was muted as my family tried to fight the sleepiness and get into the groove for a long day. My mom brought out a tray loaded with homemade cookies, cakes, pretzels, you name it. It was the one day of the year that she actually encouraged junk food before noon.

Within moments, the room was filled with the sounds of paper being ripped and crumpled, and the oohs and ahhs of happy gift recipients. Dagny sat on the floor next to the couch where I was sitting, her back resting near my legs as she watched with a look of pure delight. After a bit, Todd rose from the loveseat he and Carla were sharing.

"Um, if I could have everyone's attention?" He ran a hand through his close-cropped brown hair; his shorts and tee proclaimed the name of his and Carla's school. Everyone stopped what they were doing and gave him their full attention. I looked at my mom and could see she was nearly vibrating out of her seat. When I looked back at Todd, he had turned to my sister, bending down on one knee. My eyes got wide and I held my breath. Todd picked up a small package he had set near his pile of gifts.

"Carla, this is for you."

He handed it to her, and Carla took it, turning the wrapped packaged this way and that. Finally she opened it, careful not to rip the beautiful ivory paper. She held up a dark green velvet jeweler's box, looking at him, then back to the box. The lid squeaked ever so slightly as it was slowly opened.

"Oh, Todd," she breathed, her hand going to her mouth.

Todd said nothing as he watched. I could see him sweating, and felt bad for the guy. I looked down at Dagny, who was also watching with bated breath.

"Will you marry me, as soon as we both finish school?"

Carla looked up into his eyes, which I imagined were expectant and hopeful. *Leave it to them to throw school in there.* Her eyes filling with tears, she nodded. My mom sobbed quietly across the room; my father looked like he'd already walked my sister down the aisle. Todd let out a sigh of relief and gathered her into his arms.

"How sweet," Dagny whispered. I looked down at her and sighed.

* ~ * ~ * ~ * ~ * ~ *

My mom started getting the early dinner together as Carla showed us her ring. It was beautiful, a white gold band with a larger diamond in the center and two smaller stones to either side. Simple and elegant. Dagny caught my eye and nodded toward the French doors that would lead to the back patio. I followed.

"Some day, huh? Your mom's dinner smells so good." She took a deep breath, exhaling with a smile. "I can't tell you the last really good home cooked meal I had."

I nodded. "Yeah; know what you mean." We walked to the side of the pool and stared down into the crystal clear water. "Did you like the satchel my parents gave you?" I finally asked.

"Yes. It came as quite a surprise. I really didn't expect anything, but, it was a truly nice gesture on their part." She reached into her pocket, withdrawing a piece of folded paper, handing it to me with a smile. "This is for you. I guess you could kind of say it was my gift to you."

I took the paper and unfolded it to find a computer print out of my records for her class. I scanned the page until my eyes found my final grade. 96% — A. I looked up at her, my eyes wide. She nodded. "No shit?" I looked at it again. She put her hand on my arm to get my attention. I looked into beautiful green eyes.

She pointed to the A. "I want you to know that you earned that grade, Chase. You and I may be friends, and have a past, but I gave you no extra favors. You pulled that off all on your own. Merry Christmas."

"Merry Christmas. Oh, I guess this will be my gift to you: I've decided to go into psychology."

Her eyes lit up. "Really?" I nodded. "Oh, Chase, that's wonderful. I think you'll do great things with it. What made you decide?"

I shrugged, beginning to walk alongside the pool. "I don't know. Great teacher, I guess."

She nudged my shoulder playfully. "Thanks." We were both quiet for a few moments. "So, you never learned to swim, huh?" I shook my head. "Hm. Interesting."

*∼*∼*∼*∼*∼*

Comfortable in my own bed, I hadn't slept so well since before finals. Eager for my dream to continue, I smacked my lips and wrapped my arms around my pillow.

"Chase?"

My brow knit as I felt my body being shaken. Deciding to ignore it, I hugged my pillow more tightly.

"Chase, wake up."

I didn't want to wake up; I was happy as I was. My eyes opened slowly. Dagny was standing over me, her hand on my shoulder. I wondered what the hell the deal was.

She smiled when she saw that I was awake. "Come on. Come with me."

I saw she wore her bathing suit with a pair of shorts over it, a towel hung around her neck. "Why...where?" I mumbled, trying to convince myself that it wasn't still dark out, that I wasn't being pulled out of sleep during my vacation.

"Just come on." She grabbed my arm and tugged. With a groan I finally got up. "Get your suit on," were her last words before she sauntered out of my bedroom. *Is she serious?*

I followed Dagny down the stairs and out the back door where she took off her shorts and tossed her towel onto the lounger at poolside. She pushed some loose hair back behind her ear, her suit molded to the perfect shape of her body. I could not take my eyes off of her: her breasts, slightly pushed together from the tight fitting Speedo, her legs muscular and gorgeous, her butt—

"Come on."

Shaken out of my observations and feeling guilty for getting caught, I laid my towel next to hers. I had noticed that spending this one-on-one time with Dagny over the last week had sent my mind into frequent side trips into outer space. My confusion grew daily; my attraction grew hourly. I stopped for a moment, staring at her as she dipped her toe into the pool to test the water. *My attraction? What does that mean?* Did it mean like girl/guy attraction? As in physical? What Carrie felt for every single person she came into contact with? What did that say for me? Was it possible that I, that I... I shook my head. I didn't want to think about it. I wanted to find out why the hell Dag had dragged me out of bed at five in the morning.

"Is there a point to this?" I pouted.

"There sure is." Without further ado, Dagny dived into the deep end, disappearing beneath the surface of the illuminated water, her body black in silhouette before she broke through the surface, eyes squeezed shut, hair plastered to her head as she shook off the water. "Oh, that felt good."

I just stared at her, arms crossed over my chest, feeling very uncomfortable and vulnerable standing on the edge of my parents' pool in a bathing suit. I hated such attire and had had to dig to find it as I didn't really have a use for it. I thought about the last time I had worn it. *Why did I buy the suit?* Like lightning, my thoughts evaporated as I returned to the moment. *More to the point, why does Dagny want me in it?* I turned my attention back to my former TA and was surprised to see her looking at me. She wasn't looking into my eyes, or looking at me like I was a moron like she sometimes did when I got lost in my own world. She was actually looking *at* me, as if for the first time. I suddenly felt very uncomfortable.

"Dagny?"

Shaking her head, she looked up at me. Seeing I had her attention again, I knelt down as she swam to the edge of the water and rested her forearms on the cement apron surrounding the pool. "Why did you drag me out here?"

"I'm going to teach you to swim."

I was taken aback. "You're going to do what?"

"Yup. So, come on in. The water's great." She smiled at her own cliché and pushed off the wall to float on her back toward the middle of the pool.

"No, Dagny. I don't think that's such a good idea." I stared out over the water, thinking about how much of it could be in my lungs in a matter of seconds.

"Come on, Chase. I felt so bad I couldn't teach you when you were eight. Let me teach you now." I shook my head. "Please?"

The pleading in her voice and the hope in her eyes made me nod, reluctantly.

"Yay!" She clapped her hands and swam to the edge of the pool by the ladder.

I walked over to it, slowly stepped down into the water, holding my breath as I got used to the cold. *This would definitely wake you up in the morning.* "So, do I get the little orange float things again?" I muttered, my words slurred as my teeth rattled against the cold. "God, this is cold."

"I know. You'll get used to it, I promise. And, no. You're taller than I am now, so you'll do just fine in the five foot end."

I grinned. *How things change.* "Okay, I'm in. Now what?" I looked at her for guidance. She made her way over to me in that slow-motion walk that always amused me.

"Okay, now first of all you have to trust me." She looked into my eyes. "Okay?" I nodded. "Good. Know that I'm not going to let anything happen to you, and we can stop at any time." Again I nodded. Good to know, though I seriously doubted I'd take her up on it. I didn't want to disappoint her.

Dagny went over the ways to breathe, different strokes that I could do, ways to not panic. Just as in the classroom teaching her love of psychology, she clearly conveyed her passion for the water. She made it seem less scary, and easy to conquer my fears of swimming.

"Okay, are you ready to try?" she asked, her hand on my arm.

"I think so." I looked down into the depths of the water, glittering gold with the rays of the rising sun.

"You sure?"

I nodded. If I didn't try this now, I'd never do it.

"Okay. Want to copy me, what I do?"

"Okay." I watched her as she pushed off of the bottom of the pool with the ball of her foot and let her body submerge, her head above the water as she looked back at me, nodding that I should follow. I did. I felt the air in my lungs seem to thicken as my body took on the burden of the water pressure, and for a second I wanted to panic. But then all of Dagny's instructions and words of advice came back to me. *I can do this; I can do this. I can; I can.*

I kept Dagny in sight. Seeing her was my source of strength, knowing I was doing this for her and that she could save me should anything go wrong. Then suddenly, as if by a divine intervention, I felt my drive coming from inside me, not from fear. I wanted to do this...for me, and I knew that I could. I threw myself into it, letting my head turn to the other side as I came up for air, pulling myself through the water with a grace I had never before experienced. I put out my hand, just as Dagny had taught me, and felt the wall. I stopped, putting my feet down and turning to find Dagny standing by the wall, watching me with a proud expression. Her eyes were shining, arms crossed over her shoulders.

"I did it," I whispered.

"Yes, you did."

She walked over and took me in a monster hug, her body pressed to mine. It nearly knocked the wind out of me, which wasn't good, since I was kind of short on wind, anyway, but I went with it. I wrapped my arms around her, holding her tight, grateful for her faith in me. She always made me feel I could do anything. "Thank you," I said in her ear, hugging her tighter.

After a few moments, Dagny slowly pulled away, her hands on my arms. She looked up into my eyes. "I'm proud of you, Chase, for so many reasons. You have turned into such a wonderful woman, and I'm proud to have been your babysitter ten years ago, and I'm proud to have been your teacher last semester, and I'm proud to be your friend now."

I stared at her, stunned. "Thank you, Dag. Um, I don't know what to say."

"There's nothing to be said." She patted my arm with a smile. "Just keep being you. You're doing one hell of a job."

I chuckled. "You, too. You're a pretty cool chick."

It was her turn to laugh. "Care to swim a lap with me?"

"You're on."

* ~ * ~ * ~ * ~ * ~ *

The last of our stuff put inside, I closed the trunk of my car. I knew my folks would be all right with Dagny and me leaving earlier than planned because they had so much to discuss about Carla and

Todd's wedding plans. I was sure they would be glad not to have any distractions.

My mom came outside with a box loaded with Tupperware dishes of Christmas dinner leftovers. "You two have a safe drive," she said as she hugged me.

"Thanks, Mom. We don't have far to go."

"I know, but I miss you already." She kissed my cheek and pulled away. "Dagny, honey, it was truly a pleasure to have you. You are welcome here anytime." To my surprise, she hugged Dagny. Carla and Todd stood at the front door watching our goodbyes, waving. I waved back as my father hugged me.

"We'll see you on your birthday," he said, patting my shoulder.

"Oh, honey, I nearly forgot to ask. Are you coming home for your birthday?"

I really didn't want to, but knew my mom would be absolutely devastated if I didn't. "Sure. Let me know what time you want me."

"Okay, love." She hugged me again. "Don't forget what we talked about concerning your future, honey. You really have to think these things through," she said in my ear.

I squeezed my eyes shut, but nodded. I got into my car, thrilled to be going back to school. Who would have thought I'd ever feel that?

# Chapter 5

I put my stuff back in my dorm room, glad to be back. It would be so nice to have a few weeks to do nothing. I smiled as I flopped down on my bed, not as soft or comfortable as the one at home, but mine all the same.

It was getting late, but I wasn't tired in the least. I hated to admit it, and certainly probably would never admit it to Dagny, but our swim that morning had been invigorating. Who knew?

With a sigh, I stood, intending to put away all the clothes and gifts that I'd brought back with me from the holidays. Christmas morning I had been beyond shocked and excited when I had unwrapped an electric guitar, complete with amp and strap. I really hadn't thought my folks had listened to my requests for more musical equipment. I pulled the beauty out of its case, its glossy black body perfect and smooth as I ran my fingers over it.

"Perfect." I remembered Dagny's face as when I had seen it sitting under the tree. The look in her eyes had been priceless. She knew my secret at Gotfry's, and I'm sure she was thinking all the things I was, imagining me up there on stage rocking along with my music. Yeah, that would be good.

Carla and I had pretty much always gotten whatever we wanted our entire lives, and I think our parents only bought certain things for us because they thought that soon enough we'd lose interest in them and it wouldn't be an issue. I had to smile as I looked at my new guitar. They had no idea what they were supporting and would freak if they knew. It made me sad that I couldn't tell them or share with them my passion and what some said was my gift. I wasn't one to boast or brag, but I felt good, confident about what I did up there on that stage. I was proud.

I wondered who we'd get as a drummer. Doug had called me up just before the break to tell me Mike had left Tucson, going back home to Phoenix. I felt bad, wondering how much of his decision I was responsible for. I knew he had gotten himself into academic trouble, but had I pushed him over the edge?

I sighed as my thoughts went to Carrie. I hadn't seen or heard from her all during the break. Her family only lived a few blocks away from mine, and the thought had crossed my mind more than once to call her or go over there, but I couldn't make myself do it. I loved Carrie and always would, but I felt the need to start over, as if I'd outgrown my old life and my old self. I was molting.

Suddenly I was hit with an inspiration. I grabbed my notebook and began to scribble away. I looked at what I had written, tasting the words on my tongue, then settled Melo in my arms. I placed my fingers on the notes and began to strum softly.

> *You touch my hand, you touch my soul*
> *You touch my heart, I am all yours*
> *You make me strong, tell me I can win*
> *I'm comfortable in my skin.*

I sang the lyrics again, then again, finding the right rhythm and tune. Putting down my guitar and staring down at the page, I realized I had just written the chorus to my song. I just needed another stanza or two to finish it, but didn't want to rush it. It would come in its own time.

* ~ * ~ * ~ * ~ * ~ *

It was my first full day without class and parents. No roommate, no parties, just me and the book I'd stolen from my folks' house. I was curious. I looked at the cover of Ayn Rand's novel, wondering what lay within that had captivated Dagny's mom so much.

I made a comfy spot for myself on the bed, back against the wall, a can of Dr Pepper between my legs. I flipped through the first pages until I got to page one of the story. I felt the weight of the hefty book, wondering how I'd ever finish the thing. It was nine in the morning, and I had no plans for the day, so, brushing my hair out of my face, I began to read.

I jumped when something banged. My head jerked up, looking around the room, which had grown dark. I looked down at the book in my hands, a thick slab of pages on the left, a sliver on the right. I blinked rapidly, my eyes burning from the hours of reading. The banging again. Someone was knocking on my door.

Tempted to growl at the ceiling, I felt a surge of power flowing through me. Why couldn't there be real people and leaders out there like Dagny Taggart? This book was filled with empowering thoughts, ideas. No woman would be stomped by man or society. I grinned and stood, stretching my arms above my head, my back screaming at me. "Who is it?" I called out in the middle of my stretch.

"Dagny."

I quickly put my arms down, looking about for some place to hide the book. Shoving it under my pillow, I hurried to the door. "Hi," I said, feeling foolish, like I'd been caught doing something.

She smiled. "Hey. You okay?" She leaned in a little, looking around the room, then at me. "You alone in here?"

I nodded. "Yup. All by my lonesome."

"Can I come in?" I stepped back, leaving her space to walk by me. She spotted my newest baby leaning against the wall with Melo.

"I bet you're thrilled about this, huh?" She grinned knowingly.

I looked at the guitar with pride. "Oh, yeah. You can definitely say that again. My eyes nearly bugged out of my head when I saw her."

"I know. I was there." She walked over to my bed and sat, to my consternation, near the pillow. She put her hand down, looked to see what she'd hit with it. "Ow. What? You have rocks under here?" She lifted the pillow, then looked up at me with a grin. "Did you steal this from your parents?" Thoroughly uncomfortable, I held my hands behind my back and didn't say anything. "Are you reading this, Chase?" She picked up the book and flipped the pages, looking at me all the while.

"Well, I saw it, and you picked it up. I was curious why your mom would read such a huge book, and wanted to know about your namesake. It took up lots of paper to print that sucker, and well, yeah." I looked down shyly, feeling like a little kid. I couldn't look her in the eye. I knew she was looking at me expectantly.

"Is this because of what I told you?" She stood, book in hand. I nodded. She didn't approach me, apparently seeing my embarrassment. "Have you been reading this all day?"

I finally looked up to see she was sitting on the bed again. "Yeah."

"Chase, this book has," she turned to the last page, "one thousand, one hundred and forty-seven pages in it. My Lord! You only have around a hundred to go." She looked up at me with concern. "Have you eaten today?"

I thought for a moment. Had I? I noted the three empty Dr Pepper cans at the end of the bed and realized I had gotten up from the bed once, to go pee and get two more sodas for my all day read-a-thon. I shook my head.

"Chase Marin!" Dagny put her hands on her hips. "I tell you, some people's kids." She stood, grabbed my hand and yanked me toward the door.

We headed to Magpie's Gourmet Pizza on 4th. It wasn't as busy as usual; most of the college kids who hung out there on Tuesday nights were gone for the holidays. We found a little table near the back and sat down. We were looking over the menu when Dagny peered at me over the edge of hers.

"So, what do you think of it?" I looked at her, not sure what she was talking about. "You know, Dagny Taggart and the book."

"Oh. Well, I think it's great. I mean, who would have thought that the removal of certain people in the world could have such a detrimental impact on things. It's a fascinating idea, really."

"Yes, it is. Ayn Rand was a bit before her time." Deciding on her dinner, Dagny put the menu down.

I also put my menu down. "Has she written more?"

"Oh, yeah. I have them all, um, if you want to borrow them."

"Maybe."

Two empty plates sat at the end of the table ready to be picked up, driblets of sauce falling to the table below. Magpie's had the best calzones anywhere. My meatball calzone was resting happily in my stomach, and all I could do was sit back and smile.

"Good stuff, huh?" Dagny sipped her Coke.

"Oh, yeah. I love this place. I used to order one of those bad boys when I'd study."

"Me too. Still do, actually."

I sighed, sated and content.

"Good thing I'll be swimming this off in the morning. That's one of the great things about swimming. It increases your appetite so you eat more, but then you swim it off." Dagny stretched, her arms high above her head, neck arched as she made little squeaking noises.

My eyes were drawn to her body, breasts thrust out, back arched. *God, what's wrong with me?* As the stretch came to an end, my eyes quickly found themselves something else to look at, my napkin. I piled my napkin and used fork onto the stack of plates and sat back. "When do you go? And where?"

"I usually go around six at the YWCA."

"Hm." A plan was already brewing in my head. "So what did you think of the nutty world of the Marins?" I sipped my Dr Pepper.

"Actually, I thought they were nice." She shrugged. "I hope you don't get angry at me for saying this, but I don't think they treat you and Carla very equally."

I was surprised at her perception, and I didn't know how to react or respond. I was ashamed of the fact, but at the same time there was always that "loyalty to your family" that I just couldn't shake. I wasn't angry with her for pointing out something that was simply an observation, so I just shrugged. "Everybody has their problems."

We walked back to my dorm. It was late, but I was looking forward to finishing the Rand book. I had gotten so far into it, it had been torture to leave it, but considering the cause of the absence, it was sweet torture.

"Well, that was fun. Good dinner, too."

I smiled, not sure what to say. I didn't want to seem rude by just kicking her butt out the door, or making her sit on Natalie's bed not making a noise until I finished the novel. She looked at me, the slightest bit of a knowing grin on her face.

"It's late, and you do need your *sleep*." She glanced at the book on the bed and winked. I looked down, again shy. "I'll see you later, Chase. Have a great night." She patted my shoulder.

"Thanks. You, too. Oh, and thanks again for dinner. You really didn't have to do that."

"I know, and you didn't have to invite me to your family's home for Christmas, either. Sleep well." With that, she was gone.

I stared at the door for a moment, missing her already. With a sigh, I took up my favorite spot on my bed and started to read.

* ~ * ~ * ~ * ~ * ~ *

It was still dark outside when I rubbed my eyes open, the feeling of sand in them just not dissipating. I snatched the towel out of my closet and slung it over my shoulder, my bag in hand, hoping this was the right thing to do.

The parking lot was nearly empty, only a few early birds having managed to get out of bed at such an hour. The lady at the desk pointed me in the direction that my nose probably could have led me. I knew the Y well, as I'd been going there for Natalie every week, but I had yet to make use of their swimming facilities.

I checked the time; it was five 'til. I hoped I could catch Dagny in the locker room, and that she wouldn't be mad about me just showing up. The room was steamy and smelled like chlorine. It looked like any other locker room I'd ever seen in my life — shower stalls off to the left, tall metal lockers painted red lining three of the four walls with rows of them in between. I was looking around when I heard a shower go on. I couldn't see who it was, so I looked for Dagny's things. Bingo. Her tennis shoes and backpack, along with the same towel she'd had at my parents' house, sat on the bench by the last row of lockers. I knew I had the right girl.

I set my bag down, unzipping it to bring out the bathing suit I'd brought with me from home, and flip flops. I changed quickly, running pants flying in one direction, tee the other. I wanted to hurry before Dagny returned to her stuff so I could be ready to join her. I was pulling up the last strap of the suit when I heard footfalls not ten feet from the row of lockers, then someone sucking in their breath.

"Chase."

I turned to see Dagny looking at me, dripping wet from her rinse off. I greeted her with a small wave as she walked past me to her own stuff.

"What are you doing here?"

I could see the hope in her eyes and was pleased to be able to give her good news. "Well, I mean, since it's taken you ten years to teach me how to swim, I figured I should put that knowledge to good use, you know."

Her smile lit up her face. "I'm so excited!" To my surprise, she lunged at me and wrapped me in a wet hug. "Sorry, but this is wonderful."

Yay, she's not mad.

Dagny swam laps around me but I did my best, working at my own pace. She was terrific, patient, giving me pointers now and then. In an Olympic sized pool where she had room to really stretch out her legs, and arms, and torso — and everything else it seemed — she was amazing to watch. I pulled myself up to sit on the edge and indulged myself. I had never in my life seen anything so beautiful. She was graceful, plowing into that water with a powerfully built body as easily as if she were slicing through Jell-O. Back and forth, back and forth. I felt tired from just watching the insane number of laps she did.

"You okay?" she asked, finally coming up for air and swimming over to me.

"Yup, just fine. I wanted to watch. You're really good at this."

She pulled herself up to sit next to me. "Well, you do this for nearly twenty years and we'll see how good you get." She nudged me with her shoulder.

"Wow. You started young."

She nodded. "My mom got me into lessons when I was about three, and let's just say I took off like a fish." She grinned. "I'm really glad you came, Chase. I wanted to ask, but didn't really want to push you or make you feel obligated."

I shrugged, staring out into the water that rippled slightly. "Eh, it was a last minute decision. I didn't think you'd mind, but I wasn't sure—"

"Wasn't sure? Are you kidding? I was so happy to see you in the locker room that I nearly kissed you!" she exclaimed.

*Really? Oh, I wish, I wish...* I shrugged it off. "Well..."

"Dare I ask if this will be a more than a one time thing?"

"Well, um, actually I was kind of thinking I could join you every morning. That is, if—"

"I don't mind. Nope. Don't mind at all. In fact, I'm thrilled. Please do."

I smiled. It felt so good to be welcomed and accepted. Even appreciated. "Thanks. I will."

"Well," Dagny slapped her knees, "I'm going to do one more lap, then, if you want, we can get out of here. That is, do you want to do something today?"

I looked into the beautiful green eyes. *Can I just stare into those forever, Dagny?* "Yeah, sure."

She smiled, slapped my leg. "Great. Be right back, then we can talk about what to do." She hopped back into the pool, and was off.

* ~ * ~ * ~ * ~ * ~ *

The week wore on and Dagny and I spent every day together. I was slowly beginning to see what Dagny Robertson was all about as a person. Until then, all I had seen was Dagny the babysitter and Dagny the teacher. She was neither of those things to me now, so she had the freedom to let her full personality shine through. I felt my attraction to her growing daily, having now accepted the idea that it *was* an attraction. I didn't fully understand it, but I didn't let it scare me anymore, either.

Doug had called the band together to try out a new drummer. I was excited to get performing again; I wanted to try out my newest baby. I had yet to come up with a name for it, but Dagny had promised she'd think of some great names. That is, I got her to promise right after she looked at me as though I'd lost my mind.

"Don't you name things?" I asked.

"Sure, like my dog, even the pet fish I had when I was nine, but a guitar?"

"You don't name your car?" I was shocked and appalled. She was equally so.

"Why would I?"

"Oh. I thought everyone did." I name everything.

This would be the first time CID would be getting together without one of its founding members. I was sure the mood would be quiet, maybe sad. Even I would miss Mike's presence. I was glad he had decided to leave, but it was a shame to lose such a great drummer.

"Hey, girl." Doug gave me a hug, then indicated the black case in my hand. "What's this?"

"This is Santa Claus." I grinned and he chuckled with an understanding nod.

"Can I see her?"

"Sure." I pulled the black beauty out of the case and handed her to him; he gave her a careful inspection.

As the rest of the group arrived, we all laughed and caught up with one another. A Ford pick-up pulled into Doug's driveway, and all eyes turned to the late arrival. She looked to be a little older than us, maybe in her mid-twenties, twenty-seven at most. She had short brown hair, sunglasses, and wore tight fitting jeans and a sleeveless shirt.

I turned to Doug to see if he knew who she was. She headed toward us with a confident, almost cocky stride, her head held high, each step long and deliberate.

"Hey, Dougey," she said, giving the big guy a hug. She turned to look at each of us in turn. I wondered what was going through that head, her dark eyes nearly unreadable.

"Guys, this is my cousin Terrie. She's hell on the pads, so she's going to play for us."

Doug's cousin made her way to the drum set behind me, excusing herself as she squeezed between me and the wall. I moved, allowing her plenty of room. She had a pair of sticks in her back pocket and brought them out, rubbing them together. She looked around. "Someone want to accompany me?"

"Here," Doug said, handing me my guitar with a grin. "Let's hear her."

I hooked her up to the amps and got myself ready, then took a deep breath. I had yet to play this guitar in front of anyone. *Please don't let me make an ass out of myself.*

"You start, I'll join in."

I nodded and began to play something simple, not the greatest song for drums, which I saw clearly written on Terrie's face when I turned to look at her. *Okay, take two.* I thought for a moment, then began to play some Pink. Within minutes, we had the garage rocking. The other members slowly began to join in until we had a full out jam session going. It was great fun, and this chick's playing blew Mike's clear out of the water and onto land. The last chords of the music echoed in the garage, and in everyone's ears, but I knew we had found our drummer.

Dagny was waiting at my dorm when I returned from practice. Somehow she had talked me into going shopping. We jumped into her car, and off to the Tucson Mall we went. Hi ho, hi ho, er, something.

We found a parking space near Dillard's, and Dagny skillfully inserted her little 2-door, ivy green Suzuki Vitara. It was a cute vehicle, somewhere between a car and an SUV. She patted it lovingly on the right fender and smiled at me. "I wanted to get something that would be reliable. Isn't it cute?"

"I can't believe this poor little guy doesn't have a name," I muttered as we headed toward the building.

For me, the mall was like any other not fun place to be. Dagny, on the other hand, looked as if she were in Heaven. Some of the people passing by stared at us; others were off in their own little shopping worlds.

Dagny needed new shoes, so we went to locate all the shoe stores the mall offered. We looked at boots, from motorcycle to knee-high leathers, clear down to hiking boots. Tennis shoes, high heels, you name it, we looked at it.

"Um, Dag? What exactly are you after, anyway?"

She shrugged. "Originally tennis shoes, but now I think I may want some boots."

We laughed at all the crazy new fashions, laughing even harder as Dagny tried some of them on. They were hideous, serving no real purpose except as fantastic joke material.

Carrying the bag that held her new shoes over her arm, Dagny tried to drink the last of her Orange Julius, but wasn't real successful. We'd made a lunch stop at The Olive Garden, stuffing ourselves with bread and pasta.

"I'm so full," she said, patting her stomach.

"I don't know how the hell you've gotten any of that drink down." I looked at the cup with disgust. "I mean, those things are great and all, but my Lord." I pointed at her stomach. "Just how big is that thing, anyway?"

She grinned. "You'd be surprised."

"I *am* surprised."

We had been at the mall for hours and I had actually enjoyed every single minute of it. Dagny was fun, charming. I watched the way she was with the people there, whether they were sales clerks or other shoppers. Everyone loved her. Walking down the main hall, we saw a video store up ahead. She turned to me, a mischievous smile on her face.

"Want to go?"

I nodded vigorously, movies being another of my passions. And this place sold nothing but. I had officially found my current candy store. I could spend time in a movie store the way most people could spend time in a book store or library. I was a virtual fountain of useless movie trivia and knowledge.

"Gee, good thing your parents are spending all this money for you to go to college," Dagny said sarcastically after I admitted my movie addiction.

I glared then grinned. "Isn't that the truth." I turned to look down another aisle and halted abruptly, stopping Dagny with a hand on her arm. "Look at that." It was a rack of movies priced from $3.99 to $10.99.

"No, Chase. Don't do it," she muttered.

"I must." I nearly ran to the rack, a laughing Dagny on my heels. My eyes were the size of saucers as I perused the titles priced ridiculously low. "God, I've died and gone to Heaven," I said as I spotted one of my favorite movies, though I rarely admitted it. I grabbed it and held it possessively against my body.

"May I?" Reluctantly, I handed her the double VHS of *Titanic*. She looked at the title, then at me. "Tell me you're not one of those mush balls?" I grinned shyly. She shook her head and laughed.

An hour and five movie selections later, Dagny and I almost made it out of the mall. We each had a couple of bags, but she needed to make a stop at the GAP before we could leave. She managed to coerce me into buying a pair of jeans. My first GAP apparel. We loaded all of our treasures into the back of her little SUV and headed out.

"How do you feel about a movie night?" She looked at me, her eyes twinkling. I grinned and nodded. "Cool. But we have to get popcorn."

"With lots of butter," I added.

"And of course lots of Coke and Dr Pepper, and a box of Junior Mints. Can't have a movie without them."

"No, ma'am."

We stopped at a small grocery store and stocked up on cholesterol city, ready to begin. We decided that Dagny's apartment would be the best place for our viewing pleasure, since she had more room and, I assumed, a hell of a lot better television than the one Natalie and I suffered with. Not to mention I thought it was cool she had her own place off campus.

Her building was fairly large, and brick, but didn't look like it had originally been planned to house apartments. As if reading my mind, she explained.

"This used to be a mansion that belonged to the Swanson family in the 1800s." She stared up at the beautiful structure. "Turned it into apartments when the last of the family died in the mid-fifties. I think it's a shame they'd tear it apart like they have. Hell, I'd rather just live in the old mansion with a whole bunch of people." She grinned at me.

The walkway was made of stones, though some of them had become dislodged over time and were missing. The grounds were immaculate, obviously professionally maintained. We walked in through the double front door that was off the wraparound porch. The stained glass in the doors was also etched.

"Um, Dag, isn't this place kind of expensive?"

"I got lucky. The professor I'm working with for my doctorate, Levy, owns the building. The grad he picks to work with gets to live here, and the rent is quite cheap. He just charges the shit out of everyone else." She chuckled evilly as she led the way to the stairs.

The walls of the main floor were covered with rich dark wood paneling. Its highly polished surface reflected the lights. The wood floors, covered with beautiful rugs, squeaked a bit, but seemed to be holding up very well. I could imagine where priceless vases and works of art would have been placed and beautiful furniture scattered. Dagny was right, such a shame.

Finally we reached the second floor, the stairs opening up to a wide hall where you could look down at the first floor on one side, and head up another staircase on the other. Closed doors made of the same highly polished dark wood were located on either side. Dagny led us up the smaller, very narrow staircase.

"I bet this was a real pain to push furniture through," I muttered.

She chuckled. "You have no idea."

At the third floor there were only two doors, one to the left and one to the right. Dagny led me to the right. She pulled out her keys, inserted one, and we were in business.

The apartment was small, but had lots of character. The floors were like those I'd seen in the rest of the house, though she had large rugs in important areas like the living room and under the dining table. As you walked inside a few steps, directly to the left was a fireplace, white stone with a mantel of marble. Wow. I was impressed.

"I should go after my doctorate just so I can live here." I grinned.

Dagny laughed as she carried our goodies to the kitchen. It was toward the back of the apartment, and quite small. It only had space for the necessities and a small table with three chairs that fit into a little nook in front of a bay window. Just past the fireplace was an open door that led to the bathroom with its old fashioned claw-footed tub and pedestal sink. To the right of the room was another door, which I assumed led to Dagny's bedroom.

"This is beautiful, Dagny," I said, turning in circles. She had framed posters of abstract art hanging here and there, along with some metal sculptures. The muted figure of a human stood proud in the center of the mantel, twin crystal candle holders on either side, beautiful ivory candles in each. I figured the fireplace didn't work or wasn't used much, since there was a wooden figure of a penguin standing in the middle of it with little strings of light wrapped around him. I knelt down to get a closer look, then started as the lights came to life. They twinkled tiny spots of orange. I turned to see Dagny grinning.

"Left over from my dorm. I just couldn't throw Ozzy away."

I shook my head as I stood. "He's cute. I can understand why you'd want to keep him."

"Be right back." Dagny headed for her bedroom.

The furniture was black leather, a little worse for wear, and I figured it had been handed down. She had a couch and a chair, and an entertainment center with a 27-inch TV. A small coffee table stood in front of the couch, water marks from drinks in a couple of places. All in all, it looked like Dagny did well for herself, and the place was great.

"Okay, ready for movie number uno?" Dagny had changed into a pair of sweat shorts and sweatshirt. I nodded. "Pick one."

I looked through the quintet that I'd bought: *The World Is Not Enough, Titanic, Silence of the Lambs, Labyrinth,* and *Girl, Interrupted.* I couldn't decide, so had to close my eyes to choose. I held the Winona Ryder, Angelina Jolie great.

I turned to Dagny, who sat on the couch, socked feet tucked up under her. "Have you ever seen this?"

She took the movie from me, shaking her head. "To be honest, I've never seen any of these."

I looked at her, stunned. "You're kidding!" I took the movie from her. "I'm shocked and disappointed in you, missy." I waggled my finger at her and she chuckled.

"I know, I know. I'm a disgrace to my generation." She leaned forward and grabbed another movie. "And, what is this — *The World Is Not Enough?*"

"That's a James Bond movie." I put my hand on my hip. "Tell me you know who that is?"

She gave me a mock glare. "Of course. I'm not quite *that* out of the loop, you know."

"Okay, well, you'll be forgiven if you go make popcorn." I gave her the best puppy dog look I could muster.

"Aw, you are so cute." She chucked me under the chin and headed toward the kitchen.

I watched her go, my fingers going to my chin, gently touching the spot where her fingers had been for just a moment. I loved it when she touched me. It made me feel good, important. I smiled and slid the movie into the VCR.

Dagny watched, transfixed, as the movie progressed through Susanna Kaysen's problems and Lisa's societal dysfunctions. When it came to the part where Susanna's therapist diagnosed her as borderline personality disorder, Dagny shook her head.

"I disagree. I don't think there's a damn thing wrong with that girl except for being spoiled and self-indulgent." She popped a Junior Mint into her mouth.

I grinned. I was surprised that had been the first comment she'd made.

As the movie played on, I found myself not watching much of it. It was one I'd seen several times, and besides, something more interesting was sitting right next to me. I watched as she leaned forward a bit during a particularly exciting scene, her eyes riveted on the screen. She was so endearing — everything she did, everything she said, every move she made.

I thought about Carrie and how she reacted to women, how she called herself bi-sexual. I'd thrown that word around in my head a lot lately, and had come to the realization that I wasn't a label, and neither was Dagny. It was Dagny who had caught my attention: her beauty, her personality and mind, not her sex. I'm sure I'd figure out more things about myself as time went on, but for the moment I was content with this realization, and I didn't need to know anything else.

The movie came to an end, and Dagny didn't move, staring at the TV. Finally she turned to me. "That was really good." I nodded. "Those poor girls. Especially Daisy. My God, how could Lisa say such awful things to her to make her kill herself? That girl truly was crazy."

I grinned evilly. "I thought psych majors weren't allowed to use the word crazy."

"Har har." She turned back to the screen, watching as the credits rolled. "Well," she slapped her hands on her thighs, "what's next?"

"You pick this time."

"Hmm." She put a finger to her chin as she stared at the other four movies. "Let's try this James Bond thing. Tell me about it. I know there's about a hundred of these things, so is there something I should know ahead of time?" She picked up the box and read the back.

"Nope. Not a whole lot to think about in these, so just sit back and enjoy." I stood. "Want a Coke?"

"Oh, yeah. That sounds good." A huge smile spread across Dagny's face. "I put a Coke and a Dr Pepper in the freezer so they'd get cold faster."

Sure enough, there they were. Cans in hand, I headed back out to the living room. Dagny was taking the first movie out and putting in the second. As I resumed my seat, I realized how comfortable I felt around Dagny. Generally when I'm in someone's place, somewhere I've never been, I feel as if I don't know what to do, and I get quiet. But with her, all that flew out the window. I felt more like myself around her than I did with just me.

Dagny reacted beautifully to the movie, cringing in all the right places, laughing at others, and blushing at others. She was more fun to watch than the movie. I told her so. She glared.

"Who was the woman who played Elektra King?" she asked. "She's beautiful."

"That is the talented Sophie Marceau."

"Has she been in anything else?" Dagny hit rewind on her remote.

I nodded as I took a sip from my soda. "Yup. *Braveheart* is probably the best known."

"Okay, now I have got to see this one."

She held up the Jodie Foster, Anthony Hopkins classic. I nodded with a smile. "You're on."

"Levy has told me to watch this numerous times," she said, plopping back down on the couch.

"And why haven't you?" I looked at her, my hand on my hip.

She gave me a sheepish grin. "Because it looks scary."

I smiled, trying not to laugh because I knew she was serious. "Really?" She nodded, scooting a little closer to me. "Well, I'll protect you," I said with a chuckle.

"You spread that around and I'll pop you one." She put a fist in my face to reinforce her point.

"Yeah, I'd love to see that."

It didn't take long before Dagny had taken my hand in both of hers, setting it in her lap. I could tell exactly when she was scared, because she'd squeeze my fingers in an almost pulse-like grip, bearing down really hard when she jumped. Though it hurt, I was thoroughly enjoying the contact and the fact that I could make her feel better. I briefly considered that anyone would have had the same effect, then just discarded that notion out of hand.

I loved this movie and was excited to be with Dagny when she saw it for the first time. She was completely engrossed, loving Hannibal Lecter and his brilliantly psychotic mind. I'd known she would. I jumped, but bit my lip to stay silent as Dagny reacted to the scene at the end where the brilliant FBI agent, Clarice Starling has finally found the bad guy and is searching for him in his dungeon-like basement.

"Oh, God, turn around, Clarice," Dagny whispered, squeezing harder as she brought her legs up, curling herself up into a little ball. It was too cute. "Oh, God. He has a gun to her head and she doesn't know it. Turn around!"

"Whoa, down, girl. It's just a movie."

"No! She's... Woohoo! She shot him." She threw her arms up in victory, mine going up with them as she still had my hand in a death grip. I cried out. "Oh, Chase, I'm sorry." She quickly brought her arms down, releasing my hand only to gently take it in hers to examine it. "Oh, hon." My hand was red and smooshed. "I'm so sorry."

She looked up at me with concerned eyes. I smiled. "It's okay. I'll live. I mean, I offered to protect you."

"And you did a great job."

Keeping my hand in hers, she turned her attention back to the screen, all the while rubbing my hand, massaging it back into shape. Waves rushed through my body, ending up somewhere that surprised me. I was studying her profile when I was suddenly met with beautiful, crystal clear green eyes. She smiled. I smiled back. She stared at me for long minutes, and I couldn't read her. She took a deep breath, then turned back to the movie.

"Damn, that was good," Dagny exclaimed as the credits rolled. She looked at me, a contented smile on her face. "I have a problem." My brows drew together in confusion. "I'm out of Junior Mints." We continued to stare at each other for a moment.

"Ice cream run?"

"Ice cream run."

The little grocery store where we'd gotten the other goodies was still open, but only for another twenty minutes. We ran in, searching for the frozen foods aisle. Rows and rows of ice cream brands and flavors stared back at us; it was hard to choose.

"What do you look for in your ice cream, Chase?" Dagny asked from halfway down the aisle, a finger to her chin as she looked at all of them.

"Well, I'd have to say chocolate. Definitely important in any sort of ice cream relationship. You?"

"Sounds about right. How about this? Häagen Dazs fudge marble."

I walked over to her. "Sounds good. We have about seven minutes before they kick us out of here." We ran to find whipped cream in a can, then Hershey's chocolate syrup, and finally, and most importantly, sprinkles. Loaded down with our ingredients, we hurried to the cashier, then out into the cool night.

We made a little carpet picnic on Dagny's floor in front of the TV, all our ice cream accouterments spread out around us. I watched as Dagny piled scoop after scoop of the ice cream into her bowl, then stacked it even higher with whipped cream, adding sprinkles as the final touch. She looked up from her work of art.

"Just keep thinking swimming." She winked. I grinned and made my own sundae.

"So, you still think psych is right for you, my little protégé?" Dagny asked around a mouthful of ice cream.

I shrugged, swallowing enough so that I could talk and be understood. "I've always thought people were really fascinating and loved to try and figure them out, you know? I like to figure out what makes them tick."

"Well then, you are definitely in the right business." She patted my knee.

"I should hope so. I never really thought about my interests being in psychology. I didn't really know exactly how it could be characterized." I dug deeper into my bowl, trying to find the mother lode of chocolate syrup. "Also, I have to admit," I looked down at my bowl, embarrassed, "your class really got me thinking, too." It was silent and I wondered what Dagny was thinking. She had the sweetest smile on her face.

"Thank you, Chase. That means a lot." She rubbed my knee. "I'll miss having you in class this semester. You have some wonderful ideas, Chase."

It was my turn to put the goofy smile on my face. "What about you? What got you into it? And what do you want to do once you're out?"

She chuckled. "You make it sound like prison." I shrugged. "Well, my mother is a teacher, as you know, and when I was a kid, she demanded that I learn a little about everything. My God, some of the stuff I had to read." She rolled her eyes. "Anyway, she gave me a textbook about psychology that was scaled down for kids. It just stuck with me, and I've been hooked ever since." She took a deep breath, then took a bite of her ice cream as she thought. "As for what I want to do with it once I'm out, as you put it, well, I've thought a lot about teaching. I've had some wonderful professors and I'd love to be like them."

"You're already on your way. You're a fantastic teacher, Dag. Really, your passion for the subject comes through in every class. You're good at what you do. You make people want to learn, want to understand and love it the way you do. You did with me, anyway."

Dagny sat back, looking at me in obvious surprise. "God, that is the nicest thing anyone has ever said to me."

"Wow. Then you're missing out on life." I smiled. Finally shaking herself out of her surprise, she smiled, too.

I spent the night at Dagny's place and we went to the Y to swim early the next morning, both of us dragging from too little sleep and my back hurting from sleeping on the couch. The swim was great, just as fulfilling as it had been the previous two times, and I felt wonderful for doing it, not to mention the chance to spend more time with Dagny and to see her in a bathing suit.

The last couple of weeks before school started were great. Outside of the time I spent practicing with the band, Dagny and I did something together just about every day. Often we found ourselves sitting around somewhere talking. We didn't need anything else. She was quickly turning into a truly cherished friend.

*∼*∼*∼*∼*∼*

"Put your hands together for Casually In Debt!" The crowd in Gotfry's, mostly regulars, cheered and whistled. The band was excited and ready to go, ready to try out our new drummer. Terrie showed outstanding ability and talent, and I knew the place would go into a frenzy at some of the solos we had planned for her.

We rocked the place, playing music from the Stones, Pat Benatar, even a Paul Simon song. It was a terrific night, and the mood in the bar was perfect for really letting go. It was kids coming back from the holidays wanting to have one last hurrah before classes started up again.

After our set was over, my throat felt raw. I should have been rehearsing the entire break, but I hadn't and was paying for it. I left the stage and hurried to the bar, craving the glass of ice water I knew Greg would have waiting for me.

"That drummer of yours kicks some serious ass!" the bartender exclaimed, looking at Terrie with adoring eyes. "She single?"

I rolled my eyes and took the glass from him. Within a few seconds I felt a hand on my shoulder. I turned, expecting to see familiar green eyes, but was surprised to see dark instead.

"Great set, Chase," the drummer said, ordering her own water.

"Thanks. You, too. You nearly brought the house down all by yourself on those things." I indicated the set on the stage.

She shrugged and took her glass, swigging about half before ordering a shot of tequila. "Can I get you one?" She lifted the small shot glass. I looked at it and shook my head. Shrugging again, she downed the clear liquid fire, barely raising an eyebrow as it slid down her throat. She slammed the glass down, wiped her mouth with the back of her hand.

I noticed the way people looked at Terrie, men and women alike. Tight clothing fitted over a nice, lean body, with a very sensual quality. She was beautiful, and she knew it, too.

"See you back on stage." She put her hand on my back, trailing her fingers across my shoulders as she walked away. I followed her with my eyes.

"Hey."

I turned, an immediate smile coming to my face. "Hey. Did you like it?"

Dagny smiled. "I did. Who is that woman?" she asked, the smile quickly dropping from her face. I followed her gaze, wondering who she was talking about. It was Terrie.

"Oh, Doug's cousin, Terrie. Isn't she great?" I smiled in her direction, more and more impressed with her playing every time I heard her.

"Yeah. Great."

I looked at Dagny, surprised. I'd never seen that particular look on her face before and couldn't quite read it. She seemed to shake herself out of it and turned to me with a big smile.

"I'm so thrilled you guys are playing again. You got me spoiled." She took my arm, shaking it a little to emphasize her point.

"I know. I missed it, too. Hey, what did you think of Thanatos?" I grinned, nodding toward my electric guitar on its stand near the microphone. Dagny had finally capitulated and come up with a name for my newest baby, and Thanatos, the Greek personification of Death, was it. "Than" for short.

Dagny looked at me with pride. "Your baby rocks this place, girl."

"Chase," Doug called.

"Shit, gotta run. Talk to you after the show?" I glanced over my shoulder as I turned to hurry to the stage.

Dagny nodded. "I'll be here. We're over there." She pointed to the table where her friends sat drinking and laughing.

The show went on, the second half just as good as the first. I felt as if I were flying up there, high as a kite, free as a bird. I was back and with a vengeance.

We decided to try out a new song Doug had written that had heavy drum and guitar. This was my spotlight, just me and Than. There wasn't a great deal of vocal in the song, just a heavy beat.

Terrie and I had spent a lot of time together the previous week, since it was mostly us on this song, everyone else falling into the background. She and I would get to Doug's early just to practice my riff and her solo. We had gotten a chance to talk a little, and I had found out she was originally from Oklahoma and had moved to Tucson two years earlier for a job. She was in the computer business, doing music on the side. She owed Doug a favor, so offered to play for us until we found someone else. Now she was thinking she'd stick around.

I turned to her, Than in my arms, my fingers moving as fast as they could, sliding across the neck and chords, making my guitar talk. Terrie's head was bobbing with the music, her entire body into the beat. I smiled at her; she smiled back. We were in our own little world, and the crowd was loving it.

When it came time for me to start singing again, I turned back to the mic and belted out the lyrics. Some people had gotten up and started to dance. That was a first. I smiled into the music as I sang, the little black beauty humming in my hands.

When the song ended, the crowd was on its feet. I couldn't stop smiling. I turned back to Terrie and held out my hand to her. "Come on, let's hear it for Terrie Cannavo." The crowd continued to clap. "Our new drummer." They clapped even louder. At that point I probably could have told them that I had to go to the bathroom and they'd have loved it. Too much adrenaline and booze.

Our second set over, the lights were turned off and finally the stage didn't feel like the bins under warming lamps at a fast food place. Melo already put away, I packed Than away in her case and ran a hand through very sweaty hair, trying to get it off my forehead. I reached into my pocket to find my hair tie, then gathered my hair into a pony tail.

Most of the band were on their way out the door; I was usually the last one to leave. I grabbed both my guitars and turned, startled to see Terrie leaning against the bar, her sticks in her hand, drumming out a simple beat against the wood. She smiled when she saw I was looking at her.

"Hey." I walked down the stairs and leaned my babies against a barstool. "You waiting for Doug?"

"Yep. You did great tonight, you know. You really take control of those people out there." She pointed to the remaining audience with one of her sticks. "You've really got talent."

"Thanks. So do you. I mean, the way you beat those things. Hell, I couldn't do it."

"Sure you could. You've got rhythm; that's all you need. I could show you if you want."

"Leave her alone, Terrie. She's not your kind." I turned to see Doug coming up, his guitar strapped to his back. He playfully punched me on the chin. "Great show, kid."

I grinned. "Thanks. You, too." He saluted, pushing Terrie in front of him as he headed out of the bar. I watched them go, wondering what their exchange was all about.

"I bet you're tired."

I turned to see Dagny headed in my direction. "Oh, yeah. You can definitely say that again. Man, my throat hurts." I massaged it, waving Greg over.

"Good show. See you Wednesday." The bartender smiled, winked at Dagny, then went to another customer at the other end of the bar.

Dagny's brows drew together. "Why Wednesday?"

"He asked us to start playing on the underage night." I shrugged. "More play time. Works for me."

She smiled. "That's great. Is it going to be too much with school, though?"

"I hope not. I already told Greg that if it got to be too much we'd kill the idea."

"Sounds like a plan. Want to join us?" She nodded toward the table she was at with her friends.

I knew full well that they were all grad students like Dagny, some of them already graduated. I felt small and inadequate. "Um, are you sure? I mean, I can barely vote, let alone drink."

My friend smiled encouragingly, nudging my arm with her shoulder. "I wouldn't have asked if I didn't want you to, you nut."

"Well, okay. Can I put these two to bed first?" I indicated my guitars. She offered to help me load them into my car. As we headed back into the bar, I felt slightly nauseous. I didn't do real well with people I didn't know, even if there was only one or two at a time. This was an entire table full. I took a deep breath and followed Dagny.

"Hey, guys. This is Chase Marin. Chase, Steve, Tanya, Adam and Laura."

I nodded at each person as they were introduced. When she finished, I brought my hand up in a little wave. "Hey."

"Hey, you kick some ass with those guitars," Adam said. He smiled and gave me a double thumbs up.

I grinned shyly. "Thanks. You guys come here a lot?"

Three hours and two pitchers of beer later, Dagny and I walked out of Gotfry's, still laughing. I had had the time of my life. They had treated me like anyone else, and not like a kid the way I figured they would. They had been curious about me at first, asking me questions about school and the band, then conversation had moved around to any number of different topics, most ending up with someone telling some sort of horrible story that was very funny.

"So, what did you think of the useless ones in there?" Dagny asked, hooking her thumb at the bar.

"Very cool. I liked them a lot." We reached my car.

"Well, I think they liked you a lot, too. You have so much to offer, Chase. It's a shame you're so shy."

She leaned against the next car while I rested against my own and crossed my arms over my chest. "I know. Can't help it. I always have been."

"You seem to do okay once you're there for a little while. You shocked the hell out of me a few times, kiddo." She lightly punched my arm.

I shrugged. "Eh, what can I say."

"So, you coming tomorrow morning?"

"Of course."

"Well, how about doing something now? You too tired?"

I looked up at the night sky, black and filled with stars, and shook my head. "Nope. Tired, but wide awake."

"Me too. Let's go for a drive." Dagny smiled like she'd just come up with the greatest idea in the world.

"You're on."

We ran my guitars home, then I hurried over to her Vitara. I patted the hood of the small SUV. I had been astonished when Dagny had finally relented and let me name her car. "So, how is ol' Freud?"

"She's doing just fine." She unlocked her door, then mine. "Don't you think it's a little odd that a 'female' car is named Freud?"

I got in and shut my door. "Yeah. And? Freud would love it!" My grin was large and exaggerated.

"Nut." She put her key in the ignition, then stopped, turning to me. "Hey!"

I was startled. "What?"

"Let's take the top off the back."

My grin matched hers. "Yeah."

We quickly got out, unzipped the rag top, and tucked it into the back. The night was beautiful as January flowed into its third week. Dagny drove us everywhere — through town, then out past it into the darkness. Neither of us said a word, just enjoyed the scenery beautiful rock formations of the desert, the plant life, and seemingly endless sky and the feel of not having to say anything.

It was late, but I didn't care. These were the days I knew I'd look back on some day and say "I remember when..." The times I wanted to remember. Just me, Dagny, and the Tucson night air.

# Chapter 6

School was back in session for my second semester at the University of Arizona, and I was ready for it. None of my classes this semester was as early as the first semester, and that was a definite plus. I hadn't seen much of Carrie, only passing her on the way to my Music From Around the World class. She looked at me, ducked her head, and quickly scurried away. I felt sad, but I still wasn't ready to talk.

Part of me missed her. After all, it had been nearly two months since we'd spoken. I didn't know what to do to reconnect with her, but figured it'd hit me on the head when I did.

* ~ * ~ * ~ * ~ * ~ *

"Thank you very much. Good night." The lights lowered, and we were clear to pack up our gear and head home. It was CID's first night playing at Gotfry's on Wednesday, and it went off pretty well. We had to break them in fresh; very few Friday regulars hung around with a bunch of teenagers. We also toned down our music a bit, trying to stick with contemporary favorites so we wouldn't lose our audience.

I packed up Than and Melo and headed to the bar for my end of the night glass of water.

"So, what do you think, Greg? Were we a hit?" I slammed the cooling liquid.

"Yeah, I think so. Obviously the weekend crowd is better business, but I think they liked it fine. But, I have to say, I never in my life thought I'd hear you pop off a Britney Spears song." He grimaced.

I laughed. "Yeah, me either. We'll catch you Friday."

"Later, kid."

I put the empty glass on the bar and grabbed my babies, ready to head out.

"Hey."

"Hey." I was surprised to see Dagny standing at the end of the bar. "What are you doing here?" I looked over her shoulder to see if any of her friends were sitting at their usual table. "Where's everyone else?"

"Nope, just me." She took Melo from me. I gladly relinquished half of my load.

"Why?" We headed out the door into the cool night.

"Me? Miss one of Casually In Debt's performances? I don't

think so." She smiled and winked. I felt as if I were flying.

"Really? You just came to see us play?"

"Well, actually, more to hear you sing." She looked a bit shy, which surprised me all the more. We reached my car, and she helped me load my babies in the trunk.

I turned to her, utterly flattered. "That's really sweet."

"Well, hey." She shuffled her feet. "Oh, um, do you have plans now?"

I shook my head. "Nope."

"Cool. Earlier today I made some homemade potato soup. Want some?" My mouth began to water just at the idea of it. Dagny smiled as she could see my jaw already starting to work. "It's really yummy," she enticed.

"Oh, okay." I grinned as we headed for Freud.

"So, how are classes going? It sucks not being able to see you much anymore." She turned to look at me briefly before turning her eyes back to the road.

"I know. I have to admit, um, I miss you."

She smiled warmly, reaching over to rub my arm. "Me, too, Chase. Hey, isn't that your friend over there?"

I turned to look at the park we were passing. On a bench, not far off the road, a couple appeared to be making out in the glare of a streetlight. It was Carrie and the guy she'd had in her room the night I had gone to talk with her. He slid his hand up her leg, under her skirt. She stopped his hand, but kept kissing him. I turned away in disgust.

"Yeah. That was my friend," I said quietly, ashamed that Dagny had seen that.

"Have you seen or talked to her lately?" Dagny asked, her voice quiet, sad.

I shook my head.

"I'm sorry, hon."

"Happens."

I was quiet the rest of the short drive to Dagny's apartment, my thoughts solely on Carrie. I had noticed a liquor bottle on the bench. What was she doing? Tears built up behind my eyes, and I tried to push them away. I didn't need to cry, nor did I want to. It was her life, right?

"Come on in." Dagny unlocked and opened her door, letting me enter first. She flicked on the overhead light, and I headed straight for the couch. The apartment was almost like a second home to me after all the time I'd spent there during Christmas vacation.

Dagny sat next to me. "Here, lean forward." I did. She put her hands on my shoulders and began to work the tight muscles there. "God, you're so tense, Chase. Want to talk about—"

I exploded. "I mean, we've been best friends since we were two years old, Dag. Two!" I held up two fingers for emphasis. "And never in nearly seventeen years did we go a day without seeing each other, and definitely not without talking on the phone." I swiped an impatient hand across my eyes as I felt the stinging returning. "We didn't even see each other on Christmas! Didn't that bother her, Dag? Didn't it?"

"I don't know, honey," she answered, still working magic hands on my back and shoulders.

"I mean, how can she let this happen? We started partying together in high school, nearly got kicked out as I told you before, but then I slowed down. I did!" I put my hand on my chest. "Why can't she? Why can't she grow up and see what she's doing to so many people? She's hurting not only me, her parents, her grades and chances at college, but herself. Mostly herself. She is going to end up pregnant, or get into some kind of accident, or worse. God, she's a goddamn alcoholic at eighteen. She turns nineteen the day after I do, Dag. In three weeks. That's seventeen years of friendship down the drain." I snapped my fingers. "Just like that." I pulled away and turned to face her. "What do I do? How can I save her?"

"I don't know, Chase. There may be no way for you to. She's on her own self-destructive path right now, sweetie, and only she can stop it." She put her hand on my knee.

I loved the contact, needing to feel connected to someone, connected to Dagny. "But isn't there something I can say, maybe someone I can talk to?" I ran a hand through my hair, pushing it back from my face before I gathered it into a ponytail.

"Well, you could talk to her advisor, I suppose, or even her parents." Dagny shrugged. "What do you think? Would she be receptive to something like that?"

"I just don't know anymore, you know? She's a totally different person than when we started here."

"So are you, Chase."

I ended my tirade abruptly and just stared at her. Had I changed? "Why can't she change?" I asked, my voice pitifully quiet. Then the stinging became too much for me to handle and it bled out my eyes, releasing the pent up pain of nearly five months of a slow, painful wedge that had inched its way between me and my best friend. I was feeling the division. I lunged into Dagny's arms as the sobs burst from me, erupting from my chest with vicious strength.

"Shh, baby. It's okay."

I could hear Dagny's soothing voice from somewhere above me as I let myself go, allowing myself to reveal a most inner part of myself, knowing that my secrets were safe with Dagny.

She held me, her arms strong and comforting as she gently rocked me, petting my back, brushing back hair that was sticking to

my tear-streaked face. I was amazed that I didn't feel alone anymore.

An hour or so later I stood at the door, a Tupperware dish of
potato soup in my hand. My eyes were red and swollen. I felt a little awkward, but not ashamed, which was shocking. I hated to cry
in front of people. I hated to cry at all. "Thanks, Dag," I said quietly, holding the cold dish of soup against my chest. "I really appreciate it."

"No problem. You can have my homemade soup anytime." She
smiled, winked.

I grinned. "Yeah. Well, I'm going to go. I'm beat."

"I bet. You take care, and if you need *any*thing you let me
know, all right?"

I nodded, holding out my free arm for a hug. Dagny stepped
into it, wrapping her arms around my neck, squeezing me. We
stayed like that for a moment, neither moving, almost not breathing.

Dagny smiled as she pulled away, gently patting my shoulder.
"I'll see you in the morning, Chase. Sleep well."

"Thanks." I took one last look and left the apartment.

* ~ * ~ * ~ * ~ * ~ *

I couldn't hit the pillow fast enough for my eyes to slam shut,
game over. It was after one in the morning when I finally got to
bed, and not two hours later when I heard voices in the room.

I opened an eye, my back toward the room, so I listened.

"Please, I need to talk to Chase." The voice was faint, but
nearly hysterical.

"Hang on." I heard footfalls, then felt Natalie's hands on my
back. "Chase, some girl's at the door for you. I think it's your friend
Carrie."

Both eyes flew open, and I rolled over and looked up at my
roommate. Her long hair was a mess, and she looked as if she were
about to fall asleep on her feet. Looking over at the door, I could
see Carrie in the hall. As soon as I saw her face, I shot out of bed.
Her heavy eye make-up was all over her face, as well as her lipstick,
which she wiped at with her hand as I watched. I barely noticed
Natalie staring as I hurried out to my friend.

"Carrie?"

Her head jerked up, her eyes wide, almost wild. As soon as she
saw me she broke into tears. "I'm sorry to come here, Chase, I know
it's late, I didn't know where else to go."

"It's okay. Come on." I went out into the hall and closed the
door behind us, then looked up and down, trying to decide what to
do, where to take her. Deciding on the bathroom, I gently took her

by the arm and led her toward it, hurried into a shower stall and pulled the curtain closed around us. I looked her over, trying to figure out what the hell had happened. Her make-up was smeared all over her face and I saw that her dress was torn in several places, and she was dirty. A wave of nausea flooded through me, but I had to hold it together. "What happened?"

Carrie looked down at her hands, which were playing with a fringed edge on her dress. She leaned back against the tiled wall and took a deep breath. Finally garnering her courage, she looked up at me. I noticed that there was some blood mixed in with her lipstick at the right corner of her lip.

"I was raped," she said quietly, then quickly looked down again.

"The guy you were with on the park bench?" I asked, just as quietly.

Her head jerked up. "You saw us?" I nodded. She swallowed hard, her eyes beginning to fill as they looked everywhere but at me. "I didn't mean for it to happen, Chase. I...we were just kissing, and he started to try things, you know, and I told him no, threw his hand off my leg, I didn't want him that way. I just wanted to have some fun, you know?" She looked at me, her eyes begging for understanding. "I didn't want this." Her voice broke, and so did she.

I wrapped my arms around her heaving body, my eyes squeezed closed as I fought my own emotions.

"You have got to go to a doctor, Car," I whispered.

"No. I can't," she sobbed, holding onto me painfully tight. "I'm sorry, Chase. I didn't want to disappoint you. I didn't have anywhere else to go." Her cries echoed around the tiled room and I sucked in a breath as I heard the heavy bathroom door squeak open. Carrie lifted her head, biting her lip to try and keep her tears in check until the most inopportune arrival left. We listened to the stall door open, shut, and the lock slide into place, then the agonizingly long peeing session.

"God, finish already," I growled. Carrie, under control, fell into me again, her head resting on my shoulder as she clutched at my shirt. The girl sat there for a minute, waiting for I don't want to know what, when finally we heard the toilet flush, the water ran as hands were washed, and the person left. I let out a breath and gently pushed my friend away so that I could look at her. "Carrie, you have to get checked. If nothing else, they can give you a morning after pill. Please? I'm begging you."

"No, Chase. I can't." She began to cry again. "I don't know what to do."

I hugged her, staring up at the showerhead, praying to its chrome brilliance for guidance. Dagny. She'd know what to do.

"Carrie, listen to me for a second. Do you remember my friend Dagny?" She nodded against my neck, calming a bit. "Let me call her. She'll know what to do, okay?"

She pulled away from me, shaking her head. "No! She's a teacher, Chase."

"She's one of the kindest people I know, Car. She'll know what to do, I promise." She stared at me, dark eyes so tired, worn out. Finally, reluctantly, she nodded. "Do you have your cell?" Again she nodded and handed me her purse. I dug through it, finding a rolled up joint and a travel-size bottle of Jack Daniels. "Carrie," I chided, pocketing both. Feeling the smooth plastic of my friend's phone against my fingers, I pulled it out and dialed Dagny's number. It rang three times. I was worried she wouldn't hear it.

"Hello?" came a barely intelligible voice.

"Dag?"

"Chase?" Her voice sobered immediately. "What is it? What time is it?"

"It's really late. Put it this way, we go swimming in three hours." I could barely force a smile. "Dag, I need you here now. Please."

"Are you okay, hon?" She was awake now. I could almost imagine her sitting up in bed, already scanning her room for clothes to throw on.

"I'm afraid you'd have to define 'okay'. Please, Dag. Just come." I looked at my friend who had curled herself up into a little ball in the corner of the shower stall.

"Be there in five minutes."

The phone went dead in my hand. I clicked it off, sticking it with Carrie's other possessions, and knelt down to her. "She's on her way, Car. She can help."

"I'm sorry, Chase." Carrie looked up at me with sad eyes, fresh tears waiting to fall. "I'm so ashamed."

I gathered her in my arms and rocked her gently. "We'll work it out, Car. We always have." I kissed the top of her messy, dirty hair. "We have to go, Carrie. We'll meet her downstairs, okay?" She nodded. I helped her stand, since she was not at all steady on her feet. We went back to my room where I stuffed a pair of sweats and a sweatshirt into a bag. We then headed out, my arm around her waist and me playing Cloak and Dagger around every corner, making sure no one was there until we reached the cool night air.

"Do you hate me, Chase?"

I looked at my friend. She looked dejected, like she was resigned to the fact that I did. I smiled as reassuringly as I could and shook my head. "I could never hate you, Carrie. You're my best friend."

She threw herself at me, sobbing for different reasons now. I could hear the relief in it as opposed to the earlier devastation.

"I love you, Chase."

"I love you, too."

True to her word, within a few minutes I saw Freud taking the corner into the parking lot at a ridiculous rate of speed. The little SUV pulled up beside us, and Dagny was out in a flash, running around the front to the bench where we were sitting. She was dressed in a pair of black soccer shorts, tennis shoes with no socks, and a sweatshirt, hair hidden under a baseball cap.

"What happened?" She went immediately to Carrie, kneeling in front of her and looking up into the tortured face. "Oh, honey." She looked up at me with questions in her eyes.

"She was raped," I said, my voice low, doing my damnedest to hold it together. She nodded as if she had guessed as much. I stood away from the bench, allowing Dagny to take my place and talk to Carrie.

"Carrie, honey, do you hurt anywhere?" Dagny put her hand on my friend's hand where it rested in her lap. Carrie nodded. "There may be some damage, hon. We really need to get that looked at." She stared into Carrie's eyes to make sure she had her attention. "By a doctor, Carrie. He may have torn you, okay? If you don't get that fixed up, there could be problems later. Also the doctor can give you a pill to prevent pregnancy." She looked into Carrie's eyes. "Will you let us take you, hon?"

"I don't want to get in trouble," Carrie whispered.

"You won't, honey, the bastard who did this to you, will. They will want to know his name, okay? Will you do this for me, Carrie? For Chase?" She looked up at me for a second, our eyes meeting, both filled with worry and both scared for Carrie. Dagny looked back at Carrie, pleading with her to let us take care of her.

As I watched them, my mind raced back to earlier times, happier times with me and Carrie. I saw us together at five years old, playing in my mom's flower bed, throwing dark, rich potting soil around until we were both covered head to toe, our eyes the only things visible on our faces. Next came my tenth birthday, when I got my first BMX dirt bike — silver and blue, just like Carrie's. We rode day and night, as far as our mothers would let us go. Then when I fell off my bike at thirteen, skinning my knee, and Carrie took me home, me riding on her handlebars, nearly dumping me into my father's car as she turned into the driveway. Getting drunk for the first time together at sixteen, and finding out we had both been accepted at UA. What went wrong?

"Okay," Carrie whispered, clutching Dagny's hands tight. "Will you guys stay with me?"

"The entire time, won't we, Chase?"

"Absolutely."

"Okay. I'll do it."

* ~ * ~ * ~ * ~ * ~ *

Carrie filled out all the appropriate forms, then was taken into a little examination cubicle where neither Dagny nor I was allowed to go. Wanting to stay with my friend, I tried, and nearly got thrown out of the hospital. Finally resigning myself to the ER waiting room with Dagny, I paced back and forth as she sat, legs crossed, looking the picture of calm. The toe of her left tennis shoe tapped non-stop on the white tile, and she kept sucking her bottom lip into her mouth, only to let it go seconds later. I didn't know what to say, wondering what was going through her head. I felt very protective of Carrie at that moment, like a mother bear and her cub. I knew Dagny wouldn't say anything, more than likely feeling much the same way I did.

"Are you okay, hon?" I turned, looked at her. She beckoned me over. "Why don't you sit, Chase? Come here."

I did as I was told, plopped down in the black vinyl chair next to Dagny's. My head seemed to weigh a ton all of a sudden, and it found its way onto her shoulder. I felt an arm come around me, pulling me closer.

"Yeah. I'll live. I keep thinking about all the times when we were kids." I smiled. "God, we were evil together, constantly getting into something, some kind of trouble." I sat up, my mind focusing on the memory but my hand straying to Dagny's, needing to feel the warmth of her skin. "One time we got home from school before my mom did, and we found a bag of marshmallows that I knew were to be saved for a fruit salad my mom was going to make." I chuckled. "We grabbed a candle from the table and lit it. Now keep in mind we're like eleven. We lit the candle, stuck those big, fat marshmallows on the end of dinner knives, and roasted them. We made the biggest mess." Dagny broke into laughter and I joined in. "My mom nearly killed us over that one."

"What did she do?"

"She grounded me for a month, but she only made me stay grounded for about a week, and I had to buy her a new bag of marshmallows." I shook my head, the smile still on my face. "We used to steal Carla's lunch money all the time, right out of her backpack. She had no idea. That lasted for about a year until she finally caught on. And they say *she's* the smart one?" I grinned. "What do they know?"

The swinging doors opened, and a female police officer entered. She headed straight for the ER doors and disappeared. Part of me wondered if she was there to talk to Carrie. I looked at Dagny. The look on her face told me she was thinking the same thing.

"How long does this stuff usually take?"

"I really don't know." She looked at me, her eyes sad.

"You don't have to stick around, Dag. It's so late, and I know you have a busy day. Really, we can—"

"There is no way in hell I'm leaving you, Chase." Her look was stern, warning me not to ask again.

I smiled. "Okay. Just giving you an out."

"Well, I don't want one. But I do want a Coke." She indicated the machine near the door. "Want one?" I nodded. "Okay. Be right back." She patted my hand and a few minutes later brought back two cans. I opened and drank from mine, more for something to do and to get my mind off everything than from thirst.

We sat for another half hour, neither of us speaking, my head resting on her shoulder. Finally the doors opened and the police officer came out, joined by a woman in scrubs and a white lab coat.

"Chase Marin?" They walked up to us, the only people in the waiting room. I stood, Dagny by my side. "Hello. I'm Officer Campbell, and this is Dr. Williams. We examined Carrie."

"How is she?" I asked.

"She's fair. As well as can be at least from what we found during our examination of her."

"Was there any damage?" Dagny asked, holding my hand a bit tighter as we waited for the answer.

The doctor nodded. "There was a bit, but nothing permanent. I put in two stitches and it should heal up just fine. Physically there wasn't much evidence of trauma, except of course for the usual bruising and small cuts here and there."

"It's the mental and emotional aspects, though," the officer finished. "She's really going to need her friends." She looked from one of us to the other. "She will go through some depression, nightmares, that sort of thing. She has agreed to press charges, and that will be another ordeal for her."

"What can we do to help her?"

The officer looked at Dagny. "Just be there for her. She probably shouldn't be alone tonight."

"She was given the morning after pill. That shouldn't have any serious side effects," the doctor added. "We did some blood work, but it will be about two weeks before we get the culture results. Often it takes a while for things to show up in the system."

"Um, you mean like diseases?" I asked, feeling sick. The doctor nodded. "Oh, God." Dagny's hand tightened around mine.

"Any more questions?" We both shook our heads. "Okay., Chase, she's asking for you." The doctor smiled encouragement, and headed back through the double doors; the officer left the ER.

I followed the doctor, change of clothes in hand, my stomach churning. Only one person could see a patient at a time, so Dagny went to get her car and pull it up to the curb. I took a deep breath as I got closer to cubicle number 33. Quietly sliding the curtain aside, I saw Carrie sitting on the side of the narrow bed wearing a hospital gown. She looked up, relief shining in her eyes when she saw it was me. They had washed her face and tended to the cut at her mouth. She was pale and looked so tired.

"Hey," I said, at a loss for words. She gave me a weak smile. "Are you ready to go?"

"Yeah. I don't want to be alone, Chase." Her voice was quiet, hoarse.

"I know. We're going to Dagny's place. Is that okay? I can't take you back to my room with Natalie there, and you've got Rachel in your room." She nodded. "Good. Here, here's some clothes."

"Thanks." She took them, staring down at them, but not moving.

"Are you okay, Car?" She looked up at me, reached out her hand. I took it; it was cold and clammy. I wondered if she was in shock. "Can I give you a hug?"

"Please?"

I took the few steps that separated us and enfolded her in my embrace, wanting to take her inside me and protect her, save her. She took a deep breath, releasing it in a shaky sigh.

"Are you okay?"

I felt her nod against my chest. "I want a shower."

I smiled.

* ~ * ~ * ~ * ~ * ~ *

It was after five by the time we reached Dagny's apartment. She had insisted that Carrie take her bed, with me beside her.

"You can't leave her alone tonight, Chase," Dagny explained as Carrie took a shower. "She needs you."

"God, I don't want to kick you out of your bed, Dag. We're already intruding—"

"Don't ever think that, Chase. You are always welcome here, and Carrie is too, especially after this. Really, do it. Please?"

I sighed in resignation. "Okay." I was wiped out, sleeping on my feet.

Carrie got out of the shower, the towel wrapped tightly around her body, her arms over her chest. "I want to go to bed," she murmured.

"Okay. Come on." I put my hand on her shoulder and led her to Dagny's bedroom. I looked over my shoulder at our hostess. Dag was standing by the couch, a pile of sheets and blanket in hand for her makeshift bed. She smiled, nodding encouragement. "Goodnight," I called.

"Night, Chase."

* ~ * ~ * ~ * ~ * ~ *

My head lifted slightly from the pillow, my nose leading the way. *Waffles? Have I died and gone to Heaven?* My eyes cracked open, grating over the sand of too little sleep. I glanced at the alarm clock on the side table to see it was after ten. Five hours of sleep. I'd had worse, but I felt emotionally drained. I turned to look at my friend; she was still asleep. Carrie's sleep had been fitful, restless. She had cried out once, and I had wondered if it had been from a nightmare or from pain. She had been in my arms most of the night.

I slowly, quietly, got myself out of the bed and snatched my jeans off the floor, having slept in only a tee and underwear. I could faintly hear the clanking of dishes in the kitchen and made my way out to the noise.

Sure enough, Dagny was standing at the counter — one hand on her hip, the other on the top of the waffle iron, waiting for it to finish.

"Hey," I said quietly. She looked at me over her shoulder and smiled. She looked just as bad as I felt.

"Hey. How did it go? Is she awake?"

I shook my head. "It was okay, I guess. I think she had a lot of bad dreams, but other than that, she slept for the most part." I took the carafe of fresh coffee from the coffee maker, and poured myself a cup.

"How are you doing?"

I looked at her, shrugged. "I'm fine. Why?"

She turned to me, her head cocked to one side. "Chase, you witnessed the results of a brutal attack on your best friend. That's sure to cause some problems, affect you deeply."

"I don't need a psychiatrist, Dag." I glared at her. I didn't want to be bothered. I was fine. She was taken aback, nodding and looking back at the waffle maker. I sighed, feeling horrible. What had I done? "I'm sorry." I took a couple steps toward her, not sure what to do or say. "I'm really sorry." I set down the cup, my head hanging.

"It's okay, Chase. I won't push."

I felt a hand on my head, fingers running through my hair, and leaned in a little toward her, wanting a hug but not quite knowing how to ask. She got the picture, and her arms slid around my neck. She rubbed my back; I buried my face against her neck, inhaling the smell that was Dagny. She slowly ran her hand up my back to my neck, resting her fingers on the warm skin there. I didn't want to part, didn't want to move from that spot, ever. I knew I had to, though, so reluctantly I drew away, looking into her eyes to see if she was still hurt or mad at me. I couldn't stand the thought of her being either. Her smile reached her eyes. We were fine. I smiled back.

"Breakfast is ready. Do you think we should wake Carrie?"

I glanced down at the waffle maker, then out toward the closed bedroom door. "I don't know. Maybe?" I looked at her, unsure. Our question became moot when the door opened and Carrie stumbled out, still dressed in the sweats and sweatshirt from the night before. She didn't look at us as she made her way over to the bathroom.

"We should try and keep her busy today. How is your schedule?"

I looked at the clock on the stove. "Um, well I should be in Biology right now."

She nodded. "Yeah, I understand that."

"You're right, though. We can't leave her. Shopping? Don't most girls like that?" My brow knitted as I thought.

Dagny chuckled. "Yeah, I think most do." She nudged my arm, turning to breakfast, serving it up.

* ~ * ~ * ~ * ~ * ~ *

To my surprise, the mall was fairly busy, even though it was a Thursday afternoon, and I had figured most people would either be at work or at school. I was wrong.

Carrie had been pretty blasé about the idea of taking her out, not really caring much, but Dagny and I knew if she sat around, she'd do nothing but think about her ordeal all day. She walked around in a borrowed pair of Dagny's jeans and my sweatshirt, her shoulders hunched, hands buried in her pockets, looking almost painfully stiff. Her eyes were in constant motion, looking at every person that we passed, especially guys. She looked like a rabbit caught in a trap, with Dagny and me on either side of her to try and give her support.

"Where do you want to go, hon?" Dagny asked, looking around for some store that might be of interest to Carrie.

Carrie shrugged. "I don't care."

Dagny looked at me behind my friend, her eyes filled with question. I shrugged. "How about See's Chocolates?" I pointed, knowing that chocolate was Carrie's weakness. She glanced over at it, shrugging again. "Come on." I tugged at her arm, Dagny following.

"Oh, it smells so good in here." We looked at the cases of delectable treats. I was thoroughly stuffed from the waffles Dagny had made, but these sweet treats could make my stomach growl, regardless. I was pleased to see that Carrie was actually looking around, seeing what was available.

"Can I help you?" the salesgirl said, smiling. "Some samples, maybe?"

"Oh, look at that, Car." I pointed out a tray of dark chocolate wedges, her favorite. "Can we get a sample of these, please?"

The girl handed my friend a little paper cup with some of the dark chocolate. Carrie took it with a small thank you and looked at it for a moment before nibbling a tiny piece.

I smiled, glad to see that she wasn't too gone. I looked at Carrie's face to check the bruising. She looked like she'd been in a small scrape, but nothing major. She was still pale, which made the bruises stand out more, but her mouth looked better, the cut being much smaller than I had originally thought. She would be okay.

Carrie seemed to have perked up a bit by the time we left See's. We walked around, looking at clothes, books and music. Dagny bought Carrie the newest CD by Pink, which made her a very happy camper. She actually looked like she was enjoying herself, only getting quiet intermittently. We took her to a late lunch, then settled in for a movie, a light-hearted comedy that she laughed at. Dagny and I breathed a sigh of relief, a little too soon.

We were walking down the main hallway of the mall, talking and chatting, when a group of high school-aged guys started walking toward us. I didn't think anything of it, but apparently it got Carrie thinking, and thinking got Carrie upset and scared. She stopped dead in her tracks, staring wide-eyed at the guys, most of whom were ignoring us, a few checking us out but not saying anything.

"I can't, I can't," she said, pulling away from us. Her body got tense as she morphed into that "fight or flight" mode.

"Carrie? What is it? What's wrong? Was it those guys?" I looked back at them to see if they were doing anything, but they were headed into the music store, not giving us another glance.

"Did you know them, Carrie?" Dagny asked, just as concerned and confused as I was. Carrie shook her head vigorously, really starting to get upset.

"I think they reminded her of, well..." I looked at Dagny. She nodded understanding, and we led Carrie to a bench in a secluded nook. I gently pushed her down to sit, then sat close by with my hands on her back. Dagny sat on the other side, caressing her leg.

"It's okay, Car. It's okay." She leaned into me for a moment, quiet. I could feel her hot breath against my neck, then wetness. She was crying, silent and soft, just letting the tears come. I pulled her close, gently rocking her. "I know, Car. It's okay."

Dagny watched us, just lending support with her touch, sensing that this was a moment between Carrie and me. Carrie's soft crying quickly turned into sobs that racked her entire body, pushing her against my neck even harder. I closed my eyes, my heart aching for my friend, knowing there was nothing I could do but be there for her. My heart was heavy, the sting behind my eyes returning, but I swallowed it down. She needed me to be strong, not fall apart on her.

"I didn't mean for this to happen, Chase," she whispered through her cries. "I swear I didn't. I never imagined that it could."

I nodded, still rubbing her back. "I know, Car."

"I'm sorry. I never wanted to disappoint you." She took a deep breath, trying to get herself under control. She pulled away a little, looking at me.

I tried to school my face, knowing she didn't need to see how bothered I really was, nor did I want her to see that deep down I was disappointed. I knew that what had happened to her was not her fault, nor did she ask for or deserve it. But maybe if she had calmed down her reckless lifestyle, taken some responsibility for her actions...

"I don't know what to do." She pulled a Kleenex out of her purse, wiped at her eyes and blew her nose.

"Do you want to talk to your parents, Car?" I asked gently.

She looked at me for a moment, then sighed. "I don't know. Part of me does, but another part of me is so ashamed."

"Don't be, Carrie. This was not your fault," Dagny said, rubbing Carrie's knee. "It was that sick bastard who did this, not you."

Carrie looked at Dagny, her eyes like a child's, wanting so much to believe. "I just don't know."

"Well, if you do, I'll be there for you, okay?"

She looked at me, a small smile on her lips, then she leaned in to me for a hug, reaching her other arm out to Dagny, pulling her into our embrace.

* ~ * ~ * ~ * ~ * ~ *

Carrie wanted to try a night by herself, so Dagny dropped us off at Carrie's dorm. "Give me a call later, Chase," Dagny called from the car.

"Thanks, Dag. You've been wonderful."

She nodded. "Anytime."

Carrie walked around and leaned in the window to give Dagny a hug. "Thank you, Dagny," she said quietly.

Dagny talked to her for a moment, their voices low, until finally Carrie nodded and stepped away from the SUV. With a final wave, Dagny drove away. I watched until her lights disappeared, already missing her comforting presence.

"Come on, you." We went into the building and hurried to Carrie's room. "Do you still want me to drive you home this weekend, Car?"

"Yeah. I think they should know, especially when it all comes down and we end up in court."

"I think it's smart, Car. Your folks could probably really help you right now."

She nodded slowly. "Yeah. I think so too." She grinned weakly. "My father is going to fucking freak."

"This is true."

When Carrie unlocked the door, Rachel was at her desk studying. She glanced at us, smiled a welcome, then turned back to her books. It wasn't uncommon for Carrie not to show up in their room for days at a time, so Rachel apparently wasn't worried or surprised that she hadn't come home the night before.

I took my friend in my arms and hugged her close, wanting to convey all the love and friendship I had for her in that hug. "Get some sleep, Car. I'll see you tomorrow." She nodded, then stepped away from me and went to change out of my sweats, and to give me a chance to talk to Rachel.

Carrie had asked me if I'd tell her roommate. Even though they were friends, she couldn't bring herself to talk about the rape, certainly not to explain it. I took a deep breath and took the plunge. "Rachel?" The girl turned, looking a bit irritated that I was interrupting her studies. "Would you come out here with me for a few minutes?" I moved toward the door.

Rachel looked confused, but she rose from her desk and met me in the hall. "What's going on?" she asked, pushing strands of brown hair behind her ear then crossing her arms over her chest.

"Something happened to Carrie last night. Now, you've got to promise to keep this to yourself, Rachel. It could really be hurtful if it got out. Okay?" She nodded, her face serious, eyes riveted on me. "Last night Carrie was out with a guy, and well, things got out of control. She was raped."

Rachel's eyes got big, tears welling. "No," she breathed.

"She's really going to need your understanding, Rachel. Can you be there for her?"

Shaking herself out of her shock, she nodded. "Yeah, of course. Why isn't she staying with you?"

"She did last night, but today she decided to start trying to get her life back, you know? I think it's a good thing, but she knows she can come to me anytime, for anything. Can she count on you, too?"

"Oh yeah. Definitely. God, I'm so sorry." She glanced at the closed door, then looked at me with a sigh. "Thanks for telling me, Chase. I'll do what I can."

"Thanks. I better get going. See you." I turned and headed out of the dorm.

I was a bit nervous as I walked to my own building, constantly peering into the night shadows that hid the campus, the overhead lights unable to dispel all of them. I tried to put myself in Carrie's shoes. What had she felt? What had gone through her head as that son of a bitch forced himself on her? Had she just tried to lose herself? Did she feel anything physically? I would never know the answer to my questions; I'd never ask. It wasn't my place.

Soon the familiar lights and sights of my building were right in front of me, and I breathed a sigh of relief. I just wanted to be surrounded by lights and familiarity. Part of me wished I was back at Dagny's apartment. I felt so safe with her.

The room was empty. Natalie was at a revival for her Bible study. Part of me was sad, but another part was glad. I knew she'd want answers, understandably so. After all, my best friend had come knocking at our door at three in the morning, make-up smeared, broken and bruised. I didn't want to be the bearer of bad tidings anymore; I didn't want to have to explain. I wished someone would explain things to me.

I flopped down on my bed, back against the wall. I felt strange, as if I were so heavy, yet filled with something that was expanding and needed to be released. Spotting the cordless phone sitting in its charger on the desk, I took it in my hand, the seven numbers I dialed came to mind as easily as my own.

"Hello?"

"Hey." I reclined on the bed, then turned on my side.

"Hi. Some day, huh?"

I grimaced at the phone. "Yeah. How are you?"

"I'm okay, I think. You?"

I thought for a moment. *How am I?* "I don't know, Dag. I feel so strange, like something's squeezing my middle. My heart hurts."

"Are you okay, honey?"

Her voice had lowered to an intimate level and I could almost feel her presence in the room with me. I needed her to be, but didn't dare ask. She had done too much already, given too much. "I'm...I just..." To my horror, my voice had me; it coming out shaky and unsure.

"Chase?"

"Yeah?" I whispered, feeling that stinging again. *No, no, no.*

"I'm coming over."

"No, Dag." The dam was finally breaking. I could feel the emotions that had been pent up for two days come rushing through its disintegrating walls.

"Be right there."

The phone was dead in my hand, and I hated that. Couldn't she take her phone with her and talk to me the entire way? I knew that was ridiculous, but I wished it all the same.

I was trying to get myself together, swiping my hand across my face, trying to rub the tears out of my eyes and make them go away. It wasn't working, but I was calmer. Until I heard the knock on the door. The lump rose in my throat again. This time it wouldn't be swallowed. I walked to the door and let Dagney in.

"Hey, you," she said quietly. She got a little wave from me, as I didn't trust my voice. "You alive in here?"

I shrugged, headed toward my bed where I plopped down, back against the wall. She sat next to me, her hand on my arm. "Why?" The word just blurted from my mouth like water from a spring, unstoppable but necessary.

Dagny knew what I was talking about. She shrugged. "I don't know, Chase. Sometimes things happen that we just don't understand, but I do believe everything happens for a reason."

"That's it? That's it?" I was surprised to feel my anger rise, though I knew deep down it wasn't directed at Dagny. "'Things happen'? Bullshit! What could be the reason for 'things' to just happen? She didn't deserve this. I don't care what she's done, she didn't deserve this." My voice was shaky again and Dagny's hand moved from my arm to my shoulder, squeezing. I reveled in the contact, so glad she was there. I began to calm. "Want to hear something horrible?" I turned to her, almost afraid to admit my innermost feelings, but knowing that Dagny would not judge me for them.

"Sure." She smiled encouragement.

"Part of me almost feels relieved." She looked confused, so I explained. "I mean, I never wanted this to happen to Carrie; it's horrible. That guy should pay big time for what he did, but at the same time, I think this made Carrie finally hit rock bottom. I think maybe she needed to do that to see where she was headed." I looked at her with sad eyes. "Does that make me a total bitch?"

She shook her head. "No, Chase. It means that you care about her and want the best for her. It's also a sign of tough love."

I smiled weakly. "Yeah, I'd say."

"Sometimes people need that. You know the whole — 'can't appreciate anything if it's all given to you'? This is along the same lines."

"Yeah." I hiccupped as a sob tried to escape but I held it back.

"Don't stop yourself from crying, Chase. It's healthy, you know."

"Yeah." The hiccup again.

"Come here." Dagny tugged gently on my neck until I fell over sideways, my head lying in her lap. I felt the tears tickle my nose as they slid down my face, gathering into a little wet spot on Dagny's jeans. She didn't seem to mind. My chest heaved as her fingers played in my hair, smoothing it back from my face and then returning to caress my skin.

My shoulders shook as the sobs got closer together and louder, a little more violent. I cried for Carrie, the loss of any innocence she had left, the violation of her body and emotions. I cried for our friendship, seemingly lost to me, only now feeling that there might be some sort of hope for its resurrection. I cried for myself, so lost in turmoil, my emotions a tempest of confusion. The woman who held me now was part of that, never knowing she comforted her stalker. It was my hunger, my fault. Was I defective?

"Shh, Chase. It's okay, sweetie," Dagny whispered in my ear over and over again as I continued to cry, letting go of so many years of pain and sadness. I cried for my friend, I cried for myself, and I cried for what would never be.

# Chapter 7

I gathered my gear for Tuesday night Bible study. I had to admit, I had missed it during the holiday break and was glad to get back into it. This was the third Tuesday since school had been back in session. Those were my favorite.

Natalie held the door open for me so I could lug Melo through. "How's your friend doing, Chase? Poor thing."

"She's okay, I guess. She finally told her parents, and wow, were they not happy." I'm sure that the look on my face emphasized my point. "Her dad wanted to go hunt the guy down and pull off his... Well, you know."

Natalie grinned at my attempt to be polite. "If it had been my daughter, I would have wanted to pull his dick off, too." I stared at her, my mouth hanging open. "Well, it's true."

I shook my head in astonishment. That girl never ceased to amuse me. "And now court procedures have begun. Carrie's parents talked with the DA yesterday." I butted open the door to the building, holding it open for Natalie with my foot.

"Thanks. At one point you mentioned that you and Dagny might have to testify. Do you?"

I nodded, unlocking my car. "Yup. I got my subpoena the other day. Not looking forward to that, let me tell you."

"Bless your heart. Okay, see you there."

My roommate smiled at me as she got into her car. We always drove separate cars, since I left way before she did. I was not in the mood to stay for the actual lessons. Natalie was great about respecting that.

As I drove to the Y, I thought about Carrie. She had kept a pretty low profile for the past couple of weeks. I saw her often, but mainly because I went to her dorm on a daily basis, though she did call me almost every night, usually around two in the morning when she woke from a nightmare during the "anniversary time," as she had started to call it. From what I had heard from her friends, she still went out periodically to have fun, but avoided bars and parties, mainly sticking to more mundane haunts — restaurants until the wee hours, or going to movies. They said she rarely drank and had stopped doing pot altogether. I wondered how long that would last.

Dagny was so busy with her school schedule, I barely saw her. I missed her and felt the weight of all the time apart. I sighed. At least she'd be there tomorrow at Gotfry's for the underage night. Well, I hoped so, anyway. She had told me Sunday that there were no guarantees with that. She would do her best. I sighed again. My birthday was tomorrow, and I might not be able to spend it with her. I had been a real shit and lied to my parents so I wouldn't have to go home. I wanted to be selfish with that day and be with Dagny.

The usual group was at the YWCA when Natalie and I walked into the room, Melo slung across my back like, as Natalie put it, "my sword to do battle for God". I set up, looking over the music for the evening and getting myself mentally prepared.

As I played, I thought back to the previous night's rehearsal at Doug's. We had just run through our music for Wednesday and were packing up to go. Terrie walked up to me, a smile on her face.

*"Hey," she said. I smiled back as I packed up Melo and Than. "What are you doing tomorrow night?" I looked at her, my brows drawn.*

*"I have plans to help out a friend, but other than that..." I shrugged.*

*"Good. What time do you finish up with your friend?"*

*"Whenever I decide to leave."*

*"Wow, you don't make it easy on a girl, do you?" I just stared at her. "What do you say to getting something to eat with me? You know, when you're done. I'm free all night, so you could just call whenever." She leaned against the wall, her hand on her hip.*

*I looked at her, her jeans tight as usual, the shirt she wore also tight. Low cut, but not slutty. She looked good. I looked back at her face, the long earrings she wore brushing against her neck. "Well, um, I guess. We could grab something, yeah."*

*Her smile widened, looking almost predatory. "Great. Do you have a heavy day of classes on Wednesday?"*

*"No."*

*"Even better." She pushed off the wall and took her sticks from the seat behind the drum set. "Give me a call." As she passed by, she handed me a little card. It was her business card with her name, work number and address, as well as her home number. I watched her leave.*

*"Hey." I turned to see Doug standing next to me, also watching his cousin. "Be careful, Chase. I don't want to see you get hurt."*

*"What do you mean?"*

*"Just watch yourself. I love my cousin, but she's dangerous. I think your friend from the bar has sensed that." He patted me on the shoulder and walked away.*

*Shaking my head, I shouldered my guitars and headed to my car. I didn't understand why people felt the need to warn me. I could handle myself, and I could certainly handle Terrie*

Shaking myself out of my reverie, I got ready to "rock with

Jesus".

* ~ * ~ * ~ * ~ * ~ *

I really needed to study because I'd be at home over the week-end and wouldn't have much of a chance, if my mother had anything to say about it. I decided go to dinner with Terrie anyway.

I buttoned my jeans and slipped my sweatshirt over my head, then looked into the mirror behind the door. I looked good. My hair was down, freshly washed and brushed. If I had been meeting Carrie, I wouldn't have bothered. I mean, I had taken a shower that morning, but I felt the need to make a good impression tonight. I didn't know what it was about Terrie, but she intimidated me.

We had planned to meet at Gentle Ben's at eight, and a glance at my watch told me it was five 'til. *Oops.* I pocketed my wallet and keys and was heading for the door when the phone rang. With a growl, I scooped it up off my bed. "Yeah?"

"Well, that's unusual."

I could hear the smile in her voice, and the smile on my face was instantaneous. "Hey, Dag. What's up?" God, I wanted to stay and talk. I hadn't seen her for two days, and I missed her.

"Not much. I reached a break point in my paper, I so decided to see if you wanted to get a bite to eat." My heart sank; my stomach felt like it was filled with razors. I could cancel with Terrie, or just not show up. What would be the big deal? That would make me a total bitch; that was the big deal. I sighed into the phone. "I'm sorry, Dagny. I've already got plans."

"Oh. Uh, I'm sorry to be so last minute." I could hear the dis-appointment and surprise in her voice. "I guess you do have other friends." She laughed quietly, but I knew it was forced. "Well, I hope you have fun."

"Yeah. Damn, I wish I'd known." I lightly smacked my wallet against my leg. I felt guilty somehow.

"What are you going to do? I mean, hell, I'm sorry. It's none of my business. Forget I asked."

"No, it's okay. During rehearsal yesterday, Terrie invited me to dinner." The phone was silent. "Dag?"

"Sorry. Really? How nice."

I could hear something in her voice, but couldn't quite put my finger on what it was. I knew she was trying to hide it, and was doing an exceptional job. "Listen, I can cancel."

"No! No, you go out and have fun, Chase." There was a genuine smile in her voice. "I'll catch up with you later. Okay?"

I nodded, realizing how stupid that was, considering I was alone. "Yeah. Okay. Hey, maybe I can stop by after we're done? It's not far from you; we're going to Gentle Ben's."

"Oh, yeah. Sure. Oh, wait. I have a meeting with Levy at seven in the morning."

"Oh. Okay." My spirits fell. "Okay. I guess I'll see you. When are you free? This sucks." I felt like a pouting child, not getting my way.

She chuckled softly. "I know, Chase. I'm sorry. This year and the second are the worst. If we can get through these..."

"Yeah. Okay, well I have to go. I'm already late."

"Okay. Talk to you later."

"Bye." I felt horrible. I knew Dagny was bummed, and I sure as hell was.

I parked in the lot of Gentle Ben's, seeing Terrie's truck already there. The microbrewery was busy, but I saw Terrie waiting for me by the door.

"Hi." She smiled warmly.

I smiled back. "Hey."

She looked me over, making me feel a little uncomfortable. "You look nice."

"Thanks." I looked at her: well-fitted black jeans and a button-up shirt, the top three buttons open. I feared if she bent over, she'd fall out of it. "Um, you too."

"Come on. I already got us a table."

I followed her through the place, all eyes on her as she wove her way through to an empty table near the wall. I sat across from her at our three person table.

"Have you ever been here before?" Terrie asked me as she smiled at the waitress who handed her a menu. I shook my head as I took mine and thanked the woman.

"Can I get you something to drink?" The waitress looked at each of us in turn.

"Yeah, get me the house brew," Terrie said. They both looked at me.

"Um, I guess just a Dr Pepper."

"Okay."

"How old are you, Chase?" Terrie asked once the waitress had walked away.

For some reason I didn't want her to know that my birthday was tomorrow. "I'll be nineteen soon."

"Well, a little birdie told me you turn nineteen tomorrow. The day before Valentine's Day?" She rested her cheek on her hand and smiled at me. "So, I guess you were born for love, huh?"

I was surprised she knew my birth date and realized how stupid I must have sounded since she already knew. But if she did, why had she asked? "Yeah, I guess I was." I smiled. "My best friend Carrie's birthday is actually on V day."

"V day? Victory day?" She smiled again.

"Well, victorious for a highly paid delivery room doctor, anyway."

"This is true." Terrie sat back and opened her menu. "I am so hungry. I had the longest day today at work. I'm telling you, there are some really stupid people in this city. Don't know a damn thing about computers." She looked at me over her menu. "What about you? Know much about them?"

"I got my first computer the day I left for college." I grinned. "I've learned a lot about them since I've been here, I can tell you that. Some trial and a lot of error."

"I'm surprised at you, Chase. Aren't you supposed to be part of this new generation of kids born with a computer chip implanted in their brains?"

I chuckled. "I guess. I kind of missed that boat, I'm afraid. My parents didn't want us raised by technology. We weren't allowed to watch much television, either." The waitress came back with our drinks and took our dinner orders.

"That's good, smart. Do you watch much now?"

"No. But I do love movies. I used to sneak over to Carrie's house, she lived a block away, and we'd watch movies until the wee hours of the morning. I still do that when I get the chance."

"I love movies, too." Terrie ran a hand through her hair, the dark strands falling perfectly back into place. She really was an attractive woman. "Maybe we should go sometime."

I shrugged. "Sure." I sat back in the chair, trying to figure the drummer out. I sensed something about her, but wasn't sure what it was. It was almost predatory. That was the feeling I was getting. It didn't matter, but it made things a little more interesting.

As the night went on I found Terrie to be intelligent, funny, and a good listener. I talked about my family, school and my thoughts on the subject, and what I wanted out of life. Terrie was quite insightful, telling me about her own childhood growing up not far from where my parents lived now.

"My mother was very demanding, but I really don't think it was because she wanted the best for me, more of an 'if I have to be miserable, so do you' sort of thing." She smiled, as did I, nodding my understanding. "So, after college, I ditched this place and made a new life for myself away from Tucson."

"So, why are you back?"

She smiled as she sipped from her beer. "Good question. My mother used to tell me that no matter how far I went or what I did, this would always be home. I guess she was right. I don't intend to stay here forever, but I got a great job offer that I just couldn't refuse."

"I bet she was glad."

"Well, she's a mom, forever protective and controlling. Yes, she was happy about it." She put down the beer and pushed her dinner plate away, a few bites of her steak left, mixed with some loose peas. "So, how about you? Get along with your parents, even with all their demands?"

"Eh, I guess. I find that now I spend a lot less time there than I figured I would. To be honest, when I left for college, I was afraid. I really hadn't spent much time away from home, or away from them. I figured I'd be home every single weekend." I smiled. "I've been home twice since school started last fall. I'm rather proud of that fact."

"You're growing up, Chase."

"Yeah? Tell my family that. They think I'm just being rebellious."

\* ~ \* ~ \* ~ \* ~ \* ~ \*

I sat in my car for a moment, thinking about the dinner. It had gone so much better than I'd expected. Terrie was an interesting person, though I didn't understand her. I think that was her aim: stay mysterious and an enigma. I could handle that.

She had insisted on paying for dinner, saying it was my birthday gift. I reluctantly accepted, hating when people paid for me, even Mike. He used to get so irritated because I'd fight him every step of the way.

With a sigh I put the key in the ignition and pulled out of the space. It was just before ten, and I was wide awake. I drove around for a bit, with no particular place in mind but one particular person on my brain. I wondered what Dagny had done with her night. I hated that I had had to pass up an opportunity to see her, spend time with her. Because of her schedule, we hadn't even been able to swim together for the last week. I understood, but it didn't mean I had to like it.

I turned right and, to my not so surprise, saw Dagny's building right in front of me. I felt like a stalker as I pulled to the curb and stared up at the third floor. Lights illuminated one of her two windows that faced this side of the street. I took a deep breath, my hand caressing the steering wheel as I thought about what to do. I knew she had an appointment with Levy early in the morning, but she was still up.

I put the car in gear and swung around to the parking lot, pulling in right next to Freud. There was a spring in my step as I made my way to the stairs that would take me to the second and third floors. The door that I knew so well loomed before me, and I knocked softly. On the other side I could hear music, and a muffled "Hang on!" I smiled as I waited. Finally I heard the locks disengage, and the door opened. I chuckled at what stood before me: Dagny, dressed in baggy sweat shorts and tank, barefoot, her face covered in some sort of cleansing cream. Her hair was slicked back as if wet from a recent shower. She looked up at me, surprised. "Hi."

"Hey." I waved with a grin. "New look?"

She grinned, slightly embarrassed as she shuffled her feet. "Yeah. Night mask."

"Cute." I grinned, leaning against the door jamb. "I hope it's not too late. We just finished with dinner."

"No, not at all." She moved away from the door, motioning for me to enter. "So, what's up?" She sat on the couch, moving some textbooks and notebooks to the floor so I could sit.

I sat down, shrugging. "Well, um, to be honest, I just really miss you." I avoided her eyes, looking everywhere but at her. I felt a hand on my arm. My eyes went to it, then trailed up to Dagny's eyes.

"That's so sweet. I've really missed you, too, Chase." She rubbed my arm then took her hand away, to my definite dismay. "I have my own little confession to make. I was really bummed when you told me you were going out to dinner with that drummer." Her face wore a sheepish grin.

God, she was beautiful, even with all that pore cleansing crap on her face. I was surprised to hear the bitter tone in her voice about Terrie, though.

I know. I'm sorry." I looked down.

"No, no, Chase. Come on, you have other friends, just like I do. But...you know." She shrugged.

"Yeah, I do." *More than you think, Dag.*

"Come on. I have to take this stuff off."

I followed her to the bathroom, plopping down on the toilet lid. "Hold." She handed me a towel and I played with it, looking at the embroidered duck, faded yellow, as Dagny scrubbed her face and splashed cold water on the red skin. I watched in fascination, my heart pounding just to be next to her. I think I had really started to take my time with her for granted, and now that it had been taken away, I missed her fiercely. I wanted to be with her all the time, and hated when we had to hang up or when I had to leave her. Every morning that I had to swim alone was terrible. I decided I should keep up with the swimming so I wouldn't want to die when Dagny started up again. She had told me she was proud of me. That had been enough incentive.

"Thank you."

I was startled out of my reverie when Dagny took the towel out of my hands and dried her face. She smiled. "Bet you didn't think I needed a nightly regimen to keep my utterly beautiful perfection, did you?" She grinned. "Yeah, right, huh?"

I smiled. She didn't need to do anything; nature had done

enough.

"I was just about to have some hot tea. Want some?"

"Sure." I followed her as she through the apartment to the kitchen.

Dagny went on talking about her advisor and her classes, and how she was looking forward to being finished with classes so she could concentrate more on client experience and working full-time on the research for her dissertation. I watched her work, her hands strong, as she fixed her cup of tea, stirring in the sugar and then bringing it up to her mouth to blow on the hot liquid, finally sipping.

She looked at me, curious. "Are you okay?"

I shook myself out of my direction of thought. "Yeah. Sorry." I took my cup off the counter and poured myself some.

"So, are you still going to play tomorrow, even though it's your birthday?" Dagny leaned against the counter, holding her cup between her hands.

I nodded. "Yeah. It'll give me something to do. I think Carrie is finally going to come in to hear me play."

"Great." She smiled. "I know she'll love it." She looked down, seemingly bothered by something.

"Are you okay, Dagny?"

Her head jerked up, eyes wide. "Huh? Yeah. I just got an interesting call tonight."

"Come on." I nodded toward the living room. Dagny pushed off the counter and followed me to the couch. Facing each other, our knees nearly touching, I waited for Dagny to continue. She was quiet for a moment, sipping her tea, but I knew it was just a delay to avoid talking.

"Darrel." The way she looked at me, I knew the call had bothered her. Her ex-boyfriend, who had gone to California for his job. He had been completely in love with her, wanting her to keep up the relationship, even across the miles. She had refused. "He wanted to see what I was up to, how I was." Dagny set her cup on the table and sat back against the arm of the couch, running a hand through her hair, which had begun to dry.

"Were you okay with that?" I also set my cup aside, wanting to focus all my attention and energy on her.

She shrugged. "What could I do? I would have loved to stay friends with him, but we all know that's usually not possible. Especially when you hurt the other person so badly." She sighed. "God, I felt so strange talking with him. Apparently he's doing well with his job, moving up in the company quickly. He just bought a condo and a new car, a BMW." She smiled. "He used to talk all the time about getting a Beemer."

"Well then, it's good he finally got one." I was confused. Why was she upset about this? My stomach fell as something occurred to me. She must still have feelings for him. I swallowed, trying to hide my emotions.

"He wants me back, Chase."

I swallowed hard. *I knew it. She's going to go off to California, leave Tucson, finish her degree over there somewhere...*

"I felt so bad having to let him down again."

My thoughts stopped mid-sentence. *What? Let him down again?* That meant she didn't want him back. He didn't still matter, and she wasn't leaving. Right?

"He was so disappointed. You know, I think he really thought that the money and success he's achieved is what I was after. It's not. There's so much more to it than that, you know?" I nodded, as I didn't trust myself to say anything. "I want love, and I want to be happy. Is that too much to ask from life?" She ran her hands through her hair again, almost as if she was nervous about something. She was getting agitated and I didn't understand why.

"Dag, it seems like he loved, or loves you, right?" She nodded, staring down at her hands in her lap. "Isn't that what you just said you want?" *Stop! Why am I trying to help this guy out?* But then, I cared more for Dagny and her happiness than my own. I loved having her friendship, she meant the world to me, but if she was unhappy... The thought made me feel sick. *How on earth did I get so cheesy in just a few months?*

"I don't know, Chase. I'm wondering that myself. I ran from him at every turn, always have. Hell, why not? Running is my specialty."

Her voice was bitter, and I didn't understand it. My brows drew together as I looked at her, so wanting to help, to take her in my arms and make her feel better. I wanted to touch her, but couldn't bring myself to do it. I hated myself for that, too.

Dagny took another sip of her tea, which seemed to calm her some. She smiled at me, reaching out to touch my hand. I took that opportunity and took her fingers. Better late than never.

"I'm sorry. I just feel really bad, I guess. I wish I was never put into this sort of situation, but I can't blame it on him. He always said that I never could commit. Is that my problem? Or was *he* the problem?" She looked at me as if I could give her the answers. I didn't know what to say. She smiled again, shaking it off. "I'm sorry. I don't mean to lay all this on you."

"Hey, after what you've had to go through with me and my friends? Shit, don't worry about it. Keep talking if you want to. I honestly don't mind."

"Nah. I'm done ranting. For the moment." She smiled. "Oh, about tomorrow night." The smile left her face. "Bad news. I can't come, Chase. I'm sorry."

My shoulders fell, but I tried to swallow my disappointment. "Hey, I understand. I know you're really, really busy right now. It's not a problem." I hoped she didn't see right through the lie.

She put her hand on my leg. "Are you mad?"

I shook my head vehemently. "God, no. I totally understand, Dag. Really, it's okay."

"Okay." She looked uncomfortable. "Unfortunately, I really should be getting to bed."

I glanced at the clock on the VCR and saw it was pushing midnight. "Aw, jeez. I'm sorry." I stood, grabbing my keys off the table and headed for the door, followed by Dagny.

"Look, um, I may be able to come by Gotfry's on Friday night. I'm really pushing for it."

I smiled. "Cool. I hope you can." I opened the door. "Well, see you later."

"Good night, Chase."

Dagny slowly closed the door behind me, the light shining into the hallway getting smaller and smaller as the door-shaped beam turned into a sliver, then finally just darkness.

* ~ * ~ * ~ * ~ * ~ *

As I set up my equipment, getting Melo and Than ready for another night of rocking, I was bummed. Dagny had never missed a performance, not even before we became friends. I knew it couldn't be helped, but that didn't make me feel any better.

"What's gotten into you? You look like your dog just died."

I turned to see Terrie settling herself behind her drums, smiling at me. "Nothing. I'm fine." I forced a smile and quickly turned back to the mic. I didn't want to have to try and explain something to her that I didn't fully understand myself.

Greg had the place decked out for Valentine's Day the next day, red paper hearts hanging on fishing line overhead, pink and red balloons decorating the walls and helium-filled ones bobbing around the ceiling. There was a special on strawberry daiquiris or any other red or pink drink, too. It was nice.

The crowd had already swollen to a decent size as we started our first set, playing a number of old rock songs as well as contemporary. We had started to cut down on the teeny-bopper stuff, for which I was forever grateful. It was hard to make myself sing it. I finished off a duet with Doug of *You're the One That I Want*, a fun song that got the crowd going. Doug put his arm around my shoulders and hugged me when we finished.

"Great job," he whispered in my ear.

I smiled at him, then moved toward the center of the stage, ready to start the next song, when he took the mic out of its holder and turned back to the audience. "Ladies and gentlemen, today is Chase's birthday." He grinned at my stunned expression. "So, one, two, three..." The band played the traditional song and sixty drunk patrons sang along. I think the hue of my face matched the hearts on the walls.

Still singing, Doug put his arm around my shoulder and led me down the stairs to the main floor, where a huge cake bearing nineteen lighted candles was being carried toward me. The stunned expression on my face turned to a broad smile when I saw who held the cake. Dagny winked as she sang, the candles throwing eerie shadows on her face as she carried the cake to the bar, followed by Carrie.

"Make a wish!" Doug ordered when the song ended.

I glared playfully at Dagny; she smiled with no apparent remorse. I leaned over the cake, my wish made a long time ago, and blew out the candles in one breath. The crowd, which had completely surrounded us at the bar, clapped and cheered. I turned to Dag, wagging my finger at her.

"What?"

"Yeah, drop the innocent act."

She smiled and hugged me. "Happy birthday, Chase," she said in my ear. I closed my eyes and hugged her tighter. When we parted, Carrie was there, holding something behind her back.

"Chase, Dagny and I got together to get you something you can really use. We wanted to add to your family, so here you go. Happy birthday." She brought out a life-sized blow up electric guitar, bright pink with a red bow around it.

I threw my head back with laughter, my arm going around Dagny's neck, pulling her against me. "You guys are bad." Dagny hugged me again, laughing along with everyone else.

We cut the cake and then Dagny dragged me over to the table where all her friends had gathered, along with a new guy that I didn't know.

"Hi. I'm Paul Reilly." He smiled and shook my hand. "Happy birthday." He was good-looking, dark hair nicely cut, casually dressed but very well put together.

"Chase, Paul is a transfer student,, so I thought I'd bring him along to meet everyone."

I nodded with a smile. "Thanks for coming, Paul." I indicated Carrie who stood next to me, looking around. "This is my friend, Carrie."

"Carrie." Once she turned her attention back to us, he shook her hand as well.

She said a quiet hello. This was one of the first big public outings for Carrie, and I could tell she was nervous, constantly looking around to see if that bastard was near, which was completely irrational, since he was in jail. She knew that, but couldn't help it.

"Chase, come with me." Dagny grabbed my hand and pulled me toward the door and out into the night. We walked to her car where she opened the door to bring out a wrapped gift, handing it to me with a nervous smile. "I wanted to give you your real gift...alone," she finished shyly. I accepted the present, with the card in a red envelope lying on top. I set the gift on top of Freud and opened the card. Normally I would have waited to do that until I was back in the dorm, hating to have to react in front of the expectant giver, but I couldn't wait.

On the front was a picture of an old woman wearing a long house dress, jamming on an electric guitar, her legs spread wide. Her face was pale and covered with a street map of wrinkles, excited, with her mouth open. In large, black letters it read:
*"You know you're getting old when..."*
I grinned, opened it.
"You get your guitar chord mixed up with the oxygen hose."
I laughed heartily. "Oh, Dag, you are bad. What's gotten into you?"
She laughed with me, shaking her head. "Who knows?"
I read what she had written in her neat, small hand writing.

> *Chase,*
> *You have truly made a difference in my life and made me remember what life is all about. I never forgot the precocious eight year old who made my summer one of the best I've ever had. Now, eleven years later, that same person is in my life again. What Power had the foresight to bring us together and turn you from my charge to my best friend? Whatever it is, karma, divine intervention, or sheer coincidence, I'm grateful.*
> *Happy Birthday, my friend.*
> *Love,*
> *Dag*

I looked up from the card, speechless. I took a step toward Dagny and pulled her into a massive hug. I said nothing, and neither did she. There wasn't a need for words. I felt, more than heard, her sigh as she held me. I wanted to second that with my own contented sigh. Standing there, being so close to Dagny, there was nowhere else in the entire world I wanted to be. She embodied everything I strove to be. Nope, my hero worship hadn't gone anywhere.

"Don't forget this." Dagny pulled away from me and handed me the wrapped gift. I smiled, shy, ripping into the paper, tossing it aside to be yelled at by Dagny for temporary littering. The paper removed, I looked down at the leather-bound notebook in my hands. My name was stenciled in gold, dead center. I looked up at her in confusion.

"Someone told me you're quite the songwriter and poet." I was shocked, my open mouth making that plain. She chuckled. "You have a brilliant mind, Chase, and I want you to write all those wonderful thoughts and songs in here." She placed a hand over mine that rested on the book. "Someday this will be worth something. I hope I'm around to see it."

I could feel my throat tightening up, but didn't want her to know just how touched I was. No one had ever taken my writing seriously, certainly not someone who had never read or heard anything I had written.

"Thank you, Dagny," I finally said, my voice quiet. "I don't know what to say."

"You don't have to say anything." She brushed back some hair from my face. "Happy birthday, Chase." She squeezed my hand and turned toward Freud. "Oh, um, I can start swimming again."

My grin was huge, excited. "Really?"

"Yeah, but," she paused for effect, "it has to be at five."

"In the morning?" I squeaked.

She laughed. "Yes, in the morning. I would love to see you, but I do understand if that's too early."

"I'll see what I can do." I smiled; so did she.

"Great! Well, I do have to go."

"I can't thank you enough for coming, Dag. You really didn't have to." I held the notebook to my chest as I leaned against the car next to Freud.

Dagny looked at me for a moment, her head cocked to the side. "Yeah, I did. See you."

She stepped in, closed the door, and started up the engine. I watched her until the SUV disappeared, then with a sigh, I headed back into the bar.

* ~ * ~ * ~ * ~ * ~ *

Sitting on my bed with my back against the wall and my knees drawn up, I transferred the song I was writing from various pieces of notebook paper to the journal Dagny had given me. With careful strokes, the song came to life, and I even added a few stanzas, until I realized that it was finished. I read my handiwork.

*Comfortable In My Skin*

> *Lessons learned, as days go by*
> *I test my wings, learn I can fly*
> *I test my heart, find I can soar.*
> *Every day you believe in me*
> *I can do more.*
>
> > *Chorus: You touch my hand, you touch my soul*

*You touch my heart, I am all yours*
*You make me strong, tell me I can win*
*I'm comfortable, in my skin*
*I'm now aware of who I am*
*My place in this world, I can understand*
*It took your faith in my ability*
*To open my eyes and allow me to see*
    *Chorus*
*All my life, I didn't have a voice*
*Others made decisions and left me no choice*
*Then someone listened to what I had to say*
*And made me realize I could make it my way*
*I was too young to truly know*
*The ache in my chest when you let me go*
*But now I have you to hold me near*
*And the ache I once felt has disappeared*
    *Chorus*

I read and re-read, singing in my head. This was my anthem, my theme song.

The door to the room opened, and Natalie strolled in. She had a vase full of flowers, three balloons bobbing off the ceiling and doorway, and a white box under her arm. She smiled when she saw me.

"Happy birthday!" She handed me the gifts.

I smiled up at her. "Aw, that is so sweet." I put the journal aside and took the flowers, which looked to be a summer bouquet of a little bit of everything, and the balloons that were tied to it. "Mm, they smell good."

"And this is from the kids. They are so bummed that you won't be there tomorrow at the Bible study, but they do understand. I mean, Carrie is your best friend, and all." She handed me the white box.

Intrigued, I opened it up to see a small cake in the shape of an old country guitar. The words Happy Birthday, Music Lady were written in blue icing. I was truly touched. "This is too much. How did they do this?" I looked up at my roommate, who took the flowers from me and set them on the desk, then sat across from me on her own bed.

"Well, they wanted to do something nice for you. You give up every single Tuesday night for them, and they appreciate it. So do I." She reached under her bed to pull out a long, skinny, wrapped box. "This is also from me." She handed it to me, then sat expectantly with her hands in her lap.

With glee, I tore into the paper to reveal a music stand. I looked at the box, reading the multi purposes of it. I was thrilled.

"Oh, Nat, thank you so much."

"Do you like it?" she asked nervously.

I nodded enthusiastically. "Oh, yeah. This will definitely help on Tuesday and Thursdays."

"I figured. Plus, I'm sure as time goes by, you'll be doing more and more with music."

I put the box aside, and knelt in the narrow space between our beds and hugged her. "Thank you, Natalie. You really didn't have to."

"I know, but I wanted to." She gave me another smile, then gathered her things and headed to the bathroom and a shower before bed.

I picked up the journal again and re-read my lyrics. It was how I felt. It was good; I was happy with it. With a sigh, I closed the cover, set it on my desk and re-set my alarm, then lay down, my hands over my head as I stared up at the ceiling.

I had made the room more my own, putting up posters and goofy sayings. I looked at Natalie's side of the room. So barren. She had a cross hanging on the wall over her bed, and a poster of a beaker filled with different life forms, dolphins swimming around, babies walking, and plants and animals. Underneath the beaker, in large white letters, it read: Got Biology? I chuckled as I stared up at my water-stained ceiling.

I glanced over at the music stand Natalie had given me, very pleased. When I played for her Bible study I always had to get creative when laying out my music. This would help.

I thought about tomorrow. I was excited to be spending some quality time with Carrie. Being on Valentine's Day, her nineteenth birthday could be a blessing or a curse, or so she said. She wasn't dating anyone, thus the curse, but then again, with her birthday, she had something to celebrate. I laughed at my friend's twisted logic. I didn't know what we were going to do, but I did know it would just be me and her. I needed that time with her, time to re-connect without a tragedy being the connective tissue.

The door to the room opened, and I could smell my roommate before I even saw her, her Herbal Essence shampoo and Irish Spring soap. She never deviated from either.

"Did you have a good birthday, Chase?"

I looked up at Natalie as she took the towel from her head and dried her hair. I nodded. "Yeah. It was good. Dagny came." Such a simple statement, and yet a goofy smile immediately appeared on my face.

"Well, good. You were worried about that." She sat on her bed, starting to comb through the long brown strands.

"Well, I don't know if worry is the right word. I wanted her there. I mean she's a good friend of mine." Natalie stopped brushing and just looked at me. My brows knit. "What?"

"Nothing." She shook her head with a smile and continued brushing. "You guys have certainly gotten close fast." She looked down at the floor and began to brush her hair upside down.

"Well, she's cool to hang out with." I stared up at the ceiling again, thinking of my friend's face, seeing her smile before my eyes. I smiled back at the phantom image. "She's so nice and caring. I mean, look how she handled the Carrie situation. The woman has the magic touch with people." My roommate was silent, so I looked over at her. She was staring at me, a grin on her face. "What?" I asked again, starting to get a little irritated.

"If you speak so highly of all your good friends, let me get in line." I rolled my eyes and stared up at the ceiling. "Goodnight, Chase."

"Night." I heard Natalie pull out her two towels, plop them on the floor and kneel down on them.

* ~ * ~ * ~ * ~ * ~ *

The image was getting closer: the skin pale and smooth, beautiful legs, strong and powerful. The darkness began to part to reveal more, moving up to a flat stomach, shadows dancing and playing as she moved, coming closer and closer. The darkness parted even more, rising up...

BEEP BEEP BEEP

Smack!

I leaned over the desk from the end of my bed, my hand still on the alarm clock. My eyes were heavy, and I just wanted to fall back into the warm bed and go back to sleep. I wanted to finish my dream. My dream...

My eyes shot open as I remembered my dream and where it had been heading. I knew it had been Dagny's body that I was trying to see, that I imagined walking toward me, naked and glorious. My body burned, my fingers itched. Taking a deep breath, I stood, stretching to help wake myself. I glanced with envy over at Natalie's sleeping form.

"Swim. Must swim."

I pulled into the lot, which was empty except for one vehicle. I smiled at Freud. The engine was still warm and ticking, so I knew Dag hadn't been there long. The lady at the desk smiled at me, then went back to her computer screen.

The place was eerily quiet. I was amazed at how much more traffic it would have in an hour. *God, why am I here at frigging five in the a.m.?*

"Chase!"

I turned to see Dagny walking toward me, the biggest smile on her face. I smiled in return, my eyes automatically dropping to where my dream eyes had stopped. She looked great in a pair of baggy running pants and a tank. Realizing what I was doing, my eyes popped back up to hers.

"What on earth are you doing here so ridiculously early?" she teased.

"I could ask you the same question."

"Come on. I forgot my towel in the car."

I walked out with her, back into the chilly morning air. "I can't promise that I can do this real often, but, well, I miss swimming with you." I glanced at her and saw a strange look on her face.

"God, you are so sweet." She put her arm around my shoulders. "I am definitely appreciative." She got her towel and we headed inside for our swim.

As usual, I was done in long before Dag, so I waited at the edge of the pool for her to finish her marathon of laps. The only reason I didn't feel bad was that she had twenty years of swimming to my couple of months.

"God, this is so exhilarating," Dagny gushed as she pulled herself up to sit next to me. She smiled at me, running her hands over her hair to slick it back. "I'm so glad you came, Chase. It's amazing how much you take someone's presence and company for granted, you know?"

I nodded. Yup, I knew exactly what she meant. Then to my surprise she laid her head against my shoulder.

"I'm so tired. They say this part of the doctorate program ends, but I'm not so sure, anymore. Why am I doing this to myself, Chase?" She glanced up at me with heavy-lidded eyes.

I put my arm around her shoulders. "Because it's your dream, Dag."

"I could just get my masters; I'd be fine with that." She pulled away with a sigh.

"No you wouldn't. You and I both know that you won't be happy or content until you finish." She looked at me for a moment, her eyes staring into mine. I stared back, wanting to turn away for fear that she'd be able to read me. She'd never understand; hell, I barely did. Either way, I couldn't risk it. I stared back out over the water, but I could feel her eyes on me.

"Oh, Chase, life is a funny place, isn't it?"

I nodded, smiling. "That it is."

"Come on; let's go get a bagel."

\* ~ \* ~ \* ~ \* ~ \* ~ \*

The second semester flew by, and I was approaching the end of my first year of college. I saw Dagny rarely during the last couple of months. She came to Gotfry's on Friday nights, but had to leave at the break. It was hard not to see her more often, but I knew she did what she could. On Valentine's Day I had been surprised by a card and a pink carnation taped to my door. I nearly missed it in the dark. It was from Dagny, and I had been cheesed beyond belief.

Carrie and I had managed to rebuild things, and she was doing well. I had caught her going to a party one time, but let her go. It was her life, and she had to make her own choices. Later that night she had called, crying. She had gotten drunk and felt like she was disappointing me.

"Car, it's your life. There's nothing wrong with having a good time, but it's all a matter of being responsible."

"I know." She sniffled. "It was stupid. I didn't mean to." She sighed into the receiver. "I just feel like shit, Chase. Like I don't really matter anyway, so why bother?"

"Carrie! Don't you ever say that again. You matter to more people than you realize. And you know if you did something stupid, you'd have to deal with me killing your ass for you." She laughed quietly. "You have so much going for you. You're very talented and good with art, and there's that class you're so excited about next year. You just have to think of the future; use your head."

"Okay. I can do this."

I heard her blowing her nose. "Of course you can. I never doubted you, Car."

"Thanks, Chase."

"Not a problem. Get some sleep."

"Okay."

I carefully hung the phone up with a sigh. *What am I going to do with her?*

* ~ * ~ * ~ * ~ * ~ *

The summer was here, and I was thrilled. I had gone home the day after finals ended, after doing one more show at Gotfry's. I promised Greg I'd come back for Friday night shows, but wouldn't start up Wednesdays again until I came back for my summer class in July. My parents had been thrilled at the prospect of my wanting to do additional work — English 273. If only they'd known it was a class on lesbian literature. I'm such a rebel.

When I got home I was received by happy parents, but also given lists of chores to do while I was on break. I did them, but usually watched soap operas during the day when my mom was gone, quickly vacuuming and dusting minutes before she got home. Just like old times. My mother asked me daily if I'd gotten my grade report. I was nervous about it, so I went online to UA's website and found my grades. I breathed a sigh of relief when I saw them, knowing I wouldn't have to try and beat my mom to the mailbox every day. I had done well — two B's and four A's. Life was good.

I would only be at home for a few weeks, and I was glad about that. My life was now at school, and I wanted to get back to it, I also wanted to get back to Dagny. She was class-free this summer, but had gotten a job at Rincon Market, just east of campus. She worked in the market area sometimes, and other times worked in the restaurant. I also wanted to get a job.

"You don't need a job, honey. Soon enough you'll want to stop working," my mom said as she put on her make-up.

I sat on the toilet lid watching her. This was a ritual we had shared since I was a child. "But I want a job. What's the problem?"

She turned to look at me. "We give you a monthly allowance for a reason, Chase. Right now your priority should be school and school alone."

"This is just for the summer, though. I want some independence!"

My mother's eyes bugged at my defiance. I didn't know what to do; I had said it, and I meant it, but wasn't sure I was ready for the backlash. She stared at me for a moment, her hand on her hip as she sized me up. I managed to keep eye contact, letting her know I was serious.

"Mom, I've got to grow up at some point. Do you know how much of a slug I feel like, still living off you guys? I mean, damn, I am pushing twenty and still live off your money." I shrugged, hoping to take the sting out of my words. "I love you guys, and really appreciate all you do for me, it's just time for me to start helping myself out, you know?"

"Carla never had a job during her undergrad years," she said quietly, turning back to the mirror to apply eyeliner.

"Yeah, well, that's Carla. I, however, am not her. We're two very different people, Mom." I stood. "When are you going to see that?" I stalked out of the bathroom.

I got so tired of my older sister, the saint, being invoked in every conversation that I tried to have about me with my mom. Why couldn't they just take me on my own merit? When would I come into my own?

* ~ * ~ * ~ * ~ * ~ *

My mom had managed to get me to go shopping with her. I needed some new clothes, and she was willing to pay for them, so who was I to say no?

We walked the halls of the mall, each of us carrying a bag loaded with clothes and a new pair of tennis shoes.

"Your father and I talked last night," she said finally after a while of silence. "I heard what you said the other day, Chase, and you're right. I've been trying to stop you from growing, and I'm sorry. We've had our problems in the past, but I feel we're working through those."

She gave me that look that mothers are so good at. The look said that I had been a loser and a disappointment before, but now had managed to get my head out of my ass and make them proud. I knew there was a compliment in there somewhere, and was willing to take it where I could get it.

"Okay," I said into her prolonged pause.

"You can get a job. I think it would be best if you kept it to fifteen hours or less during the school year, however."

I turned to her, stunned. "You mean I can keep it?"

She nodded. "Yes. You've done well this year, and I'm proud of you. Your grades were outstanding." She set our packages down on a nearby bench and hugged me, her voice shaky. "You are so smart, honey. I just never understood why you refused to use what God gave you." She pulled back, her hands still on my shoulders. "The only thing I ask is that you keep an open mind concerning your future. You still have some time before you really need to be deciding on a career path. Give it the summer. Please?"

I stared at her, my previous glow of pride dimming to a mere 15 watts. "Mom, I like psychology. It's what I want to do. My schedule is already made up for next semester, and I've got a pretty heavy load of psychology classes, electives I'm taking to make sure."

Her eyes shadowed and she sighed, took her bag and handed me mine. "Let's go."

I walked on beside her silence. I knew she was upset with me, again, but I was proud of myself. I had never disagreed with anything to her face, and I was stunned. I was nervous about it, but elated at the same time.

When we got home, my father was sitting on the couch reading the newspaper. He smiled at us as we walked in. "Oh, Chase, your friend Dagny called when you were out. She called twice, actually."

"What did she want?" I asked, my foot on the bottom step of the stairway.

He shrugged. "She didn't say."

I hurried up to my room, anxious to call her back. I almost felt obsessed with her. She consumed my thoughts; the mention of her name sent chills up my spine. I dropped my shopping bags on the floor, flopped down on my bed, and grabbed the handset on the nightstand. I quickly dialed the familiar number. The phone rang and rang; finally, her answering machine picked up. I even loved the sound of her voice over the machine! God, how pathetic.

"Um, hey, Dag. My dad said you called, so I was calling you back. I'll be here all day if you want to call back. Um, bye." I gently set the receiver back in the cradle, staring down at it.  I missed her.

* ~ * ~ * ~ * ~ * ~ *

*Cocoon*
   *The rare words of devils*
   *Tempt me to vicious dreams*
   *There's nothing left to glean*
   *From these visions*
   *Watching with half-closed lids*
   *The recorder of my life*
   *Shows the happy times or strife*
   *That have risen*
      *Chorus: So I think I'm all alone*
      *Only reaching for the stars*
      *Never trying for the moon*
      *Wrapped up in my cocoon*
   *Like the turning of the tide,*
   *Always changing but the same*
   *Try to keep a simple rein*
   *On each day*
   *How can I keep this face*
   *When behind it lies the truth*
   *And everything has moved*
   *Another way*
      *Chorus*
   *At times I feel my friends*
   *Are all growing around me*
   *They have turned into large trees*
   *And I'm an acorn*
   *Or feel my jagged sides*
   *There's no flow to smooth them over*
   *Sometimes changing, always older*
   *With the storm*
      *Chorus (fade out)*

I chewed on my pen as I read what I had written, my hand never stopping until it was all out.  A tune popped into my head as I automatically set the lyrics to music.

The sun had set, leaving the land in darkness.  I sat on my bed, my knees drawn up, back against the headboard, pillows thrown off the bed.  I had brought my journal home with me.  It was like an American Express card; I never left home without it.  I was making a slight change when I was startled by the shrill ringing of the phone beside me.  I picked up the receiver.  "Hello?"

"Hi.  What are you doing?" the familiar voice asked.

An instant smile spread across my face and I felt my body relax against the wall, my legs stretching out. "Using the journal, actually." I glanced down at the book lying in my lap, traced a fingertip over the smooth, cool page.

"That's great, Chase."

My brows knitted. "What's wrong?"

"Nothing. Why?"

I knew she was full of it. I could hear it in her voice, the way she spoke; something was wrong. "I don't believe you, Dag." I set the notebook and pen aside and sat up.

"What's to believe, Chase? Nothing is wrong."

She sounded so tired, her voice thick, as if she had a stuffed up nose. Either she was sick, or she had been crying. I was worried on either count.

"Okay, Dag. I won't push." I sat there for a minute, playing with the phone cord, twisting it around my fingers. "How are you? I really miss you."

"Oh, Chase, I miss you, too." I could hear her moving around, material being handled. "What are you doing?"

"Lying down."

"That sounds good."

I pushed myself down the bed and snagged a pillow from the floor. I curled up on my side, listening to the sound of Dagny breathing. "How's the job going?"

"Believe it or not, I actually love it."

I smiled. "I do believe it. You love people, and well, there's about as many people there as you could ever want."

She chuckled softly. "This is true. How is it going there? Are you ready to kill the parents yet?"

"No. But I'm close. They're going to let me get a job."

"Oh, Chase, that's great. I know how much you wanted that." She was quiet for a moment. "Do you have regrets, Chase?"

My brows drew together at the non sequiter. "Some, yeah. Why?" I pushed myself up on an elbow.

"I don't know. Life is so short, and sometimes I wonder if I've always made the right choices. Could I have prevented things? You know, thoughts like that."

"Dagny, I know something's wrong." I was frustrated, knowing there was nothing I could do from here, wanting desperately to be with her.

"I'm just tired. In fact, I'm going to go to bed. Talk to you in the morning?"

"Yeah. Okay. Sleep well, Dag."

"You, too, Chase. Oh, and Chase?"

"Yeah?"

"Don't let yourself have too many regrets. They come back to bite you in the ass."

I stared at the dead receiver in my hand. What was the deal? I was really worried now. I got up and threw on some clothes. I was going back to school.

My parents were as understanding as they could be, not wanting me to leave any earlier than I already had planned, but liking Dagny enough to care that something might be troubling her.

I packed my little car as quickly as possible and sped away toward the university. The short drive felt as if it took forever. Finally Dagny's building came into view in my headlights, and I whipped into the parking lot and then hurried inside.

I could see the light under the door, I knocked. Silence, then I heard the muted footsteps of someone walking in socks. The locks clicked as they were undone, and the door opened. Dagny stood there in flannel shorts and a tee. Her face was flushed, her eyes red, which made the green stand out all the more.

"Chase," she whispered, a mixture of disbelief and relief in her voice, but she quickly pulled herself together, wiping all expression off her face.

"I came as soon as I could. I was really worried. Still am."

"Come in." She moved to the couch, leaving the door open for me. I closed it softly behind me, following. When I had myself settled next to her, she took a deep breath. "Darrel's dead."

I was stunned, the air escaping me in a sigh. "Dagny..." I reached out to touch her, but she put her hand up. I was stung, but let her talk.

"It happened yesterday, on his way to work. Some asshole wasn't paying attention, and well, he died a few hours later at the hospital." I could tell she was trying to hold it all inside. "I just talked to him, Chase. He called me again last week, begging me to at least go out to see him." She swallowed. "I told him no, I had too much to do."

I watched the struggle she was having, the battle raging between her heart and her brain. Why was she fighting it? "Let go, Dag," I said as gently as I could.

She looked at me, shaking her head. "No, I'm fine." She smiled weakly. "I have to stay strong."

"For who?"

Her eyes narrowed as she looked at me. "For me! I have to stay strong for me, Chase. No one else will get me through this." She stood and began to pace.

Feeling like I was watching a tennis match, I ran my hands through my hair and stood as well. "Dagny, why won't you trust me to get you through this?" An impatient hand swiped at her eye, and I knew she was cracking. I walked over to her, tentatively reaching out. "Please? You have helped me through so much, and my friend through the hardest thing she'll ever have to go through." I pleaded, my eyes saying it all.

"I can't, Chase," she said softly, her voice cracking. She looked longingly at my hand resting on her arm.

I sensed the yearning and took a step closer. "Please? Let me help." The closer I got, the softer and more gentle my voice became. "Trust me?"

"I..." A tear began to slowly make its way down her cheek. "Why, Chase? Why did it have to happen this way?" A small sob escaped.

"I don't know, Dag. Things just happen and we have no idea why. Come here." I put my hand on her shoulder, easing it around her neck until I pulled her to me. She rested her head against my neck, her body relaxing against mine, her arms going around my waist. We had issues to talk about, but not right now; they could wait. I needed to know why she wouldn't trust me and let me in as I had her.

I felt the tiniest bit of wetness against my chest, through my shirt. I put my hand on the back of her head, stroked her hair as I held her, everything in the world disappearing except Dagny and her pain. Finally the dam broke and she really began to cry.

"Shh, I know, Dag. We'll get through this."

\* ~ \* ~ \* ~ \* ~ \* ~ \*

I slowly ran my fingers over the right chords on my guitar, feeling the music in my soul. I wanted her to know just exactly how I felt, and what I wanted to be. I wanted to sing this for her, just for her.

The words of "Bridge Over Troubled Water" were written by Paul Simon, but they said everything I ever felt for Dagny, they said what I wanted her to know. Just me, Melo, and my promise to Dagny.

I kept my eyes closed as I sang, never before singing so purely. The song built, and so did my emotions, nearly seeping from my eyes. I put my entire soul into the song, letting my voice and the music die off, my eyes still closed as I took a breath. Thunderous applause brought me back to the now, and I finally looked around. The bar's patrons were on their feet, but I was only looking for one. I saw her at her usual table, her hands gripping her drink like a vise. I noted the tears on her cheeks, and I smiled. She smiled back.

# Chapter 8

Feeling something soft and warm, I opened my eyes. For some reason my vision was blurry and I could only see something pale. I inhaled, musky, spicy scent. I looked around using just my eyes, saw the blue material that met the pale something. I directed my attention to my fingertips and felt softness beneath them, soft and squishy.

Oh my God!

I seemed to be curled up with Dagny. My mind raced to the night before. I had stayed at her place with her for the past few days for a couple of reasons. One, she was still upset and had asked me not to leave. Two, I didn't have a dorm yet for my summer class. We had gotten back there after the show at Gotfry's, and she had been really upset, the song having tapped into something deeply emotional.

We had walked into the apartment and Dagny had headed straight for her bedroom. I had moved to the couch to make up my bed.

"Chase?"

I looked up, surprised to hear my name but nothing else, so I wandered into Dag's bedroom, where I saw her sitting on the bed, her head down, hands in her lap. She looked up at me, her eyes red.

"Hey, you," I said, leaning against the doorframe. She smiled weakly and patted the bed beside her. I quickly sat, putting my arm around her shoulders as she leaned into me. She was so vulnerable, almost child-like. "Do you want me to stay?"

She nodded with a quiet, "Yeah." So, she had lain on her side and I had spooned up behind her, trying to give her as much comfort and security as I could with just the heat of my body.

Which brought me to my current situation. How did I end up lying on Dagny's shoulder, my body pressed against her side, hand resting on her stomach, when I was supposed to be holding her? Was she awake? When she did wake up, would she freak out like I was doing? I had to see, had to know.

My head popped up and I found myself staring into two very open green eyes. She seemed surprised by my sudden appearance, but she said nothing, nor did I. I smiled weakly and laid my head back down.

*Shit! What do I do?* If she had been asleep, I could have quietly moved myself away and she would never have known the difference. *Maybe I can go back to sleep and then she will, too, and I can move then. She'll think it was a dream and never be the wiser.*

But I had to admit, it felt wonderful. I reveled in it. I closed my eyes, a small sigh escaping me. I felt Dagny's arm, that I suddenly realized had been around me the entire time, tighten, her other arm coming around to encircle me completely. *God, did I die sometime in the night and go to Heaven? Couldn't be. Natalie once told me I was too evil for words, and she seems to be an expert on this stuff, so perhaps this is hell, and when I look again, the person holding me will actually be Mike.*

I grinned at my own thoughts, knowing just how silly they were. In all honesty, I didn't think Dagny would freak out. We weren't doing anything wrong, just two friends who were holding each other. Just because one of them thought about the other on an almost illegal basis, and obsessed constantly, didn't mean anything.

I turned my brain off and just enjoyed the feeling. I felt Dagny swallow, could hear her heartbeat, slow and steady. I cuddled in a little closer, feeling the softness of her breast against my shoulder. I had never noticed just how safe and comforting those things could be. *Guess it goes back to the whole mother/child thing. Freud would have a field day with me.*

We laid just as we were for a good half hour when I got to wondering again. I popped my head up for a second look and saw the same thing. This time, Dagny grinned at me, thoroughly amused.

"Hey," she said.

I smiled back. "Um, hi?"

She chuckled, running her hand along my back. "Thanks for staying with me last night, Chase. I really appreciate it." She pushed some wild strands of hair away from my face, tucking them behind an ear.

Though she was smiling, I could tell that Darrel's death was still having an effect on her. I knew there really wasn't anything for me to do; I'd just do my best to be there for her. "You're welcome. Um, I'm sorry about this, though." I indicated our present positions.

She shook her head. "Why? Aren't you comfortable?"

"Well, yeah, but..."

"But what?"

*I'm too comfortable, Dagny. Therein lies the problem.* I wisely remained silent.

She chuckled at my obvious discomfort. "You're so cute."

"Thanks, I think." I pulled away, and to my horror noticed a small bit of slobber on Dagny's neck, the edge of the collar on her shirt slightly discolored. *Oh my God.* I reached out and wiped it away. "I'm sorry." She laughed, adding to my hell. I scooted to the edge of the bed and stood. Dagny started to get up, but I turned, putting up my hand. "Nope. You stay." She looked at me, obviously surprised and confused. "I'll be back."

"Ah." She piled the two pillows behind her and leaned against them. "Well, can I at least have the textbook that's setting on the dresser over there?" I saw the book and handed it to her. "Thank you. I'll read while you do, well, whatever."

I nodded and headed toward the kitchen. *What to make, what to make?* I saw the waffle iron on the counter and thought about it, but I didn't want to burn down the apartment like I nearly did the last time. I opened the refrigerator and saw the bag of bagels she kept. *Perfect.* Taking one from the bag and slicing it in half, I stuck it in the toaster and dug out the fat free cream cheese.

"Tray, I need a tray." I looked around again, in search of something that would work. I was making a great deal of noise as I rummaged through Dagny's cupboards.

"You'd better not be tearing up my clean kitchen!" came the yell from the bedroom.

"Yeah? Bite me," I yelled back, hearing laughter as I looked at the cabinet that was now in shambles. An idea sparked and I went to the drawer under the stove, where I found a big cookie sheet. *Hey, it might not be conventional, but it will serve.*

As the bagel halves toasted, I poured a glass of orange juice and got out everything she could possibly need: plate, knife for the cream cheese, even a straw for the juice. All my offerings loaded onto the cookie sheet, I headed into the bedroom.

Dagny was immersed in her reading, knees drawn up, hair tucked behind one ear. *God, to wake up to that every morning...* Shaking the thought out of my head, I strode in with a flourish.

"Oh, no way. I can't believe you did this!" Dagny put her book aside and sat up a little straighter, her legs stretching out.

I shrugged, embarrassed by such exuberance over what little I had done. I set the cookie sheet over her lap, my choice of tray earning me a chuckle. "Oh, this looks good." She looked up at me with shining eyes and a wide smile. "Thank you, Chase. You have been so wonderful."

"Eh, well, you know." I smiled stupidly as I shrugged and shuffled my feet.

"Come here. I'll share."

* ~ * ~ * ~ * ~ * ~ *

Having decided not to go to the funeral, Dagny sent Darrel's family flowers and a card. She didn't feel it was her place to attend the service; she didn't belong there anymore. She didn't want to have to think about it, wanted a day to just have fun, and so she took me job hunting.

I had never had a "real" job, you know, the kind where you get a steady paycheck and not the few pence the bar paid. The tips were good, though. I had done some babysitting in my early teens, but that was about it. I was nervous, excited, and felt like an adult for the first time. I picked up some applications and filled them out, not knowing half of the information I apparently should be able to supply.

"This is pathetic. I don't know my own damn social security number." I was frustrated, and felt stupid.

"Hey, it's okay, Chase. It's not exactly something you use every day, you know. Don't worry about it. Do you have a copy of it somewhere? In your wallet, anywhere?"

I dug through it, looking for anything that looked like it might be important. "Damn, I need to clean this thing out." I made a small pile of old receipts, movie ticket stubs, and even an old gum wrapper. "Nope."

"What's this?"

Dagny pulled something out that was hiding behind my school I.D. Holding the blue and white paper card between her fingers, she grinned at me. The nation's seal caught my eye. I snagged it from her hand, glaring as she laughed. I wrote down the information and went back to the previous application to re-write the entire thing. "I am never going to get a job, Dag," I muttered.

"Why not?"

"Look at this. How pathetic is it?" I showed her the mostly blank spaces for previous experience.

"You have to start somewhere, Chase. It probably won't be your dream job, but if it pays, it's worth it." She smiled encouragement. "It'll give you at least one more thing to fill in one of those spaces in the future."

"Yeah, yeah." We were parked outside the fast food place where I was applying. I opened the car door. "I'll be right back."

"I'll be here."

I gave the application to the sixteen year old assistant manager, feeling queasy thinking about having to work for that pimply faced kid. I felt like such a loser.

"I just got the greatest idea while you were in there," Dag said as I climbed back into the SUV. I looked at her, hoping lightning had stuck in the few minutes I had been gone. "Gotfry's."

I frowned. "I'm not twenty-one, Dag."

"So? You're over eighteen." She grinned, wiggling her eyebrows.

"Let's go."

*～*～*～*～*～*

"Hell, yeah! Why are you even asking for an application, Chase?" Greg leaned on the bar, a glass of cranberry juice in his hand. "You're hired."

"Are you serious?" I leaned in a little closer, making sure I'd heard him right.

He sipped the drink, nodding. "You'd be great for business. People already love you, and if you serve their drinks, too — shit, I've got a gold mine in you, kid. Even though I'm already paying you and CID a king's ransom."

He punched me lightly on the arm as I rolled my eyes. I felt proud and glanced over at Dagny to see she was also wearing an ear to ear grin.

"Oh, I talked with Doug the other night. I want you guys to be my main act over the weekends this summer. Kill Wednesdays until school starts up again, but do Friday and Saturday nights instead. You cool with that?"

"Yeah. Sounds great. What did Doug say?"

"He said to talk to you." He downed the rest of his juice, slamming the glass down with a satisfied grin. "Okay, you be here tomorrow night, Chase, and we'll get this hiring business wrapped up. For now, you two get lost or spend some money." He smiled as he walked further down the bar to where a middle-aged, balding man was sitting, looking Dagny up and down. He smiled suggestively. Dagny glared at him, and we left the bar.

Back at the car, I ripped the other applications in half, thrilled that my search was over. The only negative was that I couldn't be totally honest with my parents about it. I guess into everyone's life little white lies do fall.

I was nearly jumping up and down with my excitement. Dagny and I hadn't been able to spend much time together since the beginning of second semester, and now we had the whole summer. Carrie planned to come back a little early so she and I could do some things, too, which I looked forward to. We also had an appointment to talk with her lawyer in mid-July. I knew she was nervous about it, but ultimately she'd be glad to get it all over with.

Since Dagny and I both had the night free and clear, we decided to make the most of it. I bit my lip as I checked out the newest movies that had arrived at Blockbuster. As I read the titles, I thought back over the day. It had been incredible. Dagny had been a little quiet compared to her usual enthusiastic self. She had been very touchy and affectionate. I think she needed that human contact, and I certainly didn't mind. She had said she wanted a night to forget sorrow and have fun, spending some quality time with me. Of course I got all gooey at that, and I was prepared to do anything in my power to make her have fun.

"Hey, Dagny, come here," I said as I spotted a new movie I knew she had been wanting to see.

"'Kay," she said absently.

I glanced over my shoulder to see her reading the back of a box in the Drama section. I waited. She continued to read, then put the box down and picked up another. "Hello? Earth to Dagny Robertson."

"I'm coming."

"Uh huh, I can see that." I walked over to her, grabbed her from behind and lifted her off her feet.

"Chase! Put me down!"

She giggled like a schoolgirl as I carried her over to the New Release wall, setting her down right in front of the movie I wanted her to see. Getting her bearings, she saw the box and snatched it up.

"Look! *Lord of the Rings, Fellowship of the Ring* is finally out!"

"No shit, Sherlock."

"And they have one copy left!" She snatched the video off the shelf, waving it in the air victoriously. "Why didn't you say something, Chase? We could have lost this." I glared at her, my hands on my hips, toe tapping on the floor. She grinned sheepishly. "Oh, the reason for the...and you set me down in front of... Okay. I got it."

I grinned. "You're such a smart girl."

"I try."

Armed with three movie rentals, we headed to Dagny's apartment to relax and enjoy, picking up a pizza on the way. Moving the coffee table to the side, we spread the box, plates and napkins aplenty out on the floor. Dagny took the comforter off her bed and laid it out so we'd have a nice space to eat and lie down on. Both vibrating with anticipation, we watched the teasers before Tolkien's great epic began.

We scarfed down the pizza, then shoved the box aside, and I leaned back against the front of the couch. To my surprise, Dagny scooted next to me, putting her head on my shoulder. I put an arm around her shoulders and sighed. If this was the way summer was going to be, I didn't want school to start.

* ~ * ~ * ~ * ~ * ~ *

After finally getting my key for my summer room, I ran over to the dorm. I was thrilled to see I had managed to get a single. I thought it was a mistake, but wasn't about to say anything. I was glad to have somewhere to put my stuff again, but by the same token, I hated leaving Dagny's apartment. I had been staying there for a week, and it had been wonderful. It was her space, however, and I really didn't want to encroach on it, so I went to find out about my dorm as soon as I was notified.

I had started up at Gotfry's two days earlier, and so far absolutely loved it. Greg had me do whatever needed to be done — from clearing tables to covering waitress's breaks to standing at the door one night. Oh, that had been great fun. Never in my life had I thought I'd be a bouncer, or any good at it. One guy came in who was already drunk, and I had a bad feeling about him so I kept an eye on him. It didn't take long for me to be proven right. He tried to start a fight, and I got to be the lucky girl to throw his ass out. Next Greg was going to start teaching me how to tend bar. I wasn't sure if that was legal, but whatever.

It was coming up on Friday and time for rehearsals. Doug went over some new songs with the guys in the band while Terrie and I sat on the grass in Doug's front yard, catching some sun. It was late June and beautiful out. The sky was as blue as a robin's egg and the temperatures were hot, but not scorching. I rubbed suntan lotion on my legs as Terrie leaned back on her elbows, ankles crossed, watching me.

"You have nice legs, Chase."

I glanced back at her to see that she had lowered her sunglasses a bit and was looking over the tops.

"Thanks." I smiled shyly. I didn't take compliments well, and wasn't real fond of them.

"Do you work out?" She sat up and ran a hand over my left shin.

"Uh, well, no. Not really. Dagny and I swim every morning, but that's about it."

She nodded. "That's good exercise, but I bet you're one of those people who are just lucky to have a good metabolism and don't need to do a thing." She smiled. "Am I right?"

"Well, I wouldn't go that far, but I've been pretty lucky, I guess."

"I'll say." She patted my leg and leaned back again, her head back, neck arched to the sun. "God, it's blissful out here." She sighed. "I must say, this is one thing I missed when I left, the sun. Where I went back East, oh, it was cold and dreary or simply hot and humid. Miserable."

I set the suntan lotion bottle aside and lay back, my hands behind my head. I stared up at the clouds, seeing what shapes I could find in them. I felt her presence as Terrie scooted over, putting her head next to mine so we were touching.

"How is your summer going?"

I turned to find she had moved onto her side, holding her head in her hand.

"It's going well, I guess. I started my summer classes already."

"Really? What are you taking?"

"Just a literature class. You know, knock down another of my core classes." I smiled. I felt strange about what I was taking, almost like I had to hide the fact that we'd be reading lesbian erotica and literature. It wasn't a bad thing, and I was looking forward to it, the curiosity nearly killing me. But all the same, I didn't want it to be common knowledge. I wasn't ready for the questions just yet.

"I loved literature in college." Terrie smiled at me. "All the great classics. This may seem strange, but one of my favorite authors was always Rand."

My head popped up. "Ayn?"

"Yes. You know her work?"

"Well, actually I just read *Atlas Shrugged* last semester." I grinned sheepishly, remembering why I had read it. My mother had yet to ask where that book had gone.

"Are you a fan?" Terrie sat up, pulling her legs in Indian style, her hands resting in her lap.

"Well, I actually read it at a friend's urging."

"That's wonderful. I read *Atlas Shrugged* many, many years ago. *Fountainhead* was always my favorite. Ayn always wrote such strong female characters, so far ahead of her time for a woman in the fifties. Especially the main character in *Shrugged*. Oh, what was her name..."

"Dagny Taggart."

"Yes! That's right." She stopped, cocking her head to the side. "Your friend, isn't her name Dagny?"

I smiled, nodded. "Yup. She was named after Taggart. Dag's why I read the book in the first place."

"It's wonderful that she could influence you like that. She's very cute." She turned to look toward the garage. "It looks like we're being called back into the den."

Surprised by her comment about my friend, I got up to follow her into the garage.

*~*~*~*~*~*

Dagny offered to help me move into the dorm, and I was grateful. I had a lot of stuff and only two arms to carry it. This would be our first night apart in seven days, and I was not looking forward to it. I would miss her, and felt too childish to admit it to her. *Big girl, Chase, afraid to stay alone.* Well, afraid wasn't the right word; I just wanted to be around her. I had been having odd dreams almost nightly, and though they all centered around Dagny and I enjoyed them immensely, I was confused by them.

A heat started in the pit of my stomach whenever I was around her, or just when I thought of her. When we went swimming every morning and I'd see her in her bathing suit, I felt like a twelve-year-old boy seeing a nude picture for the first time. She made my body burn, and I ached for something foreign to me. I understood, yet I didn't, but I had the feeling the explanation was just around the corner.

My clothes were spread out on the unmade bed, all dresser drawers open as I carefully re-folded the garments, sticking them in their appropriate places. Dagny watched me, an amused smile on her face.

"I had no idea that you were such a perfectionist, Chase." She leaned against the wall, her arms crossed over her chest.

I shrugged, carefully smoothing the wrinkles out of the Henley I was folding. "Well, you know, I don't have a huge selection of clothing, so I should take care of what I have, right?"

"I suppose so." She pushed off, walked to the desk that was piled with stuff — notebooks, books, CDs, and the tiny movie collection I had at school with me. "What is this?" She picked an old, ratty notebook off the pile.

I glanced at it. "Oh, I've had that since I was ten, if you can't tell by all the doodling."

She nodded. "Yup, I can tell. I can't imagine a college aged Chase would be drawing Rainbow Brite."

"Hey, I was ten. You do stupid things at ten." I pushed the drawer closed as I finished with my shirt drawer. Time for the shorts.

"Why do you still have this?" Dagny sat on the bed, looking at all the doodles, turning the notebook this way and that to read all the goofy messages that were written in every direction. She chuckled a few times, shaking her head.

"Well, I started writing when I was about nine. I started with simple poetry, not quite getting the idea of writing a song until I saw a documentary on Elton John that summer." I leaned against the dresser, remembering the day the light bulb went on. I ran upstairs immediately and wrote my first song. "My parents bought us a whole bunch of school supplies for that year and I liked the color of that notebook, thought the aqua was cool." I smiled. "It quickly became my writing notebook. Kind of like my diary, I guess."

"May I?"

I suddenly got a sick feeling in my stomach at the thought of Dagny reading my work. No one had ever read a word. My reluctance must have showed on my face.

"If you don't want me to, Chase, I understand."

I hated being so damn easy to read. "No, it's okay. Go ahead."

Dagny looked back down at the notebook, then over at me. I think she knew the significance of my letting her read my thoughts, that she was the first. "Thank you."

She moved from the bed to the floor, resting her back against the side of the mattress, slowly opening the cover, trying to be careful as the flimsy cardboard was already pulling from the wire spiral. She ran her hand down the smoothness of the first page, filled with more doodles and written in really bad cursive:

Chase's Award Winning Writings

She chuckled. "That so?" She looked at me, trying to hide the grin that was itching to get out.

"Yeah, yeah. I told you I was stupid when I was ten."

"Come here, you goof. Sit with me."

I tossed the shorts I had been folding into the dresser and plopped down next to Dagny. I was so nervous, my heart was about to pound right out of my chest. At the same time, I was curious to see what she would think of the songs. She'd get to see a special part of me that no one had ever seen.

Dagny turned the first page to my first real song. It was short, didn't make a whole lot of sense, obviously written by a child who was trying her musical wings. Dagny read it, smiling the entire time.

"This is so adorable. I can just imagine you as little Chase, lying on your bed on your stomach, chewing on the eraser of your pencil." She looked at me, mirth twinkling in her eyes.

I smiled back. "That's about it, too."

Dagny continued to read, eventually turning herself so she had her back to me, leaning against me. I could read over her shoulder, and I put my hands on her upper back, massaging to get out any kinks.

"Oh, yeah. Keep it up," she breathed, her head leaning back for a moment as she enjoyed it, then turned her attention back to the page before her. "Misfit."

My stomach clenched when she read the title. This song meant a great deal to me and it would kill me if she didn't like it. I hoped she could understand it and not find it strange or stupid. I read over her shoulder:

> *Tarnished and tattered*
> *Stained colors battered*
> *Why don't I seem to fit in?*
> *Diff'rent as night and day*
> *Never seem to go their way*
> *Someone's got to be kidding*
> > *Chorus: Maybe the postman's*
> > *That could explain a lot*
> > *Or left on their doorstep*
> > *And they decided to adopt*
> > *If that's the case,*
> > *I wish they'd left me instead*

> *In a family of crystal, I am lead*
> *Alienated*
> *Young and too jaded*
> *Can't play the part they expect*
> *Too independent*
> *Don't have a remnant*
> *Of their so-called great intellect*
> > *Chorus*
> *Chipped and abused*
> *Worn out, too, and used*
> *I feel too old for my years*
> *Rags to their dress clothes*
> *Stale to their fresh loaves*
> *I don't let them see any tears*
> > *Chorus: (repeat last line)*

Dagny said nothing, and I waited, holding my breath. She slowly leaned away from me and turned. I was surprised to see her eyes shimmering with tears.

"How old were you when you wrote this, Chase?" she whispered.

"Thirteen."

"Sing it. Please?"

I looked at her for a moment, then nodded. I stood, grabbed Melo from the corner where she was tucked in with Than, and set her up. I sat on the edge of the bed, took a deep breath as I found the tune in my head again, and softly began to sing, telling of the confusion and pain in my early years, pain that had not gone away with the years. The feelings of not being worthy enough for the Marins, not being who they had always hoped and wanted me to be.

Dagny listened from her seat on the floor, hands in her lap as she studied me, her eyes traveling over my face. I wondered what was going through her mind, what was she thinking? I was thinking that finally I had found someone to accept me for me, who wasn't expecting me to create the moon from a rock on the beach.

It hit me in that moment, as I saw a tear slide down Dagny's face, lazily making its way to her mouth. I saw those green eyes looking at me, at who I was and what I was capable of. This was what I wanted in my life, what I needed to keep me going and make me keep wanting to try and be me. I needed this in my life; I needed her.

I nearly stopped playing as it hit me, but I kept going. I couldn't think about it, couldn't let it seep into my conscious thoughts quite yet. I filed it away for further processing. I ended the song and looked at my friend, not sure what to say or ask.

"God, Chase. You are...I had no idea. I'm blown away."

Another tear squeezed its way out of her eye.

"Why are you crying, Dag?" I asked quietly, putting Melo aside.

She stood and gathered me into a huge hug. "I had no idea you felt this way, Chase. No idea."

I put my arms around her and held her to me. *God, what am I going to do?* I knew there was no way in hell this would ever work. Dagny would have to stay my friend and I'd have to figure out something else. For now I'd have to play it safe, keep everything locked inside. That wouldn't be a problem. I'd been doing that my entire life.

"Are there more?" Dagny asked when she pulled away, her hand still on my shoulder as she looked down at me.

I nodded, then stood and took the leather journal from the desk. "There's really only one in this journal. Well, one that's finished, anyway." I didn't want her to read *Comfortable In My Skin*. That song was just for me. It was my heart and feelings splayed out there in black and white, and I didn't want the humiliation of Dagny reading it, seeing right through me. I flipped through the pages. "Here. This one's called *Confusion Abounds*."

Dagny took the journal from me. "Thanks." She began to read, I again reading over her shoulder.

> *What is this feeling*
> *That gnaws at my heart*
> *What does this mean then*
> *Now that we're apart*
> *Why can't I see quite*
> *What is chaining me*
> *Why can't life be right*
> *And just let me be?*
> > *Chorus: I can't understand*
> > *What's going on inside*
> > *But it's a feeling I won't deny*
> > *I can't seem to find*
> > *A word for this ache*
> > *But I'm not about to break*
> *So many questions*
> *So many things I don't know*
> *Part of me wants to run*
> *But I'll never let you go*
> *Though it can't be identified*
> *I don't know where to start*
> *True meanings always seem to hide*
> *From head but not from heart*
> > *Chorus*

Dagny slammed the journal closed and smiled at me. "Wonderful, Chase. Really, really great." She ran her hand over the soft surface of the cover. "What were you talking about in that one? What inspired you?"

I stared at her, trying to come up with something to say. How could I tell her she inspired all of my more recent songs? "Well, um, just life, I guess." I smiled nervously. "You know, things happen to you and you put them away in your brain until they all spill out in one form or another."

Dagny handed me the journal and I put it back on the desk. I suddenly felt very nervous, my palms sweating. I didn't know what I was afraid of. "So, we've worked hard today. Want to get some dinner?" I smiled, hopeful that she would take me up on getting out of there, and getting her away from my writing.

"Yeah, that sounds good." She sniffled one last time and we left the room.

Magpie's was quiet; after all, it was the middle of the week. Dagny and I sat at the table that had become ours. She looked at the menu, and I looked at her.

My small epiphany tonight had felt strange, yet exhilarating. I didn't fully understand the importance of it, yet I knew. Part of me felt sad, however. I knew chances were good that Dagny would never see me the same way I saw her. What could I possibly offer her except being a good friend — someone to watch movies and eat pizza with. That was it, nothing more. Fifteen years from now, when we had both graduated college, gone our separate ways, she would not think of me, would not wonder what I was up to. But I knew the same would not be true of me. Dagny would always be with me — the woman who had changed me and my perception of myself.

I was snapped out of my thoughts by the waiter asking for our drink orders. I got the same thing every time, drink and food-wise, so there wasn't a big hurry for me to figure out what I wanted.

"So, what started you writing?"

I looked at Dagny to find she was staring at me, her chin resting on her hand. I shrugged and grabbed the little glass shaker filled with parmesan cheese.

"I guess it was because I had so many thoughts and feelings running through me as a kid, and I really didn't know how to deal with them. I wasn't creative like Carrie, couldn't just draw it out on a piece of paper, and I couldn't talk to my parents, really. So one day I sat down and wrote that poem. I figured out it was helpful, so I didn't stop. Whenever something would happen in my life, good or bad, I'd write about it. There you go."

"You're wonderful. I must say, I'm truly impressed. You wrote with more clarity and intelligence at thirteen than I do now." She smiled, thanking the waiter for our drinks.

I sipped from my soda. "I don't know. I enjoy it. I would never want to do it for a living or anything, but nothing works better for me to get things out."

"That's good, Chase. We all need something."

We had walked to Magpie's from the dorm, and it was time to head back.

"What do you say we just walk...for a while?" Dagny asked, looking up into the clear night. I nodded my consent and we turned left at the end of Magpie's parking lot and began our stroll. The night was beautiful, summer turning out to be warm, but mild, the night was perfect. I glanced down at Dagny's hand, her thumb tucked into a belt loop on her shorts. I wanted to reach down and take it, hold her hand, feel connected. I tore my eyes away, tossing the thought out of my head.

"I have to confess, I've tried to write a time or two."

Dagny's voice surprised me, caught my attention. She looked at me to see what my reaction was. I looked at her, letting her know she had my attention.

"It sucked. I think I'm too analytical to be poetic."

I chuckled. "Well, then, am I screwed as far as psychology goes?"

She laughed. "No. I think you're one of those people who make me sick, who are good at just about anything they try."

I liked the sound of that, even if it was not true. As we walked, Dagny told me about different friends she had had through the years who had been writers, and even a good friend from high school who had been a sculptor. "She was fascinating, saw things in the strangest of ways."

"Artists can be interesting, can't they? Carrie can be quite the eccentric sometimes."

"So, she's finally made up her mind, huh?"

Dagny took a sharp left and I followed suit without much thought. "Yeah. I'm thrilled about it, too. She decided on painting. I think she'll do well with it."

"Do you see much of her?"

I shrugged. "Yeah, for the most part. This is the first summer that we didn't spend together," I said, suddenly sad at that fact. Things change, but I didn't like change.

Dagny turned to me, her brows drawn. "Oh, Chase, I'm sorry. Here you are, stuck with me."

"Hey, no, this is not a bad thing, Dag. Really." The look on her face told me I wasn't doing a very good job of reassuring her. "Really. I'd rather be here, you know?" I looked down at the side-walk, which needed some work. I was feeling very shy. I knew Dagny didn't quite understand the impact and depth of my words, but I sure as hell did.

"Aww, Chase. That's so nice. I'm really glad you're here too."

She entwined our arms as we walked, a smile on her face. I mirrored it, staying quiet as we walked up on her building.

"Want to come in for a bit?"

I nodded. *Definitely.*

Dagny pulled out her keys and steered us to the back of the building's first floor to get her mail before we made our way upstairs. She looked through a pile of stuff, stopping at the Alumni Newsletter that was sent out to all graduates of the university. We'd made it to the bottom of the stairs when she stopped, me nearly running into her.

"What are you doing?"

"It's Darrel," she said quietly, turning toward me. "They have his obituary in here." She showed me the page. A black and white picture was next to it. I stared at Darrel, the man who had managed to get next to this incredible lady. He was very good looking, with hair that looked to be brown or light brown, clean cut and well kept. He had light colored eyes and a nice smile.

"He was cute," I commented as I began to read. He had graduated from UA last year with a business degree with emphasis on foreign affairs. He was fluent in Japanese and had worked for a large corporation in San Diego, where he was in line for a promotion. As I read all the things that Darrel had accomplished in his twenty-four years of life, I couldn't help but think what a waste it was. He was intelligent and driven, and there probably was no limit to the things he would have done.

"Come on."

Dagny started up the stairs, and I silently followed. She walked into her apartment and flopped down hard on the couch.

"You okay?" I sat down next to her, setting the newsletter on the coffee table. "Can I get you anything?" She shook her head. "Why don't you tell me about him, Dag. Tell me what you liked about him, what you guys used to do. You know, talk about it." Dagny sighed, her shoulders slumping, but she said nothing. "Come on, Dag. Talk to me. Please?"

She looked so alone and vulnerable sitting there two feet away from me. I had the immediate sense that she needed to be touched, so I put my hand on the back of her neck and tugged her toward me. Within seconds, she fell over sideways and laid her head in my lap, tucking her hands up by her face, her legs curling.

"Well, we met the first day of our freshman year here," she began, wiping at her eyes. "He was so good looking and made me so nervous." She smiled at the memory. "I wasn't really all that interested; I was more worried about my studies. He wouldn't leave me alone, and to make matters worse, we had some classes together." I smiled my understanding, bringing my hand to Dagny's hair, running my fingers through it. "He kept asking and asking until finally I agreed to go out with him. He was so cute. On Christmas Eve, he took me to dinner at this really expensive place. Oh, man, did they have good steak." She smiled again.

"What made you go with him?"

She shrugged with a sigh. "I think mainly, so he'd quit asking. I got so tired of being inundated with calls from him; he even went so far as to get his friends involved. I knew a few of them from classes and they talked to me constantly about him. I was about ready to start opening fire." I laughed. "Anyway, he was a complete gentleman, and my parents absolutely loved him. He was smart, driven, treated me like a queen."

"Why did it break up?" I asked softly, staring down at Dagny's profile, her soft hair tickling my fingers as I brushed it back.

"It wasn't what I wanted. You know, it's funny." She turned to lie on her back so she was staring up at me. "I have asked myself this so many times. I mean, don't get me wrong, the guy wasn't perfect, but he was a good guy. Why didn't I try to make it work?" She took a deep breath, staring up at the ceiling. I stared down at her, studying her face and features. The delicacy of her astounded me, yet she had so much strength. "Money and success were so important to Darrel."

"Why?"

"It was how his father had made it. His father, Rob, is in the heavy-hitter business world, the type who has his fingers in every kind of pie you can think of. Darrel was on his way to being the same way. He was sharp, smart as a whip. He knew what would work and what would drop out. I think that's why he called me again." She looked at me. "He thought that his success and money could get me to go to him."

"That's really sad," I said, stroking Dagny's arm. She straightened her arm to give me more access to it.

"It is, but that's what he knew. He was always supportive of my undergrad degree and my love for psychology, but when it came down to it and he was headed off for California, he couldn't understand my need to finish. He thought that I had my BS, so why did I need to go on? I could always find work out in California. After all, his father knew just about everyone and could get me into some lucrative job." She shook her head. "Not for me. I want to get some place in this world on my own." She sighed. "Life is interesting."

"Yes, it is." I ran my fingers through her hair again as I stared down at her, smiling back as she smiled up at me.

"I remember Darrel used to take me to this little totally hole-in-the-wall café called Jillian's. Man, this place was hard to find, and had the cheapest food you've ever seen. I'm talking like a dollar fifty for a hamburger."

"Damn! I want to go." I laughed. She laughed with me.

"God, he was such a wonderful listener. I really have to say, until you, I had never met anyone who heard so much of what I had to say. We used to talk all the time. He was like no other guy I'd come across. You know, most feel the need to play the big, bad strong stud." She grinned. "Not Darrel. He was sweet and sensitive."

"Why did you let him go, Dag? It sounds like you really loved him."

Her brows knit as she thought about that for a moment, sucking her bottom lip in to chew on it. "You know, I really did. I loved Darrel very much, still do, actually. But I think the problem was I never was *in* love with him. It just wasn't right for me. Sometimes I see myself as quite defective because of that." She looked at me. "Do you think I am?"

I shook my head vigorously. "God, no. It just wasn't the right time or person for you. It happens, and it does not make you a bad person."

She smiled, bringing her hand to my face to gently caress my cheek. "Thanks, Chase. What would I do without you?" She winked. "You may be right, but I still have to live with the guilt that I never apologized to him, was never totally honest with him, and now it's too late."

I saw tears forming in her eyes and I leaned down to gather her head in my arms, holding her close, letting her know she wasn't alone. She cried silent tears, her body shaking slightly with the sobs. I stroked her hair, whispering comforting words.

Within a few moments, Dagny had calmed and was wiping at her nose. I reached across her to the coffee table and pulled a Kleenex from the box. "Here."

"Thanks." She wiped her eyes and blew her nose, then took a deep breath.

I smiled at her. "Better now?"

"Yeah. I'm sorry. I didn't expect to react that way." She sat up and reached for another Kleenex, wiped her face.

"Don't you dare apologize, Dag. You do that anytime you want to." With a sigh, she lay back down, her head in my lap again. I looked down at her. "Want a pillow?" She nodded with a smile. I grabbed the black throw pillow that sat next to me on the couch and put it under her head.

"What do you look for in a relationship, Chase?"

The question threw me for a moment, but I quickly recovered. "Well, I don't know."

"Oh, come on. Tell me."

"Okay. Well..." I looked away, staring at the entertainment center across the room. I couldn't dare look at Dagny as I answered this question. "I want someone who loves me for me, you know?" I felt her nod. "I want someone who can be fun yet serious, who listens to me when I talk and is willing to talk to me in turn." I glanced down at her; her eyes were on me. When she caught my gaze, she smiled. I smiled back. "I want to be able to build a life with someone, have all the great things in life — a house, a dog, and a pool table." She laughed. "You think I'm joking, but if whoever doesn't like to play pool, I'm sorry, no sale."

"Okay, okay. Each to his own. What else?"

"Um, let's see." I bit my lip as I stared up at the ceiling, trying to think of all the things I'd ever wanted for myself. "I want someone who respects what I do, and may even enjoys it a little."

"Like your music?"

I looked down at her and nodded. "Or whatever else I decide to do."

"Mm, I know what you mean. If you think I'm crazy for continuing on for my doctorate, deal with it."

"And if you think I'm nuts for not wanting to go to college at all, it's my choice."

She smiled up at me. "We're not bitter or anything, are we?"

I grinned, shook my head. "No, not at all. What about you?"

"What about me," she sighed. "Hmm. Well, I know I certainly don't want to be my parents."

I said nothing, just listened. I really knew nothing about her family. I had met them once when I was a kid, but that was it. I definitely couldn't have picked them out in a lineup.

"My parents love each other very, very deeply. They met in high school, the whole high school sweetheart thing. Been married forever."

"Then what's the problem?" I asked, confused.

"My parents love each other very deeply, are still in love, but they didn't have enough to go around." I looked at her, understanding hitting me. "I was a very mature kid since I wasn't really allowed to be a kid. My parents treated me as an equal once I was able to communicate and do for myself. I was bright and could figure things out on my own, so I didn't really have to be helped out with things. My parents took full advantage of that, enrolling me in classes on the weekends once I reached school age. I loved the extra challenge, but had very little time with them, you know?"

I nodded, sad for a young Dagny who didn't understand. She looked so matter of fact about her childhood as she explained it to me. "Wow." I shook my head. So much about my friend was coming into focus.

"I never had anyone else, Chase. That's why I've always depended on me and only me. You accused me of not trusting you to help when I first heard Darrel died." She smiled, understanding filling her eyes. "I understood why you'd feel that way, but that wasn't the case. I just really don't know how to lean on someone else."

I nodded. I got it now. "Do you think you'll ever learn? I mean, that would be pretty important in a relationship. People need to feel needed, Dag."

She stared up into my face, studying my eyes, her gaze trailing down my nose to my mouth, then to my cheeks and back to my eyes. "Yeah, it is important. It's something that I think will come in time; it'll come with ultimate trust." She sighed. "I do have to say, I also want the Norman Rockwell picture. I want kids, and to be happy, and to have a career."

"Sounds good." I grinned. I wished I'd be able to see her happiness unfold as time and life went on.

"Oh, I nearly forgot to tell you." She sat up, running a hand through her hair. "Levy invited me to a convention, and I have to go. It lasts for two days, but, well, if you'd like to go, I figure we could stay an extra day and sightsee."

I looked at her, stunned. "Um, yeah. When, where?"

"It's next weekend, and it's up at a little town near the Grand Canyon. Go figure, huh?" She grinned. "Have you ever been there?" I shook my head. "Chase! You live so close and you've never been?"

"Yeah. Guess I just haven't gotten around to it," I said, trying to hide my sadness. I would have gone years ago had my mother ever taken me with her.

"Cool. There's supposed to be some speaker coming in from the Washington State University. Her name is Jen something. Carlson?" she guessed, sucking on the inside of her cheek as she thought. "I don't remember for sure, but anyway, I figure you could either go with me and listen too, or just do your own thing until I'm done." She looked at me closely. "You interested?"

"Definitely!" I was excited. I knew Greg would give me the time off. "Actually, um, well do you think it would be okay if I listened in?"

"Absolutely!" She smiled, clapping her hands. "This will be so much fun."

\* ~ \* ~ \* ~ \* ~ \* ~ \*

I laughed as I pushed away from the bar, tray in hand. I had just talked to Greg about the upcoming trip, and he had been kind enough to sagely advise me to not fall over the guardrail of the Grand Canyon. As I turned to the table that had ordered the Bud and Grateful Dead, I nearly ran smack into Terrie.

She smiled. "Hey."

"Hi there. You nearly added a few more colors to that shirt you've got on."

She looked down at the jigsaw puzzle pieces that littered her shirt, each one a different color, and grinned. "I wouldn't have had to go home to change, at least."

"This is true. What's up?"

She followed me as I headed for the table that the drinks belonged to. "Well, I came by to get a drink and see my favorite cocktail waitress."

"Call me that again and I'll have to deck you."

She laughed. "My deepest apologies."

The drinks delivered, I turned to the drummer.

"So, what's this I hear — you'll be gone this weekend?"

"Dagny invited me to a psychology convention with her this weekend. We'll leave Friday and come back late Monday night."

"That sounds like fun." She crossed her arms over her chest, taking a defensive stance.

*What's up with that?* "Yeah, I'm looking forward to it. Get away a little bit, see the Grand Canyon. You know. I think it will be great."

"I hope so. You know those types of things can be a real drag. Take it from me. In my job before, I had to go to those all the time. I hope you're not bored out of your mind." She put her hand on my arm, moving in close to me. "I have to go, but you keep in mind what I said. If you get bored, give me a call." With a smile, she was gone.

* ~ * ~ * ~ * ~ * ~ *

The town of Domer, Arizona was small, with a population of about ten thousand. I wondered why the convention was to be held there, and Dagny explained it was because it was a good midpoint for the universities of Washington state and Illinois, which were coming the furthest. The rates were cheap and the scenery beautiful.

We pulled up to our motel, a quaint little place with a pool and hot tub. UA was only willing to pay for two rooms, one for Levy and one for Dagny, and we figured it would be stupid to spend the money for a second one when Dagny and I could easily share.

The room was small, with the headboard of the double bed against the center wall, a table with two small chairs to the left, and the bathroom to the right. A motel room was a motel room, not a whole lot of change there.

"The first presentation starts at eight," Dagny said, sitting on the bed and reading the schedule that had been sent to her two weeks earlier. "That lasts for about an hour or so, then we have a 'getting to know you' kind of thing with refreshments in the main hall. Um, that lasts until ten, then another presentation that will take us 'til lunch, get an hour for lunch, then another presentation starts at one and lasts until four. Sunday is pretty much the same." She looked up at me. "Are you going to be bored out of your mind, Chase?" She looked worried.

I shook my head. I found it amusing that Dag and Terrie were thinking along the same lines. *They really must think that I can't entertain myself.* I smiled at the thought. "No, I don't think so. I've never been to anything like this, so I'm looking forward to it." I sat next to her on the bed.

"Really? I hope so. I'd hate for you to wish you hadn't come."

"I wouldn't worry about that. Besides, I've only had one class so far dealing with my major, so I may actually learn something."

After getting settled in, we decided to tour the town. That didn't take long. Domer was actually a beautiful little place, with a main street filled with nothing but local shops carrying everything from tobacco to clothing to swords. We went into just about every store, stopping at a bakery for a hot cinnamon roll and something to drink. The old couple that owned the place and made everything from scratch were two of the nicest people I had ever met.

"So, what are you two ladies doing around here? I've been here for over sixty-two years and I know every living soul in Domer," the man said, leaning over one of the glass cases. "What're your names?"

"I'm Dagny and this is my friend Chase."

The old man looked at Dagny for a moment, dressed in her loose-fit jeans and tee. He rubbed his chin. "I'd be willing to bet you was here for the convention this weekend." He looked at me. "Not so sure about you, though."

We looked at each other and grinned. "Well, we're both here for that."

"Hmm. You never can read people."

"Do I look that delinquent?" I asked as we headed back out into the warm night.

Dagny laughed. "I guess. Personally I think I look younger than you are, but each to his own."

* ~ * ~ * ~ * ~ * ~ *

The morning after we arrived, I dressed in the only pair of nice pants I owned, feeling stupid. I hated to dress up, but I knew this was not a casual affair. Trying to get comfortable and loosen up, I puttered around the room. I wasn't a big fan of large events with lots of people. I waited not so patiently for Dagny to finish up in the bathroom.

A few minutes later, the door opened, and Dagny stepped out. She looked gorgeous in a dark green skirt that reached to just above her knees and a sleeveless satin top that was a lighter green. She walked out into the bedroom, and all I could do was stare. Her hair was pinned up, a few strands falling around her face.

Dagny stood in the doorway looking at me. "What?" she asked, looking down at herself to see what was wrong. I couldn't close my mouth. "Is something wrong? Am I stained somewhere?"

"Uh, no. God, no. You just look so beautiful. That's all," I finished softly. She took my breath away. Dagny smiled as she walked toward me.

"Thank you, Chase. You look beautiful yourself." She took in the black chinos and blue cotton button up shirt I wore, black Docs on my feet. "That shirt really brings out the color of your eyes." She looked up at me, staring into them. "I'm so glad you came with me. Thank you."

"Anytime." I smiled; so did she. "Shall we?"

The convention center was wall-to-wall people, and I felt like a child. Just about everyone in the room had some sort of sheepskin on their wall representing some high-level psychology degree. Here I was, barely a sophomore in college, having taken only one psychology class in my entire life. Talk about small potatoes.

Dagny saw my distress and took me by the arm to the room where we were to see Jen Carlson presenting on the inner workings of the memory. "Come on." I was excited. I was interested to see what she had to say.

Dagny found us two seats near the middle. The place was already filling up fast. The podium was set up at the front, a woman with dark hair standing at it looking over what I assumed were her notes. She was dressed in a nice suit, navy blue, the skirt reaching to just below her knees. Her hair was a bit below her shoulders, and as I watched she tucked some strands behind her ear.

"That's Jen Carlson." Dagny pointed, leaning over to whisper in my ear. "She's fantastic. I read some of her works last year. She's really into the memory and has done numerous studies on it."

"Wow. I won't need to listen to this at all now," I teased. She smacked me playfully on the shoulder.

"This year she published a paper on nature vs. nurture in regards to homosexuality." This catching my attention, I looked at her. "Fascinating stuff, from what I've read, anyway."

"Please be seated, everyone. I'm about to start." The speaker took the microphone from its holder and began to walk around, looking at her audience, smiling at those sitting near the front. Within a few moments everyone had found a seat, and it was quiet. "Hello. My name is Jen Carlson, and I'm pleased to be here. I must say it's a bit warmer than I'm used to back in Seattle." She smiled, and people in the audience chuckled. "So, let's get started."

I listened, my ears and eyes alert to her every word and exhibit.

"And what of homosexuality amongst siblings?" she asked, making eye contact with several people in the first row. "Homosexuality in families. Twins. Interestingly enough, cases of a set of twins being gay is less likely than your basic, run of the mill siblings, even though twins share thought patterns, as well as, often, a sort of," she paused as she thought of the word she was trying to think of, "a psychic connection, if you will. My department is actually working on a project right now, dealing with twins and homosexuality."

Dagny glanced over at me from time to time to make sure I wasn't bored, and chuckled under her breath each time.

"I'm so glad you're enjoying this, Chase. I was worried," she whispered.

"No need to be. She's great," I whispered back. I turned to Dagny, curious to see if she found this as interesting as I did. Of course, I had my own reasons. She was listening intently, almost as intently as I was.

The first seminar was over, and it was time to head to the get-to-know-you thing. Dagny and I made our way to a wall, trying to get out of the way of the rush of people getting out of different rooms with other speakers. Each attendee chose where they wanted to go and who they wanted to listen to.

"I can't believe how many people turned up for this." Dagny turned to me, her back to the masses. "So, what did you think of that?"

"I thought she was fantastic," I gushed. "It was so interesting, and she was so intelligent and knew so much about her subject. I especially liked what she had to say on young kids and their tendencies toward homosexuality."

Dagny cocked her head to the side. "Really? Why?"

I shrugged. *Step lightly, Chase.* "I don't know. It's just something I've always wondered, I guess. You know."

"Mamma?"

We both looked down to see a little guy tugging on Dagny's hand. She turned to look down at him and he recoiled, the confusion obvious.

"Well, hello there, little man," she said, kneeling to his level. "Are you lost?"

He nodded.

"No, you're not." The boy was picked up and lifted into a woman's arms.

The little boy looked at her, his face brightening like the sun through the clouds. "Mamma!"

"I'm sorry," the woman said, looking at us, her green eyes smiling. I understood the child's confusion. Dagny and this woman resembled each other quite a bit. Close to the same color of hair, the woman's a little lighter blonde and a little shorter. She wore a green shirt and black pants. "Hi. I'm Joie, and this is Nathaniel. He normally doesn't try and take everyone home to be his mother." She smiled at Dagny. "You should feel honored."

"And I do. Hi." Dagny smiled, shaking the woman's hand. "Hey, Nathaniel. You're so cute, I may have been tempted to take you home, you know." He smiled, bright blue eyes twinkling. He had blonde hair, a smidge darker than his mother's, and he was dressed in a pair of tiny black dress pants and a white dress shirt with a yellow tie. "He is adorable."

Joie smiled. "Thanks. Careful, though, he knows it already." We all laughed, and Joie looked at me. "Hi."

"Hello."

"This is Chase," Dagny supplied when it was obvious I wasn't going to say anything else. I was captivated by this woman, especially when Jen Carlson walked up to her.

"Hey, honey." She kissed Joie soundly on the lips. Dagny and I stood, surprised. I had liked these two immediately before, but now, wow. The presenter turned to us. "Hi there."

"These two were nice enough to corral Nate, here."

"Ah. I see. Sorry." Jen put her arm around Joie's waist and took Nathaniel from her.

As I looked from one to the other, I realized that the boy was probably Jen's son and not Joie's, but Nathaniel had called Joie mamma. I was getting a headache.

"You were great, babe," Joie said, picking a small piece of lint off of the speaker's jacket.

"Thank you." She smiled at her obvious mate.

"Yes, incredible. I had to study your work on memory last year," Dagny said, looking at the woman with ultimate hero worship.

Jen laughed. "Oh, I'm so sorry. That must have been awful." She grinned at me. I smiled back shyly.

"No, no, it was very enjoyable. I did a paper on it, actually. Extremely informative."

Jen smiled, obviously pleased. "Would you two care to join us?" Jen looked from one of us to the other, then indicated the hall where everyone was to eat.

"Oh, yes!"

We found a table for four and got Nathaniel settled in. Dagny and Jen got lost in a world filled with psychology, theories, and schools of thought. These things left Joie and me in the dust, so we started our own conversation.

"No, Nathaniel is biologically Jenny's, but he's my boy." She looked with pride at her son, and he grinned at her, offering her his half-eaten doughnut. "Nope, you eat it, Natey." He laughed and stuck the entire thing in his mouth. She shook her head as she wiped his chin and face.

"Are you in psychology, too?" I asked, taking a drink of my orange juice.

She shook her head. "Nope. I wouldn't have a clue about it, other than what I've learned from Jenny in the last eight years."

"So, you guys have, um, been together that long?" I asked, curious beyond belief whether these two were lovers.

"Yup. We met during our junior year at the Washington State University. We played hockey together."

"Hockey?" I smiled, not able to imagine Jen Carlson anywhere near a sport.

"Oh, yeah. This one here was a force to be reckoned with." She indicated her lover with her thumb. "I now coach the hockey team up there, the Cougars. My girls are the best in college hockey today." Her smile was radiant. I couldn't help but be jealous of their life. "So, are you here just to be with your girl there?"

"Oh, well, um, we're just friends, actually."

She looked at me, the surprise evident in her eyes. "Oh. I'm sorry."

I shrugged. "It's okay."

She studied me for a moment, her brows drawn, then with a slightly cocky grin, she punched my arm playfully. "Hang in there." She sipped from her juice. "So, what do you do?"

"I'm a student at UA, also. Just starting my second year."

"What are you going into?" She took Nathaniel from his chair and heaved him into her lap. The boy tried to reach for everything that was in front of Joie. She absently stopped tiny hands from grabbing her food, her juice, her wallet or sunglasses.

I was absolutely charmed and amused. "Psych."

"Aw, shit, am I keeping you from their conversation? I'm sorry."

"Oh, no, no. I just started, kind of getting into it late, so don't worry." I grinned. "I have no more of an idea what they're talking about than you do."

Joie grinned. I liked her. "What area do you think you want to go into?" She helped Nate sip from her glass, making sure the juice didn't dribble down on his tie. "Jenny will kick my butt if he gets dirty," she mumbled.

I chuckled. "To be honest, I really don't know. I'm finding that I do enjoy children, though." I proceeded to tell her about the Thursday night jam sessions I did for Natalie, and how inspirational I found them.

"That's wonderful, Chase. Maybe you could go into hospitals or schools, or something. Kids and music go hand in hand. You really should try and keep both your passions together, you know? It makes things more interesting for you and whomever you're working with."

The get-to-know-you came to an end, and it was time to move into another session. Jenny and Joie invited us to attend the cognitive learning presentation with them, and we happily agreed. The trio walked in front of us, looking every bit the happy family. I found it amazing that they had been together for so long, yet looked so happy and in love still. I couldn't take my eyes off of them. Neither could Dagny.

* ~ * ~ * ~ * ~ * ~ *

The weekend conference went well, and I enjoyed every minute of it, especially spending time with Joie and Jenny. They were so interesting, and the fact that they were lesbian partners blew my mind. To see them together was amazing. They lived like any other couple. They obviously loved each other and their two year old son very much. They owned a house together, had a dog and a cat. No different. Huh, it could work.

I had found it very interesting and strange that Dagny seemed almost obsessed with those two, especially Jenny. I mean, I understand that Jen did exactly what Dag wanted to do, but she couldn't get enough of them and the dynamics of their relationship.

Monday afternoon we decided to make the trip to the Grand Canyon, and I was excited. I had seen my mom's pictures from when she used to take her summer jaunts there, but no picture could ever get you ready for actually being there, seeing the depth of it, and imagining what would happen if you were to fall in.

We stopped in front of one of the rails and looked down into the canyon. Earlier we had stopped a couple and asked them to take a picture of both of us, standing in front of the rail with goofy smiles on our faces. That would be a good picture.

"Turn around, Chase. I'll get a picture of you," Dagny said, hurrying a good distance away, bringing up the disposable camera we had purchased before leaving Tucson. I posed, smiling, hopefully looking happy. I hated pictures and saw cameras as evil creations.

"Your turn." I grinned.

Dagny handed me the camera with a smile, her fingers brushing against mine as she passed me the camera. I took several of her, wanting to have this trip saved forever. I had had the most wonderful time. She had cracked me up constantly with her comments on everything from the town to the speakers to the cloud formations. She seemed happy; that made me happy. Mostly. I was having the most intense dreams now. Almost every time I closed my eyes, images came to play that left me breathless and sweaty when I woke. It was always Dagny, and in my dreams, she was always doing what I was yearning for more and more in the light of day.

Dag turned to look out at the expanse of the canyon, and I walked up behind her. I felt guilty now when we touched, knowing what was behind my caresses, but I could not deny myself the guilty pleasure. I hugged her from behind, resting my chin on her shoulder. She put her hands on my forearms and leaned back into me.

"You know, when I was a kid, my mom did a lot of amateur photography and would come out here during her summer breaks. She always left me home...with the babysitter." I grinned, and Dag lightly slapped my arm. "I always used to ask if I could come. I wanted to see it, to spend that time with her. She would tell me I was too young, so I stopped asking. As I got older, I still wanted to go, but she never offered to take me." I looked down at Dagny. "I'm glad my first time was with you."

She didn't say a word as she turned her head up and back and stared at me for a moment, then turned in the ring of my arms and hugged me, her head resting against my shoulder. I held her close, breathing in the smell and feel of her. Every day it was getting harder and harder to be around her. My feelings were growing, and I didn't know what to do with them or about them. Who was there to talk to? I was more and more frustrated. I didn't know what to do.

* ~ * ~ * ~ * ~ * ~ *

The drive back to Tucson was underway, Dagny pushing Freud along the roads, music playing on the radio. I looked over at her, her fishing hat in place. I told her earlier that she looked like all she needed was a pole with some bait. I had gotten a pinch for my observation.

"I love my hat, so bite me."

*Tempting.* I reached up and snatched the brimmed hat, swiping it off her head.

"Hey!" she batted at my hand blindly, trying to keep her eyes on the road. "Give me that back, woman."

"Nope. You shouldn't cover this." I ran my fingers through her hair, only to really dig in, ruffling it. She squealed in surprise. I stopped, not wanting her to crash and kill us, but could not stop laughing. "God, that was too good!"

She laughed, trying to flatten her hair. "You're evil, Chase Marin!"

"You have no idea."

"Neither do you."

* ~ * ~ * ~ * ~ * ~ *

We had been back from the convention for a couple days, and I had to start getting ready for my upcoming lit class. I was looking forward to it, my curiosity piqued, especially after meeting Joie and Jenny. I had met lots of Carrie's friends, and her girlfriends over the years, but I never took them that seriously. It seemed for them it was all about lust and rebellion. The couple at the convention was all about love and making a life together.

Dagny talked about Jen Carlson often, and how much she respected her work and liked her as a person. I almost felt jealous of Jen, though I knew how stupid that was. I mean, Jenny was basically married, and Dagny, well, that wasn't a problem there.

I sat on my bed, back against the wall, and stared up at the ceiling as I thought about her. Yesterday morning we had gone swimming, and I had turned toward the bathroom while Dagny took a shower to get all the chlorine off her body. The flimsy curtains didn't close all the way, and I caught sight of her naked back, muscles moving under smooth skin as she washed herself, then she turned slightly and I caught just the barest glimpse of her left breast, the nipple taut from the cold air and hot water.

I felt like a pervert, and it was definitely not fair to Dag. I quickly hurried to the bathroom, squeezing my eyes shut tight as I locked myself into the stall. I tried to get my breathing under control as I saw it in my mind over and over again. I imagined my hands on that breast, touching that nipple, feeling the hardness of it.

I swallowed as I felt stinging behind my eyes. Why did I have to be this way? Think this way? I just wanted to... Hell, I didn't know anymore. I didn't know what I wanted, but I did know that Dagny was in there somewhere.

I took a deep breath as I sat in my dorm room all by myself. Night was falling, and I needed to head out to work soon. I needed to calm myself, as I could feel my pulse beating in my head, fast and hot. Every time Dagny touched me, which was often, I felt the sting of her fingers, like fire licking across my skin. *God, help me!*

Dagny was to meet me at the bar, as we had plans after my shift was over. I hurried back to the employee lounge where we kept our personal stuff and quickly untied my apron, exchanging it for my wallet. The bar was loud and rowdy as I headed out, dodging dancers and drunks until one didn't let me pass.

"Hey, you."

It was Terrie, and I wasn't too surprised. She had started hanging out there on a semi-regular basis. "Hi." I smiled. "Great rehearsal today."

"Thanks. You too. Want to join us?"

I glanced at the table full of people staring at us. I shook my head. "No can do. Dagny's supposed to be here any time." I ran a hand through my hair, knowing it smelled of smoke, the only thing I hated about working there.

"Too bad."

She put her hand on my back, turning me to introduce me to her friends. As she did so, her hand began to rub my back, slipping low to just above my ass. I wondered what was up with that. The strange thing was, I didn't mind so much. I said my hellos and thank-you's as people told me they loved the band, then felt like I was being watched. I turned to see Dagny standing about five feet away...and she didn't look happy.

"Hey!" I grinned from ear to ear. She smiled at me, giving Terrie a hard look. "I have to go. It was nice meeting all of you." I pulled away from Terrie and went over to my friend. Dagny's eyes were still on the drummer, a look on her face like I'd never seen before. "You okay?"

Startled out of her thoughts, she looked at me and nodded. "Yeah. Let's get out of here."

After a good pizza at Magpie's, we headed back to Dagny's place for some relaxing time. Neither of us was in the mood for a movie, so we planned to just sit back and shoot the shit.

"So are you ready for your class to start?" Dag asked as she pulled into the parking lot of her building.

"Oh, yeah. I'm looking forward to it."

"What is it, anyway?"

She engaged the parking brake and we got out. I had a bag of fresh clothes with me since Dagny always let me take a shower to get rid of the smells from Gotfry's.

"Oh, uh, English 273." I said, eyeing her. For some reason I felt strange talking about it, almost guilty.

She drew her brows and glared at me. "You wanna tell me what that is?" she drawled.

"Well, it's a class on lesbian literature."

She stopped just shy of taking the first step up the stairs. She looked at me over her shoulder, her face unreadable. "Really?"

I nodded.

"What made you want to take that?"

She began to ascend; I followed, enjoying the view in front of me. "Well, it just, I don't know. It just looked interesting," I stammered.

She didn't seem to notice, or maybe just didn't say anything. "I thought about taking that at one point," she said absently.

I looked at her, surprised. But then, when you're as avid a reader as Dagny, you'd read anything.

I stepped out of the shower, feeling so much more alive than when I'd stepped in. As I dried myself off, the image from the other morning came back to me. I saw Dagny's body again, so beautiful. I was getting hot all over again. I glanced down at the towel I was using to dry myself off and realized that Dagny also used this towel, the soft material draping across her nakedness, worshiping the curves and soft skin. I squeezed my eyes shut as I held the towel to me, trying to calm myself. It didn't seem to take much to get me going these days.

I opened the bathroom door, dressed in a pair of sweat shorts and tank. Dagny was laid out across the couch, one leg hanging off, so I planned to sit on the matching chair.

"No, come here."

I looked at her as she scooted herself up a bit into a sitting position. She beckoned me to sit between her legs. I did, my back against her chest. She wrapped her arms around me as I laid my head back against her collarbone and sighed. *God, I could sleep like this.*

"Did you have a good shower?"

I nodded. "Very good. Thank you."

"What did you think of Jenny and Joie?" she asked, playing with the hem of my shirt, running it through her fingers.

"I thought they were great. Very interesting. Especially Joie. She was so great with Nathaniel." I smiled at the memory of the little blond boy, so obviously loved.

"Yeah." Dagny smiled, too, laying her head against the side of mine. "I had no idea that Jen Carlson was gay. They made such an adorable couple, though. So happy. God, I'd love that." She sighed. "I think it's great you're taking that class, Chase. You'll have to tell me all about it."

"Sure. Want to take it for me? Then I can sleep in." She chuckled; I could feel the rumble against my back.

"Yeah, right." She was quiet for a moment. "You know Terrie is after you, right?"

I drew my brows together, surprised by the mention of my bandmate's name. "What?"

"Yeah. She's been after you for a while, I think." She laughed, moving her head away from mine, taking the intimacy with it.

I said nothing. Could that be true? If so, how had I been so blind?

*∼*∼*∼*∼*∼*

We were getting set up on stage at Gotfry's for our performance. I was particularly looking forward to it. We had been back for a week now and I was about to pull my hair out. Dagny touched me constantly it seemed, though I wondered how much of that was my imagination. I hated the fact that I could touch her any time I wanted to, but it meant nothing to her. It was just me being an affectionate friend.

"Hey, you. Ready for a rocking night?"

I turned to see Terrie standing behind me, like *right* behind me. If I moved an inch, we'd be touching. "Hell, yeah. I wish so bad that Greg would slip me a drink," I said with a grin.

She raised an eyebrow. "Hold that thought." She hurried off the stage to the bar, leaning over it to talk with Greg.

I needed a distraction, something to fuzz my head up for a bit. Melissa Etheridge's song, *I Want You* came to mind often.

"Here you go."

I looked up to see the drummer standing next to me with a glass in her hand.

"What is it?"

"Tequila Sunrise."

"Sounds good to me." I took it and downed the entire thing in two gulps.

"Damn, girl!" Terrie smiled. "Got some problems there? If I didn't know better, I'd think you were having some nasty frustrations." She leaned close to me. "If you need help, let me know."

I looked at her in surprise as she walked to her drums and got herself situated, winking at me. I shook my head and turned toward the audience as I grabbed Than.

"Hello, hello out there!" I could feel the alcohol already traveling through me. I had little tolerance anymore as I rarely drank now. But, on the upside, my head was definitely fuzzy.

We began the night hard, playing some of the classics from the sixties and seventies. The place was rocking, and I loved it. Doug and I did a duet, then I was all on my own again. It was beautiful and helped to push Dagny out of my mind completely. She wasn't there yet, having to work late. She was going to try to make it for the second set. I felt almost free, as if I could act and think however I really felt, not having to hide it or protect it because I was so afraid of Dagny seeing through me. I put my heart into my music that night, wishing somehow Dagny could hear it wherever she was.

We finished out our first set, and I put Than on the guitar stand and headed straight for the bathroom. I wasn't feeling well, and I needed some peace. Now that I worked at Gotfry's, too, I was well known all across the board, and couldn't get away from people wanting to chat.

I sat on the toilet, my head in my hands as I tried to relax. No one would bother me in the bathroom stall. I hoped. After sitting there for about ten minutes, I took a deep breath, ran my hands through my hair, and opened the door, startled to see Terrie standing there, leaning against the sink. She had her thumbs in her pockets, her head slightly cocked to the side, the slightest hint of a smile on her lips.

"You okay?" she asked.

"Yeah. I think so." I went to the tap next to her, turning on the cold water to splash my face.

"Did that drink pack a little too much punch?" She looked at my reflection in the mirror. I nodded with a grin. "Poor baby." She brought her hands up to my shoulders and began to rub them, digging her thumbs into the tense muscle. I closed my eyes, nearly moaning. "Feels good, doesn't it?"

I nodded, my mouth open as my head fell back. Slowly I felt myself being turned, pushed gently until my back was against the wall. I opened my eyes and Terrie was standing in front of me, looking into my eyes. "Beautiful, beautiful Chase," she whispered. I said nothing, not sure what to do. She brought a hand up to brush the side of my face, her eyes following the trail of her fingers.

I felt frozen to the spot, not sure what to feel. Should I leave? Yell at her? Be upset, or sit back and enjoy? Part of me was needing touch so bad that I'd take it from Terrie, who was willing, even though I truly wanted and needed it from Dagny, who I knew would never.

"You've been so uptight and tense lately, Chase. I was quite serious when I said I'd help you out." Terrie's voice was soft and seductive. She leaned in close to me, breathing me in. I could feel the heat of her body, merely inches from mine, getting closer with every word.

I could take her up on her offer, try to forget about Dagny in *that* way and just be friends, good friends. I didn't want to be friends. I felt a pressure in my hands that were against the wall, a pressure to reach up and push Terrie away, but I couldn't get my body to respond. I was lost in the sensations.

"Let me help you, hon."

I opened my eyes to see Terrie's face half an inch from mine, her warm breath against my mouth. She placed one hand on the wall next to my head, the other on my waist. "Let me..." Her voice trailed off as she moved in.

This was not the place for this. Somewhere in the back of my mind I heard the bathroom door open and felt I should look. But what really caught my attention was the sound of breath being sucked in.

My eyes shifted from Terrie to the door. Dagny stood frozen, her hand still on the door. Her eyes were huge, mouth open. She had the strangest look on her face, like she wanted to cry or scream or laugh. She swallowed once, then without a word, she turned around and hurried out.

"Dagny!" I pushed Terrie away from me, intending to follow.

"Chase, what are you doing?  Let her go."

I rounded on the drummer like a vicious dog.  "I can't!"  I calmed down for a second.  "I love her.  I'm in love with her."

Terrie looked at me, struck dumb.  She released my arm, looked down.  Without another breath, I hurried out of the bathroom, running into the bar.  I had to find her, had to talk to her and make it right.

She was nowhere to be found.  I burst out into the hot night air, just in time to see Freud's tail lights disappear.

# Chapter 9

I ran my hands through my hair again, readjusting my body on the top stair where I sat. The steps were carpeted, but after sitting there for two hours, any cushioning seemed to disappear. *Disappear.* I couldn't stop thinking about earlier. *God, how could I have been so stupid?* But then again, what did I have to feel bad about? I was so confused.

I had left Gotfry's right away, driving around for a bit but ending up at Dagney's, waiting for her. I had no idea where she had gone, but I was getting worried. I glanced at my watch; it was after midnight. I would give it another hour. We needed to talk. I needed to understand.

Downstairs, the door opened; I could barely hear it three flights above. Silence for a few minutes, then I heard the stairs squeak as someone ascended. I stared expectantly at the door to the third flight, waiting for the familiar figure, hoping I wouldn't be disappointed, again.

Dagny turned the corner and stopped at the bottom of the third floor flight. She looked up at me, her face expressionless, then began to climb. I said nothing, nor did she. She passed by my little vigil spot and went to her apartment door; her key made the only sound as she inserted it and turned it in the lock. I waited to see what she'd do next. Would she say anything? I saw the light shine on the opposite wall when she flicked it on, then her silhouette as she passed under it. She had left the door open.

I stood, stiff muscles screaming in protest as I did so, and entered the apartment. Dagny was stock still in the middle of the room, her back to me, keys dangling from her hand before she finally tossed them to the coffee table. I watched her intently, not sure what she expected of me. I was flooded with mixed emotions, my stomach gurgling as the acids built and died, only to rebuild.

"You had me worried, Dag," I finally said, finding my voice.

She shrugged, turning her head so I could see her profile as she stared at the floor. "I drove around for a while, stopped in at a coffee shop."

I could barely hear her. *Please, turn around and look at me, Dag.* When she said nothing more, I took a step toward her. "Why?" I asked.

"I needed to think, to clear my head." She took a deep breath, then turned, looking up at me with tired eyes. "I didn't know, Chase. I should have seen it, I suppose." She looked down again, her hands fidgeting with each other.

"Should have known what? Guessed what? What are you talking about?" I tried to catch her eye but she refused to let me.

"About you...you know...you liking...well, anyway..." She ran a hand through her hair, then looked up at me, fire in her eyes. "She's wrong for you, Chase!"

Taken aback by her vehemence, I felt the fire beginning to bubble to the surface. The fear had turned into sorrow, which had turned into worry, which had turned into fear again, which was quickly turning into anger.

"How dare you tell me who is or isn't right for me?" I thumped my chest. "You have no hold on me, Dagny!"

"No, I don't, but she'll fuck with your head, Chase!" Like a switch had been snapped, Dagny was on. She was ready for battle.

"Who gives a fuck? What business is it of yours what I do or who I fuck, if I so choose?"

"I care!" she screamed.

I was stunned, but quickly got myself together. "Why? It's none of your business, Dagny. The fact that Terrie almost kissed me tonight, yeah, that was a mistake, but-"

"You should have told me! I have a right to know!"

"To know what? What gives you any rights with me? We're friends, Dag. We go out and we have a real good time, laugh and all that shit, but at the end of the day, it all boils down to - we're just friends!" I could feel the blood pounding in my head. I was so angry that I felt dizzy. *What does she care? What does it matter? I can't have her, so why should she have any say in what I do? I can never have her!* I wanted to scream into the night, but didn't dare start to scream; I might not stop.

"God damn, how do you think I felt when I opened that door to see that fucking slut all over you like flies on shit?" She took a step toward me, her voice dropping. "That woman makes me want to scream. I can't stand the sight of her. To see her that close to you made me sick." Her voice and body language were dangerous, reminding me of a tigress, ready to pounce. "You deserve so much better, Chase."

"Oh yeah? And who have you come up with in your infinite wisdom, Dagny?" I spread my arms wide, palms to the Heavens. "Who!"

She was silent for a moment, some of the tension draining from her body. "Someone else." She turned away from me, giving me her back.

I tried to calm myself. I took a deep breath, releasing it slowly. "Dag, like I said, tonight was a disaster waiting to happen, and I'm glad it didn't. There was never anything to tell you as far as Terrie is concerned." I chuckled ruefully. "I can't even say she's just a friend, 'cause she's not even that really."

"Why didn't you tell me about you?" She ran a hand through her hair, still facing away from me.

"I don't know. It wasn't something I've exactly been hiding from you, Dag." I shrugged. "I didn't know for sure, myself; I'm still so confused." Dagny didn't say anything, nor did she look at me. Further discourse seemed pointless.

"I'm going to go." I turned and moved toward the door. I was reaching for the doorknob when I heard footsteps coming up behind me.

"Don't," came the whisper from just behind me. I closed my eyes, feeling Dagny's presence surround me. "Please don't go, Chase." Her voice was low, filled with sadness. I felt her hand on my back, sliding down and over to my arm. "Please?" I turned, looked into pleading eyes. "Stay?"

I stared at her for a moment, amazed at how quickly the blaze inside me had simmered down to nothing, gone as quickly as it had come. I nodded, and she smiled weakly.

Dagny leaned in to me, wrapping her arms around me, and I did the same, pulling her in tightly, wanting her so close, inside of me. I heard her sigh, and I did the same. God, that had been so close. I had been scared that our friendship was over with, that I had gone too far. I breathed in her smell, the smell of her hair, her skin, her sweat and tears.

I knew that it was impossible to get what I wanted, so I'd just have to try and be happy with what I had. She was in my life, and wasn't that what counted? I felt my relief stinging my eyes, and didn't try to fight it. The tears slipped out from behind my closed lids and I held Dagny tighter. *How will I ever be able to let her go?*

\* ~ \* ~ \* ~ \* ~ \* ~ \*

I lay in the dark, Dagny's cheek against my neck as she slept. My arms were wrapped tightly around her body, hugging her to me. She adjusted her head a few times, still very much asleep. It had been an emotional night and she had been exhausted. So was I, but I couldn't shut off my brain.

I thought about earlier, in the bathroom of Gotfry's with Terrie. Up until now, I had not had much time to think it over, dissect it. How had it happened; how far would I have let her go? She was not what I wanted and I knew that, knew it then. I think my frustration over the situation with Dagny had driven me to new lows. And then there was what I had said to Terrie just before I'd run out of the bathroom to follow Dagny: *I love her. I'm in love with her.*

It had slipped out without thought. I don't think the admission surprised me so much as the timing. I usually thought things through, thought them to death, actually. In short, I was a dweller.

Those words had slipped out effortlessly, requiring no thought at all. I did love Dagny, very deeply. But it went beyond that. I loved Carrie, too, and had even loved Mike. But Dagny had my heart; she had my soul and my mind. I was *in* love with her. How did that make me feel? That was the million dollar question right there.

When you're little, what your parents say means everything; that's what kept coming back to me. When we were in high school, Carrie confided to me that she thought she liked girls as well as boys. Being an open-minded person, I had been fine with that. I wasn't sure where that tolerance came from because my family was not tolerant. My mother still did not know about half the crap Carrie had done and who she'd done it with. But I had been fine with it because I had been fine with my own sexuality. I liked boys, for the most part, and I didn't worry about it any further than that. So how had this happened?

I really hated labels. I wasn't about to stick one on my ass now.

After the fight ended, we'd said nothing. Dagny just pulled me by the hand to her bedroom and we both collapsed, emotionally drained. I slept for a couple hours, but it was restless, dreams and nightmares waking me about twenty minutes ago. I had so much to think about, to decide.

What would happen to our friendship? What if she suspected my true feelings for her? I'd try to hide them, do a performance worthy of the Oscar in order to keep her in my life. I could shut myself off, cut all ties with my deeper feelings so I wouldn't scare her away. What would I do if she ever started dating someone? That would hurt, but she had every right. Why should I begrudge her happiness just because I was condemning myself to a life of loneliness?

\* ~ \* ~ \* ~ \* ~ \* ~ \*

I tried to squeeze my eyes shut to keep out the determined morning sun. I was losing. I slowly opened an eye, turning away so my back was to the window, seeing little flashes of light behind my lids when I closed my eyes. *That's pleasant.* Finally, cranking both eyes open, I realized I was alone. *What the...? Where is she?* I was beginning to panic in my half dream state when I heard the bedroom door close softly. With a sigh of relief, I took a deep breath. Within seconds I heard the shower start. All was well in the world. I hoped.

I pulled my exhausted body out of the bed, running my hands through my hair and wondering what the day would bring. How was Dagny doing? What was she feeling? It was such a creepy feeling to wake up to find her gone. I found my jeans and boots from the night before and threw them on, finding one of Dagny's brushes on the dresser. My hair was a mess, all over my head. Apparently I looked as bad as I felt.

Put together and assuming Dagny would want me to leave, I headed to the living room. I was sitting on the couch for a long moment, trying to get my thoughts together before I took off, when I heard the water stop. I glanced at the closed bathroom door, not sure what to do. *Should I be gone by the time she gets out of there? Will she be mad if I go? God, I hate this feeling of walking on eggshells!*

The bathroom door opened and Dag walked out, just a towel tied around her still wet body, her hair slicked back. She looked directly at the bedroom door, saw that it was open, and scanned the room until she saw me shrinking away on the couch. She smiled, the warmest smile I've ever seen.

"Hey." Her voice was quiet, almost timid.

I smiled. "Hi. Have a nice shower?" *God, how lame.* I stood, shoving my hands in my back pockets so she wouldn't see them fidgeting nervously. Uncertainty roiling around inside of me, I didn't want her to know that I felt like I might throw up. To my surprise she hurried over to me, bare feet padding across the wood floor, and I was nearly bowled over by her enthusiastic hug. Taking my cue from her, I wrapped relieved arms around her, nearly breaking her ribs the embrace was so intense. When she groaned against my squeeze, I eased up, grinning down at her. "Sorry."

She raised an eyebrow. "Trying to kill me or something?"

"Uh, no. Just, you know, well, I just wanted you closer, I guess," I stammered.

Dagny smiled, running her hand down my arm. "Come on. I'll get dressed while you get in the shower, 'cause you smell like a damn smokestack, and we'll go get some breakfast. How does that sound?"

I smiled so big it felt like my face would split. I had my old Dagny back. "You're on."

* ~ * ~ * ~ * ~ * ~ *

Life began to get back to normal, and I had a lot of groveling to do to Greg, who didn't understand why I had taken off, and Doug, who'd had to take over for me. I explained to Greg that Dagny had gotten sick, and I had to go take care of her, and he smiled at me like I was nuts. Yeah, so I lied to the guy. How could I tell him what had really happened?

"Don't let it happen again, Chase," he said, wiping out some freshly washed glasses. I nodded and went to watch the door, taking money for the cover charge. I hadn't seen Terrie, and I didn't really want to. I couldn't quite put a finger on how I felt about her.

I wasn't angry, per se. Maybe some embarrassment could be thrown into the mix. Hell, I didn't know. I would find out soon, at rehearsal tomorrow.

For tonight, after my stint at the bar, I sat in my dorm room, back against the wall and read Anaïs Nin's *House of Incest*. One thing I had to say about my lesbian literature class was that we were required to read some interesting stuff. I turned the page, just starting to get into it when the phone rang. Absently, I picked up the cordless from the bed beside me and clicked it on.

"Hello?" I muttered as I continued to read.

"Hey, girl."

I smiled. "Hey, Car. How goes it?" I put the book down to concentrate on my friend, whom I hadn't talked to in the few weeks I'd been back at school.

"It goes well. I have been so busy. Oh, my God, I got a job at this art supply store, right?"

"Right,"

"It's like, oh man, artgasm! They have some of the most incredible stuff there."

I smiled at the excitement in her voice. I hadn't heard Carrie excited about much of anything since the rape.

"My boss, Doyle, said that I could get whatever I needed for my classes this semester for a third of their cost. Isn't that just awesome?"

"Oh, Carrie, that's fantastic!" I sat up, crossing my legs Indian style and leaning my elbows on them.

"Needless to say, I'll be all set. I plan to come back next week."

I shut my mouth, my nutty friend having answered the question before it even got out. "Awesome. We'll have to celebrate." I smiled into the phone, glancing down at the book next to me, tracing the image on the cover.

"Oh, I have a question to ask."

"Shoot."

"What do you wear on a date with a boring guy?"

I nearly choked on my bottom lip. "What?"

"Yeah, this guy called me and he wants to go out tomorrow."

"Are you okay with that, Car?" I asked, my voice low with worry.

"Yeah, I think so. I insisted we go to Conway's, you know, where I worked all through high school? Everybody knows me there, so I'll have all kinds of eyes on me."

"Sounds like a plan. Who is he?"

"Well, I don't really want to say in case things don't work out or something. To be honest, I'm not even sure why I agreed to go out. I just think I'm lonely," she admitted softly.

"Okay. I'm sure you'll be fine, but be careful, okay?"

"Yeah. So, what do I wear?"

"Carrie, just how many boring guys do you think I've gone out with?" I was trying to picture the clothes Carrie had in her closet, putting different outfits together.

"I even thought about raiding my mom's closet."

I chuckled. "Well, if the angelic look is what you're after, then go ahead. But you'll burn in hell for it." I grinned, she laughed.

"Bitch."

We finally figured out something for her to wear that would make her look decent without looking like a nun. I felt secure in knowing that Carrie was learning to be smarter and not so free and trusting. She promised me she would not drink at all on the date, volunteering that she hadn't touched pot in months. I hoped this "boring" guy could help with her turn around.

Carrie told me all about her summer adventures: going on vacation to Las Vegas with her parents, going out with some of the old gang we used to party with. She swore she stayed sober, but I couldn't imagine that, especially when she felt so comfortable around them. Carrie and I were the only ones in our little enclave of friends who had gone on to college, and I knew most of them were still heavy partiers. That made me sad.

*  ~  *  ~  *  ~  *  ~  *  ~  *

Though I had been quite nervous as I drove up to his house, the rehearsal at Doug's went well. Terrie's truck was already there, the engine still warm and ticking. I walked up the driveway between the parked cars of the other band members. Usually I was the first to arrive, but tonight, putting it off as long as possible, I was last.

"There she is." Doug grinned when he saw me, walking up to me to put an arm around my shoulders. "Where you been?" he asked in my ear as we walked into the garage.

"Sorry. Had some stuff to do," I mumbled.

He took me to the side so we could talk alone for a moment. "Is everything okay, Chase?" I nodded. "You sure? Did Terrie do something?" I glanced out to see the drummer laughing with our bassist, then tore my eyes away. "I told you to watch out for her, kid."

"Yeah. It's cool, Doug. Don't worry about it. It won't happen again." I smiled at him, letting him know I'd never again leave the band high and dry during a performance, but we both also read between the lines of my statement. I glanced at Terrie again, patted Doug on the arm, and walked toward the practicing area.

"It's the missing singer. Welcome back, kid."

I glared playfully at our keyboardist. "Yeah, bite me."

"Ohhh, tempting."

I flipped him off and everyone laughed. Including Terrie.

"Hey," she said, walking up to me.

I unzipped Than's carrying case and took out the guitar. "Hey, yourself."

"Look, um, about last Friday." I looked at her, staring into nervous dark eyes. "Look, I'm sorry. I didn't realize." She jutted her chin out defiantly, as if she was waiting for me to attack.

I shook my head and shrugged. "It's okay. No damage done." I smiled weakly.

"Was your friend pissed?"

"We worked it out. Don't worry about it." I plugged the guitar into the amp.

"Oh, I won't. But if you find you ever need anything..."

I shot a glare at her before I saw she was smiling. "Hag." Laughing, she kicked off and I joined in.

* ~ * ~ * ~ * ~ * ~ *

"Thank you! Now go to the bar and spend some money." I grinned at my audience as I stepped away from the microphone, shrugged off my guitar strap, and headed to the bar myself. It had been a good session in front of a packed house. Greg was eating it up, the biggest smile on his face.

"Here ya go, kid." He slid my ice cold water to me. "I tell you, I may yet make my million before I'm forty." He punched me lightly on the shoulder, then moved off to serve other customers.

I was leaning against the dark mahogany, downing half the glass, when I saw Terrie's eyes fixed on something, her body language stiff. She put her drumsticks on the seat of the set and headed off the stage, her eyes still glued. I looked in the direction of her gaze and my own eyes nearly popped. She had her sights on Dagny, who was standing talking to Paul. *Oh, shit!*

I almost threw the mug on the bar as I hurried to try and intercept the drummer. "Terrie? What are you doing?" I put my hand on her shoulder, but she completely ignored me, pushing by. "Terrie!"

She walked up behind Dagny and tapped my friend on the shoulder. "Hey."

Dag turned around, her eyes bulging then narrowing as she realized who it was.

Oh shit, oh, shit, oh, shit.

"I want to tell you something, Dagny. I don't like you, never did like you, and chances are good I never will. But I want to tell you something about your friend there."

"Terrie! Stop it." I finally reached them, tried to get between them. Nearly body to body, neither woman budged.

"I won't compete with you, but you'd better open your damn eyes. You got me?" She stared Dagny down, my smaller friend standing her ground. I wanted to cheer.

"Get the hell away from me, Terrie," she said, her voice a deadly calm. "Don't ever get in my face again, *and* you leave my friend the hell alone." Dagny gave her the once over, then with a grimace, grabbed my arm. "Come on, Chase."

I was too stunned to move. I glanced at Terrie in time to see her wink at me, then I turned to follow Dag outside.

The night was already warm, but Dagny's anger made it even hotter. She paced back and forth in front of me, hands balled into fists. I stood back, watching, not daring to get in her way.

Finally Dag stopped pacing and turned to me. "What the hell crawled up that bitch's ass? What did I ever do to her?" She began to pace again. "She doesn't like me, never has, and oh no, probably never will." She laughed ruefully. "There's a kicker. I really can't stand that woman. She's a bitch and a snake." She stopped again, walked over to me to slump against my shoulder. "Why, Chase? Why on earth did you let her get even remotely close to you?" She playfully nudged me in the side, drawing a reaction, as I was extremely ticklish. Dag looked at me, eyes wide with her new find.

"Dag, no. No, please, ugh!" The wind was knocked out of me as she dug her fingers into my sides, my teeth clenched as I tried to fight the little shit off. "Uncle! Stop!" I was nearly crying through my laughter. Finally I got away from her and looked at her, my body crouching as I got ready to pounce.

"Chase, come on, now. You're bigger than me. Be kind, be kind...no!"

She took off running as fast as her legs would carry her, which was pretty impressive, considering I did have about four inches of height on her. I chased her to the end of the parking lot before catching her and digging my fingers into every ticklish inch of her body.

"Truce!" she yelled out, making a dog bark down the street.

I stopped, not able to wipe the grin off my face. She put her arm around my shoulder as we walked back to the bar. "Oh," she began, still out of breath, "Paul told me he had a fantastic date the other night."

"Oh, yeah?" I ran a hand through my hair, sweaty from the vigorous activity. "With who?"

"I don't know. He won't say."

"Huh. Good for him."

*∼*∼*∼*∼*∼*

The summer began to fly by, and the new school year was drawing closer and closer. Dagny and I became inseparable. I stayed at her place most of the time, her couch my new best friend. Either she picked me up, or I picked her up after work or my class, and we'd head to her place, or once in a while, mine. I was fully entrenched in my literature class. The material we read was wonderful, definitely nothing I would have read otherwise. But then, that was usually the case with me and books.

Dagny was getting things straightened out for the next semester. Her class load would be cut back slightly, but she would be doing more outside work with her degree, working at the University of Arizona Counseling Center under Dr. Bernard Fantine, as well as seeing clients on a part-time basis. She was looking forward to it, since it would be getting her closer and closer to practicing her profession, but it would be taking a lot of her energy, and we would have much less time together. I dreaded that.

We were having a quiet night in Dagny's apartment, each of us with our own book to read as we stretched out on the couch. We had just finished off a fantastic dinner of chicken breast and rice with peas that Dag whipped together, and now it was time to relax.

In my lit class we had started on the poetry section, so I was reading *Warrior at Rest* by Jane Chambers. I was enjoying the poems very much, able to relate to many of them.

"What are you reading?" Dagny asked, changing position so that her head was lying in my lap. I looked down at her.

"Comfy?"

"Yes, very." She grinned. I showed her the book and waited for her reaction. "Is this for your class?" When I nodded, she looked up at me with pleading eye. "Read to me?"

"This is lesbian poetry, Dag," I warned.

"So? I told you I wanted to take that class. I'll take it vicariously, through you."

I shook my head with a grin and began to read, my voice soft and steady as I flowed through the stanzas of thought and experiences and ideas. I could feel Dag's eyes on me, like electric heat. As I read the author's words, my mind began to wander. It felt wonderful to have Dagny so close, just a breath away. If I really wanted to torture myself, which I did often, I could almost think of our friendship like a relationship. She was my best friend, my confidante, my teacher, and sometimes my student. We shared space and time, often putting our ideas and money together to have fun. We had it all, except one thing. Well, two. The other thing I didn't have was Dag's heart.

* ~ * ~ * ~ * ~ * ~ *

June was long gone, and July was half over. My English 273

was finished, and I looked forward to the new semester with new classes that centered around my major. Carrie and I spent a lot of time together, and I was beginning to notice a change in her, a good change. She was becoming more serious about school, actually buying her books this semester. The clothes had started covering more, the make-up covering less. She still had a ways to go, but I was pleased with her progress.

"What has happened to you?" I asked as we stood in line to see a movie. She shrugged with a secretive grin. "Come on, Car. Talk to me."

"It's nothing. I just, I need to try this on my own first, Chase." Her eyes searched mine for understanding. "Please? I don't mean to shut you out or not be honest with you, but for the first time in my life there may be something to it, and I'm just afraid of fucking it up."

I studied her for a moment, then it dawned on me. "It's a guy, isn't it?" She nodded. "Will I not approve, or something? Is that why you won't tell me about him?" Despite all of her disclaimers, there was a part of me that was hurt.

"No. That's the funny thing. I think you'll approve a little too much." She smiled ruefully.

I frowned in thought. "Boring guy?" She nodded. "Holy shit." I smiled a mile wide. The line moved up, and we moved with it, my mind still trying to process her disclosure. "How the hell did boring guy manage to tame you, Car?"

She laughed. "Oh, I wouldn't say I'm *tamed*. That'll never happen, Chase, you know that."

I grinned. "How did he do it?"

"He takes me seriously." She looked down, her face filled with pain. Finally she looked up and met my gaze. "He listens to what I have to say and doesn't laugh or make fun of me. Plus, he's cute, and we have the most fun. Completely sober! Who would have thought?" She nudged me with her shoulder and grinned.

"Yeah. No kidding. But I do understand." I couldn't keep the dumb ass smile off my face.

"So, what's the deal with you and Dagny, anyway?" She gave the guy her money for the movie and I handed her mine to give to him also. Tickets in hand, we headed for the concession stand.

"She's just a friend," I said, my voice a little sharp.

Carrie stopped, looking at me as if trying to read me. "What's up with that, Chase? What's going on? I rarely see you now. If I do, you're usually talking about her. Now don't get me wrong, I like her. And I still think she's hotter than hell." She grinned and winked.

I considered for a moment. This was as close to a heart to heart as Carrie and I had gotten in a long time, and I felt she deserved to know the truth. At least part of it. "I don't know, Car. I think that maybe my feelings for Dag run a little deep." I looked at her to see if she was catching my meaning. She looked perplexed. Damn, I didn't want to have to spell it out. "They go beyond friendship."

Carrie's eyes jerked to mine, open wide with surprise. "No way, really?" I nodded. "Wow." She turned to the girl waiting expectantly behind the counter. We ordered drinks and candy, and headed into the theater. "Does she know?"

"No! And I don't want her to, Carrie. Promise me?"

She nodded. "Oh, yeah. Definitely." We found two seats, and Carrie's feet went right to the seat in front of her. "What are you going to do?"

"What can I do? I'll just get over it." I opened my box of Junior Mints and popped two into my mouth.

"You know, this doesn't surprise me, really." Carrie opened her box of Sour Patch Kids. "I've always wondered about you, Chase. You know what they say: birds of a feather flock together."

"Yeah, thanks, Car. That's going to do me a lot of good right now."

"I'm sorry, Chase." She covered my hand with hers. "I'm here for you, okay?" She turned and drew me into a hug. "It'll be okay, Chase. I promise."

* ~ * ~ * ~ * ~ * ~ *

The next few weeks flew by quickly, Carrie spending a lot of time with Dagny and me. We were set to meet with her lawyer at the end of July, which was in a few days, and I could tell the pressure was starting to get to my friend. She was becoming quiet and withdrawn, and I was worried. Dagny kept telling me that it was natural and to give her time. Once the legalities of it were over with, Carrie would be through with it forever and could just concentrate on moving on.

Me and Dag were in her apartment playing a game of chess on the floor when the phone rang. The pawn she was about to move in hand, she hurried to the phone that we'd left in the kitchen.

"Hello? Hey, Carrie. What's up?" She smiled into the receiver as she walked back into the room to sit cross-legged in front of me again. She put her hand over the speaker and looked at me. "Carrie wants to meet us at—" she took her hand off the mouthpiece, "at where? ... Cafe Paraiso? At? ... Okay." She covered the mouthpiece again. "At eight." I nodded. "Sure, we're there. 'Kay, bye." Dag tossed the phone to the couch. "Well, that's interesting."

"Yeah. I wonder what's up. She never goes there." I checked my watch. "We've got about an hour. And, I was in the process of kicking your ass, so if you'd be so kind as to put that pawn down so

I can liberate him from your evil thrall..." I grinned, cocky to the core. "Don't even try to beat me at chess, 'cause it just ain't going to happen." She stuck her tongue out and looked down at the board to see what her next move would be

* ~ * ~ * ~ * ~ * ~ *

Dressed casually, Dagny and I made our way toward campus to meet our friend. It was a beautiful night, so we'd decided to walk to the café, breathing in the fresh air.

"God, it's gorgeous out." Dagny lifted her face to the sky, her eyes closed and a smile on her face. I watched her. I had the urge to take her face in my hands and just stare into her eyes before I kissed her. I clenched my fists. I had been fairly successful at keeping those kinds of thoughts at bay, but certain times, in certain situations, Dag would catch me all over again. It could be agony. Like right now. I decided to try to send my thoughts north to my brain.

"So, this was a bit odd of Carrie."

"Yeah, it does seem odd." Dagny smiled at me, brought her arm up to entwine it with mine.

I smiled, loving the contact of her warm skin. "Who knows?"

We reached the little café, and I saw Carrie right away. She was sitting at an outdoor table, facing us, having an animated conversation with someone whose back was to us. She looked good, wearing a summer dress with spaghetti straps and sandals. Her hair was pulled back and up, her make-up scant, just a touch of fire engine red lipstick to show her unshaken defiance. She saw us over her companion's head and waved with a huge smile. I grinned back; Dagny waved. My eyes went directly to the guy, who had yet to turn around. He wore what looked to be a white tee shirt and cargo shorts; his feet were in Tevas. His dark hair was combed back neatly, cut short around his ears. I thought he looked familiar but couldn't place him.

"Hey, Car. What's up?" Dagny and I sat in the two empty chairs, facing each other. I turned to the guy; it was Dag's friend, Paul. "You?" He grinned, nodding. I turned to my friend. "This is boring guy?" Carrie turned bright red, her complexion nearly matching her hair. I heard Dagny chuckle; Paul looked confused. I felt really stupid. "Uh, sorry, Paul."

He smiled, shaking his head and putting up his hands. "Hey, doesn't bother me."

"I can't believe you said that," Carrie muttered between clenched teeth.

"I'm sorry. It just came out," I muttered back.

"Anyway, this is Paul, as you both know. And um, well, we're kind of together." She smiled at him in the sweetest way.

I looked from one to the other, then back to Dagny. Her eyes were already on me. She had a strange look on her face, but it disappeared as soon as she noticed I was looking at her. She smiled, nodding her approval of the pairing. I looked back to my friend.

"We didn't tell you guys before 'cause we wanted to make sure...you know." Carrie looked at Dagny, then at me. There was hope in her eyes.

I smiled, communicating with her through that look that I was thrilled. From what I had heard, Paul was a great guy, and maybe just what she needed. "I think it's fantastic." I smiled at Paul. He was beaming at his new lady love. I heard Carrie actually let out a breath of relief, and I squeezed her hand under the table.

As we talked with the couple, I began to think, being honest with myself, how fair was it that Carrie, who had lived wild and out of control since she was fifteen, had found her happiness? Here was me, trying to do good for myself, doing what was asked of me, and my happiness eluded me. Well, actually my happiness was sitting right across from me, but she was unattainable.

I felt a hand on my knee under the table and turned to see Carrie smiling at me, understanding in her eyes. She patted me, and joined the conversation that Dagny was having with Paul about school starting up.

Paul was a great conversationalist. He knew a little about everything and was interesting. He was the polar opposite of the idiots that Carrie had dated in the past, and I didn't understand, even though Carrie had explained it to me. I guess it was just one of those things that I would push to keep up and going. She needed some steady guidance in life, and Paul seemed to be settled on his path and secure in himself. I trusted him

\* ~ \* ~ \* ~ \* ~ \* ~ \*

The law offices of Ronald McDivitt, the D.A. for Tucson, were furnished with plush carpeting and expensive furniture. Seemed pretty ritzy for someone working for the city. Dagny and I sat on the couch; Paul and Carrie huddled on the love seat. He held her hands, trying to keep her calm. Today Dagny and I were to talk with the lawyer about what we had seen that night — Carrie and the guy on the park bench.

Dagny had her arm on the back of the couch, her hand on my shoulder because I was also pretty tense. I had been dreading this, not wanting to have to relive the events of that night in our pre-trial visit. We'd been through it all before with McDivitt, but I dreaded it this time as much as I had the first few times. We had talked about it a lot lately, trying to jog both our memories, as it had happened nearly eight months ago.

My leg was tapping up and down, getting rid of some of my nervous energy. Dagny put her hand on my knee. "Chase, hon, you're making the entire couch vibrate." She grinned at me, understanding on her face. "This will be over soon, and that bastard will be taken care of for a long time." She caressed my knee through the material of my khakis.

Stilling my leg, I looked at her. "Sorry. I hope so." I looked over at Carrie, who had her head on Paul's shoulder. I was glad she had him, but at the same time, I couldn't help thinking that it would have been my shoulder she'd have leaned on. I missed her not coming to me. I knew it was selfish, but she had never taken anyone she dated seriously enough to lean on them. It was a strange feeling. My baby was growing up.

I felt numb as I walked out of the office, Ronald calling us in one at a time, Dagny going in next. We passed each other in the hallway, and she gave my arm a quick squeeze of comfort before releasing it and going into the office.

Carrie and Paul were nowhere to be seen. I wondered where they had gone. Then the door to the lawyer's space opened and Paul stuck his head in. He scanned the room, stopping when he saw me.

"Chase, can you come here, please?" He sounded rattled. I hurried out to the hall where Carrie was curled up on the floor, crying. "I can't get her calmed down. I don't know what to do," he said, his hands in the pockets of his cargo shorts.

I knelt down next to my friend and gathered her in my arms. "Car, listen, I'm here, Carrie. Come here." At the sound of my voice, she looked at me and lunged into my arms, nearly knocking me over backward. I held and rocked her as she cried.

"I was doing fine, Chase. I had gotten over it, you know? Ron showed me a picture of him to make sure it was him, and I saw it all over again: the look on his face as he pushed me to the ground, the sound of my clothes ripping, all over again. God, I don't want to have to go through it again."

"Shh, I know, Car. I know. It's almost over. The trial is in a month, then it'll all be behind you. I promise you, okay? They'll put that son of a bitch away for a long time. Okay?" She had calmed considerably, beginning to take deep breaths, wiping at her eyes.

"You okay, Carrie?" Paul sounded like a lost little boy as he knelt down next to us, his hand on her arm, rubbing the skin gently. He looked at me, and our eyes met. I nodded to reassure him she was okay. He looked back at his girlfriend, moistening his lips as he decided what to do.

I knew that Carrie had told Paul about the rape a few days earlier, and he had been wonderful, patient and kind as he held her, listened to every gruesome detail. So now, I gently nudged her away from me and toward him. Surprise in his eyes, Paul took her in his arms. That's where she should be now.

*~*~*~*~*~*

Dagny and I snuggled together on her couch that night, the TV unwatched in the background. I lay between her legs, my back to her front as I stared up at the ceiling.

"I should have done something, Dag. Even if it was just hunting the guy down and chopping off his dick. I feel responsible somehow. I mean, we *saw* them, Dag." I turned enough to see her face. "Right?"

She nodded. "I know, Chase. Sometimes I think about that too. We were right there. But you know, she's okay. This was a horrible thing, Chase, but Carrie learned a harsh lesson from it. Remember, life is filled with lessons. My mom always told me that."

We both started at the knock on the door. I sat up. "Pizza's here."

"Get my wallet off the TV. I have a twenty."

I opened it up to get the money. Dagny's driver's license picture smiled at me. I grinned. "Nice mug shot, Dag." I showed her the picture; she rolled her eyes.

"Yeah, yeah. So I can't take a picture to save my life. I have never in all my twenty-four years seen a good driver's license picture."

"You haven't seen mine." I went to the door, gave the guy the money and took the pizza. When I went to stick the money back into the money pouch, I saw the birthdate on the license. My brows drew together. "Dag, why didn't you tell me your birthday is next month?"

She shrugged. "Guess I didn't think about it." She took the pizza to the kitchen to get plates and napkins. I followed her.

"You didn't think about it? What, don't you celebrate birthdays or something?" I grinned, closing the wallet and tossing it onto the counter.

"Nope."

I stared at her in surprise. "Why?"

"My parents stopped doing anything for that years ago, Chase. My mom will call, but that's about it. Here."

I took the plate she offered. "Thanks. That's so fucked up." I was angry. How could anyone not celebrate the birth of their child?

"Yeah, well, that's just the way it is." She took out two slices for herself and got the parmesan cheese from the refrigerator. "Since it's at the end of the summer, my mom was usually gone with my dad. It's just not that important."

I heard what she said, but I sensed she wasn't telling the whole truth — that she was in fact bothered, but just too damn proud to admit it. That was okay. The wheels in my head were already turning.

*~*~*~*~*~*

Summer was ending and the weather was cooling off a bit, with the monsoon season tapering off to an occasional brief shower. I loved the night air, cool but nowhere near cold. It was perfect walking weather, and Dagny and I often took advantage of it.

School was to start in a week and a half, and some students were coming back to start moving into their dorms and prepare. I had received my dorm assignment and was glad to see Carrie was in the same building this year. We'd decided before coming to college that we wouldn't be roommates, since we knew that if we were together nothing would get done.

She lived on a co-ed floor, of course, so she could have Paul up whenever she wanted to. I asked her if they were having sex already, and she said no, but it was getting close to that point. Now, I'm no prude, but I did worry about her.

It was amusing. There were all these double bunked, female-only dorms. My entire way of thinking had changed over the last few months, and I wondered how many of those roommates were or would be lovers. Whenever I saw two women walking down the street together, I wondered. I laughed about it often, thinking what a pervert I must be.

Dagny was helping me set up my dorm room, making sure we left plenty of space for Natalie when she returned in a few days. I had enjoyed having my own space in the single dorm over the summer, but at the same time, I had missed my roommate. I wondered if she would be doing the Bible study thing again this semester.

"Tell me you are not going to put this back up?"

I turned from hooking up my computer to see Dag looking at me over her shoulder, a tattered poster of two Hostess Twinkies posing against a fence. Their faces were drawn in with magic marker, their smiles made from the cream that filled their bodies. "Well, yeah. I've had that since I was twelve."

"And it shows. Come on, Chase. This belongs in... I don't know what."

I walked over to her and took the poster out of her hands. I held it out from me, looking at it with amusement. It was in horrible shape, and I had been thinking of trashing it, but now I decided to hang it, just on principle. I stuck some poster gum to the back and placed it above my bed. Dagny shook her head and started on another box.

"You know," I started casually, "the other day Greg had me go pick up a shipment of Corona for him and I passed that little place you talked about. Jillian's?" I looked at her briefly before turning back to my computer.

"Uh huh," she said distractedly as she hung clothes in the closet.

"Would you ever go back there?" I sneaked a glance at her.

She stopped what she was doing for a moment, thinking. "Well, I'd say yes. I don't believe in dwelling on things and having places or people stir up bad feelings, you know?" She looked at me; I nodded. "So I think I would, just to get new memories of the place and relive the good ones I had there with Darrel."

"Makes sense."

"God, I haven't been to there in at least two years." She smiled. "We had so much fun there. There was this woman who worked there named Marty, who was a hoot." She shook her head. "She used to flirt with Darrel incessantly, just to make him blush. Now, he wasn't the kind of person to be shy or threatened by a flirtation, so she had some gift."

As I sat there on the bed, listening, I realized it was really, really hard for me to hear. She was a bigger person than I was, because Darrel was definitely starting to take on negative connotations for me. I was sad the guy had died, for sure, but I hated the fact that he had been such a large part of Dagny's life for so long. I hated the jealous streak that ran through me sometimes, but since Dag was so out of my grasp, I couldn't help but feel insecure. I sighed.

"How's my bestest friend in the whole wide world?"

I was surprised to feel arms come around my neck, warmth along the back of my head and upper back. I reveled in the hug and leaned back into it. "She's fine. And yourself?"

"Can't complain." She set her chin on top of my head. "I got a call from my mom yesterday."

"Really?" I pulled away and turned to look at her, taking her arm in my hands, rubbing and massaging it.

She nodded. "Yup. She's coming up to Tucson for Thanksgiving."

"Really? Oh, Dag, that's great!" It had been over a year and a half since Dagny had seen her mom, and longer than that for her father.

"But she's still going to be with my father for Christmas." She looked down briefly, then smiled at me, but I could tell it was forced.

"I'm sorry." I brushed some stray hair away from her face.

She shrugged. "What can you do? I can just go to your house." She winked.

I brightened immediately. "Yes, you can."

"Chase, I was kidding." She pulled away to continue unpacking my junk.

"Well I'm not. My parents loved having you there last year, and my sister won't be here. They're spending Christmas with Todd's family in Oregon."

"Wow. How's your mom dealing with that?" Dagny began folding the clothes she was taking from a box.

"Are you kidding? Her perfect little angel is going to be gone and she'll just be left with the oops child."

"Chase," Dagny looked at me from under her bangs, her voice chiding, "that's not true."

I shrugged. "Either way, I won't be Carla."

"I really hate the fact that you feel that way." Dagny moved back to me, standing over me, running her hands through my hair.

"So do I, but that's just life."

Sometimes it amazed me just how much alike Dagny and I were, the things we had to deal with. I had never felt closer to anyone.

* ~ * ~ * ~ * ~ * ~ *

The month marched on; the trial finally convened. Carrie did well on the stand, managing to hold it together, and Dagny and I both testified as scheduled. Paul was always there, never leaving Carrie's side. It made me sick to look across the courtroom at the smug bastard sitting at the defendant's table. He was a slimy little man, and my mind was filled with many and varied thoughts of what I would like to do to him.

When the guilty verdict was read, we were thrilled. We found ourselves back in court for the sentencing, which was pathetic. He received five years in prison, with ninety days probation after he was released. And he would have to register as a sex offender, wherever he lived. I looked over at Ronald McDivitt. He was staring down at his legal pad, scribbling something. He didn't look happy.

I turned to my friend. Carrie was looking around, for what, I wasn't sure. I think she was trying to digest it, but I knew it would hit her later. Paul would have some interesting stuff to deal with. I felt for him. I could hear Carrie's mom crying in the seats behind Dagny and me.

* ~ * ~ * ~ * ~ * ~ *

"How did it go?" Natalie asked when I opened the door to our room. She was putting up some new posters, the question muffled around the roll of tape in her mouth.

I shrugged, flopping down on the bed. "The guy got a slap on the wrist. I mean, he did get time, but I doubt he'll serve much of it." I watched her as her Got Biology poster went up next. Natalie had chopped her hair over the summer and had highlighted it, which had surprised me when she'd walked through the door last week. She looked good, but different.

Every summer my roommate went to a retreat with her parents, this year being her first to actually teach some classes herself to kids ten years old or younger.

"That's really too bad." Natalie sat on her bed across from me, her hand on my knee. "At least it's over, Chase. Think of the positive."

"Yeah, I guess so. I don't think Carrie is doing too well. Her lawyer asked her whether she wanted to file a civil suit, and she told him to leave it alone; it didn't matter anymore. I think she had it in her head that this son of a bitch would be put away forever. The justice system is just so fucked up."

"Yes, it is. I'll keep her in my prayers."

* ~ * ~ * ~ * ~ * ~ *

"Okay, now you have to keep your eyes shut, Dag, or I'll staple them shut."

"They're shut, they're shut! I only saw which highway we were on. Jeez."

I had known she would peek, so I had initially gone the wrong way on purpose. I grinned as I turned the car in the opposite direction. I had called ahead and the staff remembered Dagny well and were sorry to hear about Darrel's death. I explained what I wanted done for Dagny and they had happily agreed to help out. Greg had been a godsend, too, giving me extra hours at work. I had saved nearly every dime I'd made since I had found out about Dag's birthday.

The scenery flew by, and Dagny sat in the passenger seat of my little black car, affectionately named after my favorite character in a musical, Phantom. Dagny had laughed at my explanation for the name. Not only because *Phantom of the Opera* was my favorite musical, but also since the car was black and had two white hubcaps on the front tires. The originals had been thrown off in a little fender bender I had the first day I got the car, and the replacements served as the mask, making my Phantom complete.

"You're a nut," Dagny had said after I had related the tale.

"Yeah, and—?"

I glanced over at my friend now, amazed that she was twenty-five today. I used to think of that as old, even though it was just six years older than me. But, Dagny had taught me that age is a state of mind. You can be old and used up at nineteen, or young and vibrant at ninety.

"Okay, we're almost there." I pulled into the parking lot, mine the only car there as I had reserved the entire place for two hours. A huge, colorful banner was strung across the front that read "Happy Birthday, Dagny" printed in different colored letters surrounded with confetti and balloons. I hoped she'd like it. I pulled the car to a stop and got out, hurrying to the passenger side to help her out. I took her hand, closing the door behind her.

"Can I look yet?"

"Nope." I knew this was torture on her, as she hated to be out of control. I led her to the front door that was opened by Marty, a mischievous smile on her face. She mouthed a hello to me and I smiled with a little wave.

The inside of the café had been transformed into a birthday toyland. Inflatable birthday candles the size of small children were strung up everywhere, as were colorful streamers. A table was decorated with confetti and noisemakers and coned birthday hats with the rubber band straps. A birthday cake sat on the counter, a rice paper picture of Dagny decorating the center of it. Her smiling face looked radiant against the purple frosting.

Dagny was taking deep breaths, smelling the air. "Smells familiar. Are we in Magpie's?"

"Nope."

Her brows drew together as she concentrated. The staff of three — the cook and two waitresses — stood behind the bar-like counter, smiling wildly.

"Are you ready?"

"Yes." She was bouncing with excitement, her curiosity reaching fever pitch.

I turned and spied the juke box in the corner. "Oh, hang on."

"Come on, Chase!"

I hurried over to it, quickly finding the selection I'd hoped for: *Bridge Over Troubled Water* by Simon & Garfunkel. I slipped my quarters into the slot and pushed play, then hurried back to my friend.

"Okay. Open your eyes."

Without delay, green eyes opened to look around. She knew instantly where she was, and her mouth fell open. "Oh, Chase." She looked at the people grouped around the counter. "Marty! You're still here?"

The waitress came around and gave Dag a huge hug. "Happy birthday, kiddo," she said, patting Dagny's back.

"Rick and Mary. My God, you guys are loyal." She laughed as she hugged the other two, then she turned to me, wagging her finger. "You..." She smiled, pulling me into a warm, full hug, laying her head on my shoulder. "Thank you, Chase."

"Happy birthday, Dag."

After a wonderful lunch with Dagny's every need met, sometimes before she even asked, her unfinished piece of birthday cake still before her, Dag looked at me from across the table and smiled. "You did good, Marin. You really didn't have to go to all this trouble, but you did good."

"You don't mind? I wasn't sure whether or not you'd be upset."

"Oh God, no. I was stunned, and so grateful. This is the best birthday I've had in at least ten years."

"Really?" I couldn't keep the smile off my face. She smiled and nodded. I was so charmed by that smile, absolutely captivated by the look in her eyes, the way the light shone in, making the green nearly translucent. "Well, the day isn't over yet."

"What? Chase, no. You've done more than enough."

"Nope. Just tell me when you're ready to go, 'cause we have somewhere to be." I leaned back in my chair, patting my stomach. "I have to say, that was the most awesome cheeseburger I've ever had." I sighed, content.

"I told you. I love their food here. And I can't believe Marty remembered my favorite meal and had it ready for me." She looked at the pile of our dishes on the counter. "Meatloaf and me don't usually get along, but, oh man, theirs is good."

I stood by the door, the remaining cake in the box under my arm, and I watched Dagny say her goodbyes and thanks to the folks at Jillian's. I had a good feeling, as if I had done something really extraordinary.

We dropped the cake off at Dagny's place on the way to our next and final destination, and I suggested Dag change into a pair of jeans. It might get cold later.

The Arizona-Sonora Desert Museum was a bit of a drive, but so worth it. The look on Dagny's face was priceless.

"Oh, Chase. Is this where we're going? I've always wanted to come here!" Her excitement was infectious, and I found myself nearly vibrating out of my seat. I had been there several times as a child, but being with Dagny as she experienced it for the first time would be better than any of my previous visits.

I paid for our tickets and watched with glee as Dagny looked around, her mouth open. We walked along the paths, starting at the Cactus Garden. Dagny read the little map we were given at the gate.

"Wow. More than a 140 different species are grown here," she read. We looked at them all, taking pictures with the disposable camera I had picked up.

Hours and hours went by, looking at everything from Cholla and Beavertail cactus to hummingbirds and Coatimundi in Cat Canyon. It was beautiful, and as the sun began to descend, we made our way up to the overlook to gaze out over the Sonoran Desert. I knew this was the most awesome place to be as the sun set. We got settled, Dagny sitting next to me, her face alight with happiness.

"Did you enjoy this, Dag?" I asked quietly, feeling shy.

She turned to me, staring into my eyes with the slightest bit of a smile on her lips. She searched my entire face as she nodded, her arms hugging her knees to her chest. "Oh, yeah," she whispered, her eyes still on me. People climbed up behind us, and at the sound of their voices, Dagny looked away, looking out over the scenery.

"Look at that," one of them said to someone in their party.

So I did. Off in the distance, storms were raging, vibrant as they lit up the velvet-like sky. It was one of the most incredible things I had ever seen. The undersides of the heavy rain clouds could be seen as lightning flashed, spreading across the sky in a web of electricity. I reached out and put my arm around Dagny's shoulders; she laid her head against mine and watched the show of nature.

* ~ * ~ * ~ * ~ * ~ *

That semester was my busiest yet. I was hopping between Bible study on Tuesday and Thursdays for Natalie, working and playing at Gotfry's on Friday and Saturday nights. And then, with my load of classes, I didn't know which way was up. I rarely saw Dagny. Though her class-load was lighter, she was even busier. Go figure! She went to class on Monday, Wednesday, and Friday, then worked at the counseling center on Monday, Thursday, and Friday afternoons. The University of Arizona Counseling Center was basically a place where students of the university or the poor from the community could go for counseling help from doctoral students supervised by professionals. On one of the rare mornings when we were able to swim at the same time, Dagny gushed about how much she loved the work, and yet how frustrated she was with a little boy she could not get through to.

"He's adorable, Chase. He's nine years old, has these great big black eyes that always look like they're searching for someone to help him." Dagny's client was a full-blooded American Indian who had seen his father murdered. His grandmother, who was raising him on a nearby reservation, was gravely worried about him, as he had stopped talking after that the trauma. She had brought him in to the counseling center for help.

"He won't say anything? What kinds of things is he into?"

She shrugged, splashing the water with her feet as we sat at the edge of the pool after our swim. "I don't know, and I'm not real sure how to find out. I've talked with Levy about him, and he's given me some pointers, but I'm just a little frustrated. I feel useless, you know?" Her face was filled with sadness. "I care about this little boy, and can't stand the thought of him being so traumatized for the rest of his life. He's destined for trouble if no one can get through to him." She sighed. "But I don't want to talk about that. How are your classes going?"

I couldn't stop the grin that came to my face as I thought about all the fascinating things I had learned in my psych classes. For the first time in my life, I looked forward to school. I told Dagny so, talking at breakneck speeds about my professors and what I thought of the information and the project I had to do. A smile on her face, Dagny watched me speak, my hands animated to try and get my point out there all the faster.

"God, you're so cute, Chase," she said. I looked down, suddenly feeling really stupid. She seemed to sense it and she put her hand on my arm. "Your enthusiasm is wonderful, Chase. You shouldn't be ashamed of that. And trust me, Gilder will love you more for it. Don't hide it in her class. You'll be her class pet in no time." I grinned and nodded.

* ~ * ~ * ~ * ~ * ~ *

Before long, the weather began to change, and shorts were replaced with jeans and sweatshirts tied around the waist. Midterms came and went, and the holiday break loomed before us. I hadn't seen Dagny in over two weeks and I was starting to feel the withdrawal. She wasn't even able to go to CID's shows on Friday nights, and that bothered me more than I ever would have imagined.

I sat on my bed, back against the wall, studying. I had been keeping to myself. Carrie was not available, as she was so wrapped up in Paul. Other friends I made in my classes invited me places, and sometimes I went. Mostly I didn't. I appreciated the offers, but there was only one person who could lift me out of my doldrums, and she didn't have the time.

The door to the room opened, and Natalie entered, dropping her heavy backpack to the floor before flopping down on the bed. She looked over at me, hands behind her head. "Wow. I think you're in an impossibly worse mood than you were yesterday." I looked up and glared at her. "What is it, Chase? Dagny?" She sat up. "You've been moaning and groaning about her lack of time all semester." She stared at me, but still got no response. "At least Christmas break is coming up." Nothing. "You know, it amazed me when I got back from summer break that you guys had gotten impossibly more close than last year." She studied me, sizing me up.

I didn't want to talk about it. I knew I was being childish, that it was out of Dagny's control, but I still hated it. I managed to find time for her whenever I could, even skipped a class or two when she had time off. Yeah, she had done the same for me, but I wanted more of her. I missed her.

Something was going through Natalie's head. She tucked her bottom lip into her mouth as she thought, the wheels smoking. "Cheer up, kid." She stood and patted my knee. "Come on, come get some dinner with me."

I shook my head. "No, thanks."

"Chase, get up off your ass and come down to the cafeteria with me."

I looked up, surprised at the forceful tone in Natalie's voice. She usually reserved that for our Bible study kids who were getting out of hand. "Did you just curse?"

"Yes, I did, so get up."

Amused, I shook my head as I stood. "I'm telling."

"Yeah, right. As often as you pray, I'm sure God wouldn't even bother listening to any message you left."

I smacked her as we both laughed.

* ~ * ~ * ~ * ~ * ~ *

Friday night came around, and so did another performance for our local barflies. "So, what did you ask for from Santa?" Terrie asked as she got settled behind her drums. "Would it be a little blonde headshrinker?"

I glared at her. "Fuck you."

"Okay." She laughed, whacking me on the butt with a drumstick as I strapped Than over my shoulder. I glared again before I flipped her off.

As the first set wound down to an end, I saw Dagny come in. She smiled up at me as she walked by. I nearly jumped off the stage right then and there to give her a hug. Instead I kept the pace of the song I was singing slow, true to form, trying not to rush it just to finish. Finally, what seemed like an hour later, the song ended.

"We'll be back." I threw the guitar strap off me and set Than down in the holder, then headed down the stairs. I heard Terrie's laughter behind me.

"Hey, you," Dag said as she stood up from her table to hug me. "You sounded great."

"Thanks." A few of Dagny's friends were already there, and we chatted a bit, but my eyes were on Dagny. I felt as if I were getting a hit of the drug I was most addicted to.

"Okay, folks, I'll be back." Dagny stood up and took my hand. "Come on, Chase." I followed, confused. We went outside, where she stopped and leaned against Freud. "I needed to get out of there," she said, looking at me. "I wanted some time with just me and you."

My heart began to soar. "I was surprised to see you come in."

"Yeah, I gathered. I wondered if you were going to forget the words to the song." She grinned evilly.

*God, was I* that *obvious?* I just chuckled. "Yeah, well..."

"So, are you excited about Tuesday?"

I nodded vigorously. That was the day we were going to my folks' house for Christmas break. "God, yes." I leaned back against the SUV next to Dag. "I am so tired."

"Oh, yeah. I hear ya. I'm looking forward to a Calgon vacation." She grinned at me; I smiled back.

After we finished up our sets, Dagny and I went out to get something to eat and talk. We had to play catch up. She told me all about working with that little boy, and how she was still not making much progress.

"I got him to acknowledge his name the other day. He just barely nodded, but I was so proud." She smiled.

I patted her on the back. "Go, you!"

"Thank you, thank you."

I kept my hand on her back, rubbing. "You'll get through to him, Dag. I have faith in you."

When I got back to the dorm, Natalie was already asleep, her back to me. I undressed and was about to get into bed when I saw a piece of paper lying on my pillow. Taking it and holding it under the light shining in from the streetlight below the window, I saw it was a clipping from a scientific magazine. The article was titled: *New Scientific Evidence On Why More And More Teens Are Coming Out Of The Closet.*

I looked at my roommate; she hadn't moved. Curious, I read on. When I asked her about it the next day, she said she had found it interesting, and thought I might, too. This was said with a wink, of course.

* ~ * ~ * ~ * ~ * ~ *

Christmas went off without a hitch, even though Carla was in Oregon. I think my parents were just as glad having Dagny there as they would have been with Carla. The holiday went over even better than it had last year. Even I enjoyed it. We played teams in board games such as Cranium and Trivial Pursuit. Dagny and I nearly won, but in the end, my father was too much for us. It was great fun.

Dagny and I swam daily, and my mother was shocked and immensely pleased that Dag had been able to turn me into a fish. Christmas morning, my parents surprised me by having nearly as many gifts for Dagny as they did for me. All of Carla's gifts waited in the corner to be opened when she came home the following week. I received a music system that would allow me to make my own songs and compose my own music. Dagny watched me intently as I looked it over, imagining all the wonderful things I could do with it. God, I just wanted to be able to be open and honest with my parents, to show them what I was doing with my life and how much I loved it.

We were surrounded by a forest of wrapping paper. I'd started to clean it all up when Dag stopped me with a hand on my arm. I looked at her questioningly.

"I have a surprise for you, Chase," she said. My parents were smiling, holding hands. *Okay, so they know about it.* "All right."

"I'm taking you to a cabin in the Rockies that belongs to a family friend. Last year you said you wished to see a white Christmas, so I want to hopefully grant your wish, though we'll need some cooperation from Mother Nature."

I looked at her; was she serious? "Are you serious?"

She nodded. "Yup. You interested?"

"Hell, yeah!"

"Chase, your language," my mother chastised.

"Sorry. When do we leave?"

"Two days."

I couldn't keep the smile off my face. I would actually be able to see and touch snow in person. I had only seen it on TV, and the few times we'd had a flurry or two in Tucson. I was beyond excited.

*~*~*~*~*~*

We started our drive ridiculously early in the morning, wanting to reach the cabin by mid-afternoon. Dagny's SUV was packed with warm clothes and some playthings we'd bought: a sled, snow shovels, and provisions to make a snowman. I was giddy, like Dorothy off to see the Wizard.

"So were you surprised?" Dag asked as she navigated the roads.

"Hell, yeah." I grinned.

"Watch your mouth, Chase," Dag said, her voice low and stern, but her face breaking into a wide smile.

"Yeah, bite me. Anyway, yeah, I was shocked. What made you do this?"

She sighed. "I don't know. I guess because over Thanksgiving my mom and I talked about when we used to come here when I was a kid. I took my first steps in this cabin." She turned to look at me, and I smiled, imagining a tiny little Dagny taking that first wobbly step to the awe and amazement of her parents. "I haven't been here in years and years. I wonder how small it will look to me now. You

know, when you do something as a kid, it seems so huge to you."
She smiled. "Then, when you do it again as an adult, it's almost disappointing."

"Yeah. I doubt this will be, though. I mean, it's memories that
endeared the cabin to you, not the grandeur of it."

"True."

As we drove out of Arizona and over the Colorado state line, the
weather became noticeably colder. I looked around in amazement.
The huge rock formations that lined both sides of the road were not
new to me. Arizona was filled with the likes of those, but these were
frosted with a thick layer of snow, little rivulets of ice hanging off
the edges. I looked out the window, wide-eyed and open mouthed at
the beauty of it all. The sparse grasses on the side of the road were
also tipped with ice and snow, the sky, gray but not foreboding.

We turned toward the huge Rockies that loomed ahead. It
looked as if you could run into them at any moment, but as you got
closer, they simply fell away, until suddenly and without warning,
we were surrounded by barren slopes and snow-covered trees
threaded by narrow, winding roads. I was impressed with the way
Dagny was able to maneuver through the curves and twists, as if
she'd done it thousands of times, turning off to flatter land, higher
up, the mountain dropping off the road on Dagny's side. I looked
over and down into a snow-covered valley.

"Wow," I breathed.

"Incredible, isn't it?"

Not able to speak, I nodded.

* ~ * ~ * ~ * ~ * ~ *

We made good time, reaching the cabin at just past three.
Unloading everything from the car and into the small structure, we
headed to the nearest little town of Bud to pick up some supplies for
our week long stay. The store was tiny, filled with about five rows of
shelving, packing in as much merchandise as possible. We got food,
candles and matches, as well as some batteries.

Back at the cabin, I took some time to explore. It had two bedrooms, though only one had a bed in it; the other served as storage.
One bathroom, living room, and a small kitchen with a round
wooden table large enough for four completed the cabin's layout.
The floors were wood, but large area rugs were scattered everywhere to keep feet warm on cold winter nights. A large stone fireplace took up the entire west wall.

"This is just too awesome," I said, standing in the middle of the
room with my hands on my hips. The furniture was made of logs,
very rustic. My only beef was the pair of antlers hanging over the
fireplace. What on earth was so decorative about that?

"Well, I'm glad you like it. Are you going to help me or not?" Dagny had been zooming back and forth, putting stuff away and getting dinner started. With a final sigh of contentment, I jumped in.

Walking around outside the cabin that night was magnificent. The snow was not too deep yet, maybe six inches. Dagny said it was usually three times that deep, but with Colorado's drought, the snow was not as plentiful. I didn't care; it was snow.

I picked up a handful, rubbing the cold wetness between my fingers, reveling in the beauty of its white crystals. There was so much brown and red in Arizona, this was definitely a nice change. I stared up into the sky, the snow falling lightly, just enough to tickle my face rather than make it wet.

"Come on, you. Let's go in for tonight. We'll come back out tomorrow during the day, when it's a bit warmer."

* ~ * ~ * ~ * ~ * ~ *

The cold was something for me to get used to. I hated having to wear so many layers of clothing, but Dagny made me, nearly dressing me each time we went out. We made a fire in the fireplace every night. Dagny cooked some fantastic meals. Though I tried to help her, she did most of it. She definitely had talent in the kitchen. I had brought Melo with me, and sometimes I played for her, singing whatever popular songs popped into my head.

There was no television, so we were totally cut off from that sort of intrusion, instead making our own entertainment. We played endless games of chess and cards. We read to each other and took walks, waiting for the big snow that was promised by the end of the week. I was so excited, I nearly bounced.

It was the most incredible week of my life. Dagny was so much fun, and interesting. We had needed some good bonding time after the hectic last semester and before the one that would start shortly after our return to school. I wanted to savor this time, revel in it. I had Dag all to myself, and it spoiled me. She was so affectionate with me, always rubbing my shoulders or lying with her head in my lap as we listened to the radio and watched the fire dance.

My favorite part was playing in the snow. I was amazed at just how creative you could be with it. I made three snowmen, each with its own distinct personality and attitude. Dagny stood back, watching me finish my last masterpiece, covering her mouth as she laughed. I looked at my creation, loving the bulge in his arms. I knelt down, working on the legs, getting them just so before standing to work on the face a bit more. He had to be just right.

She laughed. "Oh my God! Never in my life did I think I'd see a buff snowman."

I grinned, standing back from him to review my Arnold

Schwarzenegger look alike. He stood with his legs spread wide, arms pressed to his sides because of the limits of snow. He was good; his icy muscles pronounced and obvious. I stood in front of him, taking the same pose, my face hard and drawn. Dagny laughed harder when I brought my arms up to flex for her, my biceps lost in the impossibly large bulk of material in the coat I wore.

I had never in my life felt so close to another person. Dagny looked at me as if I were special to her, as if I were the only other person in the world, which I was in our little part of the woods. I felt my heart beating just a little bit faster that week. But the thing that I found interesting was — though, yes, my body burned for her — it was mostly my heart that was calling out, not my hormones. My chest actually hurt, as if my heart were being pumped up too large for the space it was allotted. I wondered how she felt. I knew it was nothing like that, but I hoped. I wanted her to feel it, to want it.

I shoved those thoughts away, relegating them to the recycle bin in my brain.

\* ~ \* ~ \* ~ \* ~ \* ~ \*

The bright light from the full moon shining in, we lay in bed together, talking about the coming semester. I looked out the window and saw the snow beginning to fall, to my delight. "Dag, check it out." I pointed.

"Holy cow!" She got out of the bed and padded over to the window; I followed. The snow floated down, like a feather pillow sliced open — large flakes, and lots of them. She turned to me. "You thinking what I'm thinking?"

Giggling like schoolgirls, we dressed in sweats, sweatshirts, and boots and ran outside. It was cold, but we didn't care. There was already a thick layer of old snow on the ground, but all of our tracks were already nearly covered by the new fall. We played, throwing snowballs at each other, pushing each other into the cold blanket of white. Finally, in an all out snowball war, we pelted each other, hiding behind trees, trying to dodge icy missiles.

"Wait, wait!" Dagny cried out, laughter following each icy breathed word. "Truce! I'm soaked."

She peeked out from her hiding place. Her hair was plastered to her face, water dripping down her nose. Her normally light gray sweatpants were nearly black from being so saturated.

I laughed. "Oh, Dag. Come on."

We hurried back inside, and I quickly got a fire going. Dagny stood on the thick rug in front of the fireplace, stripping out of her wet clothes. I did my best not to look, not to notice the incredibly beautiful body, toned by years of swimming, smooth skin glowing in the firelight.

To distract myself, I hurried to the cabinet in the bathroom and grabbed a large, thick towel to help dry her off. When I returned to the main room, Dagny stood in just her soaked bra and underwear. I could see nearly every detail of her body through the thin material. I felt guilty for looking, but that didn't stop me. She was just so beautiful. Clothes could never do her figure justice.

"Here." I wrapped the towel around her shoulders. She took the ends of it in icy hands, her entire body shivering. "I'm sorry, Dag. God, you're going to get pneumonia." I began to rub her arms to try and rub some warmth into her body and get the blood flowing.

"It's okay," she said, her teeth chattering. "It-t-t was m-my idea."

I smiled, amused by her attempt at speech. She turned in my arms, burying her face against my neck, moaning at the warmth her ice cold nose found there.

I wrapped my arms around her, pulling her into me for more full-body warmth, when it occurred to me that Dagny's half-naked body was pressed against me. I could feel her breasts against mine, the softness and fullness. Like a match to a wick, my body was suddenly on fire. My stomach began to do flip flops as my body responded to the contact. She was so close. This must be what it would feel like to be with her, to hold her and touch her.

Dagny's arms were around my waist, but they began to move, her hands sliding around my body to my hips, her face leaving my neck. Green eyes looked into mine.

I stared down into Dagny's face, searching her gaze for the message that I felt was there. Her eyes looked into mine before trailing down my nose to my mouth, my lips slightly parted to bring in more air. I was having trouble breathing. I noticed the way the firelight caressed her skin, turning it bronze, the side of her face that was away from the fire in shadow.

My eyes were drawn to Dagny's mouth as it opened slightly, the tongue licking along the inside of her bottom lip. My gaze flicked back up to hers as I felt myself moving. It was like a dream, her eyes getting closer just before they closed, or was it mine that closed?

Softness pressed against my lips, the exquisite softness of Dagny's lips. The barest touch before they were back, pressing harder but still just as soft. So amazing, as the fullness gave in to the pressure, making me feel lost in it. The softness parted slightly, just enough for my lips to fit perfectly, like the pieces of a puzzle, drawn together as a match, then torn apart when the puzzle was shaken.

My eyes opened as I felt the softness leave. Dagny was looking at me, bringing her hand up absently, her fingers touching her lips.

I could not read her expression, beyond surprise, and I was afraid. I said nothing, just stared, waiting for her next move.

Dagny took a step back, her eyes dropping to the floor. "Um, I'm going to take a shower and get warm," she said quietly, then turned and went into the bathroom, shutting the door behind her with a soft click.

I felt the familiar stinging behind my eyes and turned to stare into the flames. *What just happened? Did I do that? Did she?* I had no clue. One moment I was standing there trying to warm Dagny up, and the next I was kissing her. How had that happened? My heart felt heavy; my lips still tingled from where Dagny's had been moments before. God, I wished they were still there. *Stop it, Chase! Haven't you done enough?*

Taking a shaky breath, I headed for the bedroom where I slowly changed into dry clothes, my mind in a haze, my body on autopilot. I couldn't deny that I had wanted that for so long, and now that I'd had it, I felt sick. *Never would have imagined that.*

I turned to look at the wall shared by the bedroom and bathroom. I tried to imagine what Dagny was thinking, what she was doing in that shower stall. Washing herself and warming up, with no thoughts and blocking it out? Or was she leaning against the wall, as stunned as I was?

It didn't matter. I felt empty, like some part of me had been ripped out, taken away. I had trod on ground that was strictly forbidden. The line had been crossed, and I was sure our friendship had been damaged because of it.

I plopped down on the mattress, trying to lie as close to the edge of the bed as possible, giving Dagny more than enough space away from me. I was sure she'd want that when she finally came to bed. I stared up at the ceiling, my hand behind my head, the stinging still very present. I was holding it back. She didn't need to see my pain or sorrow or frustration.

The water turned off, and many minutes after that, the bathroom door opened. My stomach lurched, like that of a kid awaiting her father's wrath. I tried to control my breathing, but it didn't do a whole lot of good. Minutes went by, then more minutes. I started to get concerned. Where was she? I quietly slipped out of bed to stand at the doorway of the room. Dagny sat on the couch, her back to me as she stared into the fire. I had the feeling she was not coming to bed.

I crept back to the bed and lay down, pulling the comforter to my chin as I let the tears come.

# Chapter 10

I watched him as he watched me, chewing on the earpiece of his glasses, sizing me up.

"So, last time you mentioned that you liked girls, or perhaps just one girl. What did you mean by that?"

What did he mean, what did I mean? Wasn't it pretty self explanatory? "Well, I mean that I dated guys for years. Well, a few, anyway. But then I came across this one girl, and she turned my world upside down." I looked down at my fidgeting hands as I talked, played with the strap of my backpack that sat on the couch next to me.

"You don't look so happy about that, Chase. Why not?"

I took a deep breath, knowing why I had come, knowing that I hadn't been able to get it out in the last two sessions, so I might as well do it now.

"Picture this: you're in a secluded cabin in the Colorado woods in some butt-fuck back area where there is no civilization except for a tiny store ten miles away. You plan to behave, not do a fucking thing, then next thing you know, you're kissing this girl of your dreams." I took a breath to get myself under control.

"Did she kiss you back?"

"Yeah. But she pulled away, then took off to the bathroom to take a shower. We had just come in from playing in the snow, so we were both cold, and she needed to warm up."

"It sounds like you're trying to make excuses for her, Chase." He shifted in his chair, crossing his right leg over his left. "What happened next?"

"She slept on the couch, and I slept in the bed. The next morning, we shared a fucking silent eight hour trip back here."

"You're very angry, still."

"Wouldn't you be? Fuck, yeah, I'm angry." I looked at him, frowning. "I just want to understand." I stood, went over to the window to look at the campus stretched out before me. "I haven't spoken to her since."

"So you're avoiding her, then?"

"Nope. Other way around."

"Interesting." I could hear him scribbling something on the pad balanced on his thigh. "This happened during Christmas break, you said?" I nodded. He glanced over at the wall calendar. "That's been well over two months now."

Again I nodded. "I know."

I walked around the small, neat office, feeling eyes on me the entire time. A large desk stood near the far wall, and I wandered over there. On the desk were several framed picture — a snapshot of a large golden retriever in one, and in another, a studio picture of two men. I turned to him. "Who's the other guy?"

"That's my partner, Jerry," he said matter-of-factly.

I looked back at the picture, at the two men frozen in time. Jerry was a good looking guy, darker skinned, with the slightest bit of a beard, dark hair trimmed neatly. Samuel was also a good look-ing man, getting older, maybe in his mid-forties. He had dark hair, also, but it was beginning to gray around the temples, making him look quite distinguished. They both appeared to be in wonderful shape. I looked at Samuel. "Why is it that when men start to gray, it's considered sexy, and when women do, they're old hags."

He chuckled, shaking his head. "Don't you just love that double standard?"

"Yeah." I plopped down on the couch.

"Tell me more about you, Chase. Does your family keep in close contact with you?" I shrugged, leaning back, my ankle crossed over my knee, bouncing nervously. "Are you uncomfortable, Chase?"

I glanced at my foot and grinned. "No, not really. Sometimes I just have too much energy, need to get it out. Anyway...my parents. Yeah, they don't live far. I talk to them about every week or so, see them occasionally."

"Do you get along?"

"As well as most, I'd say." I glanced down at my watch. "Out of time, Doc." I grinned at him and he smiled at me.

"Yes, it appears we are. You did better today, Chase. I think I'm getting a larger picture of Chase Marin."

"Good luck, Dr. Roth." I shouldered my backpack and headed toward the door. "It's not easy being me." With one last smile, I exited his office.

Every time I left the counseling center, I was afraid I'd run into Dagny, and yet there was a large part of me that hoped I would. I had been sure to make my appointment days opposite her work days so that I wouldn't run into her. The smart part of me knew it would probably be best if I didn't. She obviously didn't want to see me, so who was I to force the issue? Apparently I'd done enough of that already.

I headed back to my dorm, thankful that I had scheduled the counseling sessions after my classes for the day, so I could just go home and veg. The semester was three weeks in, and I had not left my room unless it was for class, the sessions, rehearsals, or a gig.

The sessions. I smiled as I thought about how much I had wanted to strangle Natalie. She had cornered me one day in the room, sitting across from me and staring into my eyes.

*"Chase, what's wrong?"*

*"Nothing."*

*"That's crap and you know it. Come on, talk to me."* I looked
at her, putting my notebook aside, no longer able to write in the
leather journal Dagney had given me. It hurt too much. *"Is it
school? I can't imagine, since we just started. Your family?"* I
shook my head. *"Dagny?"* I looked down, playing with my pen. *"I
wondered. She hasn't been around, and you haven't talked about
her much. Is everything okay?"*

*"No,"* I whispered. I did not want to go into detail with
Natalie. Though she had put that article on my bed about homosexuality, I still didn't feel she'd be able to understand. Plus, I felt
ashamed.

*"Look, I think I know someone who can help you, okay? At
least he'll talk to you and understand. His name is Samuel Roth;
he's a psychologist at the counseling center."*

*"No, Natalie. I won't go."*

*"Please don't be stubborn, Chase. I know you don't have many
people you can talk to, so please do this. At least go once, then
after that, you can stop, okay?"* I finally nodded my consent,
secretly grateful that someone cared.

I walked across campus now, staring up into the sun. We were
headed into mid-March, and I was so very sad. Actually, how I felt
depended on the day and moment. Right now I was sad, thinking of
how different things had been this time last year. My birthday had
come and gone over three weeks ago. Carrie and Paul had taken me
out, and Natalie had taken me to a movie and dinner. Dagny had
sent me an email, wishing me the best and a wonderful twentieth
year, followed by a half dozen carnations the next day.

I had been surprised at that, not having expected her to do anything, but wishing all the same that I could transport myself
through time to last year and do everything all over again. But then,
my feelings would not have changed, so the same thing likely would
have happened, one way or another.

Some days I felt angry and confused. What had I done that had
been so horrible that Dagney couldn't even let me to explain, or at
least talk to her about my side or allow me to hear hers? I was experiencing a tempest of emotions, so I tried to ignore the personal and
just focus on my schoolwork. Who would have thought? My parents would be so proud, and were, but if only they knew the truth...

Suddenly I stopped, the hair on the back of my neck standing
on end and my stomach lurching. I slowly glanced over to my left
where I saw a stone bench, and Dagny sitting on it. She was leaning
over a book, her legs curled up under her, then she looked up, her
eyes seeming not to see anything, just staring into space.

My feet became rooted; I couldn't move from the spot. I wondered what was going through her head, what she had been doing. Often times I'd lie in bed, knowing Dagny was still up studying, imagining her sitting on the floor of the living room or the couch, that white gook on her face as she read.

Suddenly green eyes were on me, and I stared back. Dagny lifted her head a bit, staring into my eyes. She was a ways from me, but from what I could see, emotions swept across her face like an ocean tide. One moment she looked lost, then the next, hard as the stone bench on which she was sitting.

For a moment I thought she would get up, but then she turned back to her book. My heart sank, again, and I hurried on toward my dorm. I didn't want her to see me cry.

* ~ * ~ * ~ * ~ * ~ *

During rehearsal on Thursday I was quiet, not even wanting to be there. Luckily, after being asked what was wrong only about twenty times, my band-mates left me alone. Terrie watched me all night, and I wasn't sure why. I'd venture a guess that she was looking for me to fall apart, but since it didn't happen, I don't know for certain. I didn't know whom I could trust my pain to, so I didn't bother. I'd just learn to deal with it on my own.

I was glad when Friday night came around. The distraction of Gotfry's would be good. I only worked there two days a week now, anything more being too much with school and Natalie's Bible study classes. She had stopped doing the Thursday night child classes, which had bummed me out, but she didn't have time for it this semester.

I set up my guitars and brought the microphone up to my height. I don't know who used it between our shows, but whoever it was must have been a midget. I scanned the customers, just to see who was there. Yeah, right. I knew exactly who I was looking for, but didn't want to admit it, even to myself.

"You okay, Chase?"

I turned to see Terrie standing behind me. Her dark eyes were filled with a genuine concern, and I badly wanted to confess all my secrets, but this was not the time. I nodded, but could not look her in the eye. She reached up and put her hand on my shoulder. "It will all work out, Chase. It always does."

I felt the sting behind my eyes. I cried so often nowadays. I hated it, never liked crying. "Thanks, Terrie." I quickly turned away so she wouldn't see the gathering tears. Valiantly, I shoved it all down for another day.

The show started, and I tried to put as much into it as I could, some of the songs coming out far too harsh, but powerful. The crowd ate it up, taking it as my own interpretation of the song. Worked for me.

At the break, Greg looked at me strangely, as if he knew something was wrong but couldn't quite put his finger on it. To his credit, he didn't ask. My water and I headed outside.

The night was clear and quiet as I strolled around, one hand in the pocket of my jeans, the other holding the mug of water. I needed some air, and I didn't want to be around a whole bunch of people, and I especially didn't want to be where I had so many memories of Dagny. It hurt just to be up there singing. I'd thought about quitting the band but knew I'd regret it for the rest of my life. This was but a moment in my history, but damn did it hurt!

"Hey."

I turned to see Carrie standing behind me. I smiled, her presence immediately brightening my dark mood. "Hi. What are you doing here?"

"We wanted to surprise you. Paul's inside." She pointed to the door with her thumb.

I hugged her, happy to see a friendly face. "I'm glad you came."

Carrie stared at me for a moment. "What's going on, Chase? What's happened between you and Dag?"

I was surprised, as I hadn't said anything to her. I stared at her but couldn't come up with an answer.

"Come on, no tough girl shit. We took her out to lunch yesterday, Chase. She was sad and withdrawn. Paul had to pretty much force her to go with us. Now I look at you and see the same, so I'm asking again, what happened?"

"I kissed her, Car," I said quietly. "Well, at least, we kissed." I fiddled with my mug. "I don't know what happened. She flipped out."

"Oh," Carrie breathed, stepping back in shock. "I'm...wow. I'm sorry, Chase." She put her hand on my arm. "So, what do you think?"

I shook my head, looking out into the night. "I'm thinking that the greatest thing to ever happen to me is fucked up beyond repair. I don't understand why we can't just go back to where we were." I looked at my friend. "Why does it have to be as dramatic as us totally avoiding each other? I saw her in the park the other day. She looked right at me, then turned back to her books. She hates me, Car."

"I didn't get that impression at all, Chase. She said that she's been really busy with school and all, but she... God, I can't even explain it to you. If I didn't know better, I would have thought her dog died. Hell, her entire family." She leaned back against a nearby car. "She looked unbelievably lost."

I sighed. *I'm right here, Dagny. I can lead you back.* But I said nothing.

"It kind of makes sense now. Anyway, you guys sounded great in there," Carrie said finally.

I smiled and turned to her. "Thanks. I think I sucked, but hey, you can keep on praising if you like."

"Well, I don't think Poison ever intended *Every Rose Has Its Thorn* to be so harsh, but other than that..."

I laughed. "Yeah, bite me." I dodged the smack that she aimed at my arm. "So, how are things going, you know, you and Paul."

"Oh, Chase, we can talk about that some other time, huh?"

"No, it's okay. Really, I'm okay. How is he?" My friend's face lit up, though I could tell she was trying to hold back. I put my hand on her arm. "Car, really. It's okay. Just because my life sucks I'm not going to begrudge you your happiness."

She looked at me, gauging my sincerity, then finally smiled full out. "He's wonderful, Chase. I think this is what I've been looking for, you know?" I nodded. "We're taking it slow, you'll be happy to know, but things are kind of getting serious. Last weekend I took him home to make the formal introduction to my parents."

"Really? The parent moment, huh? How did that go?"

"Well, I was nervous as hell, but I have faith in my choice, so no matter how it turned out, I knew what I wanted. But all my worrying and analyzing were for naught. They loved him." She smiled again, wrapping her arms around herself.

"I knew they would, Car. You've got a great one there."

"Chase, can I ask you a question? If it's too soon, tell me to go fuck myself, but, well, if this doesn't work out with Dagny, will you go back to guys or stick with girls?"

What a fine question, one that I had no answer. I hadn't even thought about it. I sighed as I considered. "Well, I mean, I like guys as a whole, and Mike was great, but I don't know. There's something about women that you just don't get with men, you know?"

She nodded. "Oh, yeah. I understand. They're so gentle and soft."

"Yeah, but it's more than that. I mean, I haven't slept with one, so I don't know shit about that part of it." I stared up at the night sky, trying to get my thoughts in order. "It's more of a connection that I have never experienced in my entire life." I looked at my friend. "You and I are close, right?" She nodded. "But even so, and you know how much I love you, it's different. Now I don't know if this is with all women or just Dag, but there is a connection there, like I don't even have to say a word, and she understands me." I could feel the familiar stinging and looked down to hide my face from Carrie. I felt a hand on my back, rubbing in slow circles.

"It's okay, Chase," she whispered.

My chest heaved as a sob tore free. "God, I feel like I'm pregnant. I get the weirdest emotional outbursts at the oddest times." I tried to smile through my tears, wiping them away as fast as they poured from my eyes.

Carrie smiled. "Yeah."

"What did I do that was so wrong, Car?" Realizing that wiping the tears away was a losing battle, I stopped trying. "You know, I find it ironic that the same person who gave me a purpose, made me feel strong within myself, has made me question my every move. I feel like my touchstone is gone."

Carrie took me into her arms, whispering loving words into my ear and rocking me slowly.

\* ~ \* ~ \* ~ \* ~ \* ~ \*

I arrived at the counseling center a bit early. Dr. Roth's door was closed, so I took one of the chairs in the waiting room. There was a little boy already there, no older than eight or nine, and an older woman next to him reading a magazine. When I sat, his dark eyes focused on me. I smiled at him, and the look in his eyes became fearful as he moved closer to the woman.

Surprised, I sat back and waited for my appointment, and then a song popped into my head. It was an old camp song my sister had taught me years ago. I began to hum it, just for something to do. I felt the boy's eyes on me, but did not look directly at him for fear of scaring him further. If I looked at the picture hanging on the wall above their heads, I could see the child out of the corner of my eye. As I hummed, I got my feet into the action, moving them this way and that, at first very subtly, to the rhythm of the song.

The boy's eyes followed my movements, his face stone still. I brought my hands into the little dance, doing an almost 70s style disco move. I kept my face empty of expression except for my eyes, which moved back and forth with my hands, and I began to bob my head along with my humming. To my immense surprise and delight, I saw the slightest bit of a smile flit across his lips and reach his eyes to make them sparkle like black marbles.

"Chase?"

I stopped abruptly in mid-dance and looked up at my doctor, who was staring down at me with amusement on his face. I smiled and stood, following him into his office.

"Entertaining the little guy there?" he asked.

I sat down with a smile. "He looked like he could use a little pick-me-up."

"Indeed he can." He shook his head as he flipped through the pages of his notebook, then looked at me. "So, how have you been, Chase?"

I shrugged. "Okay, I guess. Not much to tell. Been pretty typical days. But, there is some good news." I smiled.

"Oh?"

"Well, two things, actually. My sister and her fiancé have set a date to get married. It will be this fall. Also, I decided not to quit playing music."

"That's wonderful, Chase." Sam leaned toward me and patted me on the knee. "I think that was a wise, mature, healthy decision."

He leaned back in his chair and studied me. I had been coming to see him for three months, now, and was so glad I did. He was awesome professionally, and his honesty about his own gay life had been beyond helpful.

"Do you compose music, Chase? Music can be such an extraordinary outlet for feelings and emotions, whether good or bad."

"Yeah, it can, and yes, I do."

"Have you written any pieces about this girl who hurt you so badly?" I nodded, not meeting his eyes. "It's nothing to be ashamed of, Chase. It can be very therapeutic."

"Yes, but to be honest, sometimes I almost feel like a voyeur. Like, I know she will never read or hear any of these songs, but they're about her. It's like talking about someone behind their back." I chewed on my bottom lip as I stared at the doctor. "Does that make sense?"

He nodded. "Yes it does. But what's important is how they make *you* feel. Do they make you feel better?"

"A little, yeah."

"Then that's what counts. Do you allow anyone else to read your songs?" He took his glasses off to polish them with the ever-present Kleenex he had in his pocket.

"No. No one reads them." I recollected that one happy occasion and corrected myself. "She's the only one who ever read any of my songs." I felt deflated and the stinging started again. *Dammit! I don't want to cry anymore.*

I heard some movement, but didn't dare look up. I would be mortified if Sam saw me crying. The couch next to me lowered with the added weight of the doctor, then I saw a Kleenex come into view. I took it, quickly trying to wipe the tears away.

"I really shouldn't be so personal with you, Chase, but I want to tell you a story." Sam's voice had gone from the strong, professional tone to a much softer, comforting one. "When I was younger, just starting college, so about an eon ago," I smiled as he nudged me, "I met this man. Shawn. We had a class together. The first time I saw him I was drawn to him, but he treated me like dirt for a good long time. So I decided he was an asshole and threw my feelings out of my mind." He brushed some hair away from my face, but I still stared at my lap.

"What happened?" I finally asked.

"We ended up having to do a project together for the class. He showed up at my apartment with breakfast from a fast food place, and we sat down to eat and talk. We talked about the project for maybe an hour, then the rest of the day we discussed our lives, our pasts, any and everything. See, at that time I thought I was still very much straight, even had a girlfriend. Imagine that." I looked up at him and grinned; he was already smiling at me. "Anyway, the long and short of it was we became best friends, inseparable. I fell in love with him. I was surprised, and so scared. What would happen? What would my family think; would my career be ruined? So, we stayed like this — Shawn showing me all signs pointed south, but us never doing anything, never following through." He grinned. "Neither of us had the guts. Eventually he transferred to another college, and I was left heartbroken. I had changed my entire life for him, Chase. Came out to my family long before I was ready, broke up with my girlfriend, which ultimately ended up being the right thing. But at the time, I was shattered, devastated."

I wondered how the tale would end, and why the hell he was telling me. "Are you trying to depress me more, Sam?"

He chuckled. "No, Chase. Time passed, and my heart mended to the best of its ability, and I met Jerry. He was the best thing that ever happened to me. My point is, with this girl, whether you ultimately win or lose, she's playing a part in your life for a reason. It's up to you to figure out what that reason is and to use it to your benefit. Life throws us curves, Chase. I know you know that, but you have to respect and learn from the bad in order to appreciate and deserve the good."

I looked at him in a new light. He wasn't just the psychology guy that I came in and talked to every week, he was a human being who had feelings and experiences, too. I hugged him. "Thank you, Sam," I said, the words muffled against his shoulder.

He hugged me back, rubbing my back and neck. "You'll get through this, Chase. I promise."

* ~ * ~ * ~ * ~ * ~ *

It had been weeks since I had seen Dagny sitting in the park, which was one of three times I saw her over the entire semester. The pain was lessening some, but it was turning into the anger and frustration that went along with having no closure. What was I supposed to do? There was no way I could move forward with the rest of my life without knowing why things had happened as they had, at least trying to understand.

One night I had gone to Magpie's for dinner. Yes, I know, I must be a masochist. It hurt to sit in that booth, looking across the table at where Dagny should have been. I never really understood why I went in there, except maybe on the off chance that she'd come in. Then what? If she did, what would I say? Anything? I didn't know.

I was writing fairly regularly again, which was good, and as Sam had said, it was extremely helpful, even if the songs were only for me. The crying was also less frequent, thank God. I sat on my bed, back against the wall, my notebook in my lap as I wrote. I stared out the window as I thought about how I felt, or what I might say. Then, like being hit by lightning, the entire thing came to mind. I wrote as fast as I could, which wasn't always as fast as my brain composed. A few minutes and many writing mistakes later, I was finished.

I sat back and read over my creation, trying to think of a name for it. A smile broke out over my face. Maybe I'd even let Sam read this.

* ~ * ~ * ~ * ~ * ~ *

I had to visit Sam on an off day, since I had finals on my regular day and was too brain dead to walk, let alone talk. I worried about possibly bumping into Dagny, but what could I do?

In the waiting room, the little boy sat beside the older woman, his feet dangling several inches above the floor. That jolted me into an awareness of just how little we are when we're kids. Someday that little boy would be taller than I was.

I sat in my usual spot waiting for Sam. The boy watched me intently, and when I got situated, I heard the tiniest little sound. I listened, realizing it was the little ditty I'd been humming the week before. I looked over at him, and the humming stopped. Picking up on the game, I looked away, keeping him in my peripheral vision. I heard the quiet humming again, and his eyes were glued to me. I began to hum along, tapping my toe with the beat. I saw a tiny smile curl the corner of his mouth, then it was gone. As his humming got louder, so did mine. The woman watched us both, a look of astonishment on her lined face.

The boy looked over toward the office doors and abruptly stopped. I turned too, and stopped just as abruptly. Dagny stood in an open doorway, her eyes riveted on us, going to me when she saw I had seen her and was looking at her. She wore a black skirt that reached to just above her knees and a tight knit shirt with capped sleeves. She looked thinner, her hair a little longer. She looked good, but very tired.

We shared the contact for several minutes, neither of us having expected to see the other and neither knowing what to say. I gave her the faintest of smiles, and she returned it, but then she turned around and disappeared into the office.

It was the closest I had been to her since the drive back from Colorado in January. The life and light that I had so loved in her eyes was absent. I was probably just fooling myself, but that's what I saw. I felt my insides gurgling as if I would be sick, and I wasn't sure I could control it.

"Chase?" I looked up, startled. Sam stood at his open door, his brow furrowed. "Are you okay?"

"Uh, yeah." I walked into his office, my notebook in hand. I handed it to him, opened to the appropriate page. "Um, I brought this for you to read."

He took it, still looking at me with concern. "You look like you've just seen a ghost. My God, you're pale." He sat me down on the couch, and I batted his hands away.

"I kind of did." I smiled weakly. "I'm fine. Just read."

He shook his head, then sat in his chair across from me and began to read. I watched the expressions that crossed his features. Finally, he put the notebook down and looked at me. "Chase, this is exquisite work. Is this recent?"

"Yes. I just wrote it about a week ago."

He handed the notebook back, and I tucked it away next to me. "You really should allow others to read your music, Chase. You may have a future in it."

I shook my head. "Nah, I enjoy it, love it, in fact, but I have no interest in making a career out of music. It will always be in my life, but..."

He smiled and nodded. "Probably wise. No matter how intelligent or talented you may be, that sort of business is very difficult to get a proper foothold in."

"Yeah." I looked down for a moment, trying to decide whether or not I should tell him about just seeing Dagny. I did not want him to know who she was, for her privacy as well as my own, but all the same I felt I should tell him I had seen her. "Um, I just saw her. That's what was wrong when I came in."

He nodded. "I figured as much. Is there anything I can do? What are you feeling?"

"I was a little shaken, but I'll survive."

My doctor nodded at me. "Yes, I believe you will, Chase."

"I hope so." I patted my chest. "I hurt so bad, Sam. I hurt here. It's so hollow."

"It will be filled again."

\* ~ \* ~ \* ~ \* ~ \* ~ \*

It was to be our last show of the semester, and for me, the last performance for a while. I planned to go home for a couple weeks, get some distance from the campus and this part of Tucson. I needed to be someplace where there wasn't a memory staring me in the face every time I turned around. My parents' house wouldn't be ideal, but at least I had lived there for eighteen years and had all that familiarity to fall back on.

Sam had talked to me about possibly singing my new song at this last show. I didn't know if I could do that. Not only was it intensely personal, but also I had yet to sing any of my own music in public. I had made copies of the music for the band in case I decided to do it, and knew the song I would cut out of our program to make time for it, too.

As I drove to the bar, I noticed heavy clouds rushing in the late-day sky, turning it a gun-metal gray. A storm was coming. In spite of the threatening weather, we set up in front of a large crowd. It was the first weekend after finals, and everyone needed to just have a good time.

"Hello, and good evening, everyone. Finals are over!" That drew a resounding cheer, and I grinned as I turned toward the band, handing them the music, just in case.

Doug took his copy, finding the melody in his head. He nodded. "This is good stuff, but, um, well, where are the lyrics, Chase?" I smiled as I tapped my head with my finger. "Is this yours?" I nodded; he grinned. "Wow. Cool."

"This is not definite, but maybe, okay? See how much nerve I can get up."

"You got it."

Than securely around my neck, I turned back to the microphone and began the first set. The crowd became rowdier and more responsive the more they drank, and I actually found myself having a good time.

"Thank you! We'll be back." I put Than in her stand and headed to the bar for my water.

"I'm going to miss you guys, Chase," Greg said, leaning over the bar. "You still going to work for me this summer?"

"Hell, yeah. I just need to get out of here for a bit."

The bartender looked at me, then surprised me by patting my arm. "It'll all be better, Chase." He winked at me, then moved off to wait on a customer.

I leaned against the bar, staring out at everyone, trying to see who had shown up. Pretty much the same groups of people and guys playing pool toward the back by the bathrooms. Everything felt all right, as if it were supposed to be happening this way. I didn't know exactly what *everything* was, but I knew I'd be fine. Yeah, right.

The second set was just about to start. Than was around my neck, ready to rock, when I glanced around at the nearly full bar.

There was a small table back by the door, where, to my shock, Dagny sat. She had a mug of beer in front of her. I was shaken. *When the hell did she get here?*

"Ready?" Doug asked, and I nodded, exhaling a very deep breath. The next song was to be a Def Leppard hit, and the music for it had started. I didn't want to sing, just wanted to run, but I knew I couldn't. I had to stay and struggle with my emotions, try to get a semblance of my normal life back, and that meant singing. I began to sing. It was not the best I've ever sung, but I managed to get through it.

My eyes kept drifting to that distant table with its single patron. Dagny's eyes were on me, her face nearly expressionless as she listened. I felt the anger I had been trying to deal with start to bubble up. I felt all the frustration and pain of the last five months coming to a head, and I knew I had to sing the song. I had to let her know how I felt.

"Okay, the next song I'm about to sing for you is, well..." I grinned. "I consider all of you my good buddies now, so here's one I wrote. You be nice to me, now!"

This drew a roar from the crowd, and I smiled. I turned to look at the band, who were all looking at me as if I'd lost my mind, but they were scrambling to get out the music I had given them.

Terrie started out slow with the drums, the only instrument playing. I closed my eyes, holding on to the microphone until it was my turn to start playing.

"This song is called *Should I*," I said, my voice breathy. My eyes still closed, I began to sing.

> *Behind closed lids*
> *We both feel the same*
> *You love me or I hate you*
> *At least there's no one to blame*

I started in softly with the guitar, everyone quiet behind me, and in the bar. I took a breath, then continued.

> *It's not just your rejection*
> *That crumples me inside*
> *The tears I shed for you*
> *Serve only to remind*
> *What we had just weeks ago*
> *Was not felt by me alone*
> *But one touch has changed all that*
> *Your eyes to ice, your heart to stone*

As the song picked up in the chorus, I opened my eyes and looked at Dagny, my eyes burning a hole in her. She stared at me, her face intense, but she bit her bottom lip as if she were trying to stay expressionless.

> *I see you peering at me*
> *Across the width of fence*
> *Your eyes filled with wonder*
> *Your body so tense*
> *Your face next to mine*
> *Now what should I do?*
> *With the touch of your lips*
> *I was gone...and so were you*

I said the last line slow and deliberately. The crowd went nuts; Dagny didn't move an inch. I continued, the music coming down to just Terrie and me again.

> *Sometimes it gives me pause*
> *Would it be simpler to forget*
> *That few seconds of bliss*
> *Silence turned into regret*
> > *I see you peering at me*
> > *Across the width of fence*
> > *Your eyes filled with wonder*
> > *Your body so tense*
> > *Your face next to mine*
> > *Now what should I do?*
> > *With the touch of your lips*
> > *I was gone...and so were you*

As the band played, I stepped back from the microphone, lifting my head in defiance. I would not be torn apart by this. I closed my eyes as I lost myself in the music, playing Than for all I was worth before stepping back up.

> *Do I chalk it up*
> *To a year-long mistake?*
> *Move on with my life*
> *Let the memories fade?*
> *Or do I give you control*
> *That which you always had*
> *The key to my heart*
> *For good or for bad*
> *With the touch of your lips*
> *I was gone...and so were you.*

"I was gone," I looked right into Dagny's eyes, "and so were you."

The bar was as silent as a tomb as the words and their powerful message seeped into alcohol-saturated brains. Dagny pushed back her chair, a horrible screech echoing through the silence as the wooden legs scraped along the wood planks. She looked at me for a moment, then turned and stormed out of the bar.

I threw Than's strap off my neck and handed the guitar to whoever was standing there before I raced after her.

I burst through the bar door and saw Dagny standing in the middle of the parking lot, not far from me, her back to the building. I stared up into the sky at the rain that was coming down in torrents. "Why did you sing that?" she asked, her voice low, muffled by the rain.

"Why not?"

"Leave it to you to make a slap in the face sound so poetic."

"It wasn't meant as a slap. I had no idea you'd be here." That was a lie. I hadn't even known if I'd sing it or not. *Turn around, Dag, I need to see your face.* Perhaps she heard my plea. She turned around, and I saw how her eyes glistened, but I couldn't tell if it was from the light or from...something else.

"What do you want from me? What do you expect from me?" Her voice rose as she spoke, her body tensing.

"I don't want anything from you," I said, my voice low, dangerous. "I did not ask you to come here. I have not asked anything from you or of you."

"Why did you kiss me, Chase? What happened back in that cabin?"

Tears. I could tell Dagny was crying. They were falling and mingling with the raindrops. I felt my own eyes stinging, but was not about to give her the satisfaction. Not anymore.

"I didn't kiss you, Dagny. I don't know what happened. It *just* happened. That's life."

"I don't know what to do, Chase. I'm so goddamned confused."

"*You're* confused?" My anger was rising. "What the hell do *you* have to be confused about, Dag? Personally, I wanted that kiss to happen. There, I said it." I looked away, then back. "I didn't mean for it to happen, though. That had not been my intention — to go with you to the remote woods of Colorado and then seduce you! God, give me more credit than that."

"I never thought that, Chase. Honest. I just...I wanted it, too!" Her words echoed in my head, leaving me stunned with my mouth open. Dagny threw her hands up into the air in exasperation. "My whole life I've wanted what my parents have. I wanted a love that strong, someone to love me like no one else ever had." She looked at me, cocking her head to the side. "And it was right before me all along. I don't understand it, Chase, but it was there. *You* were there."

I could only stare, shell-shocked and too afraid to say anything. "I can't do this again, Dag. I cannot go through this with you again."

She smiled, shaking her head as if she hadn't heard me. "You know, I always thought I was the strong one — independent, intelligent, driven, you name it. And look at you, the willpower and strength all along."

She took a step toward me; I took one back. I didn't trust her, didn't trust what I was feeling.

"All these months that we've been apart, I've been thinking, discovering. Before the break I was getting to a point where I couldn't imagine life without you in it. I loved having you in my apartment, snuggling up with me in my bed, keeping me warm." She smiled weakly. "I needed you. These past months I wanted to see if I could live without you, if I could just pick up where I had left off, lose myself in school and work, in life." She shook her head. "I couldn't do it, Chase. Sure, I was fine, but there was something huge, something monumental missing." She took another step forward; this time I held my ground. When she looked up at me, she was standing no more than six inches away.

"Why are you doing this, Dag?" I asked, my voice hoarse. "I can't do this again, can't allow you to fuck with my head again."

"I can't guarantee you that I won't hurt you again, Chase, or that you won't hurt me. But I want to try. I've realized that I don't want a life without you in it. You *are* my life." Her eyes pleaded with me. "Don't you see?" She placed her hand on my chest. "I want to be in here."

I almost smiled at the irony. Just hours earlier I was telling Sam how much my heart hurt, and now it hurt because it felt like it was about to explode with hesitant hope.

She placed my hand over her heart. "Say yes," she whispered. "Please, say yes."

I stared into her eyes, tears running freely down my face, as they were down hers. I couldn't find my voice for a moment; I nodded, and she smiled. "Yes."

Dagny dropped my hand and threw herself into my arms. I closed my eyes, squeezing them tight as it felt like everything in my life had just clicked into place, as if I had found me again.

"I'm so sorry, Chase," she whispered into my ear. I nodded against her neck.

Dagny pulled away and looked up into my eyes, caressing my cheek, pushing a few wet strands away from my face. She placed the softest of kisses on my lips. I tensed for a moment, then relaxed. She came back for another small kiss, then pressed her lips more firmly to mine, holding us together before her head tilted slightly to the side, mine following suit. I felt her hand wrap around my neck, her arm encircle my waist. My lips opened just the slightest bit, allowing our lips to fit together perfectly. Then to my surprise, I felt hers open a bit more, and a very tentative wetness brushed against my lips. I opened for her, allowing her tongue to explore.

My arms pulled her to me, our bodies pressed tightly together. I shivered as our tongues touched, slowly gliding against each other, making a promise in that kiss.

I felt Dagny's hands begin to run up and down my back and we slowly pulled apart, staring into each other's eyes, silently communicating all that we weren't ready to say. Dagny fell against me with a sigh that I imagined was partly contentment and partly relief. I held her tight, reveling in the feel of her, knowing that she felt it too, and that she accepted it.

"Come home with me?" She smiled at my look of confusion. "Just to sleep. I'm cold." I grinned, and nodded.

As we headed for Freud, I turned to see that the bar door was open and a group had gathered to watch us. Someone was herding everyone back inside, and then turned to look at me. Terrie winked, then closed the door behind her. I smiled, shaking my head.

Dagny pulled out of the parking lot, smiling over at me as she held my hand in hers on her thigh. I smiled back, squeezing her hand. The lights of Gotfry's disappeared in the rearview mirror.

# Chapter 11

Entering the apartment I felt as if I were coming home. Nothing had changed since I'd been there last, yet so much was different.

Dagny stood in the middle of the room and looked at me, her wet clothes clinging to her body, her hair pushed away from her face. I could hear the rain still falling outside. "What do we do now?" I asked, my voice quiet. I held my breath, a terrible feeling inside me just waiting for her to start laughing, telling me this was some elaborate hoax. God, please, no.

"I don't know," she said, just as quietly.

She was the same person I had fallen for, the same person I wanted in my life forever, but she had also changed. It seemed as if she had become impossibly more mature, more wise over the past five months. I saw an old soul standing before me, her eyes deep and filled with knowledge. She came to me and took me in her arms, laying her head on my shoulder. I held her close, my eyes closing as I thought about all the what ifs. Neither of us said a word as we hugged, both reveling in the feel of things returned.

The embrace ended, and Dagny stepped back, her hands slowly trailing down my arms, and then the contact was broken. I stared at her, looking into tired eyes. She smiled; I smiled back.

"It's been a long day. Um, are you interested in going to bed?" She looked hopeful, nervous, like she was afraid I'd tell her to go to hell. I nodded; she sighed. "Okay, good. Um, well," she glanced toward the doorway to her bedroom, "you're welcome to come in there with me, if you want. I mean, if you don't want to, I'd completely understand, but I'd like you in there."

I smiled, completely charmed by this precious woman. "No, I'll join you."

"Good. Okay, um, well, shall we?"

*~*~*~*~*~*

Feeling a weight on my chest, I opened my eyes. Dagny was lying on me, her face buried against my neck, her breathing deep and even. We had slept like this many times, but this morning as I ran my fingers through her hair, it took on an entirely new meaning for me. She felt the same way I did.

I smiled and pulled her a little closer, her body instinctively cuddling closer to my warmth. The morning sun streamed in through the blinds. Staring up at the ceiling, I thought of Natalie. Maybe she had something with this God stuff. I mean, apparently someone up there saw fit for my life to not be miserable. I chuckled at the thought. Natalie would be so proud.

"What are you laughing about? Are the voices talking to you again?"

Green eyes were peering at me from beneath tousled bangs. I grinned and nodded. "You know it. They're telling me that I should be in charge of the world and cause mass destruction and chaos."

"Ah, I see. Sorry, there are others out there who already have that job." She pushed herself up so her head rested on her hand, and she stared down at me.

I started to feel uncomfortable under the intense scrutiny. "What?"

She shook her head. "Nothing. Just looking, still not quite sure of what's happening." She smiled shyly. "You know, when I went into Gotfry's last night I had no intention of anything happening, or really even talking to you."

"So why did you go?" I asked softly, reaching up to play with a strand of hair that was sticking straight up in the air from sleep.

"To indulge in a passion that I hadn't in too long."

"What was that?"

"Listening to you sing."

I suddenly felt painfully shy. "Really?"

"Really."

She leaned down and gave me the softest of kisses. I looked at her as if she were the savior of my life, the love I had no idea existed. I had never felt so corny in my whole life, having always thought that all those sappy commercials and movies were just created from the imagination of Hollywood. Who knew?

"I bet this time yesterday you didn't think you'd be doing that, did you?" I asked with a grin.

She shook her head. "Um, that would be a no."

"Are you glad?"

Dagny nodded, stroking my face with the backs of her fingers.

I had been ruled by different factors at various times in my life: my parents, greed, hunger, and my passion for music. But never in any sort of relationship outside of family and Carrie, had I been ruled by just a look or a touch. As I lay there with Dagny, I found that I'd do just about anything for her, and I had the distinct feeling that as time went on, I would do *anything*. Why was that? I didn't understand.

In all the songs I had written, not one of them was about love, or how love touches your soul and makes you want to sing, yadda, yadda. My songs were always dark and about how life can affect you, not about love. I never understood why so many movies and songs were written about this unfathomable emotion. But now, as I looked into the face of the most beautiful woman I had ever known,

I finally got it.  Now I could be a sap along with the rest of the world.  Go me.

"Um, Chase?"

"Yes?"

"Would it be okay if I start swimming again?"

"Can I go with you?"

"Please."

I grinned.  "I'll kick your ass in laps today."

* ~ * ~ * ~ * ~ * ~ *

I was beating myself up for telling my parents that I would be staying at home for a couple weeks.  Now that was the last thing I wanted to do.  I found it ironic in the extreme that the reason I had decided to go was the same reason I now wanted to stay.

Dagny was in my dorm, helping me pack up my stuff, and Natalie was sitting on her bed, grinning.  In a rare few minutes without Dag, I had managed to fill Natalie in on the events of last Friday.  That is, I told her Dag and I had managed to patch things up.  Natalie had been a wonderful friend, surprising me on several occasions, but I still did not feel comfortable telling her the *exact* status of things.  She was thrilled nevertheless, and I thought her face would split open with the size of her grin.  I'd asked her to keep her mouth shut, and she hadn't said a word, but the way she kept looking from Dagny to me and back again said it all.  When Dag turned her back, I'd glare, which only earned me a bigger smile.

"So, what are your plans for the summer, Natalie?" Dag asked as she started taking down my posters.

"Well, for the first time I'll be going on our annual retreat without my parents."  My roommate smiled proudly.  "However, this time it won't be in Montana, as it has been since I was twelve.  I'll be heading to South Africa."  She sat back on her bed with a brilliant smile.

"That is so interesting," Dagny said, turning to look at Natalie, then sitting on the edge of her bed to ask her questions about it.

I had heard about the entire project several times, and continued to pack as they talked.  My mind wandering, I thought about my own family.  Should I tell them about Dagny and me?  Was there enough to tell them yet?  What did I tell them — I had fallen in love with my former babysitter?  Before, there was nothing to tell.  But now...

The thought of letting my parents know anything had not even occurred to me until last night when I had been curled up with Dag.  We had discussed my staying at her place over the summer and me not even bothering to get a dorm room for my class, which would start up in about a month.  I was surprised when she broached the subject, but happily agreed.

I could not get enough of Dagny — her touch, her mind, the sound of her voice. We had not been apart for more than an hour in the week since our reconciliation. If this was what life loving a woman could be like, count me in. Never, even in the earliest stages of Mike's and my relationship, had I ever felt this way. I had never felt so connected to him. Granted, Dagny and I had been friends first, for nearly two years, and Mike and I had just started to date outright. Even so, this was different.

* ~ * ~ * ~ * ~ * ~ *

I sat on the couch, my legs stretched out in front of me as I dug into my Styrofoam container of beef fried rice from Lucky Kitchen, one of the Chinese food places on campus. Dag tore into her lemon chicken. I frowned as I thought about the question of telling my parents. I knew the time was coming. In just the short time since Dag and I had confessed our feelings for each other, things were already speeding forward at an incredible rate, feelings and emotions becoming all encompassing, leading to the inevitable — Dagny being the center of my world for a very long time to come.

"Dag?"

"Yeah, babe?"

I looked at her, a smile spreading across my face. *Did she just call me "babe"? That is so sweet.* I had found myself wanting to call her some pet names, the words just on the tip of my brain but unable to get out.

"Chase?"

"Oh, sorry. Anyway, I've been thinking about something."

Dag put her container of chicken aside and leaned toward me, her hand on my thigh, her chin resting against her other hand. "What's that?"

God, when she looked at me like that, I just melted. "About my parents." I set my lunch aside. "I wonder if I should tell them."

"Tell them what?"

"Well, you know, about," I gestured at her, then at myself, "us." I had gone home for the hiatus two days earlier, but had managed to invent an excuse to return tonight. I only wished I could stay overnight, but I had no idea what lie I could come up with to explain that kind of time away.

"Oh." Dag leaned back, sitting up straighter. "Oh." She looked around the room, now with my two guitars leaning against the wall by the fireplace and some other things that belonged to me littering the room.

"What do you think?" I turned so I was facing her, reaching out to play with the hem of her tee shirt.

She looked at me, then sighed with a nod. "Well, obviously it's up to you, Chase, but I think they have a right to know, you know?"

"Yeah. Kind of what I was thinking."

I couldn't keep the smile off my face. She smiled back. Even though I knew what the situation between us was, still, every day there were thoughts and feelings running through my head that I didn't understand, that I didn't know what to do with. Like a boy just going through puberty and discovering the wonderful world of girls, I was excited and overwhelmed. Nothing had really happened between us, just a kiss here and there. Neither of us was ready to take it any further, yet.

"I guess I should tell my folks, too." She ran a hand through her hair, then reached down and took my hand. She gently brushed the tips of her fingers over my fingernails and the skin on the back of my hand. Like whisper touches. I loved it when she did that. "Chase?"

"Yeah?"

"When did you know, about me. I mean, when you figured out how you felt...you know."

I nodded. "Yeah, I know. Well, let's see here." I stared up at the ceiling, and only moments later Dagny climbed into my lap, her head resting against my shoulder. I straightened my legs to give her more room to cuddle up to me. Wrapping my arms around her, I laid my chin on the top of her head as I thought. "I'd have to say pretty soon after Christmas."

"Last Christmas? As in six months ago?" Dag looked at me, surprised.

I grinned and shook my head. "Nope. Before that. The first Christmas you went home with me."

Her eyes widened. "Really? That long ago?" I nodded again. "Wow. I'm stunned."

"Why so surprised? I was quite taken by you, strutting around my parents' pool in that little Speedo bathing suit."

"Hey!" She smacked me on the arm. "I was not strutting."

"Well, it was that moment that you snared me, Dag. God, you were so beautiful."

"Thank you," she said quietly, then she became silent. It was killing me, wondering when it had been for her. "You know, I think for me it had been building for a while. I can't really say when. See, at first, I felt protective of you, still seeing you as that little girl from so long ago." She began to pet my arm as she spoke, snuggling her body in a little closer. "Then somewhere along the way I realized that you were a young adult, not a kid anymore, and then I got to know you for who you were, who you've become. Certainly not the skittish kid I knew." She chuckled softly. "Suddenly you became a close friend, someone I began to trust, then rely on." She turned her head to look at me. "Thank you, Chase."

"For what?"

"For being who you are, for being what I didn't realize I needed."

She leaned up and kissed me on the lips, holding the kiss for just a moment, then backing away. My eyes opened, and I saw her gazing at me, the softest expression on her face as she looked into my eyes, at my mouth and the rest of my face. "You know, when I signed up for college this definitely wasn't what I was expecting, but I'm glad I got it."

"You are?" I asked, my eyes wide.

She laughed. "Yup. I am. Anyway, I guess when it really hit me was just before Christmas this last year. I mean, before then I knew something was going on. I was noticing you in ways that I wasn't real comfortable with. Remember all of our swimming sessions?"

"Yes," I drawled.

"Well, um, I have a confession to make." She looked down for a moment, a smile on her lips. "Um, I thought you were hot in your swimsuit." Finally she looked back up at me, then burst out laughing. "Close your mouth, you'll catch flies."

My jaw snapped shut. "You pervert," I chastised with a smile.

"I know, I know. Bad Dagny, bad Dagny. Hey, I couldn't help it, okay? It's your fault; you're so damn hot!"

"Well, you know, I just can't help that fact, and as much as I'd love to take the credit for it, I'm afraid that honor belongs to my parents." We both laughed at that. "Besides, you're the beauty here, not me."

"God, we are sappy, aren't we?"

"Yup. Did you ever think that would happen to you?"

"No."

"Good. Me either." I looked at her for a moment, then decided to risk asking the question that had been bothering me for a long time. "Dagny, what happened at the cabin in Colorado?" She looked at her hands for a long moment and sighed. "Hey, if you don't want to talk about it..."

"No. You have every right to ask, Chase." She looked at me, then reached up to caress my cheek. "That really hurt you, didn't it?" I looked down, refusing to acknowledge just how deeply her abandonment had cut. "When I saw you at the counseling center, I was confused and worried, but didn't dare ask you. I was afraid you'd tell me to go fuck myself, which you would have had every right to do, by the way." She smiled and I smiled back, though mine was weak. "I wondered if your sessions were because of me, then I deemed myself not worthy enough to send you into therapy, so I discarded the entire idea."

I finally looked at her. "I had to try and understand." My voice was small; I felt small.

"Had to understand what, honey?" She brought her hand under my chin and lifted my head so she could look into my eyes.

"I had to know why our friendship had ended, what was wrong with me."

"So you did go to see Roth because of me." I nodded. "Oh, Chase." She gathered me into her arms and I felt wetness against my neck. "I'm so sorry. God, I had never meant to hurt you like that, babe. Please believe that," she cried, pulling me almost painfully close to her. "I was so selfish. I needed to figure myself out, and while I was doing that I disregarded what you might be feeling. I'm so sorry."

I wrapped my arms tightly around her, trying to hold the tears inside. I had cried enough, and didn't want to anymore. I didn't need to. "Don't cry, Dag. It's okay." I cradled her head and let her cry, though each tear broke my heart a little. "It's okay."

"No, it's not." She pulled away, her eyes wet, face red. "Chase, I hurt you so badly. I pulled away from you at the cabin because it all hit too close to home. My feelings for you were nearly out of control, which scared me. I knew I was attracted to you, but just didn't know if I had the courage to accept that. What I said at Gotfry's was true: I wanted that kiss. Who knows," she smiled through her upset, "maybe subconsciously that's why I brought you all the way out into the wilderness, where we could be alone and be ourselves." She wiped her eyes with the hem of her shirt. "But I am sorry. The human heart is not made to experiment on." She managed a watery smile. "God, how did I get so lucky? I can't even begin to work through all this, yet."

"I know. Me neither." Using a napkin off the table, I wiped away her tears. "My parents raised me to believe one credo: fall in love, get married, procreate."

"Me, too." She laughed nervously. "God, what will my parents say, Chase?"

"I don't know."

"This would be a fine time for them to start caring about what I'm into." She smiled ruefully. "Yeah, right."

"Well you know mine are not only going to care, they're going to have plenty to say about it."

Dagny's face sobered and she cradled my neck. "Oh, Chase. Do you want me to be there with you when you talk to them?"

I took her hand and kissed the palm. "No reason you should be subjected to whatever they throw at me. Besides, I think it will go over better if I do it by myself."

* ~ * ~ * ~ * ~ * ~ *

I hung up the phone and leaned back against the pillows that were stacked up against the headboard. I had been at my parents' house for a week, and it had seemed like an eternity. Dagny and I were on the phone with each other as much as possible, and I occasionally sneaked out at night for a short visit back to campus. I hated that I felt the need to play cloak and dagger, sneaking out like a teenager. But I knew my parents would never understand, and I had not yet found the guts to let them in on my secrets.

Dagny had decided to tell her folks about us the next day, and our most recent phone session had been spent trying to figure out a way to get me away from home so that I could be there with her when she told them. I stared at the cordless that was still in my hand, my heart hurting. I did not want to be here, I wanted to be with her back at school — at Gotfry's, or anywhere else.

I started at the knock on my door. "Come in," I yelled as I tossed the phone aside. My bedroom door opened and Carla peeked around the corner.

"Hey, you. Have you been hiding in here all day?" She opened the door wider and stepped inside.

"Yup," I confirmed. "When did you get here?"

"Like," she glanced at her watch, "three hours ago."

"Oh." I grinned sheepishly. "Sorry." *Was I talking to Dag that long? Oops.*

"So, what's up?" She sat on the bed next to me. "Mom says you're gone most of the time, and when you are here, you're not. You okay?"

"Yeah. I'm fine." I ran a hand through my hair. "So, Mom told you all that within your first three hours home, huh? Gee, I should feel honored that I was the focus of attention."

"Hey, come on. They're just worried about you, Chase."

"Then why don't they just ask me about it?"

"I don't know. Why do they do half the shit they do?"

"Isn't that the truth?" I agreed with a rueful smile. "How are you? Where's Todd?"

"He's in Oregon visiting his folks. We'll catch up in Vegas in a couple weeks to finish out the summer together."

"That sounds like fun." I smiled, imagining Dagny and me there, having fun in the sun. I wished we could redo the cabin thing, spend a romantic weekend there. Shaking myself out of thoughts like that with Carla staring at me, I looked at her. "So what else did the all-knowing Mom and Dad have to say?"

"Stop it, Chase. Don't talk about them that way."

"Is it hard being so virginal all the time?"

"You know what, fuck you, Chase." She stood. "I really don't have to listen to this." She stalked toward the door.

"Wait, I'm sorry." She looked at me over her shoulder; I could tell she was hurt. "That was shitty, and I'm sorry. They just piss me off. Why don't they ever snoop into your business like they do mine?"

She shrugged. "I don't know. I guess because I'm in med school." She grinned sheepishly and I grinned back.

"Guess so. Think I could be your right-hand gal in surgery?"

"See what I can do." She winked and went out the door.

I lay back against my pillows and stared at the phone beside me. I wanted to talk to Dag, felt the need to hear her voice. To my surprise, the phone rang and was picked up on the first ring. I knew that his answering was my father's way of trying to keep me off of it. When my name wasn't called, I figured it wasn't Dagny, and got off the bed to go down and be social.

* ~ * ~ * ~ * ~ * ~ *

My hand on the railing, I paused at the top of the stairs as I tried to think of a good excuse that I hadn't used yet. *I could tell them that I'm going to the library. Yeah, right. I've never read a book voluntarily at home since I was nine. Okay, library's out. How about going to meet with Carrie? No, she went with her parents to Italy for the summer. Um, aw hell. Fuck it.*

I took a deep breath and slunk down the stairs, the front door in my sights. My folks and Carla were watching some medical documentary in the living room, just off to the right of the front door. I had the knob in my hand, just about to turn it.

"Chase? Where are you going?"

*Damn. Busted.* I took a deep breath, screwing up my courage. *Goddamn. I am almost twenty-one years old. Why the hell am I so afraid of these people?* I knew why.

"Out. I'll be back in a bit." I hurried out the door so they couldn't say anything else, reaching my car and quickly starting her up.

Dagny was waiting for me when I walked into the apartment. She offered me an ice-cold can of Dr Pepper and a smile. "Hey, you," she said, her voice low...and I felt it low.

"Hi." I took the soda, but didn't bother to open it as I walked into her arms. I inhaled, taking in her scent. Since we'd been separated so much over the last week or so, I was going through major withdrawal symptoms. Whenever we were together now, I felt her more, saw more each time we were together. It was like I was learning not to take her for granted, trying to take as much from each encounter as I could.

"I missed you," she whispered into my neck, her voice vibrating through my entire body. Her hand ran up my back, then down again, and I closed my eyes, reveling in the touch of the hot skin through the thin material of my shirt.

"I missed you, too," I said, my voice breaking. I heard her chuckle and wondered why, but didn't ask.

Long moments later, Dag stepped back from me and smiled. "I'm glad you were able to get away, Chase."

"Me, too. God, I hate this." I ran a hand through my hair. "I'm not a child anymore, and I resent the fact that I'm being made to feel like one. It almost seems as if they already know and are trying to keep me away from you." I paced back and forth, popping open the can of soda as I did.

"Do you think that's what they'd do if you told them?"

"Hell if I know."

She was sitting on the couch now and patted the spot next to her. "Come here, babe. Sit next to me." I walked over and plopped down, resting my head on her shoulder. "Maybe you should tell them so it's out." She grinned. "No pun intended. It might make you feel better. You think?"

"I really don't know. It worries me. I mean, they've never approved of anything I've ever done, so why would they approve of this?"

"They might surprise you."

I jumped when the phone rang.

"That's probably my folks. My mom said she'd call at this time. She's in England with my father for the summer." Dagny took a deep breath and picked it up. "Hello? Hey, Mom, how are you? ... Oh, Dad's on the line too?" She looked at me, apprehension in her eyes. "Hey, Dad. How are you? ... I'm doing great, wonderfully well, in fact. ... Yes, school was great, and thankfully over with for another year. ... No, it's psychology, not sociology. Yeah, well I know it's been a while since we talked."

I put my hand on Dag's leg, rubbing her thigh as she looked down, her shoulders slumping.

"Yeah, well there was a reason I wanted to talk, yes. Well..." She looked at me to gather her courage, swallowed, then proceeded to update her parents on her life. "I've met someone. ... Yes, thank you. I'm happy, yes. ... Well, you won't believe it, actually. Um," she glanced at me again, "do you remember the year we lived here in Tucson and I babysat the girl down the street? ... Yes, the Marin girl. Well, um, her name is Chase, and well...it's her." I could tell she was holding her breath, so I squeezed her leg, reminding her I was there. She listened for a short time, nodding and saying, "yes, I know" and "okay" once in a while, then she hung up.

"That's it?" I looked at her, wondering what the hell. She gently set the phone on the coffee table and sat back on the couch, staring straight ahead. "Are you okay, Dag?" She nodded. "Are they okay?" Again, she nodded.

She sighed. "A little too okay."

"What did they say?"

"That's great, honey. Be careful. You do know diseases are easily spread. We'd like to see Chase again, and how were your grades?"

She finally looked at me, and I could see the pain in her eyes. Nevertheless, I couldn't help but hope that it would go that easily with my parents. "I'm sorry, Dag." I put my hand on her arm, not sure what she wanted me to do. Did she need to be comforted?

She fell over against me, her fingers clutching the sleeve of my shirt. "Can I ask you a question, Chase?"

"Of course."

"Do you think I'm worth more? More than just a cursory phone call, and endless trust that I'll do the right thing?" I looked at her, not sure what she was asking. When I didn't say anything, she looked at me. "Am I? Do you care?"

"Oh, Dag, of course I do." I caressed her face, pushing strands of hair behind her ear.

"Why don't they care about what happens in my life? I just told them that I was with a woman, that you and I, well, we're..." Her brows knit together. "What are we?"

"I don't know. I've wondered that, too." I smiled, so did she.

"Well, whatever we are, my parents don't care. Why aren't I good enough for them to care about?"

"Oh, Dag! God, you deserve so much more than that." I pulled her to me and cradled her against my chest. "You are my everything; you got that? Your parents may have messed up priorities, but they do love you, Dagny. They honestly do, they just trust you completely." She chuckled a little at that but said nothing. "Were you nervous about telling them?"

She nodded against my neck. "Imagine that."

"Hey, you didn't know for sure how they'd react. You're strong, Dag. I know you're hurt right now, but what does it matter when it comes down to it? You've done your own thing your whole life; why would you stop now?"

Dagny took deep breaths and gently pulled away, staring up into my eyes. "Thank you, Chase." She cocked her head to the side. "This may sound stupid or corny, but sometimes I honestly wonder how I've made it all this time without you."

Embarrassed, I didn't meet her eyes, taken aback by the tremendous compliment. No one had ever said anything like that to me before. Generally I was a hindrance, not an asset. "Thank you," I whispered.

Dagny moved in and left a soft kiss on my forehead. "Anytime."

\* ~ \* ~ \* ~ \* ~ \* ~ \*

Back at home, I thought about what Dagny had done. Despite her parents' apparent indifference toward her life, I had been impressed with the ease with which she'd told her parents about us. It took guts, guts that I had yet to find. And it made me realize just how seriously Dagny took this, took us. We hadn't told any of our friends about it, well, other than those who saw the whole parking lot exhibition on that rainy night at Gotfry's.

I thought a lot about Dagny, a lot about what I was setting myself up for. Carrie hadn't ever discussed her bisexuality with her parents. I wasn't sure how much they knew about her past, but I did know they were thrilled with her choice in Paul and had embraced him like a son. My parents had embraced Dagny in much the same way, but that had been before. Would they make her pay the same price I felt I would have to pay?

Two long days went by. Dagny was with Levy at a weekend conference for grad students that I could not attend with her. Not even being able to talk with her had been absolute torture, and I had walked around the house like a zombie. My family couldn't understand what was wrong with me. When they realized there wouldn't be a straight answer forthcoming, they finally stopped asking. Part of me felt bad. I knew they just wanted to help, but I wasn't ready to talk about it.

Different possibilities paraded through my mind. How would they react to the news that my former babysitter and I were an item? I had mentioned my breakup with Mike in passing, but hadn't gone into any real detail. My mom would ask once in a while what had really happened, but I just told her that his direction in life was starting to bother me and I didn't want to go that way. She was thrilled at that answer, but as much truth as there had been in that explanation, it was not the whole truth. I knew even then that he wasn't what I wanted. The writing had been on the wall; I just hadn't gotten out my reading glasses yet.

My mom managed to get my father to take a day to go exploring around the Arizona countryside to take some pictures. As usual, Carla and I were not invited. We decided to have a pool party for two. It was hot, mid-May, and already summer temps were showing themselves. We cleaned the pool, actually having a great heart-to-heart in the process.

"Are you excited to be marrying Todd?" I asked, skimming the deep end as Carla worked on the shallow.

"Absolutely. But I'm also very nervous." She smiled. "It's terrifying to think of spending the rest of my life with just one person. Not that there's a line waiting at my door, but it's just such a strange concept." She stopped for a moment, staring up into the blue sky as she thought about her own words.

"How did you know, Carla?"

"Know what? That Todd was the one?" I nodded. "That's a good question. To be honest, I didn't especially like him at first. I thought he was a total drag." She grinned at the memory. "He didn't like to have fun, didn't like to go out or anything. But I decided to give him a chance, and he is very intelligent. Major turn on for me."

"Did it make up for the boredom?" I grinned evilly.

She glared at me. "Be nice. He can be fun once in a while. I've just learned to tone myself down." She started skimming again. "So, what about you? I know Mike is history, so who else is on the horizon? If I didn't know better, I'd say your moping around here these last couple weeks is either because you're missing someone or wishing you had a certain someone. So, out with it."

"Nice choice of words," I muttered.

"What?"

"Nothing. Well, truthfully, there *is* someone, but I don't think Mom and Dad would approve."

"Why?"

"Well, let's just say this person isn't what they would have selected for me." I looked at my sister, so badly wanting to be able to trust her, talk to her. I was proud of my relationship with Dagny and was pissed off I had to hide it.

"Hello?"

The familiar voice sounded at the back gate. My face lit up when I saw Dag, hopping up to try and see over the tall stucco fence.

"Hey!" I dropped my skimmer and ran over to unlatch the gate and let her in.

"I had to see you," she whispered.

"I'm so glad you did," I whispered back.

"Dagny? Hey, how's it going?" Carla smiled and joined us. "Long time, no see."

"Yeah. Glad to be home?" The three of us walked toward the back door of the house.

"Oh, yes. I really miss this hot weather at school. How on earth anyone can live where the weather is even the slightest bit inclement, I'll never understand." She smiled. "I just made some lemonade. You guys game?"

"Please," Dagny begged, wiping sweat off her forehead. My sister hurried into the house, and Dag turned to me. "I have missed you so much, Chase. This weekend nearly killed me."

"God, me too. How did you get back so early?" I tugged her arm and led her a little ways away from the house.

"I skipped the last lecture, telling Levy I had to go to work."

"Dag!"

"I had to see you."

I pulled her into a crushing hug, feeling like I hadn't seen her in months when it hadn't even been a full 48 hours. The hug ended and I leaned in. Her lips were soft beneath mine. It always amazed me and turned me on. Dagny's mouth opened slightly, welcoming me, and I took it. My tongue slid slowly between her lips into the warmth of her mouth and I heard the tiniest bit of a moan, so tiny I wasn't even sure it had been there.

Realizing where we were, I quickly ended the kiss, trying to get my breathing under control. "Um, I'm glad you're here," I said, smiling shyly.

"Me, too."

* ~ * ~ * ~ * ~ * ~ *

The next day, I sat on my bed, thinking about the time I'd spent with Dag and my sister. We'd had a fantastic time. Carla loaned Dagny a suit, and we swam all afternoon, splashing and laughing. My sister and I hadn't had such quality time together since before we'd understood what sibling rivalry meant.

Dag's appearance at the gate had been a total surprise, and it made my heart soar. *She really likes me.* When she was ready to leave, I walked her out to Freud, and we leaned against the SUV and talked. On Friday I was to head back to school in time for my show at Gotfry's, then the rest of the summer was mine. Yay! The stupid smile wouldn't leave my face.

I jumped when my bedroom door burst open, and my father stood there, his blue eyes, so much like my own, electric and on fire.

"Come downstairs now," he said, and walked away.

I was stunned, broadsided. *What the hell was that about?* I rose from the bed and ran a nervous hand through my hair as I made my way downstairs.

"Don't do this, Mom. Please." Carla was crying.

*Uh oh.* My stomach began to churn, and the hair on the back of my neck stood on end.

"Shut up, Carla. Your part in this is finished." My mother had also been crying, and her voice was harsh and thick.

"What's going on?" I asked as I rounded the corner to the living room. Carla and my mother sat on the couch, my father paced behind them.

"I should ask you the same thing," he said.

"I thought I had raised two daughters," my mother nearly growled.

Stunned and confused, I could only stare at her. *What the hell?*

"Instead I find out I have raised one daughter and a sick pervert. It's no wonder you want to go into psychology; you can work closely with those like you."

I felt like I had been socked in the gut. *Do they know?* "What the hell are you talking about?" I felt tears spring to my eyes at the venom just spewed by my own mother, but I was not about to give her the satisfaction of knowing how deeply she had hurt me.

"Carla told us," my father said, coming out from behind the couch to stand in front of me. "You and that...Jezebel. And to think we welcomed her into our home. It's disgusting."

My eyes swept the confines of my hell until I spotted Carla, looking away from the confrontation, crying silently. "Carla? What did you do?" What had she told them? What had she seen? And who the hell was Jezebel?

"I'm sorry, Chase. I was trying to help you."

"Help me? Jesus Christ, Carla, just how do you figure that!" I roared, a tempest of emotions surging to the surface.

"Carla saw you and that...that *female* kissing," my mother said, moving from the couch to stand next to my father, a united front against me. "How could you? You took our trust, and you violated it, twisted our love for you into something vile. How could you, Chase?" She grimaced. "Even saying your name puts a horrible taste in my mouth. Like gangrene, your poison must be excised." I stared at my mother, shocked at what I saw in her eyes. "You disappoint me. You make me sick; I wish I had only had one child."

I wanted to vomit. How could one person bring you down so low that you felt you were looking up at the carpet fibers? I felt like everything I had been working for over the past two years had just been blown out the window, as if none of it mattered, none of it was good enough for her. For her. My entire life, my mother had been the one to hold me back, to try and keep me down. My anger grew, exploding into colors behind my eyes.

"We send you to school, we clothe and feed you, give you everything your heart desires." She continued, "All we asked in return was that you to go out into the world and do us proud, make good with the talents you were blessed with." She trembled with emotion and rage. "Why couldn't you just do what you were supposed to? Why couldn't you just be like..."

She stopped herself, and I defiantly lifted my gaze to meet her eyes. "Like who? Carla? Your perfect little angel?" I glared over at my sister. "And you," I took a step toward her, "what the fuck were you thinking? Are you a spy for her now?" I hooked a thumb toward my mother. "Do you really want to be as pathetic as that? You want to know something, Carla? You're like her already. You're a clone, doing exactly what mommy and daddy want you to do with your life. Just yesterday you told me that you even changed yourself for Todd. How does it feel? Is it worth it?" I turned on my parents. "What can be so special about Carla when there is no Carla?"

"Chase!" my father bellowed. "Don't you dare talk to her that way. This isn't about Carla."

I looked at him. "Go ahead, Dad. Stick up for her again. You stand there, your face red, trying to play a part for your wife. Carla's right, as always. She's perfect, as always. And of course it's not about her. She does no wrong. That's my job." I took a step toward him. "You're no different. You know, there was a time when we were close, Dad. Remember when we'd get up early to make breakfast in bed for Mom? Remember those days?"

He looked at the floor, then at me. "It didn't have to be this way, Chase." His voice was low, on the verge of cracking.

"You're right, it didn't, but you don't have any more of a spine than Carla does. You've let her," I gestured dismissively at my mother, "warp you. You're a jellyfish!"

His hands balled into white-knuckled fists at his side, the veins in his neck bulging. "How dare you, you ungrateful child."

"I'm so sorry, Chase. I never meant for this to happen," my sister cried.

My head whipped in her direction. "Then why the fuck did you open your fucking mouth?"

I had a feeling that this was it, my family was breaking apart. I was the piece that would be breaking off, so what did I have to lose? I turned back to my mother. "My whole life you have told me I was not worthy of the Marin name; I was not worthy to be your daughter. Never, ever was I good enough. I was the disappointment of your life!" I took a step toward her and my mother actually took a step back. God, that felt good — to know I had control for once. "I wanted to be loved by you guys; I tried to be everything you wanted me to be. I tried to be fucking Carla! I'm not. I am Chase." I pounded my chest. "You said you gave me everything my heart desired? That's fucking bullshit! All I ever wanted from you was love and acceptance, but you never gave me that!"

"Despite all the times you disappointed us as you were growing up, I loved you," my mother cried.

"I sure saw that every day of my life." My voice dripped with sarcasm.

"What did I do so wrong that resulted in the creation of something like you, to raise a queer?" my mother spat.

"That is the only thing you *ever* did right, Mother. Congratulations," I said with just as much venom. "You wonder why I went into psychology? Well, let me enlighten you. I went into it to maybe be able to figure out what the hell crawled up your ass and died. I wanted to know why you are such an unbearably negative person and hate yourself so much that you have to let it bleed over into the lives of your kids."

"Give me your keys."

Without a word, I bolted up the stairs and burst into my room.

My body was buzzing with adrenaline, but I stopped for a moment and looked around. This was the first room I'd ever known, where I had slept my first night home from the hospital. The decor was now that of a high school girl, but the feel and memory was still there, and it was still strong. The journal that Dagny had given me was lying on the bed, and I grabbed it along with my keys, and the suitcase that had never been fully unpacked. Maybe somehow I'd unconsciously suspected that when I told them about Dagny and me, this would be the outcome.

My father was sitting next to Carla, comforting her, but my mother had not moved. I thrust the keys at her, my chin raised in defiance. She took them, found the house key and took it off, then tossed the ring back at me.

"You are no longer welcome here. Let that," her mouth pursed in disgust, "lesbian bitch of yours take care of you now."

I stared her right in the eye. I wanted her to know that no matter what happened to me once I left this house, my childhood home, she would not bring me down. At least not in her presence.

"Well," I took a deep breath, the enormity of what had just happened sinking in, "you've finally done it, haven't you? You've finally gotten rid of the scourge of the Marins. I hope you're happy."

I felt the smooth leather of the journal in my hand and brought it up for my mother to see. "Do you see this? This book is filled with thoughts and feelings from my entire life. Remember those poems I used to bring home for you to read when I was a kid, the great big shiny stars on the tops from my teachers? The ones you threw away, saying they would never get me anywhere?" My voice dropped to a level that was scaring even me. "I kept writing, my entire life. I wrote about how you made me feel less than human. I never shared any of it with you. Or you." I looked at my father, who I knew once upon a time would have enjoyed them. "You weren't good enough to hear them. So instead, that *lesbian bitch* listens to them. She hears me out, and accepts me totally. Oh, her and the people at the bar I've been singing at every single Friday night for the last two years." My mother's mouth dropped open, shock and, impossibly, more disgust evident on her face. "Stick that in your annual Christmas letter." I glanced around one last time, then turned and strode out of the house.

My hands were shaking as I tried to unlock my car door, but I finally managed and threw my suitcase and myself inside, sitting behind the wheel with my heart beating in my throat. *My God. I had no idea, I...* I was at a loss for even thought. It was a relief that it was finally over with. I would no longer have to hide Dagny from them, but then again, it was over altogether. My parents had cut me loose.

I snatched the plastic bag I kept for trash off the glove compartment handle, as I finally let go. My stomach emptied itself, throwing out all the pain and hurt along with it, tears springing to my eyes at the force of it.

Finally finished, I tied up the bag and laid my head back against the headrest, still feeing sick but knowing I was through. I glanced around until I spotted the large garbage can sitting next to the garage. With a small smile, I hurried over to it and dumped the plastic bag inside. My last contribution to the Marin family. I got in my car and backed out of the driveway.

# Chapter 12

Somehow I managed to drive to Dagny's apartment without incident. My emotions had caught up with me, and my eyes were red and swollen. I was unspeakably thankful to see Freud in the parking lot. Short of hunting her down, I wasn't sure what I would have done if Dag hadn't been home. I stumbled up the two flights of stairs and reached for the knob, thankful to find that it was not locked.

I stepped into the apartment to find the lights off, save for that of the TV screen. Dagny sat on the couch with her feet on the coffee table. When I cleared my throat, she turned, startled.

"Chase?" She jumped up and hurried over to me. "My God, what happened? Are you okay?" She gathered me in her arms and I sank into them. *My refuge.*

"God, it was so awful," I cried, tears streaming freely down my cheeks. Right then, I didn't care if she saw. My pride fell by the wayside to make way for my broken heart. Dagny held me, rubbing my back in slow rhythmic circles that eventually helped to calm me.

"What happened, baby?" she asked, pulling away just enough to look into my eyes. Her eyes were narrowed with concern, her finger gently brushing away strands of hair stuck to my face with sweat and tears. Now all I needed was blood and the trio would be complete. "Do you want to talk about it?" I nodded, wiping my eyes with my hand. "Come on." She led me to the couch and pulled me down to half lie on her as she stroked my hair. "Talk."

"They know." Dagny was silent, but I could hear her heartbeat, steady and slow.

"Oh. From the look of you, I'm guessing it didn't go over too well."

I shook my head, nuzzling in closer to her, the softness of her breasts under my cheek. "My parents went ballistic. The sad thing is, I didn't even get to tell them."

"How did they find out, Chase?"

"Carla."

"What!" She nearly dumped me off the couch as she jumped up. "What do you mean, Carla?"

"Apparently she saw us kissing. I guess it was the day we all swam." I took a tissue from the dispenser on the coffee table and blew my nose.

"You mean, as in two days ago?" Dag's eyes were on fire. I nodded. "I want to fucking rip her hair out! We had so much fun, then she turns around and fucking stabs you in the back like that?

That little bitch!"

"Whoa, calm down there, captain."

"Chase, don't you see? It's because of her that you're going through this." She looked at me, her arms out wide emphasizing the enormity of Carla's betrayal.

"It would have happened anyway, Dag." Why the hell was I protecting the little bitch?

"Shit." The anger seemed to seep from her as she physically deflated, grabbing me again and pulling me to her. "So, what else happened?"

"My mom took my house key." I lowered my head, feeling the crushing weight of people who refused to understand or see me for me.

"Oh, baby. God, I can't believe this. What's going to happen?"

I shook my head. "I don't know. I guess it's all up to me now. I'm just grateful that this upcoming semester of college is paid for."

"We'll figure it out, Chase, okay?"

I remembered all the things I had said to them, all the things that had been building inside me for so long, and I actually grinned. "I did get my say, though."

"What do you mean, you got your say?" Dag looked at me, unsure, a smile waiting to peek out.

"I told them everything I've felt for my entire life. The way they have shat on me, the dumpster of the family. Wow, did they not like that, but that's life. They've never liked to hear the truth. In fact, they run from it. It's really pathetic. Actually, this has been building for years; it was just a matter of time before it blew up in their faces."

"You may be right, baby." Dagny held me tighter, her face buried against my skin. I felt warm lips on my neck. "I want you to know something, Chase." She pulled away to look into my eyes. "No matter what happens with them, I'm here for you. Okay? We've come too far and struggled too hard to lose this now."

I was immensely relieved. That was exactly what I had needed to hear. I felt so lost. I knew it would really hit me later, but right now I was too busy riding the emotional merry-go-round to really have it hit home. "Thank you."

"Anytime."

Her lips on mine told me it was a promise she intended to keep.

* ~ * ~ * ~ * ~ * ~ *

"Well, Chase, I must say I wasn't expecting to see you here during the summer." Sam smiled at me, patting me on the back as he led me into his office. I sat in my familiar place on the couch, him across from me, automatically crossing his right leg over his left.

"Did I see you walk in with Dagny Robertson?" he asked, taking off his glasses to polish them.

I nodded, trying to hide the ridiculous grin that threatened to break out every time I heard her name. "She's actually the one who got me to come here today."

"Really? Why is that?"

"Well, first off, it's been an interesting couple of weeks. I need to fill you in."

"All right." He sat back, watching me patiently, his hands placed neatly in his lap.

"Do you remember the girl?" This time the grin spread across my face, smooth as butter. He nodded, an anticipatory grin curling up the corner of his mouth. "It, um..." I cleared my throat. Sam was the only person I had actually officially told. "It all worked out, and, um, well, we're together."

He looked at me for a moment, then, completely out of character, sat forward, ready for a session of girl talk. "I must ask you, Chase. Is it Dagny?" The smile again, followed by a blush and a nod. "Oh, that's wonderful." He put his hands together, then patted me on the knee. "I'm so happy for you."

"How did you guess?" I also sat forward, my curiosity piqued. "And, um, well isn't this highly unethical?" I raised an eyebrow.

"Highly, so don't learn a thing from me. And, how did I guess? When I saw you two together a few moments ago, I saw the spark of love passing between you. It's a wonderful communication that can be seen by anyone who has eyes." He sat back in his chair, taking the proper position, and smiled.

"Thanks, Doc. I'll have to remember that." My smile faded as I thought of the other thing that had me sitting on Sam's couch again. I looked down, my fingers beginning to tug and pull at one another nervously.

"Chase?" came his concerned voice.

"Yeah?" I looked up at the face of the doctor I had come to see as a friend.

"Are you all right?"

"I will be, I'm sure." I sat for a moment as I gathered my thoughts and myself. It had been over a week, and it still haunted me: the look in my mother's eyes, the hatred in her voice. I did not understand where it came from or why I was the one to bear the brunt of it. I broke down in tears on an almost daily basis, and Dagny had done her best to try and help me through it — being there for me, listening to me, threatening to beat the crap out of my parents. Nothing worked.

"I want you to see Dr. Roth, Chase. Please?" she had begged. Finally, grudgingly, I had said yes.

Now as the doctor waited patiently for me to explain, I thought about my childhood. I had felt taken care of, safe and settled. But no matter how hard I tried, or how hard I looked back, I had never felt like I belonged. I always felt like an outsider to the clique, the new kid on the block that just didn't look like the others.

"My parents found out about me, about us, last week," I finally muttered. "It didn't go well."

"So, they found this out because you told them?"

I shook my head. "No. My sister saw Dagny and me kissing. Apparently she felt she was helping me out by telling our parents."

"She wanted to tell them for you?"

"Oh, hell, Sam, Carla hates me! She is the absolute joy of my parents' lives, and what better way to secure her place in the family lore as the great white hope and make me look disgusting?" I jumped up from the couch and began to pace the office, finding my way to the window to stare out over the nearly empty campus. "My mother made me give her my house key, and she said some pretty awful things to me."

"How did you react?"

I smiled grimly. "I blew up. I told them everything I had felt and thought for so long. I called my father a jellyfish." I chuckled and looked at the psychiatrist over my shoulder. He was smiling, his fingers thoughtfully stroking his chin. "Did you forget to shave for, like, the last twelve mornings, there, Sam?"

He smiled and nodded. "I'm growing my yearly beard. Soon I'll get tired of it and shave it off."

"I don't get men and their fetish with facial hair. And women liking chest hair. What's up with that?" Sam looked at me like I was crazy. "Sorry. Anyway, I gave my mother the key, said some mean things, and left the house."

"How long ago did this happen?"

"Last Tuesday."

"Your sister?"

"What about her?" I made my way back to the couch and flopped back into the soft cushions. *Why am I here? I really don't want to be talking about this at all.* I liked Sam a whole lot, but I just wanted to push this all down and forget about it. I wanted to attempt to get my own life started with Dagny, finish school, and start carving out my niche.

"Chase?"

I looked at Sam, irritated at being ripped from my reverie. "What?"

"Maybe we should end the session for today. What do you think?"

He leaned forward, smiling at me with understanding. I lowered my head, feeling bad, but nodded. "I'm sorry, Sam."

"Don't be. This is not an easy thing you're going through, hon.

Listen, do you have anyone you can talk to? Anyone, perhaps, who's a little older, that you trust, maybe who has gone through the same thing?" I shook my head. "Well, if you need to talk to someone your own age, let me know. I know a few people." He smiled and stood, as did I.

"Thanks, Sam. I really appreciate what you're trying to do for me. I'm sorry I'm being a pain in the ass."

He patted me on the back as I opened the door to his office. "Don't you worry about it. You're a good kid and deserve better than this."

I snorted. "Says you."

With another pat, he sent me on my way, then called me to him again. "I hear you're a psych major. How far do you plan on taking it?"

"I don't know yet. I just recently figured out that I was a closeted psych major." I smiled and winked.

"Well, if you decide to take it all the way, I'd absolutely love to be your mentor."

A grin spread across my face. "Really?" He nodded. "That's really cool," I muttered. "Thanks, Doc."

* ~ * ~ * ~ * ~ * ~ *

I drove to the apartment, my mind working on what Sam had said. Who did I know that I could talk to? Dag had said something similar, thinking maybe I should talk to someone who had gone through this crap with their family. Where does one go to find such a friend? Advertise in the local paper: Calling All People With Assholes For Parents? Worked for me.

I was ever grateful to whichever god had given me great foresight, however unexpected. I had taken very little with me to my parents' house, since I had only planned to be there for two weeks. Most of my stuff I had left at the apartment. Having grabbed my mostly filled suitcase on my way out, I only lost a few articles of clothing. Better that than Than or Melo. I would have really had to hurt someone, then.

I parked toward the back of the lot at the apartment and took my keys from the ignition, tossing them up in the air and catching them on their descent. They shone in the sunlight, one new key in particular shining the brightest. An instant smile spread across my face as I recalled Dag presenting me with my very own key. I ran my finger over its newly sharpened teeth. How could some aspects of your life be so fucking awful, yet others so incredible they didn't seem real? I didn't get it.

Dagny had gone to work with Levy on a project for the upcoming year. As I looked around the empty apartment, I felt totally at home.  Dagny went out of her way to make it feel as if it were my place, too.  I would start helping her with rent soon.  I still needed to talk with Greg about getting more hours at Gotfry's.  I needed to save up all the money I could for expenses during the year ahead.  I would start my junior year come September.

The energy draining from my body, I plopped down on the couch.  What was I doing?  Was it the right thing?  Why the hell couldn't I just be like everyone else — my parents supporting me in everything that I did.  I knew my mom wanted Carla and me both to get married and give her grandchildren.  We were not kids to her, just trophies.

My hands covered my face, but I was unable to hide from the painful truth that my mother did not love me for who I was.  She loved me for what she could get out of me, how proud I could make her, and how much she could brag to her friends.  How had she become that kind of parent?  And how had my father, a strong man in his own right, allowed her to drag him down just as low?  Carla and I had never had a chance, but he had.  Why did he stay with her?  He was the primary breadwinner, so it sure as hell wasn't for the money.

I felt the tears coming, again.  I had cried more in the past six months than I had in the previous twenty years.  This time, I let them come.  I wanted to wash out all the memories, all the pain and disappointments, all the pressures.  There was absolutely nothing I could do now, outside of maybe turning into mini Carla in the night.  That wasn't going to happen, and I knew it.

Dagny had told me to unpack all my stuff today, to settle in.  So, I swiped impatiently at my eyes and blew my nose, then started the most unpleasant task.  I hated moving, and since I'd started college it seemed as if that's all I had done.

Throughout Dagny's life, her family had moved all over the country, once even doing a nine month stint in Italy when she was a baby.  She was used to packing and unpacking.  I had always lived in the house on Ute Drive, and had lived there until the day I left to live in the dorm at UA.  It was strange to think that I would never live there again, probably never even visit.

I shook the thought out of my mind, put a Melissa Etheridge CD in the stereo, and started in on the first box.  I unpacked it and started on a second, leaving the flattened boxes in the middle of the floor.  I sang along with the lyrics at the top of my lungs, really in the groove, when I came upon some loose papers and trash in one of the boxes.

Sitting on the floor with my legs stretched out in front of me, I began to go through the pile, tossing aside old notes and tests, and scrap pieces of paper with doodles that I could no longer decipher.  Hey, I was a singer, not an artist.  Under the Ayn Rand book, which my mom would never see again, I found a small white card. Picking it up, I realized it was a business card, Jenny Carlson's, and when I flipped it over I saw Joie had written her name also and their home phone number.

Tapping the card against my thumb, my wheels began to turn. I pocketed the card and continued unpacking, trying to find a place for everything. The problem was that the apartment was small, and Dagny and I both hated clutter, so making everything fit was a challenge. Like solving a jigsaw puzzle, I worked steadily throughout the day. I even managed to find a place for my Care Bear, a relic left over from childhood. I stuck him in the fireplace next to Dagny's penguin.

Loaded down with the flattened boxes, I made my way noisily down the flights of stairs to the back door and out to the dumpster, where I disposed of the detritus. Wiping my hands on my shorts, I glanced up at the sky, which was steadily becoming darker. It had taken me nearly six hours to get everything put away.

I leaned against the building, my mind going to Dagny. I knew she'd be home soon, and I couldn't wait to see her. I thought of her face, her eyes, and especially her mouth. My eyes closed as I imagined her kissing me, her lips soft and pliant, on my neck, my shoulders, everywhere. I wanted her so badly my body boiled at least a hundred times a day.

We slept in the same bed every night, our bodies entwined, but I never made a move. I didn't think she was ready for that, and I had no clue what the hell I'd do if given the chance.

"God, make me behave!"

With a very heavy sigh, I pushed off the wall and took the business card out of my back pocket, re-reading it as I made my way inside. My palms were sweaty as I picked up the phone, my eyes locked on the numbers written in blue ink on the card. Would she be mad? Presumably not, otherwise why would she have given me her number? I bit my lip almost painfully hard as I dialed the numbers. It was early evening their time, so I hoped they'd be home.

Ring...

*Am I doing the right thing?*

Ring...

*God, I feel like an idiot.*

Ring...

*Okay, not home.*

I was taking the phone away from my ear when I heard the click of the receiver being picked up.

"Shit." I put the phone back over my ear and heard a woman's voice yelling at someone. "Nate! Let go of the dog, let go, now. Good boy." A sigh. "Sorry about that, whoever you are. Hello?"

I smiled, thoroughly amused. "Um, hi. Is this Joie?"

"Cameron, is that you again? Now, I told you I'd have to bench you if you called for Jenny one more time. She's taken, hon."

I was nearly giggling, at least I was once I got past the surprise. *Wow, what a psycho this Cameron must be.* "Um, well, no. This is Chase Marin." There was silence from the other end of the line. I felt really stupid; Joie obviously had no idea who I was. Why would she? Hell, I'd met her a year ago! "Aw jeez, I'm sorry for bothering you."

"No, no. How goes it, Chase? How's Dagny doing?"

A smile slowly spread. *She remembers me, yahoo!* "Uh, well, I hung in there." I grinned into the receiver.

"You dog! Good for you. So, all's well, then?" I could hear Nathaniel running around and laughing in the background, along with a barking dog. "Wow, it must sound like World War III around here, eh?" She laughed.

I nodded, then realized she couldn't see me. "Yeah. New dog or something?"

"Well, kind of. Anyway, what's up, kiddo? It's great to hear from you. How did it happen?"

I told her the entire story from beginning to finish. Joie made comments or laughed or sympathized as I went along.

"Wow, that is awesome that she finally got a clue. I tell you, when I first saw Jenny at a party...oh man, she had me right there." Her voice was filled with awe and I hoped that Dagny and I would be an eighth that happy in another nine years. "It was worth the wait, Chase. I'm sure you've found it was, too."

"Oh, yeah." The love was evident in my voice, and she chuckled at it. "But, there is one problem." I took a breath, looking around for something to play with as I sat on the couch talking to Joie. I saw my inflatable guitar not far, so I grabbed it. " My parents know."

"Uh oh."

"Yeah,"

"Are they talking to you?" Her voice was low, concerned.

"Talking to me? Hell, they took my house key away."

"Aw, man. Listen, can I tell you a story?"

"Sure." I found the little tube that pulls out of the guitar to inflate or deflate it. I picked at it with my fingers, needing somewhere for my nervous energy to go.

"My folks live in Florida, have for many years. My dad was some bigwig in his time and made lots of money, which meant lots of friends and lots of people to impress. My older brother Tommy and I were so close; I mean this guy was my hero all my life. He was eight years older and protected me from parents who weren't happy that their only daughter wasn't the perfect little debutante they had tried to raise. Tommy was the good kid; I was the stupid one."

I understood that. "Oh, yeah. I hear you."

She chuckled, then continued. "Hockey was our lives. My brother got into it first when we were kids, then when I got old enough, I played against him until I got as good as he was." She sighed sadly. "Then he went off to college in Washington state, and I was lost without him. I had centered my identity so much around him that I didn't know what to do with myself, and my parents had no idea what to do with me, either. I mean, check this out — rich man has a gay daughter who likes to have fun and play hockey."

"I'm sure their friends were in awe."

She laughed outright. "You got that right. You should have seen. I would steal clothes from Tommy and my father. I was the perfect little boy-wannabe." I erupted in laughter, imagining little Joie dressed up like big brother. "Now, if you think I'm lying, I should send you a picture of me in college. God, what was I thinking?"

"Comfort?"

"Oh, Chase!" she roared. "You hit it right on the head, girl. Oh man, you're fun. Anyway, so, Tommy left home, and that's when the shit really started to hit the fan with my parents. My mom tried and tried to turn me into a miniature version of herself. You know — like Dr. Evil and Mini Me or something."

I laughed, totally understanding. "For me it was them trying to turn me into my sister, Carla."

"Oh, that's bad. So I fought with them constantly, started getting into trouble, doing stupid stuff just to piss them off." I chuckled as I heard Jenny yelling at Joie not to curse in front of the baby. "Oops. Anyway, so then when I was fifteen, my world was absolutely shattered." Joie's voice lowered and I could tell a sense of seriousness was coming into the conversation. "Tommy was playing in a game, kicking butt as usual, when he got blindsided by an opposing player. The doctor counted thirteen cracks in his helmet."

I sat back against the back of the couch, my fingers stilled on the plastic guitar. I could almost feel the pain radiating off of Joie in waves.

"He was all I had."

"Ah, Joie. Damn, I'm sorry."

"Yeah." She was quiet for a moment and I swore I heard her sniffle. "After he died, the family tensions grew even worse, and I decided that in order to get out of there and not end up on the street, I'd have to go off to college. Besides, I wanted to play for the Cougars at Washington State University. So, that's exactly what I did. Of course, my folks helped things along by kicking me out after I graduated from high school." She chuckled.

"So what happened?"

"My father sent me money every single month, an incentive to keep me away. If I stayed clear across the country, they'd pay for me to live and go to school."

"My God. They, like, bribed you."

"Exactly. Hell, I didn't care. By that point I was so bitter." She snorted. "They hated me playing hockey."

"Because of Tommy?"

"Hell, no! Because it's not a lady-like thing to do. My mother has not said a nice word to me since I was twelve. They do come up once a year for Nathaniel's birthday, though."

"That's something."

"Yeah. I saw them for the first time two and a half years ago. Chase, they had no idea what was going on in my life; they didn't even show up at my college graduation."

"You're not giving me much hope here, Joie."

"Hey, I won't lie to you, kid, it's tough. What I've learned of life is that when your own family turns their backs on you and don't support you, you have to create your own family. That's exactly what you've started to do with Dagny."

"So, this is it, then?" I asked, feeling abandoned all over again.

"Who knows? I don't mean to be a downer, Chase, but I don't know your folks or what's up their asses, oops, I mean their rear ends. Sorry, babe."

I grinned. *Can I have your life someday, Joie?* "How have you dealt with it?"

"Don't have much choice. I tell you, if having my family in my life on a normal or regular basis meant that I had to change my life and who I am, I wouldn't do it. Jenny and Nate are my family. I love them with all my heart; I'd do anything for them. They're what matter. I promise you, Chase, you will get to that point, too. This is still a raw wound for you."

I tossed the guitar aside, wishing I had Dagny with me. "Thank you, Joie. I really appreciate you talking to me. I'm sure you're busy and didn't really wake up this morning with the desire to relive your life."

"Hey, not a problem. I will gladly talk to you anytime, got it?"

"Yeah."

"Jenny says hi, too."

"Hi right back at her. Well, um, I better get going. Thanks again."

"Anytime."

I hung up with the hockey coach and stared out at the room. *Come home, Dag. I need you.*

Dagny had warned me earlier that it would be a very long day, so I was not worried yet, just agitated. I wanted her with me. Joie's words and experiences had served two purposes. First, it gave me hope for my future. Second, it made me realize my relationship with my family was probably screwed beyond redemption.

I lay down, staring up at the ceiling, my inflatable guitar back in hand. I strummed the plastic strings molded into the face of the guitar, imagining in my head what I was playing. I thought about our conversation, feeling better for knowing that I wasn't the only defective kid out there. It still hurt, and I knew it would be one hell of an uphill battle, but all in all I was free; I didn't have to hide or play games anymore. Plus, I had Dagny in my life.

I took a deep breath and let it out slowly. It was time for me to stop concentrating on the negatives. There was nothing that I could do to change their minds, so why beat myself up over it? Feeling like I had found some peace for the first time in weeks, I snuggled against the soft cushions and closed my eyes.

Her skin was soft and smooth beneath my hands, almost hot to the touch. She moaned my name as I explored her body with just my hands. I traced the lines of her face, then trailed down her throat to her collar bone, lingering only a moment before my fingertips slid downward. Her fingers tightened on my arm as I cupped a breast in my hand, amazed at how impossibly soft it was. She pressed herself up into me. "Oh, please, Chase, yes."

"Chase? Wake up, baby."

My eyes popped open to see Dagny sitting on the edge of the couch, her hand on my stomach. I smiled. "Hey, you. I missed you today."

"I missed you, too, baby." She leaned down and kissed me. My dream coming back to me, I brought my hand to her arm, trailing my fingers down it until I reached her fingers, tracing the skin, over her knuckles to her fingernails, back up again. I looked up into her eyes; they were gazing back at me. She adjusted herself so she was closer to me. She brought her other hand up to my face, pushing hair behind my ear, then caressing the line of my cheek.

"How was your day?" I asked, my voice breathy and sounding like it belonged to someone else entirely.

"It was good, long." She leaned down just the tiniest bit. "But it's so much better now." She brushed her lips gently across my forehead, my eyes closing as I took in her scent. "Much better," she whispered as her kisses made their way down my temple and across my cheek, stopping at the tip of my nose, then moving down. "How was yours?"

"I don't know," I mumbled just before her lips met mine. I brought my hand up and tangled my fingers in her hair, gently pulling her down, aching for the kiss to deepen. Dagny moved herself so she was nearly lying on top of me, her upper body pressed against mine. Her lips opened, mine did the same, but the kiss was kept at a slow, luxurious pace, our mouths working together, a bottom lip sliding in between top and bottom then out again, only to find its way back into the warmth.

Dagny moaned as she opened her mouth further, just brushing my lips with her tongue. It was my turn to moan as I responded, my tongue meeting hers before it slipped inside her mouth.

"Baby," she whispered as she slid more of her body on top of mine.

My mind and body were reeling at the kaleidoscope of sensations whirling through me. I was kissing Dagny, hell I was making out with her. I was kissing a woman. Whoa. That was a strange thought. All that lovely childhood conditioning struggled to the fore, but I blocked it out. This felt right and true. More right than anything in my life.

I slid my hands from Dagny's hair down to her back, running my hands all over her, feeling the material of her tank under my fingertips, fingertips that itched to feel the bare skin beneath, but not daring. If Dagny gave me the go ahead, I'd gladly go where no woman had gone before.

And then the telephone rang.

Dag broke the kiss and leaned her forehead against mine. "Saved by the bell, huh?" She smiled, her breathing heavy. All I could do was nod. Pulling herself together, Dag stood and grabbed the cordless off the coffee table.

As she answered it, I sat up, trying to get myself under control, straightening my hair and the shirt that had become wrinkled by the weight of Dagny's body. Oh, Dagny's body. I closed my eyes as I recalled her lips on mine, her hands on me, her body on mine. Oh, cruel, cruel world to interrupt so thoughtlessly.

Dagny sat down next to me, turning off the phone and setting it back on the table.

"Who was that?" I asked, doing my damnedest to keep my hands to myself. I finally had to resort to sitting on them.

"Some idiot phone salesman." She glanced at me, then down at my hands, a slow, very sexy smile spreading across her face. "You all right, there?" I nodded, probably a little too vigorously. Her smile grew wider. "I'm going to take a shower. I'll be right back, then maybe we can catch some dinner. I'm starving." She kissed my neck and then moved toward the bathroom.

I watched her go, the jean shorts she wore fitting just so, nicely emphasizing that incredible body. Her tank was black and ribbed and tight. I clenched my fists and suppressed a groan. Every day it was getting harder to control my impulses. As my feelings for Dagny grew, so did my need.

The door to the bathroom closed and my heart slowed. Sort of.

Energy surging through my body, I ran my hands through my hair, then looked for a hair tie to pull it all back away from my face. I checked my pockets; no luck. *Shit.* None on the table, either. My eyes drifted to the bathroom door. I knew that behind that slab of wood was an entire bag full of hair ties, but Dag was in there. Naked, getting ready to take a shower.

I stood, but stayed where I was, my eyes locked on the door. My legs wanted to move me toward it, and I had to will them to wait until I could think about it rationally. I could easily just open the door once she got under the water — which she had just turned on — and blindly reach my hand to the back of the toilet where the bag was. Dagny wouldn't mind. There was a shower curtain. Granted it wasn't one of the opaque variety, but still, she wouldn't get mad. Making up my mind, I walked resolutely to the bathroom door and knocked softly.

"Yeah?"

I heard her yell above the water and opened the door just enough to be heard. "Dag, I need a hair tie."

"Go ahead, babe. You don't have to ask."

*Yes, I do.* I pushed the door open all the way and stepped inside, making a conscious effort to avert my eyes. *Yeah, right, Chase. Sure you did.* Dagny was rinsing her hair — her head back, arms raised as she smoothed back the blonde strands. My eyes slid down her wet body to her neck, her shoulders, and finally her breasts. Oh my God, those breasts. The nipples were hard from the hot water, and my mouth literally started to water. Never in my life had I seen or touched another woman's naked breasts, and I had no idea what I'd do with hers, but God how I wanted the chance.

Next stop on my visual tour was her stomach, so beautiful, and then lower to unbelievably beautiful legs, one bent just slightly as she moved her head under the water. My gaze traveled back up her body, just as slowly, until it reached her face. She was staring at me. *Oh shit!* I panicked, until I saw the look on her face. She was looking intently into my eyes, her own on fire.

I was filled with a heat, a craving that I had never known. My heart began to beat double time, the blood pounding in my ears. I needed to escape, or... I grabbed the hair ties and fled.

Out in the kitchen, I opened the window above the sink, to let in some air and cool off. I scarcely recognized my body's responses anymore. Though I didn't fully understand what it was going through or where it was taking me, I definitely wanted to sit back and enjoy the ride. But damn was it taking its time.

* ~ * ~ * ~ * ~ * ~ *

After dinner and a quiet evening, we lay in bed, both on our backs staring up at the ceiling. I think we were both feeling the heat. I was afraid to touch her, not sure that I'd be able to stop, then I felt her hand on mine.

"Chase?"

"Yes?" I was almost expecting her to yell at me about the shower incident. When she finally came out of the bathroom, I was already in here, getting ready for bed. She hadn't said a word, just brushed out her hair and lay down.

"Besides that kiss with Terrie, have you ever done anything with a woman?"

I turned to look at her; she was still staring up at the ceiling. She began to caress my hand, her touch soft and gentle.

"No," I admitted. "You?" She shook her head. "Did you ever want to?"

"To be honest, I never really thought about it. I've found different women...attractive, even sexy, you know? But it never went beyond that." She smiled. "Until now."

I smiled back. "Yeah. When we were younger and Carrie would talk about this girl or that, and the stuff she'd do with them. It didn't bother me, but it didn't really do anything for me, either. You know?"

"I understand completely. I always did think the female body was absolutely beautiful. Oh, I had this swimming coach one time when I was about thirteen. Damn." She began to run her hand up and down my arm. "It amazes me how soft your skin is. Anyway, Mary was her name. She was probably about twenty-five."

I grinned. "Ah, enter the older woman."

"Yeah, something like that." She smacked my hand playfully. "She was just beautiful." She looked at me assessingly. "You know, you actually remind me a lot of her, your coloring."

"Is that a good thing?"

"Oh, yes. A very good thing." She took my hand and brought it to her lips, kissed the palm. "What do you like, Chase?"

My brow furrowed. "What do you mean? Like choosing between peas and corn?"

"You nut. No, sexually."

"Oh." That stopped me cold. Not really one to share my sexual history or likes, I suddenly felt embarrassed. When Mike and I had sex, I enjoyed it, but it never seemed to get me to the place where it took him. I was afraid it was just me, so I didn't really talk sex with my friends, not even with Carrie, though she felt the need to tell me plenty. "Well, hmm." I thought for a moment. This entire last year or so, I had been thinking specifically of Dagny sexually, and sure as hell not myself. "I can tell you one thing that I'm really not a fan of."

"What's that?"

"Well, you know, like when the guy, or whoever, or whatever goes, well, inside."

"Penetration?"

"Yeah. I'm not such a fan of that."

"Really?" I looked at her. Was that a bad answer? "That's funny, because neither am I." She smiled at me and I was thoroughly relieved.

"Oh. Good. I thought maybe I was defective or something."

"No. Maybe it just means you were meant to be with women." She smiled and winked, placing my hand on her tank-clad stomach. "Darrel always had a difficult time with me. See, I'm very sensitive...down there, but only in certain spots, so it takes a definite knowing touch, and it takes a long time." She rolled her eyes. "God, he used to get so irritated with me."

"You're kidding. Why?" I turned onto my side, leaning on my arm, suddenly intrigued, wanting to know what would please Dagny.

"Well, it took a long time, as I said, and he would get tired. He'd do his thing, you know, inside and all that, but then I was nowhere even near finished." She chuckled. "Poor guy."

"Yeah, but he shouldn't have gotten upset with you for it."

"No, probably not, but overall he handled it fine."

It felt really strange hearing my, well, I guess my *girlfriend* talking about having sex with her ex-boyfriend. It kind of creeped me out, and certainly didn't help in the jealousy department.

"What about you and Mike? Was he the only guy you ever slept with?"

I shook my head. "No, but he was the first real boyfriend I had. The other one was just to pass the time."

"Oh." She sounded surprised. "I didn't realize. God, Chase you're so young. How many people have you slept with?"

I chuckled. "Only the two."

An adorable smile spread across Dag's face, her curiosity evident. "Well, what did they do that you liked?"

"Well, sometimes Mike would be between my legs, and he'd well, he'd just kind of rub against me. Know what I mean?" She nodded. "God, I loved that. Another thing that I like, and this is kind of silly, but I love nails on my skin. Not the hard, S&M type, but just run gently along my arm or something." I closed my eyes, thinking of the sensation it caused, imagining Dag doing something very similar. *Oh, Dag.* The more we talked about sex, the more my body began to crave her.

"I also have extremely sensitive breasts."

My eyes automatically traveled there. They were so beautifully pronounced through the thin material of the tank. God, I just wanted to... Grrrr. "Mine can be, it just depends."

"On?"

"How it's done. I need a certain speed and a certain amount of pressure."

"God, I'd really like to know what."

I looked at Dagny to see if she had said what I thought she had said. She was staring up at the ceiling, biting her bottom lip. "We should get some sleep, Chase," she finally said, her voice low and husky, sending a shiver through my body.

* ~ * ~ * ~ * ~ * ~ *

A few days and restless nights later, we strolled along the streets around campus, in the mood to shop. Dag ran her hand up and down my arm as we walked and talked. I told her about my conversation with Joie and all the wisdom that she'd imparted over the phone. I also told her about Joie's own troubled past and snobbish, uncaring parents.

"God, is it just rampant? Are there no parents at all out there who accept their kids?" Dagny asked, an edge to her voice.

"I don't know. If there are, send a set my way."

She chuckled, hugged me as we walked on, turning onto 4th Avenue. "Hey, want to go in there?"

She was indicating a big glass-fronted store. Antigone Books. People were milling about inside. "Sure. You've never been in here before, Miss Reader of the Masses?"

"Well, no. I always wanted to go in, but, um, well, I just never got up the nerve."

I looked at her in confusion. "Why not?" She pointed to a stack of books near the door. *Lesbian Erotica*. "Oh." We giggled like little girls as we walked in, holding on to each other as if a huge lightning bolt would come down from the ceiling and fry us both for being in a bookstore that sold lesbian books. "Have you ever read anything like this?" I asked, looking at a rack of bumper stickers.

Dagny shook her head. "No. I've always wanted to, though." I looked at her. "Hey, I'll read anything. Besides, I was just curious."

"Uh huh."

She smacked me on the arm.

"Ow."

We wandered around, Dagny snooping through the books, me checking out the greeting cards.

"Oh, this looks good." I turned to see her reading the back of a book. "How sad. These girls have been friends for a long time, then one dies." She opened it up and began to flip through it, reading different parts of it. "Oh, I have to get this."

"What is it?"

"It's called *First*, by some woman with a very odd last name."

"So, um, will this be your first lesbian novel?" I virtually whispered.

She grinned. "It's not a sin, Chase. I want to see what they're like. My freshman year of college, my roommate used to read books like this all the time."

"Was she?"

"I don't know. Well, I didn't know at the time. Looking back on it now, I'd bet my life on it." She grinned, tucking the novel under her arm as we continued to look around.

"Oh my God, Chase, come here." Dagny grabbed my sleeve, nearly pulling me off my feet to look at the book she was poring over.

"Holy shit!" I covered my mouth and swiveled around to see if anyone was looking at us, then turned back to the book in Dag's hands. It was filled with pictures of women in a variety of sexual positions. "Can you actually do that?" I whispered, moving in so we were both huddled over the book.

"I guess. They sure as hell are."

"What *is* this?" She closed the front cover to let me read. "What is the *Lesbian Kama Sutra*?"

She shook her head. "I don't really know, but it's kind of cool."

"Can I help you, ladies?"

We both jumped, Dagny nearly dropping the book as we turned to see an amused woman standing behind us, her hands behind her back as she looked from one of us to the other.

"Oh, um, no. Thanks." Dag smiled. I was grateful she had been able to speak, because I couldn't quite breathe yet.

"If you need anything, I'll be over there."

"Thanks." The woman shot one last glimpse at the book in Dag's hands, then walked away chuckling. "How utterly embarrassing."

"Oh, come on. If she works here, she's probably gay, and you know she's probably had sex at least once."

"Yeah, but still..." Dagny looked around to make sure we were alone, then opened back up to the page we had been looking at.

I grinned. "God, I feel like a kid looking at my dad's Playboy magazines."

"I know. Me, too." Dagny giggled at our badness. It wasn't long before our heads were pressed together as page after page of pictures and descriptions passed before our virgin eyes.

An hour later we left the store, each of us toting a bag filled with books, some rainbow buttons that I planned to stick on my guitar strap, and, of course, the *Lesbian Kama Sutra*.

The time was quickly approaching, and I think we both knew it.

* ~ * ~ * ~ * ~ * ~ *

"Put something good on the stereo," Dagny called from the kitchen.

"Okay." I knelt down, turning the tuner until I found something I liked. I stood and went into the kitchen. "May I?"

Dag turned to me. Seeing my hand extended, she smiled and took it. I led her to the living room where we stopped in front of the fireplace.

"Good choice," she said. We began to dance slowly as Art Garfunkel sang about the troubled waters and how he'd be a bridge to cross them.

"It's still true, you know," I said, putting one hand on her lower back, the other clasping hers.

She smiled. "It's always been true for you, too, baby," she said, bringing her hand up from my shoulder to brush my cheek with the back of her fingers. "I'll always be here for you, Chase."

"Me too, for you." I stared down into the most beautiful eyes I had ever seen. She was amazing and gorgeous, and mine. I didn't understand it. I didn't care. To me it wasn't about understanding or not understanding, it was pretty much black and white. I was with Dagny: long struggle; I'd finally won.

"I want to spend my life with you," she said as our bodies slowly swayed together. "I want you to always be with me so that I can share everything with you. You have given me so much, showed me so much of what life and love can be." Her fingers traced the features of my face.

"Love?" I asked, my voice barely a whisper.

She nodded slowly. "Yes. Love. I love you, Chase."

My heart was in my throat. "You do?"

"Yes." She smiled.

"God, I love you, too." I pulled her to me, the music and dance forgotten.

"Say it again, Chase," she begged, her voice thick.

"I love you, Dagny. I love you so much."

She clung to me and I buried my face in her hair. In that moment I knew that what I had been waiting for my entire life was right there. Joie was right: you move on and build your own life, make your own family. Dagny was the person I wanted to do that with.

I pulled back from her a little, just enough to look into her eyes. I wanted to let her see how much I loved her. I brought my fingers up to lift her chin, my eyes trailing down to her mouth, her lips parted, a nervous tongue slipping out to run across the bottom lip. I looked back up to her eyes to see she was looking at my mouth. I moved in until our lips were brushing together, barely touching. Dagny edged closer, our bodies molding together, her hands reaching up into my hair as the kiss deepened. I wrapped my arms around her waist, pulling her ever closer, wanting her inside me, inside my spirit.

Dagny put her hands on the back of my head to press my mouth closer, hers opening wider for me, taking me in. My hands grew restless and started to move, feeling the texture of Dagny's shirt beneath my fingers. They slid down her back to her butt, the sweat shorts she wore loose-fitting and soft. I slid my hands, underneath and squeezed. Dag moaned, which turned my blood to lava.

I broke the kiss and tilted my head, homing in on the long, smooth neck. She raised her head for me, eyes closed as she gripped my shoulders. My mouth explored the planes and curves of her throat, my tongue tasting the salty skin.

"God, Chase," she groaned as my teeth nipped the skin just below her ear. She dug her fingernails into my skin. I took her earlobe into my mouth, which earned me another groan and a slight thrusting of her hips. *Oh, pay dirt.* I sucked a little harder, running my tongue all along the edge until I found a soft little spot right behind where her hoop earring sat. "Jesus!" Her body jerked in response and I did a little happy dance inside as she clung even harder, her hips trying to find some sort of purchase against me. My hands began to explore, feeling the smooth roundness of her butt, then resting on her hips as my lips continued moving from ear to neck to throat to mouth.

Dagny reached down and grabbed my hand, placing it at the hem of her tee shirt. Taking my cue, I brought my hand up slowly, wriggling my fingers under the material to feel the hot skin beneath. If I hadn't known better I'd have thought she had a fever. My other hand soon joined the first, caressing the skin of her stomach, running my fingertips over it then gliding up over ribs. I stopped when I felt the underwire of her bra. I sucked in a breath, visualizing what was hidden just beneath that silky material.

I looked into Dagny's eyes, seeing what she wanted me to do. I knew by the intensity I saw there, she wanted it all. I leaned in and kissed her softly as my fingers began to play all along the edge of that bra, following the path around to her back where I felt the clasp. I didn't want to unhook it just yet. No, I wanted to torture her a bit first.

I brought my hands back around to her breasts, my fingers brushing over the underwire to the silkiness of the cups themselves. She closed her eyes and tilted her head back as I began to massage the fullness, so pliable in my hands and against my fingers. I wanted to moan right along with her. God, the feel of them was incredible, and way beyond any daydream I ever had.

My finger explored around the breasts, beginning to form slow circles starting along the outside and moving in, around and around, until I felt the hard nipple. Dagny sucked in a breath, releasing it with a groan. I was amazed at how hard they were, how large they had become. God, I wanted to see them! I grabbed the tee shirt, about to pull it over Dagny's head when a knock sounded at the door.

"What the hell?" Dag's eyes opened and she looked around. I quickly pulled my hands from beneath her shirt and looked at the door, as if that would tell me who the hell I had to kill. "Hang on," she called out, trying to get herself together. "What on earth did you do to me?" she asked, leaning in for a smoldering kiss that left me unsteady on my feet.

She dawdled to the door and unlocked it as I tried to get myself under control, get my breathing back in this galaxy. When Dagny whipped the door open, it was Carrie and Paul that stood out in the hall.

"Hey." Dag smiled. "What are you guys doing here?"

Carrie smiled at her, then looked into the room and saw me. Her eyes narrowed in on me as I wiped the evidence of our kisses from my mouth. A slow smile spread across her face at the dawning realization.

"Hey, guys. I didn't expect to find you here, Chase. What a break."

"Yeah, we called you at home, but didn't get an answer," Paul said, seemingly oblivious to what his girlfriend had clearly figured out.

"We wanted to take you to dinner and a movie." Carrie's eyes couldn't stay on just one of us, but kept bouncing back and forth. I knew her questions were burning a hole in her brain.

Dagny turned to look at me over her shoulder. "Chase? Interested?"

*Not really.* "Sure." I smiled, taking a step closer to grab Carrie. "I've missed you." She came to me quite willingly, the hug deep and satisfying.

"You have a lot of explaining to do," she whispered in my ear.

"Later," I whispered back.

"Well, um, let me get changed." Dag disappeared into the bedroom. Alone.

* ~ * ~ * ~ * ~ * ~ *

The darkness seemed to fall all around me, the softness of her skin against me, her nails lightly tracing lazy patterns on my arm. The sound of heavy breathing, obviously female, was definitely getting to me, stirring my blood to a rolling boil. Dagny's mere presence was enough to put me in a tailspin, regardless of any of the other sensations. Finally, mercifully, the love scene came to an end and the movie played on. Carrie leaned over to whisper in my ear.

"You all right there, Chase?"

"Bite me."

I heard her laugh as she leaned back against Paul. I had managed to get Carrie away from Paul long enough to drag her to the bathroom and explain what had happened since school had ended. She had been excited for us, but wasn't sure whether to hug me or go kick my family's ass.

"God, I can't believe it. I never, ever thought your mom and dad could be such assholes, Chase. I'm so sorry."

"It happens, I guess. What can you do?"

Now, sitting in the dark theater, I wanted nothing more than to drag Dagny to the bathroom and finish what we had started back at the apartment. As the movie, which ordinarily I would have enjoyed, droned on, my mind kept racing to unfamiliar places. Dagny's nails on my skin did nothing to help matters. I looked over at her and was met with an evil gaze. She knew what she was doing to me.

"Enjoying the movie?" she asked, leaning over to my ear.

I gulped. "Yeah, it's great."

She chuckled. "I agree."

* ~ * ~ * ~ * ~ * ~ *

"Listen, we'll talk, okay? I'm so happy for you, Chase." Carrie hugged me tightly.

I hugged her just as tightly. "I've really missed you, Car," I said as we parted outside of the apartment building.

She smiled. "Me, too."

"Paul, later."

"Bye, guys." With one more wave, Carrie and Paul climbed into his car and drove off. Dag and I made our way up the stairs and into the apartment. Neither of us said anything as we went into the bedroom and changed for bed. I put on my usual boxers and tee, and she, her tank and panties. God, she was sexy.

"Part of me is glad they stopped by," she said, pulling back the sheets.

"Yeah, me too. It was good to see them, and Carrie had no idea what was going on."

"So, I take it the bathroom trip was the explanation?" I nodded. She, scooted down in the bed and I moved in behind her to spoon. "Come here, you." She reached around to grab my hand, putting it on her stomach, just like always. Her hand reached back to lie on my thigh. We settled in, my face nearly buried in her hair as I loved the smell and feel of it, even if it did tickle my nose from time to time. Longer hair was definitely something I had to get used to. Mike's hair had been so short, I barely noticed it was there.

Dagny pushed her butt out a little, which pushed into me. I ignored it, settling in, caressing her stomach through her shirt before stilling my hand for sleep. My body was still wired, but I knew I could sleep it off. She scooted against me again. My eyebrows drew together in puzzlement, and I thrust my hips forward a bit. She pushed against me again, this time her hand moving on my thigh.

I closed my eyes, inhaling the smell of Dagny, her hair — her skin, her clothes. I let it all sift inside and fill me as my hand on her stomach responded to that on my leg. My thumb began to move back and forth. The heat that was coming to my hand through the shirt was unreal. Dagny pushed herself back into me even harder, our bodies not even a hair's breadth apart.

I began to kiss Dagny's neck, slow, wet kisses across and down, finding my way to her ear again. Her breath caught, and her fingers tightened on my leg. I started to move my hand, rubbing her stomach, bunching the material of her shirt up in my hand only to release it. Dagny's hand began to move, fingertips gliding as far down my thigh as they could before moving back up and around, her palm resting on my butt, kneading and massaging.

I shifted, licking down the side of her neck, her head moving on the pillow, arching her neck for me as much as she could. Her hand traveled up a bit until it was at the hem of my boxers, a single finger slipping underneath. I sucked in a breath, as I wore nothing underneath. My stomach clenched, and that wasn't the only thing.

My hand moved further down her stomach, found the end of her tank, slipped a couple of fingers beneath. I could feel her hip bone against my hand, her leg moving as she pushed into me, like a pulse. My fingers touched the hot skin that had been burning me through the shirt, scorching me now. I rested my hand on her belly, working up to moving on.

Dag's hand moved further up under the leg of my boxers. I held my breath as her fingers, like snakes, slithered up my skin, making my heartbeat skyrocket. My hips jerked and I heard her chuckle, low and sexy. *Okay, I can play too.* I resumed kissing Dag's neck as I caressed the skin of her torso, moving up until I felt the round underside of her breasts. I closed my eyes, wanting to get lost in the feel of just that.

"Yessss," she purred.

Feeling more confident by the second, my hand explored further, my fingers running along the curve — caressing, pushing and rubbing, working their way upward. Dag's hand stilled but her hips had begun to move, her body arching, her back pressing against my breasts, her hand beginning to knead my skin, as my hand got closer and closer to that peak of heat.

My hand finally covered her entire breast, the hard nipple insistent against my palm. We moaned together at the contact. I opened my hand, rubbing my palm in circles over the nipple, the rigidity almost tickling me. Dagny was really gyrating, her butt pressing as far into me as it could, her body straining into her captive position. I took my hand from her breast and started to work on her shirt. I wanted it off, wanted to see her at last.

Dagny helped me, lifting herself up on her elbow so I could pull the tank off and toss it to the floor. She was gorgeous, her skin seemingly flawless, smooth. The one window in the bedroom sent in a bright beam of moonlight, like a spotlight.

Dagny turned toward me, her eyes locked on my face. Her hands reached down and tugged at my shirt, which I gladly whipped off, throwing it to join Dagny's. We stared, bared to one another for the first time. I had seen Dagny in various states of undress over the last two years, but nothing I ever could have imagined to fill in the blanks could have prepared me for the reality of her. She was exquisite, what everyone with a heartbeat would crave and desire.

Dagny pushed me onto my back and slid on top. The feel of skin on skin, our breasts pressing together, oh my God. I will never in a million years forget it. That alone nearly sent me over the edge. I could feel Dagny's wetness on my thigh.

Dagny's mouth immediately went to mine and I wrapped my arms around her, my hands sliding up and down her bare skin, my legs automatically parting allowing for the fitting of one of hers between. She thrust her hips down as I thrust mine up, the sensation of their meeting unbelievably intense. Our bodies began to move together, as did our mouths, Dag's hands cupping my face as the kiss got deeper, my hands wandering down to her butt, pulling her into me. I knew it wouldn't be long before I crested, my body winding higher and higher with every thrust.

My head fell back, my eyes closed as my body let go, the pulsing in my veins spreading through my entire being. Dagny continued to thrust against me then she, too, fell over with a cry. She collapsed against me, holding on to me tightly, almost afraid all would be lost again. Our breathing was the only sound in the room, hers hot against my neck, mine buried in her hair as I pressed her to me.

After a few moments, Dagny lifted herself up on an elbow and looked down at me. She traced my face, my neck and throat with a finger as her eyes followed the trail until they settled on my breasts. I watched with bated breath as her fingers got closer and closer, then to my surprise and delight, so did her mouth. Dagny kissed my breast first, then tentatively her tongue slid out and tasted the skin, then again, but this time a little closer to my nipple. The anticipation was torture, and I wanted to grab her head and deposit her mouth directly on it. Finally, I threw my head back, my mouth open as a wet tongue licked across the nipple, sending incredible sensations shooting through my body.

"God," I breathed, clutching the sheet in an iron grasp. Getting more confident, she brought her entire mouth down on it, sucking the taut skin into her wet warmth. My hips bucked as I groaned, long and breathy. *Heaven, this has got to be Heaven. I'll have to remember to ask Natalie if God is female, and if She looks like Dagny.*

Hands began to explore as I was suckled, my body being caressed and worshipped. Then fingers found my other entirely over-aroused nipple and began to play, rolling it between fingers, tugging slightly. My hands found their way into Dagny's hair, pressing her against me. She moaned as she licked me.

After what seemed an eternity, I felt my boxers being pulled. I looked down at Dag kneeling over me, her fingers hooked in the waistband of the shorts on either side, tugging. I lifted my hips, and she pulled them down over my butt, down my legs, and tossed them off the bed. Lying naked, and feeling extremely vulnerable, I decided it was time to even things out. I indicated Dag's panties and she obliged, well, actually, she lay down so I could remove them. I sat up and followed her example, sliding them down her beautiful body, tossing them aside only to linger and look at what was revealed to me. I was breathless.

Dagny gently pushed me down on my back, and I pulled her with me, my hands on her hips, but she stopped herself, wanting to prolong the feel of our fully exposed skin touching. She knelt over me, hands on either side of my head, one knee between my legs. She looked down at me, her eyes burning into mine.

"I love you, Chase," she whispered.

I ran my hands gently through her tangled hair and smiled. "I love you, too, Dagny."

She smiled and softly kissed me as she slowly lowered herself, starting with her breasts, then down from there. I closed my eyes as our bodies made full contact, our legs entwined, our breasts pressed together, everything lined up where it needed to be. She began to kiss my neck as she gently nudged my legs, wanting me to spread them. I did, and she fitted her small frame between, pushing herself up to her elbows. She looked down at me as she slowly began to move against me. I smiled in appreciation, she smiled back, and I began to move with her, pushing up against her as she pushed down, moving with me. I spread my legs a little wider, opening myself up to her. She moaned as my knees straddled to either side of her moving hips.

Our breasts rubbed against each other as she moved a bit faster, her body sliding easily against mine, bending down to kiss me. I put my hand on the back of her head to push her closer, our mouths working slowly along with her hips, but as I felt the ball of fire begin to form in my stomach and fall south, I deepened the kiss, intensified it, thrusting against her faster, my hands going to her butt, pushing her on, pushing her in. Though it was true I had never enjoyed penetration, I would have given anything for Dagny to be inside me at that moment. Finally Dagny raised herself up on her arms, pushing me to my limits until my head flew back. Eyes closed, mouth open, I exploded. My entire body arched off the bed, my breasts pressing into Dagny as my fingers dug into the skin of her back.

"Yes, baby," she whispered as she kissed me, bringing me back from my forgotten world into the present one with her.

My body still pulsing, I tried to slow my breathing. That had been the most incredible experience of my life. I looked into the face of my lover, her eyes burning, started on fire by watching me. I pushed her over onto her back and found her mouth, my hands exploring her body, touching everywhere, her breasts, finding the erect nipples, which I longed to taste.

I bent down to do just that, my hand making its way down her stomach to wiry hair. Dagny sucked in a breath as my fingers played, her legs opening for me, spreading apart to allow me all the access I wanted. I took a nipple into my mouth, letting my lips form around it, reveling in the whimpers that came from Dag's throat. Her hands wound themselves in my hair as her breathing became heavy, husky. I kept my hand where it was, waiting for her to lead me. Within a few seconds she got the picture, and brought her hand down into the copious wetness — gently placing her fingers on top of mine, placing them where she needed them —and showed me what she needed, moving our fingers together in a slow, circular motion. Her hand withdrew, and I continued.

I held myself up with my free hand as I continued to suck on her breast, rhythmically pulling the nipple in, running my tongue over it then running my teeth over its length. I tried to pay attention to what her body told me — her breathing, her movements.

Dag's hips began to move in time with my hand. As one sped up, so did the other. It did not take long; she was drenched. My two fingers were completely covered as I moved faster, my forearm feeling the pressure as I never faltered. Dagny's hips rose off the bed, and her gasps turned to breathy moans; finally she cried out. I raised my head from her breast to look at the magnificence of her body, every muscle straining as she reached climax.

"God, Chase!" She grabbed the back of my head to pull my face to hers. I kissed her with everything I had in me. She was partly panting and partly moaning into my mouth as I moved my entire body on top of hers and she thrust herself against my thigh to ride out the tremors of her climax.

She started to come down, her body relaxing, breathing evening out. I stayed where I was, body to body, our hearts beating in time, arms and legs entwined.

"God," she breathed. "I had no idea." She gently stroked my hair, kissing the side of my head.

"Neither did I." I cuddled closer, reveling in the feel of her and the thought of what we had just done. How could anyone possibly think this was a perversion? I had never experienced anything so pure. Maybe all those judgmental people out there needed to try it. Maybe my mother should.

It wasn't long before we both fell into a deep sleep, our bodies exhausted, our hearts and minds completely satisfied.

* ~ * ~ * ~ * ~ * ~ *

The light came streaming through the window, spreading across the floor to climb up the mattress, caress the sheet with its brilliance, and shine right into my eyes. With a groan I tried to squeeze them shut, but it was futile. Once I was awake, it was usually a lost cause. My lids fluttered open, and I turned so my back was to the window, and saw Dagny sitting up against the headboard, reading.

"Good morning." An instant smile bloomed on my face.

She looked at me, matching smile in place. "Hey, you." She leaned down and kissed me. "How did you sleep?"

"Like the dead. Well, that is except for when we woke up off and on to have sex again." I grinned. "You?"

"Pretty much the same."

I pushed myself up so I was sitting next to her when I realized I didn't have a stitch on. Dagny was wearing my tee shirt from the night before. "Now, this isn't fair," I muttered, tugging at the hem of the shirt.

"What?" She looked down, then grinned. "Okay, fine." She pulled the shirt off.

"Oh, yeah. Much, much better." I leaned over and laid my head on her breast. "What are you reading?"

"Um, nothing, really."

"Let me see." She tilted the book to show me the cover of the *Lesbian Kama Sutra* we had bought at the bookstore. My laughter faded as she started to read out loud.

* ~ * ~ * ~ * ~ * ~ *

I sat on the couch, the Advocate magazine I had bought at Antigone's in my hands.

"I'll be right back, babe. It's after one and I haven't even read the paper yet." Dag hurried out the door to pick up the paper and the mail from downstairs. As soon as the door closed, I grabbed the phone from the table. I was bursting and needed to talk to Carrie. I had never dialed seven numbers so quickly in my life, but it seemed like forever before the phone began to ring.

"Hello?"

"Hi, is Carrie there?"

"One moment, please." Carrie's dad handed over the phone to my friend.

"Yeah?"

"Hi!" My voice was high-pitched and chipper.

"Um, hi. Who is this?"

"It's me, Car. Damn, don't even recognize the voice of your best friend?"

"Hell no. Not when you sound like you've swallowed Disney-land."

I grinned. "How are you?"

"I'm fine. What's wrong?"

"Nothing. Why do you ask?" I glanced at the door; no Dagny.

"Come on, Chase. I've known you for almost two decades. Spit it out it."

Deciding I needed to talk or I'd explode, I brought my hand to the receiver and whispered, "We had sex last night."

"Yahoo!" I pulled the phone away from my ear, her shrill excitement too much for my tired headache. "No shit, really? Oh, man, that is beautiful! I cannot wait to tell Paul."

"No, Carrie. Please don't. I'm not even sure I was supposed to tell you."

"Where is she?"

"She's—"

"Hey, baby." Dagny suddenly, almost magically appeared through the door, folded newspaper and mail in hand. "Who's on the phone?"

"Um, no one." She looked at me, hands on hips.

"Hi, Dagny!" Carrie yelled, me ripping the phone away from my head at the volume.

"Hello, Carrie." She walked over to the couch and sat next to me.

"Way to go, Dag!"

I looked at my lover, mortified. "Carrie, I hate you and I have to go." I pressed the off bottom and set the phone down, my eyes never leaving Dagny, who stared at me, trying to hide a smile. "I'm sorry, babe. I had to tell someone."

She looked at me for a moment longer, then burst out laughing, taking me into a hug. "God, I just love you." She smiled at me, kissing my nose.

I grinned, thankful she wasn't going to filet me for lunch. "I love you, too."

"Oh, here. This came here for you." She took an envelope from the table and put it in my lap. "I'm going to start the shower, join me?" I nodded, kissing her. She walked to the bathroom as I studied the piece of mail. It had both our names on it, and my parents' return address. With thudding heart, I slid my finger under the flap and ripped it open. The ivory colored sheet inside was beautiful, with satin ribbons molded into the paper. It was an invitation, a wedding invitation. Both Dagny and I were invited to Carla and Todd's wedding in November.

With a sigh, I dropped it on the coffee table and went to join Dagny.

# Chapter 13

We walked around campus, the African mask in my hand, my fingers tracing the colorfully painted lines. The mask was large enough that I could wear it if I so desired.

"Thank you, Natalie. This is really beautiful." I smiled at my former roommate.

"As soon as I saw it, I knew it was for you. The woman told me it is a *pumzisha* mask, which means to give someone peace." She was smiling proudly.

"Thank you." I turned and gave her a hug, smiling at the contact. Before Dag came into my life again, I hadn't been one for the touchy, feely kind of stuff. She had taught me that it was okay, actually enjoyable. Oh boy, was it. We continued to walk.

"Have you found peace?" Natalie grinned, nudging my shoulder with hers.

I smiled, looking down at the ground so she wouldn't see the extent of my happiness. I felt shy all of a sudden, but nodded. "Yes and no." I turned to her. "Dagny and I worked things out, Natalie, and um, well, we're kind of a couple." I looked at her, afraid of what her reaction would be. Last fall when she'd returned to school from her summer-long missionary thing, she had been even closer to God than usual. I wasn't sure how she'd react to the news. She looked at me, then away, but a smile was firmly in place.

"You know something, Chase? Before I came to school, I was just as involved in my church as I am now, if not more so. After all, I did have more time, then. I admit that I was quite close minded, even though science is my biggest passion next to God. I think of how much I've grown, and I think I owe a lot of that to you." She looked at me, then turned to watch a group of guys playing football.

"Why's that?"

"Well, for starters, when I first saw you, when I smacked you with the door that first day, I thought, 'oh, Lord, what have you done to me?'" She laughed, so did I.

"Me, too."

"Oh, great. Thanks." She patted my arm. "But as I got to know you, and saw you with those kids that first year during our Tuesday night Bible studies, I realized there was so much more to you than what met the eye." She indicated a bench and we sat. "You're filled with depth, Chase. There's so much love inside you, and a great need that I never could quite understand. But if Dagny fills both the love and the need, then who am I to say that's wrong?" I was stunned. "And besides, haven't you guys been a couple for, like, two years now?"

"Huh?"

"Well, wasn't that what the deal was after Christmas? You two broke up, right?"

I shook my head. "Nah. We were never a couple, Natalie." I was amused. What I had wished for, and didn't think I had a chance of getting, my roommate had thought was there the entire time. I guess it made sense, though. I mean, we spent every single available moment together, and Dag was all I had talked about. Poor girl.

"Oh, well then, I'm doubly glad it worked out."

"Wow. Why couldn't you be my mother?"

She looked at me, brows drawn. "Huh?"

"I'll explain later. But, thank you. I'm not really sure what to say."

"You've said it all, Chase. I had a feeling that was the case from the start, so I'm not so surprised. You're a great person, a talented person, and I think you and Dagny are lucky to have found each other. It's too bad you're not a writer, Chase. Well, beyond music, that is. You could write your story and make millions." She grinned and winked.

"Yeah, that'd be nice." I put my arm around her shoulders. "I'm going to miss you this year, Natalie."

"Me, too. I'm glad to finally get my own place, though."

"Oh man, I hear you. Dorm life is for the birds."

"Stay in touch?"

"Oh, hell yeah!"

She smiled. "Don't say that. It's a naughty word."

"I've missed you."

"Me, too, Chase. So, tell me about this mother thing."

* ~ * ~ * ~ * ~ * ~ *

I looped Than's strap around my neck, excited to be back on Gotfry's stage. I had not played at all during the summer, and I was anxious to get back into the saddle. Greg had been wonderful about me and Dagney, and my band mates, well they had gotten used to the idea eventually.

I stepped up to the microphone, adjusting it to my height. "Good evening, everyone."

"Hey, the prodigal daughter returns!" someone yelled up at me.

I smiled and waved. "Hey there, Danny. Yup, I'm back and feeling good, so I hope y'all are ready to rock." The patrons cheered, whooping away as the band began to play, and I dug into the music. I looked around at everyone as I sang, seeing my girl sitting with her table of friends, talking and laughing. Just like old times, but better. She looked at me and my heart fell to my knees. I winked at her, receiving a smile in return and a salute before she turned back to her friends.

It wasn't long before we had the place on its feet, everyone either singing along or dancing, having a wonderful time. I had never had so much fun on stage. My heart was light, my spirit on the way to healing. Life was good.

"Okay, don't any of you go anywhere. Just spend some more money, get drunk, and we'll be back." I stepped away from the mic and set Than on the guitar stand.

"Wow, whatever you've been taking, can I have some?" I turned to see Terrie smiling at me. I grinned and nodded. "I think I should bottle Dag and sell it. I'd make millions."

"The feel good serum for the new millennium?"

I nodded. "You've got it. How was your summer?"

We headed down to the bar.

"It's been good, busy. Give me a vodka rocks, Greg." He went to get our drinks as we leaned on the bar. "I met someone."

I looked at her. "No shit?"

She smiled. "No shit."

"Oh man, that's great. What's she like?"

"Hey, baby, you were fantastic."

I turned toward Dagny. She pulled me into her arms for a monster hug. Terrie stood by, watching. I took Dagny in my arms, holding her tightly to me. Though she was right in the room, watching and listening to us, she was still too far away. I had tried to persuade her to join us on stage before the first set, but she had said that a cat in heat sings better than she does. "Thank you." I kissed her.

"Hey, Dagny. How are you?"

We turned to Terrie who stood, feet set wide apart, thumbs hooked into her belt loops.

"Terrie. Not bad, how about yourself?" Dagny put her arm around my waist, moving in close to me.

Terrie chuckled at the possessive move. "Not bad. She did great, huh?"

Dagny looked at me with pride. "Yeah, she did. Kicked some major butt out there."

Terrie laughed. "You two enjoy the break." She took the drink Greg had left on the bar, and walked away.

"She's met someone," I said, nuzzling my face in Dag's hair.

"Good. She can leave you alone."

I chuckled. "Babe, she's no threat. I think you've made it more than clear who I belong to."

She looked into my eyes as a slow smile broke out across her lips. "Do you?"

"What?"

"Belong to me. Are you mine?"

I smiled, shaking my head with disbelief that this incredible creature would want me to be hers, would care enough to ask. I caressed the side of her face with the backs of my fingers. "Oh, yeah. You've had me from the time I was eight years old. You were my gold standard."

She just stared at me. Funny time to draw the parallel, but it reminded me of when you talk to a faithful furry friend, the way they stare into your face as if you're their entire world, their reason for living. I could only hope the same was true with Dagny. "I love you."

"I love you, too." She sighed with contentment and kissed me again. I heard someone clear their throat behind the bar and turned to see Greg staring at us.

"You two wanna get a room?"

"Bite me."

He laughed as he moved away to draw a pitcher. I turned back to Dag and saw she was staring at something over my shoulder. She glanced at me, indicating with a nod that I should look. I did, and stopped cold.

There stood Carla, her hands clasped nervously in front of her. When she saw she had my attention, she smiled. "Hi."

"Want me to stay?" Dag asked, her voice low.

I squeezed her hand in thanks, but shook my head. "I'll be over at the table in a few."

"Okay." Dagny shot a glance at my sister, then walked away. I turned to face Carla and just stared at her.

"Um, can we sit?"

I nodded, still silent. I wasn't sure what I was feeling, my body suddenly cold, my emotions tying my stomach in knots. I wasn't sure if I should cry, or be angry and mean, or just fall into her arms, relieved to see a family member.

We found a table off all by its lonesome, and sat — her, a bit rigid, me, relaxed and cocky. But ready to bolt at a moment's notice.

"So, um, how have you been, Chase?"

"Been great. Yourself?"

She sighed. "Okay, I guess. Had a horrible summer."

"Funny that."

She smiled ruefully. Finally, her voice quiet, she said, "You were fantastic up there." Her eyes were moist, as if she was going to cry. "I had no idea. Why did you never tell any of us?"

"And what good would that have done, Carla? I'm the fucking leper of the Marin family. Do you think *that* can be fixed with a song? I don't think so."

"That may be true, but you have a wonderful voice and amazing talent."

I stared at her impassively. I didn't want her compliments to mean anything.

"I wasn't sure what to expect when I came here tonight. As you know, bars have never done much for me." She looked around and smiled. "But this one isn't bad. I have to tell you, you just about made mom drop her teeth when you told her you were singing in a bar." She shook her head and chuckled.

"I don't want to talk about her," I snapped, my voice like steel.

"Okay, Chase. Whatever you want."

I sat up straighter, my emotions veering toward anger at the mention of my mother. "Whatever I want? Oh, that's a bunch of bullshit if I've ever heard it. It's never been about what I want, Carla. You seem to forget, *you're* the perfect golden child, not me. You don't have the slightest clue what it's like to feel like an outsider in your own fucking family."

"Chase, please, I didn't come here to fight with you."

I glared at her. "Why did you come here?"

"I came to apologize. I never meant for...*that* to happen. I really just wanted to help you, Chase."

"How the fuck did you figure opening your goddamn mouth was going to help me? You had the balls to spend the day with me and Dagny, knowing what your little brain had decided to do? Jesus! Talk about betrayal."

"Chase, it wasn't supposed to happen that way. I know how disapproving Mom and Dad have always been. I've never understood it, but I knew it was there. I thought they might take it better if they heard it from me, that maybe it would soften the blow." She looked down. "It was shitty of me not to do anything about it, either standing up for you more or something... I don't know. I'm sorry. I think I was just so caught up in my own little world of achieving that I never gave much thought to your side of it." She took a breath, staring at me with pleading eyes. "I know I messed up, that goes without saying, but doesn't it mean anything that I'm here?"

"Does the expression 'too little, too late' mean anything to you?"

We were both silent for a moment, Carla looking down at her hands in her lap, me looking toward the stage. I really wanted to be there right now. Finally my sister sighed.

"Well, however it turned out, however you want to take it, I really was just trying to help you guys. I can't apologize for that, Chase. I admit that I went about it the wrong way, and for that, I am sorry." I said nothing and she took a deep breath. "I've been watching for your RSVP for the wedding."

"I don't know that I'm going."

The look on her face said that stung. "I'd like to make a request." She looked me in the eyes. "That's what you do with a singer, right?"

*Where is she heading with this?* I didn't ask; I just stared.

"I want you to sing at my wedding, Chase."

My jaw dropped. What? "What?"

She lifted her chin. "I want you to sing at my wedding."

"What is this, some sort of sick booby prize for fucking up my relationship with your parents? Trying to butter my bread?"

"No. You have immense talent, and I haven't been supportive of you in the past. I'm trying to say I'm sorry for that, and show it in the only way I know how, circumstances being what they are. Watching you up there tonight..." She blew out a deep breath. "You had that audience in the palm of your hand, which, with a bunch of drunks, I can't imagine is easy to do." She smiled weakly. "You're wonderful, and I'm proud of you." She swallowed and looked away as tears began to gather in her blue eyes. She swiped at them. "Chase, you're doing what I've dreamed of my entire life."

"Singing?"

"No! Living your *own* life! As far as being a doctor is concerned, I'm doing what I want to do. I've always wanted to follow in Dad's footsteps, but I've always had a spotlight on me. Hell, I should make an even better entertainer than you." I chuckled softly. "I've hated the concessions and the compromises, but I found out a long time ago that it's easier to just go along with them, let Mom and Dad have their little pride fest and then do my own thing later. Well, later never came."

"Whose fault is that? I'm sure not about to sit here and feel sorry for you because you've let yourself become a puppet, Carla."

"I know. I'm not asking for your sympathy, Chase. I'm just venting. You've ruined my chances of ever telling Mom and Dad how I really feel. How am I supposed to top what you said?" I looked down to hide my grin. I didn't want her to think she was out of the soup yet. "Well, I've said what I came to say." She looked me in the eye and reached across the table to take my hand. "Chase, please think about my wedding. If you don't want to sing, well, that's your choice, but please come. You and Dagny both."

"Do your parents know you invited Dagny, too?" I asked. My sister nodded. Wow. Maybe she *was* trying. "I have to go, Carla. It's time for the second set." Without another word or even a glance, I stood and strode back to the stage, where the rest of the band had already taken their positions.

"You okay?" Terrie's concern was clear in her eyes. "Who is that? Want me to fuck her up for you?"

Grinning, I patted the drummer on the shoulder. "Thanks, but no. I'm fine." I slung Than's strap over my neck and got myself

ready for the next song. As the show went on, I looked around to
see if Carla had stayed, and was shocked to see her talking to Dag.
They were standing near the bathrooms, having what seemed to be a
decent conversation. *What the hell is she trying to do to my life?*

* ~ * ~ * ~ * ~ * ~ *

I pulled Dagny to me, her naked body pressed against mine,
sweaty and sated. She sighed as she cuddled closer, her body wiggling a bit to eliminate any little crevice or space between us.

"Comfortable?" I asked, amused.

She kissed my neck. "Completely."

"You know, it's funny. I never thought I'd actually enjoy snuggling up with someone who was all sticky and smelly. Especially
when it gets hot." I stroked her hair. "Guess I was wrong."

"Well, good. I'm happy to have thrown a wrench into your theory."

I chuckled. "I'm sure you are. And you definitely have done
that."

"Besides, it's because of you that I'm sticky and smelly."

"Yeah, yeah. And boy, did I have a good time accomplishing
that."

"I should hope so." She pushed herself up on an elbow and
smiled down into my face. "You're so beautiful, Chase."

"No, that would be you."

"Oh, I disagree completely. I've never seen a more beautiful
spirit."

I stared at her in awe for the millionth time that day alone.
"You make me get so cheesy. You have a talent for that, I think."

"So do you." She leaned in and kissed me, running her hands
through my hair. "I love you," she said when the kiss finally ended,
leaving me breathless.

"I love you, too."

Dagny lay down against me, her head on my shoulder, body
halfway atop mine. "I must say I was shocked to see Carla show up
tonight," she said, running a finger along my collarbone.

"Me, too. I saw you guys talking."

"Yeah. She was apologizing to me."

"That was nice." I kept my voice even and low. I wasn't sure
how I felt about Carla's overtures, and didn't quite know how to act
with Dag.

"You know, babe, the wedding invitation has been stuck under
a refrigerator magnet for over two months now."

"I know."

"Well, are you going to send in the RSVP?"

"Carla brought that up tonight, too." I sighed, turning my head to look at the window.

Dag gently caressed my shoulder and arm. "Do you not want to talk about this?"

"I don't know. I don't know what to do, Dag." I looked at her. "It's because of her that my family is so fucked up and I've been kicked out of the fold."

"Babe, please don't take this the wrong way, but your parents always had a warped view of you and Carla. What Carla did definitely didn't help things, but I think you and I both know their reaction would have been bad regardless of how the revelation came about." When I didn't bite her head off, she continued. "Carla is the only sister you've got, or will ever have. I know you guys haven't been close in the past, babe, but why throw away this opportunity to make things better between you? If your mom wants to be a bitch, then let her, but Carla is really trying to make this up to you."

"But Dag, she had no right!"

"No, she didn't. I believe that she honestly thought if she broke the news to your parents first — the daughter who is their guiding light, their precious little angel — then maybe things would go easier for you. I truly don't think she thought they would react so precipitously, anymore than you did."

"Are you defending her?" I asked, my anger building.

Dagny put her hand on my chest, pushing herself up so she could look into my face. "No, babe, I'm not. I'm just trying to be the voice of reason for you, who are, understandably, emotionally driven right now. All I'm saying is: think long and hard about your decision before you make it. Obviously, you're doing that; the proof is hanging on the fridge."

"She asked me to sing," I said, my voice quiet as indecision set in.

"What did you say?"

"A whole bunch of mean things."

"Which you were justified in saying." She kissed my forehead. "Listen, Chase, I'm not trying to tell you what you should or shouldn't do, I'm just trying to give you some food for thought. Okay?"

I nodded. "Thanks."

"That's what I'm here for."

"I'm certainly hope that ain't all you're here for," I growled, flipping us over, Dagny yelping in surprise as she suddenly found herself lying flat on her back.

She grinned up at me, that sexy little smile that did me in every time. "That's not *half* of why I'm here," she purred, just before I kissed her.

* ~ * ~ * ~ * ~ * ~ *

The days got shorter as fall arrived; Halloween was just weeks away. It had been six months since I'd seen or spoken to my parents, and it weighed heavily on me. I tried not to think about it, but unfortunately forgetfulness was not a talent that I possessed. I was a dweller. I drove Dagny crazy with it; hell, I drove myself crazy. What could I have done differently, what could I do now? What should I do? Should I do anything? On and on it went. I went through a phase for a while in September thinking it was all my fault, that if I had been a better daughter none of this would have happened. Thank God Dagny shook me out of that misguided train of thought.

Carla's wedding was in a month, and though I had yet to come to a decision, I knew which way I was leaning. Hell, part of me wanted to go just to piss off my mother.

* ~ * ~ * ~ * ~ * ~ *

Since long before the start of the current semester, Dagny had been working with a young boy named Jesse, and though I hadn't realized it at the time, I had already met him — the young Native American boy who had hummed along with my singing game. She wasn't having much luck in drawing him out of his shell, so she thought maybe I should try. Dag got special permission to bring me in on the case. Jesse and I would be in a room with a two-way mirror so that Dagny and the psychologist could observe.

Jesse's file said that he was eight years old and lived with his grandmother. A year and a half before he had seen his father, a twenty-five year old drug dealer, shot to death near their house on the reservation, just outside of town. Since then, he had refused to speak. Ava, his grandmother, said he was fascinated by guns and did nothing but draw them. Dagny and I were poring over the file and discussing my approach.

"Do you think he'll be upset at seeing me instead of you?" I asked, setting Melo aside.

She shrugged. "I really don't know. This is totally an experiment, Chase. I hope it works, but I don't really have high expectations. I've been seeing this little boy for over a year and haven't gotten anywhere with him." Her shoulders slumped, and she sighed. "God, am I cut out to do this?"

"Babe, he's got some serious stuff to deal with." I put my hands on her arms. "You're wonderful with him, and you're great at what you do. You've been given a tough nut to crack. Well, so to speak." I grinned; so did she. "I have every confidence in you, Dag."

"Thanks. I wish I did."

There was a knock at the door. As Jesse and Ava walked in, Dagny closed the manila folder and put on a smile. She was really nervous and I wished that I could give her one last comforting hug, but it was not the time or the place.

"Hey, Jesse, how are you today?" He looked at her and shrugged. "Do you remember Chase?" She pointed at me, and I smiled and waved. The corners of his lips turned up in a tiny smile. Good sign. "She was in the waiting room with you a while back." He nodded, and Dag looked to me.

I knelt down to his level, but he backed away from me. I stayed where I was. "Hey, Jesse, how are you? My name is Chase Marin, but you can call me Chase, okay?" He just looked at me.

"Jesse, Chase wants to talk with you today. Are you all right with that? If we leave you in here with her?"

He looked from Dagny to me, then at his grandmother, who had been consulted a few days earlier in regards to the experiment. She nodded at him and smiled.

"She's a real nice lady, honey," Ava said. He looked back at me, his dark eyes curious but leery.

"Well, you two have a wonderful time, and I'll see you real soon, okay, Jesse?" Dag smiled charmingly at the boy, and then she and the grandmother left the room.

The boy stared at me for a moment, a good ten feet separating us. "Do you like music, Jesse?" I asked. After a long moment, he nodded, looking over at the case in the corner with curious eyes.

"Do you know what that is?" He shook his head, eyes still on the black case. "That, my little friend, is a guitar." He looked back at me, his eyes wide. "Have you ever seen a guitar before?" He nodded. "In real life?" He thought about it for a moment, then shook his head. "Would you like to?"

He cautiously watched my every move as I slowly made my way over to the guitar. I grabbed Melo and unzipped the case to take her out, watching Jesse from the corner of my eye. He kept a wary eye on me as he began to explore the room. He walked over to some toys that were set out in one corner, fingering a few but not showing any real interest.

I placed my guitar on the table in the center of the room and stepped away from it. "Would you like to touch it?" He shook his head, but his eyes told another story. "Do you like to sing, Jesse?" He shook his head. "Do you like music?" Again, no. I smiled. "I happen to know you like to hum. You did with me, remember?" His big, dark eyes just looked at me, flitting to Melo then back to me. I recollected the song that I had been humming that day, so long ago it seemed, and began to hum quietly.

Jesse stared at me, the tiniest of smiles appearing at the corner of his mouth. I hummed a little louder. It wasn't long before he began to hum, too. It was soft, barely audible, but there all the same.

I reached for Melo, keeping my movements small to avoid breaking the tenuous connection. I was shocked Jesse was doing as well as he was, considering it was just me and him in a strange room.

Getting the guitar into position, I began to play, soft and simple, something that could go with the song I was humming. His eyes large and curious, he watched my fingers as they danced through the chords. I stopped humming, wondering what he'd do. He also stopped, looking at me like I'd just stepped on his toe.

"Want to go on?" He took a moment, thinking over his answer, then slowly nodded. "How about if I sing? Want to sing with me?" He didn't respond. I started to strum again, and began to sing a simple little song that he could easily follow if he chose.

I played and sang for another half-hour until someone knocked on the door. Immediately Jesse's wall went up, and any distance that he'd walked that day was gone in a heartbeat. Dagny opened the door and smiled at me, then turned to her patient.

"Hey, Jesse, how are you?"

I said nothing, but I think Dag saw the same thing I did: there was a tiny spark in his eyes as if there were a little boy in there somewhere who wanted to jump out and play.

Jesse sat on a chair as his grandmother talked to Dagny and me. "I'm not at all surprised that he is reacting to the music. When he was a baby, his grandpa used to play for him." She looked at her grandson and smiled sadly. "I wish my little boy would come back to me." She sighed heavily. "Well, thank you. We'll see you next week, Dagny."

"See you then, Ava. Bye, Jesse."

He looked at her, then put up his little hand in a nearly nonexistent wave and walked out of the office. Dag turned to me and smiled, grabbing me in a strong hug.

"Whoa! What's that for?"

"We feel this was a success today, babe," she said, her voice soft so as not to be overheard. "You did a fantastic job."

"Really? Cool. And I didn't think I had gotten anywhere with him."

"Are you kidding? You got further in an hour than I have in a year. I don't know what your magic touch is, but damn, you've got it. Will you do this again for us, Chase?"

I looked at her, stunned. "Uh, yeah. Sure."

*~*~*~*~*~*

The wedding invitation on my lap and my sister's number in Berkley on the table in front of me, I stared at the phone. Dagny and I had talked about it again, but she had been wonderful, leaving our attendance totally up to me. I had mulled it over and over, trying to decide on the right thing to do. I knew that, ultimately, Dag was right: Carla was the only sister I would ever have, and she was doing her best to make peace between us. It would take me a while to get over the consequences of her interference, but I figured someday she and I would achieve some sort of better footing.

I picked up the cordless, tossing it from hand to hand. This would be it. I would have to see my parents and sing in front of my family for the first time. In addition, I might be subjecting Dagny to unnecessary unpleasantness. I had no idea how my mother would treat her. But I did know that she could handle herself with them, probably much better than I would.

I dialed the number and listened to the ringing of the phone. Part of me hoped she wasn't home, so that I could just leave a message on her answering machine.

"Hello?"

Or not. I took a deep breath, running a hand through my hair. "You've got one song. If the food is good, maybe two. And I will *not* wear a dress."

"What? Who is this?"

"Your sister." I sat back against the couch, my heart beating wildly in my chest.

"Chase?" The surprise was there in the higher pitching of her voice.

"Do you have any sisters I don't know about?"

She laughed softly. "No. So, are those your conditions for singing at my wedding?"

"Yes, they are."

"Does this mean... have you..."

"Forgiven you? No. It just means I'll come and sing at your wedding."

"Oh, Chase." Her voice was thick and I imagined the tears in her eyes. "Thank you, thank you, thank you. I really didn't think you were going to do it."

"To be honest, neither did I." My hands needed something to do to get rid of some of the nervousness; I grabbed the invitation and looked at it.

"Is Dagny coming too?"

"She said she'll go if I do, so I guess so."

"That's great. She's a really great person, Chase."

"I know. That's why I fell in love with her." She was quiet for a moment and I figured she was trying to process what I had told her.

"I'm thrilled for you, Chase. You seem really happy, and so does Dagny. I hope you guys stay that way."

"Thanks." I sighed. "Look, I've got to go. Send me a list of songs you'd like to hear so I can get hold of some lyrics, okay?"

"Yeah. I can email those to you. Take care, Chase."

"Yeah. You do the same."

"Um, well, bye."

"Later."

I pressed the off button and stared at the phone. *Lord, did I do the right thing?*

* ~ * ~ * ~ * ~ * ~ *

"No way. Absolutely no way in hell am I wearing that."

"Come on, babe. You won't even try it on for me?"

Dag laughed, that evil spark in her eye that I loved, but not enough to try on a cocktail dress. "Not in a million years."

"Okay, okay. You're no fun." She put the dress back on the rack and looked around the Talbots store.

"Are you sure we should be shopping here, Dag? This place is, like, way too expensive." I eyed merchandise as we walked through the quiet store.

"Sure. The thing is, you have to find a good sale. Come with me, o doubtful one. We'll get you something. If not here, then somewhere else."

"Goody."

We shopped and we shopped, and we shopped some more. Have I ever mentioned I'm not a big fan of shopping? True to her word, Dagny ended up finding us both really nice outfits for the wedding. For herself, she found a beautiful skirt set, a long, black matte jersey skirt with a slit up the side to the knee, and a sleeveless black and silver top. Definitely sexy. Me, I agreed to a pants suit in black, with pants in the same material as Dag's skirt. It was fitted and, according to my girlfriend, fit me perfectly in all the right places. A great deal of time and a hefty chunk of change later, we headed home with our bags in tow.

* ~ * ~ * ~ * ~ * ~ *

My first meeting with Jesse had been such a success, the powers that be gave me the opportunity to work with him. I was determined to get through to the boy, so Jesse and I were sitting in the room with each other for the sixth time. Melo at my side, my goal for this session was to get the boy to play with the guitar. I would happily sacrifice a guitar string or two for his mental health and well-being.

"See, this one makes this sound." I plucked a string, letting the tone die off. Jesse watched, obvious interest on his face. "Did you like that?" He nodded. "This one makes this sound." He watched me do it, then looked up at my face to see my reaction to it. "Kind of neat, huh?" He gave me a small smile. "You know what I think, big guy? I think you want to talk to me, and I think you want to play this guitar. Am I right?" He remained silent, but did not shake his head. I had come to find that this was him being indecisive. If he truly didn't want something, he shook his head outright. But if he wasn't sure, I had a chance. I put the guitar on the table and slid it over to him. "Try it."

Jesse looked at me, startled, but when he realized I wasn't coming with the instrument, he stayed where he was, staring at it. He looked up at me again before slowly reaching out to touch the neck, quickly withdrawing his hand after a fleeting contact.

"You're doing fine, Jesse. Go for it," I urged. He pulled the guitar toward him, looking at me with big dark eyes wide with surprise. "Kind of heavy, isn't it?" He nodded; I smiled. To my absolute delight, he smiled back. The small boy took the instrument and set it in his lap, against his body as he had seen me do. The thing was huge for him, his arm barely able to make it over the body to the frets. An idea struck me upside the head.

* ~ * ~ * ~ * ~ * ~ *

Later that night, as Dagny and I lay in bed, Jesse was still on my mind. "I can't believe I got him to take the guitar," I said, staring up at the ceiling. I pulled Dag a little closer, her body half lying on me, her usual favorite place.

"I know. Levy and I nearly jumped for joy, and Ava was beside herself." She laughed, kissing my neck. "You weave some magic, Chase."

"Nah. It's just trying to understand Jesse. God, I want so badly to help that boy."

"I'd say you're well on your way, baby."

* ~ * ~ * ~ * ~ * ~ *

The wedding was a week away, and I was as nervous as hell. CID had been practicing the song that I had picked from the list Carla had sent to me, a Celine Dion song that Carla had always loved. I had a difficult time singing really girlie ballads, but I was determined to do my best.

"Dude, when did you start singing for weddings?" Doug asked as we packed up our gear from rehearsal. "Did you rent some cheesy tux, too?"

"Fuck you, Doug," I said with a smile.

He put his arm around my shoulders as he walked me to my car. "You go out there and kick some serious ass, kid. Good luck to you."

"Thanks, man. God, I hate this kind of shit." I put my guitars in the trunk of my car.

"What shit? You do this twice a week, Chase."

"Yeah, but in a bar in front of a bunch of drunks, not in front of a bunch of stodgy people in gowns and tuxedos."

"Ah, it'll still be in front of a bunch of drunks, believe me. Just sing later in the evening and people will be totally sauced by then."

I grinned. "Asshole."

"I try. You'll kill 'em, kid."

"Thanks. See you tomorrow night."

"Later."

* ~ * ~ * ~ * ~ * ~ *

I paced the living room of the apartment, sweating, and afraid I might ruin the new suit. I still had an entire night to go. Dagny was still getting ready, and I was beginning to wish I had waited a while longer before I dressed.

"Babe, will you stop? Everything'll be fine," Dag yelled to me from the bedroom.

"No. I'll make an ass out of myself. Why the hell am I doing this?"

I went into the bedroom. Dag was standing in front of the dresser mirror, putting in her earrings. Her reflection looked at me.

"You'll do just fine. You know the song, you know what you're doing. Just imagine you're at Gotfry's. You have absolutely no problem singing there, right?" I shook my head. "All right then." She turned to me, looking me over. "My God, you look yummy."

The speculative look in her eyes told me that we had to get out of there before it wasn't just sweat that was making my clothes damp. As we left the bedroom, I lagged behind, looking my lover up and down. *Holy shit, is it legal to be so damn sexy?*

Dagny stopped to pick up the handbag she'd bought to go with her outfit, and I stepped up behind her, hugging her, pressing her body to mine. "You are so unbelievably beautiful," I whispered into her ear, giving it a quick lick.

"Oh, you are so mean," she moaned. I chuckled evilly, my hands sliding up to cup her breasts. "You better stop now, Chase, or we'll never get out of here."

"Okay. We'll just stay here and make love all day and stay in bed eating chocolate. How does that sound?"

Dag turned in my arms and glared playfully. "You are such a baby." She kissed me lightly. "Come on, baby. We have to go."

"Okay." I felt like a child, sulking all the way to the car. I knew Dagny was right — I would never forgive myself if I didn't go, but my stomach was in knots, and I wanted to throw up. Why had I agreed to sing? Having to see my parents again was bad enough, but having to sing in front of them? I must be suicidal.

Todd was Catholic, and Carla had converted so they could be married in a Catholic ceremony. The cathedral was beautiful. Dagny tried to get me to march proudly up the center aisle and sit my butt down with the family. I couldn't bring myself to do it. The thought of my mother staring at me during the entire ceremony was just too much for me to handle, so I made the decision to sit in the back. Besides, sitting in the back would get us out first. Yeah, right.

Man, were those matrimonial rites long! I briefly wondered if the priest thought the length of the service had something to do with the longevity of the marriage. The ceremony finally ended, and I nearly sprinted out the door, Dagny following close behind.

"Hold on there, stud. I can't run in heels."

"I'm sorry." I slowed as we got closer to Freud.

Dagny walked beside me, glancing at me from time to time. "Are you okay, babe?" she whispered.

I nodded. "God, she looked so beautiful, Dag," I said, my voice choking up. My sister wore an ivory gown with lots of satin and lace and beadwork. I was sure it had cost a small fortune. Todd and all his groomsmen were in black tuxedos; Todd's bow tie and vest were ivory satin. Together the bride and groom had made an incredibly lovely couple.

"Yeah, she did. And Todd looked so handsome." She sighed. "Did you see your mom?" I shook my head as I climbed into the passenger side of the SUV. "She was gorgeous, wearing a white and blue dress. She looked really good. Your dad, too."

"You know, I used to dream about my dad giving me away when I got married. The crazy thing is, I never wanted to get married." I smiled at her. "Now I know why." I squeezed her hand. "I remember when I was a kid, watching movies where the father gave the daughter away, and my dad'd get choked up." I felt my throat tighten as I looked out the window. "I've really hurt them, Dag."

"You have a right to live your own life, Chase."

I tried to make myself believe every word she said. I knew she was right, but it still hurt. "I know. And I want you to understand that I don't regret a moment of it, okay?"

She nodded. We pulled up to a stoplight, and she looked over at me.

"I love you, Dag. It just hurts that my family has to be such assholes, not wanting to be a part of my life unless I live it on their terms. Why couldn't today have been a great day for all of us? They love you, so why couldn't they just accept the fact that you and I are more than just friends, that we're still the same people we always were?" I looked out the side window. "I don't get it."

"Neither do I, sweetheart. Neither do I."

When we arrived at the reception hall, numerous cars were already there, and I started to get butterflies in my stomach. It would soon be time for me to sing, and I was terrified. This would officially be the largest crowd I'd ever sung in front of, but despite the large numbers, I was really only afraid of one person. How sad was that?

Carla, Todd, his parents and mine all stood at the door, greeting the guests as they came in. God, I hadn't thought about the receiving line. I had to grit my teeth to stop myself from running or crying. Dag was behind me, her hand discreetly on my back for comfort, especially as we got closer to my family. We had to go through the wedding party first. Finally it was our turn to see Carla and Todd.

"Chase." My sister pulled me into a tight hug. Finally letting me go, she looked at me. "You look really nice," she said, approval in her voice.

"What, were you afraid I'd show up in jeans and a tank?"

She grinned. "It crossed my mind."

"Yeah, yeah." I hugged her again, all the resentful feelings I'd had seeming to shrink in the face of the idea that my sister was married. "I can't believe it," I said, trying not to choke up.

"I know. Pretty amazing, isn't it?"

I looked at the two of them, so much in love. "Good luck, you guys."

"Thank you, Chase," Todd said, smiling.

"Are you ready to do this?" Carla asked.

"I don't know. I haven't seen her in months. What do you think she'll say to me, if she talks to me at all?"

"I meant the singing."

"Oh." I grinned, embarrassed. Easy to see what was foremost in my mind. "Yeah, I think so."

"I can't wait," she said. "We'll see you in there. Hey, Dagny."

"Congratulations, Carla." The voices faded as my mother came into view. She was two people ahead in the line, and her eyes were on me as she waited for the person ahead of me to pass by. The look on her face was one of contempt. That was all it took. My mushy center turned hard and cold. If she wanted to play it that way, so could I.

I congratulated Todd's parents and moved on to my mother. I passed her, then decided to stop. I turned to face her, meeting the eyes that bored into mine. Her jaw was set, her chin raised. Mine did the same. It was a silent stand-off, mother against daughter: no one would win. No one ever did.

Finally, I'd had enough and I turned away, not saying a word, moving on to my father. Dagny smiled at my mother, but she didn't see Dag as worthy of her attention. Stepping up behind me, Dagny moved away from her, seemingly unfazed by the coldness.

"Hello, Chase." My father's shoulders were slumped and he looked tired.

"Hello, Dad."

"How are you?"

"Fine."

"I want to talk to you later," he said quietly.

"Sure. I'll be around." With a nonchalant shrug, I moved on.

"Dagny," he said, his voice stern, strong.

"Mr. Marin," she said, hers just as formally polite.

As we made our way into the hall, Dag took my arm. "Are you okay, Chase?" she asked quietly.

Not trusting my voice, I nodded. Never in my life had I experienced something more pointless, so absolutely ridiculous than the way my mother had acted just now. I was appalled, surprised, hurt and angry.

Dinner was served — prime rib, salad, and incredible desserts. I had no idea how Carla and Todd had managed to pay for everything. I'm sure my parents helped out. Hell, they wouldn't help me with my college education anymore, but by God, let's give Carla one hell of a wedding.

We sat at a table with strangers. My parents were at the head table with the happy couple and Todd's brother and parents. I had never felt so uncomfortable in all my life. I just wanted to sing my song and leave.

I wasn't sure if the folks we sat with were part of Todd's family, or friends of theirs from school, but Dag started to chat with the man who was sitting next to her. Soon they had me in the conversation, and I began to feel a bit better, like people actually did see me. It wasn't long afterwards that the bride and groom were up on the stage.

"Can I have your attention, please?" Todd asked into the microphone, looking around at the guests. Silverware clattered as people stopped eating and waited expectantly. "First of all, I'd like to thank you all for coming. This has been a truly wondrous day for us." He looked at my sister and smiled. "Though I have to admit, I'm not sure which debt I'll be paying for longer — my wedding or med school." This drew a collective chuckle, even from me. "As I get older, I discover more and more about life and the people in it. People do shape your life. They can make it a wonderful experience," again he looked at Carla, "or they can make it pure hell." I glanced over at my mother, surprised to see her looking down at her hands. "I want to thank Carla Marin — yes, she's keeping her last name — for being who she is, and for agreeing to be my wife." I looked at my sister, who had tears in her eyes. He leaned over and kissed her. This precipitated a round of "awww" and applause.

Carla took the microphone. "Hello, everyone. You know, going into this, I had no idea these dresses were such a pain to get into."

Again, I chuckled. Who knew my sister and Todd both had a sense of humor? Huh.

"But, it's all worth it." She turned adoring eyes on her new husband. I felt a hand on my leg under the table, and turned to see Dag smiling at me. I smiled back, squeezing her fingers. "Thank you, Todd, for asking me to be in your life. I love you." They kissed again.

Previously I would have been plenty irritated by that point, but as I looked at Dagny, I realized just what love could make you do, and how funny you looked doing it.

"Everyone, I'd like to introduce a very special person who will be singing for us." My head jerked back to the stage to see Todd at the mic again. He smiled at me. "Carla's baby sister, Chase. Come on up, Chase." The guests clapped and I stood on shaky legs, feeling like a new colt trying to walk for the first time.

"Good luck, baby," Dag whispered. I smiled at her.

As I headed for the stage, I glanced over at my parents. My father looked surprised but interested. My mother was nothing short of furious. Climbing the stairs to the stage, suddenly my suit felt about three sizes too tight. *God, this sucks.* The band they had hired was getting set up behind me, and I took several deep breaths, trying to get my nerves under control. As I waited, I did a mental run-through of the lyrics.

"You ready?" the lead guitarist asked. I turned to him and nodded. Stepping up to the mic, I tried to focus my attention on Todd and Carla, but it was difficult. They were seated right next to my parents. The look of contempt on my mother's face was almost too much to stomach.

"Hello, ladies and gentlemen. I am so happy for my sister and Todd. They make a great couple, don't they?" I had to do something to divert my attention from what I was about to do. I began to clap for them, and the guests caught on and clapped, too. When the applause died down, I leaned into the mic. "This song is dedicated to them." The music started, and I closed my eyes, waiting for my cue and trying to get into the state of mind that I used at Gotfry's. *Just forget about what you're revealing to a room full of perfect strangers. Just do it, and love it.*

As I began to sing, my nerves melted off me like butter. The words and their meaning were taking over — love, life, and happiness. I smiled at the newlyweds as I sang of those things, forgetting about my mother and her pettiness. This was Carla's and Todd's day.

The guests listened attentively, many of them getting lost in the song themselves. I was grateful; it went off without a hitch. The song ended, and I was rewarded with thunderous applause, including my father's. My mother only stared, her mouth open, her eyes wide. *Yeah, eat it up.*

Todd stood up. "Let's hear it for Chase Marin."

There was a fresh round of applause, Dag looking as if she were about to burst with pride, her hands pounding together. I smiled at her and she smiled back at me, letting me know I had done well.

"How about another, Chase?" Todd asked

A third round of applause encouraged me to oblige. "Um, sure. Any requests?"

"Do some Elvis for us." Todd grinned, rubbing his wife's arm. My sister had loved The King since we were kids.

"Okay." I turned to the band and told them what I had in mind, and they readily complied. I stepped back up to the microphone and let the music begin. This time I looked around the room at the guests, then finally to Dag, telling her through the song how I *Can't Help Falling In Love.* I loved her with my entire heart, and I wanted her to know it. She had a big smile on her face, but I could tell she was holding back her emotions. I loved it when my singing made her cry. It meant that what I felt had successfully been conveyed to her. Like that first night, when I'd sung *Troubled Waters* to her after Darrel died. I think that night was when I first tried to tell her how I felt, even though neither of us truly realized it, or the extent to which I cared.

To my surprise, Todd and Carla went out on the dance floor in front of the stage. I watched them: young love. Life was good.

The song came to an end, and I smiled as the applause rolled in, including from the band behind me. I stood to the side, my hand out to them so they could get their well deserved recognition.

"Thank you very much. Please enjoy the rest of the night."

I took my leave of the stage, my mother's eyes following me as I made my way to Dagny. I would have given anything to kiss her right then. I needed that connection with her. Instead of sitting, I took her hand. "Come on." We found the nearest bathroom and ducked inside one of the stalls.

"You were fantastic," she whispered, her arms around my neck.

"Really? Did I do okay?"

"God, more than okay!" She leaned up and kissed me. I, of course, kissed her back. The kiss was not filled with desire or lust, just love, plain and simple. "I love you, Chase."

"I love you, too, Dag."

When we got back to the reception, my father pulled me aside and led me over to the door. I had no idea what he wanted, so I kept my guard up, crossing my arms over my chest. He looked nervous, pacing a bit before coming to a stop in front of me.

"Well, first of all, you were really good up there." There was a mixture of pride and pain on his face. I hadn't seen him in months, and he looked older and very sad. This rupture had really taken its toll on him.

"Thank you."

"Why didn't you share this talent with us before, Chase?"

I was taken aback. "Are you serious? Singing isn't med school. Would you really have given a shit?"

"Don't talk to me that way, Chase. I am still your father." He kept his voice low so he wouldn't be overheard. I seriously doubted anyone knew what was going on. As if he or my mom would ever reveal the true, evil nature of their youngest child.

"Then act like it," I growled. He looked at me, stunned. I almost expected him to slap me.

Instead he looked down for a moment and then reached into his pocket. "Well, anyway, the reason I brought you over here was to give you this. Your mother and I started a college fund for you and Carla when you were little. It's paid for your education thus far, and I see no reason why it shouldn't continue to do so. After all, it is your money." He handed me an envelope. "In there is a check for the remaining money. I hope you finish school, Chase, but it is yours to do with as you wish."

I looked at the envelope, not sure what I was feeling. Relief for one thing, but also I felt very sad. My throat tightened just the slightest bit, but I quickly swallowed it down. "Why did it have to go like this?"

My father looked at me, shook his head. "To be honest, Chase, I don't know. I do not agree with what you're doing, but, hell, I just don't know." He ran a hand through his graying hair. "Well, anyway, there you are."

I watched him walk away, wondering what would be between us a year from now, two, five, ten. Where would I be, and what would I be to them?

As the night went on, my mother continued to refuse to even look at me, but after a while I decided to ignore her childishness. This was Carla's wedding, not my chance to attack my mother, no matter how much I might have wanted to. Dag and I had a great time. We laughed with people we met; we both even danced with a guy. That was a change.

"Okay, it's time to throw the bouquet!" Carla exclaimed from the stage. "All you single women, get on out there." Dag and I looked at each other, not sure if we should bother. We weren't exactly single.

"Come on," she said, grinning mischievously. She grabbed me by the wrist and dragged me out to the middle of the dance floor. We were surrounded by a whole group of single, mostly young, really giggly women and girls. I was one of the tallest in the group, so figured I had a shot, but who knew? Carla looked at all of us, a smile on her face, the bouquet in her hands.

"Ready?" She turned around, her back to us, and tossed that puppy high into the air. I watched it, almost as if it were in slow motion: up into the air it went, then falling, falling, falling. *Crap, it's headed right for me.* I reached up a hand, feeling the soft petals against my skin, nearly letting it slip past me, but reaching up with the other one to get a better hold on it. I snatched it out of the air and brought it in to my body. I looked at the beautiful ivory roses, then turned to see Dagny looking at me.

* ~ * ~ * ~ * ~ * ~ *

When we got back to the apartment, I set down the bouquet and turned to look at my girlfriend, who was slipping out of her high heels. As I watched, I suddenly realized that she might very well be all I had left. Though it was indeed a relief, my father giving me the money left in my college fund, it was also very final. It felt far too much like a goodbye.

"Hey, baby," Dagny said as I moved up behind her, wrapping my arms around her waist. She fell back against me, her head tilting slightly as I kissed the side of her neck.

"I need you tonight," I whispered against the warm skin. I think she understood, as she always seemed to do. She ran her fingers over my hands before they ran up my arms, the touch muted over the material of the jacket to my suit. Not good enough. As I explored her neck and ear with lips and tongue, my fingers found their way to the zipper of her dress, slowly lowering it, revealing the smooth strength of Dagny's back.

Taking her hand, I led Dagny over to the couch, where I sat, knees spread. She stood between them, the dress sliding down her arms and body until she finally stepped out of it. I looked up at the perfection standing before me, running my hands up the sides of her thighs, the silkiness of her nylons tactile bliss. Reaching the waistline, I tugged the nylons down, taking her panties with them. Dagny steadied herself on my shoulders, her eyes never leaving my face. As she stood before me in her bra, I was overwhelmed with love and the relief that this precious woman was with me. She actually loved me, something I desperately needed.

Leaning forward, I inhaled the scent of Dagny's skin, nuzzling the warmth and sighing as I felt her fingers running through my hair. I could already smell her arousal, and it encouraged me. Not like I really needed it. I pulled her down to sit on my lap, her warmth nearly burning me through the material of my pants.

"You are so loved, Chase," she whispered against my lips, her fingers sliding up and down along the lapel of my jacket.

"I don't feel so loved," I whispered back, my ardor suddenly cooled by the profound sadness of the situation with my family. I felt small and alone.

"You are the most wonderful person I've ever known," she continued, beginning to slowly push the jacket from my shoulders. I helped by shrugging out of it. "Your heart is like nothing I've ever seen, your goodness shines through in those gorgeous baby blues." She smiled as she looked into the eyes in question. I closed them as she leaned forward and placed the softest of kisses on my forehead, strangely as comforting as it was erotic. "You're smart," a kiss to my left cheek, "beautiful," a kiss to my right cheek, "ridiculously talented," a kiss to my nose, "the sexiest woman on the planet," a kiss to my chin, "and all mine."

I met Dagny's heated kiss, tongue stroke for tongue stroke. I was overwhelmed, wrapped up in the love I knew Dagny had for me. It wasn't my mother, it wasn't my father, but it was love, and it was strong.

"I love you," I said, my words breathy as my arousal surged once more, my fingers expertly releasing Dagny's bra.

"I love you more," she teased, breaking the kiss to pepper my throat with hot, wet kisses. Her bra released, Dagny tossed the garment aside, fully nude now. She pressed her breasts against mine as she pushed out bodies together, her mouth finding mine again. I could feel her snake her fingers between us, quickly unbuttoning my blouse. I ran my hands through her hair, which had grown long over the past year, the silky strands soft on my skin. Soon my shirt was pushed from my shoulders, then my bra. Naked from the waist up, I pulled Dagny back to me, needing to feel her skin against mine. We both moaned, my hands running up and down her back. The heat coming from between Dagny's legs was like pure liquid fire.

Within moments Dagny had me fully naked and lying back on the couch, her body atop mine. She was unstoppable as she traced heated trails across my neck, over my shoulders, and finally to my breasts. I hissed, eyes closing as she took a painfully hard nipple between her lips and fluttered her tongue over it. I could feel her hips moving against me, her leg slipping between mine. I was surprised to feel how wet she was, her need painting my thigh. Dagny's ministrations moved to my other breast before moving further south. A long, languid grown escaped my throat as Dag nipped at the skin of my stomach, then the insides of my thighs.

"Oh, baby," I whispered, hips lifting off the couch at the first touch of her tongue. "God, yes."

Dagny hummed against me, her tongue lapping at my desire, mouth sucking in my clit. My brain shut down at the intense pleasure that flooded through me. Suddenly I realized I wanted more.

"Baby?" I managed through my lustful haze. She hummed in acknowledgement. "I need you inside, baby. Please, go inside." She looked up at me suddenly from between my spread legs.

"Are you sure, Chase?" At my vigorous nod, I heard a shaky release of breath, though not entirely sure who it was from, as Dagny brought a hand up to my slit. "My God, you're so wet," she moaned, a finger teasing my opening.

"Yes," I hissed, thrusting my hips up to encourage her to enter. I needed her as close as humanly possible, needed her to touch my very soul.

Dagny slowly slid inside, both of us holding our breath. Though not a favorite of mine, it felt wonderful, and I spread my legs wider, draping one over the back of the couch. I cried out as Dagny's mouth was on me again, her finger still slowly sliding in and out of my engorged sex. Within moments, a second entered, and Dagny sucked hard on my clit. I cried out, my entire body lurching with the intensity of my orgasm. I called out something that sounded almost like her name, my mind exploding with a euphoria I'd never before experienced.

As I regained control, I felt Dagny climb back up my body, wrapping me in strong arms. She rained kisses across my face, brushing damp strands of hair out of my eyes. She whispered over and over again how much she loved me, her embrace tightening when I could no longer hold back the tears.

"Shh," she cooed, managing to turn us so she lay on her back, me atop her. I buried my face in her neck. "It's all going to be okay, Chase. It's okay. I'm here with you."

I couldn't speak. My profound sense of loss consumed me, though somehow I knew that if anyone could make me feel whole again, it would be Dagny. Eventually my tears dried up and I felt exhausted — mind, body and soul. Dagny held me as I drifted off into sleep, her words of love soothing me into peace.

# Chapter 14

Dag put her arm through mine as we looked in the different shops. We had come to the mall to look for a student guitar for Jesse, and I had been thrilled when I found one on sale. It was adorable, just big enough for an eight-year-old boy.

"Are you sure he'll like it?" I asked, looking down at the package in my hands.

"Yes, babe. I'm positive, for the fifth time," Dag said, thoroughly exasperated.

"Okay. But only if you're sure."

With a growl she turned to me and took me by the shoulders. "Chase, Jesse will like the guitar!" She shook me for emphasis.

"Okay, okay."

Jesse and I were ten weeks into our sessions. I wanted so badly for that little boy to talk to me, to sing with me. I wanted him to have what every child his age should have. It was hard not to get frustrated, to keep concentrating on the progress we had made.

Dagny had resumed his normal sessions with her, and was surprised that he was actually responding to her. He still had not said a word, but was willing to draw her pictures, and even brought her a paper from school that he had received a gold star on. I had been excited when I'd gotten him to actually play Melo. He had let me get close enough to teach him some very simple chords, and I knew it was time he had his own.

Having made our primary purchase, we navigated down the hall toward the food court when we passed a group of benches in the middle. One person in particular caught my attention, and I did a double take.

"Hang on a sec, Dag," I said, heading over to him. He was sitting with an ankle crossed over his knee, his elbow balanced on that as he rested his chin on his hand. He looked totally bored, and I grinned. He hated to shop; I knew that from personal experience.

"So, who managed to drag you to the mall?" I asked, standing just a little to the side and behind Mike. He looked at me over his shoulder, then turned to face me.

"Hey." He gave me a small smile. "How are you, Chase?" Standing, he gave me a hug, and I hugged him back.

"I'm great." I indicated Dagny, who was standing back a bit to give me a chance to talk to him. "You remember Dagny?" He nodded, giving her a small wave.

She smiled. "Hi, Mike."

He turned back to me, and I looked him over, noting the normal clothes and hairstyle. Before, he had looked every bit the drummer, his usual attire a metal band shirt and torn jeans to go along with the spikes in his hair. Now, he was clean cut, although his usual stubbly beard was still in evidence. I had to laugh at that. He once told me he'd never get rid of that, and he had apparently been telling the truth. "You look great."

"So do you. How's school going?"

"It's going great. I'm more than half way to that degree. I've been real busy, got a job, still in CID, came out, Carla got married. You know, the usual stuff."

"Whoa, wait a second." He looked at Dagny again, then at me. "You came out?" I grinned and nodded. "Oh, does that make so much sense now." He smiled, crossing his arms over his chest. "Wow. So I take it you guys are together, now?"

Again I nodded. "It's been interesting with the folks."

"Yeah, I bet. That's great about Carla. Todd?"

"Yeah. So what about you?"

"I'm waiting for my fiancée." He glanced over his shoulder at the Gap store behind him. "She takes forever. We just got engaged."

"No shit?" For just a second, I felt pained. He had meant a lot to me at one time and I still cared about him, probably always would. I was glad he was happy, though. "That's great, Mike. Really."

"Thanks." He looked down to hide his obviously proud smile. "I also went back to school. I just finished up my associate degree in graphic design."

I looked at him, stunned. "Who are you and what have you done with Michael? Good for you."

"Well, it looks like things have turned out well for us both, I guess." He smiled.

I nodded. "Yeah, it does. I wish you well, Mike. I always did."

"You, too, Chase." He leaned down and gave me a quick kiss on the cheek. "See you around."

"Yeah. Bye." With one last smile, I turned to Dag, and we walked away.

* ~ * ~ * ~ * ~ * ~ *

I paced the room nervously, hoping this wasn't going to be too much for Jesse. I had the guitar lying on the table, ready for its new owner to take it home. Oh, I hoped he liked it. No matter how good Dag was at her job, she admitted she really didn't know how he'd react, either. I wasn't sure why I was so worried. I think it boiled down to my really caring for the little guy and wanting him to have a normal life. I had come so far with Jesse, and if too big a step at one time resulted in a setback of our progress now, it would nearly kill me.

"Hon, you have to learn some professional distance," Dagny told me one night. "It's great that you care so much for Jesse; hell, I do, too. But in the end, he will go on, and you can't go with him."

I knew that, but I also knew I would do whatever it took to get through to him.

The door to the outer office opened, and I knew it would be a matter of moments before Jesse would be here and see his gift. I had called Ava to get her input and to ask if it was okay. She had started crying; she thought her grandson would be overjoyed. We were about to see.

Jesse and Ava appeared, both looking a bit sullen.

"You guys okay?" Dagny asked.

"This one got into a fist fight yesterday," Ava said, looking down at her grandson.

I looked at Jesse and saw the slight discoloration under his right eye. *Jeez, eight and already has a shiner.*

"What happened?" Dag asked, kneeling down to look at his face. He glared at her, then at me.

"I don't know. I think some little kid made fun of him or something. The teacher said Jesse threw the first punch."

"Hey, Jess. How are you?" Dagny asked, smiling at him. He didn't respond.

"Those kids, they're so mean sometimes. They tease him because he is different from them."

Ava was obviously upset, tears beginning to well in her dark eyes as she stroked her grandson's hair. I looked at him with concern. Just the sort of thing I didn't want to happen to him. I knew as he got older it would get worse. Kids were cruel.

"Hey, big guy, guess what." I took a step forward. He watched me, but did not step away. This was good. "I got you a little something. Wanna see what it is?" He stared at me, seemingly unsure of what to do. I decided to take a different tack. "Do you like birthday parties, Jesse?" He nodded. I smiled. "So you like it when you get presents?" Again he nodded, this time with the tiniest of smiles. "Well, come here, then."

I walked toward the table, knowing Dag and Ava were watching closely. The three of us had been excited about this all week, curious to see how Jesse would react. I picked up the gift-wrapped guitar, a dark blue bow tied around it. An interaction of questions and gestures during one of our previous sessions had revealed that blue was his favorite color.

Jesse stood with his grandmother for a moment before deciding to walk over to me. He stood about a yard away, but his eyes were shining. It was good to see. I was afraid we might have a major setback as a result of the fight.

"This is for you, Jesse. Now, you have to let your sisters see it, too, okay?"

He looked up at me, then at the gift, slowly nodding. I gently nudged the guitar toward him, and he looked at it for a few moments before accepting it. I could almost read his thoughts as he tried to tell what it was by its shape and its weight, shaking it slightly. I stood back, my arms crossed over my chest, afraid to breathe. My little charge turned the brightly colored package around in his hands, studying it. I was fascinated by the way his brain worked. As I'd been working with him for the past three months, I'd thought he'd be a good scientist or even architect. He was creative, analytic, and intelligent. Now if only I could get him to say even one word.

Paper ripped as he tore into the gift, throwing the wrapping aside. When he saw what it was, his eyes opened wide, and he looked up at me.

"It's yours, Jess." He stared for a moment longer before his eyes flashed back to the guitar in his hands and a wide smile spread across his lips, seeping up into his eyes. He turned and hurried over to his grandmother, lifting his gift for her to see.

"What did you get, boy?" she asked, kneeling down. "A guitar?" He nodded vigorously.

I glanced at Dag. Her eyes met mine, and we shared one of those great moments of silent exchange. Turning back to Jesse, I saw him slowly walking toward me, the guitar held out. I wasn't sure what he was doing.

"What's up?" I asked, looking down at him. He thrust it toward me. "I don't know what you want, Jess."

"He wants—"

Dag gestured Ava to silence. "No. Let him tell her."

He refused to say anything, just held the guitar out to me.

"Do you want me to teach you how to play?" He nodded, smiling. I casually sat in a chair, my arm hanging over the back. "You know, Jesse, this guitar is yours, and it is a gift, but it does not come without a price." He looked at me, his eyes narrowing. "If you want to learn how to play it like I play Melo, you have to talk to me." He just stared, then looked down at the guitar in his hands. "Can you do that for me?" Not looking at me, he shrugged. "Jesse?" Dark eyes met mine. "Can you?" Finally, with a small sigh, he nodded.

* ~ * ~ * ~ * ~ * ~ *

I smiled as I thought back to that day with Jesse. I would never forget that little guy, no matter how many kids I talked to or helped.

"Yo, Chase. You in outer space, or what?"

"Sorry. You just reminded me of someone. You have to understand things do change, Shanita."

"Hell, my parents don't give nothing about me, though, Chase. Fuck, man, my dad kicked my ass when he found me an' Nora together. He don' care."

"You are so young, Shanita, and you have a jumpstart on your peers just because you have a clear picture of who you are. That's a great place to start."

"Man, I wish things could turn out for me like they did you. The only thing that makes me feel better is that you was screwy as a kid."

I laughed, patting the girl on the knee. "Thanks, Shanita. I'm glad I could be of service." She grinned. "Okay, well our time is up. I'll be here again next week. Same time, same channel." I grinned; so did she as I stood. "Okay, you. I have to go pick up my son."

Shanita stood and put her hands in her pockets, suddenly looking very shy. "Um, I just kind of wanted to say thank you, and all, know what I'm sayin'."

I put my hand on her shoulder. She would be tall, already standing a good few inches taller than me. "You got it. I'll see you next week."

"Oh, hey, and tell the cute blonde chick hi for me." She grinned widely as I headed out of the room.

"Which cute blonde chick?"

"The one you is celebrating a decade with. Man, you's a honky."

"Thank you, Shanita. I take my honky-ness quite seriously."

"Man, get outta here."

I laughed all the way out to my car.

As I drove to the daycare center, I thought about my day's session with Shanita, and it made me angry to think of what that poor girl had to go through. Her parents were not the richest people in Portland, but they were not living on the streets, either. Shanita was one of five children, the second to the oldest. She was a gay teen who had been caught with her girlfriend. Her father had beaten the crap out of her and then kicked her out. Shanita was now at a shelter for runaway teens.

I was working with four other girls there at the shelter, but Shanita was the only one who was a lesbian and struggling with its effect on her family and life. This shelter was on my schedule three days a week. I also worked with kids at the detention hall outside town, visiting them twice a week, then off to Green Meadows, the alternative high school. Four times a month, I also worked with the kids at a local elementary school.

"Hey, Chase. How are you, hon?"

I smiled at Martha, Hunter's daycare lady. "Not too bad. How about yourself?"

"Pretty good. Our little man here got into a spot of trouble today, though."

I looked down at my two year old son who sat with a group of kids playing cars. He looked at me with his big blue eyes, trying to get the puppy dog look in there. I grabbed him up under the arms and lifted him high into the air as he squealed with delight.

"What did you do, big guy?"

"Nothin'." He smiled when I set him down again.

I looked at Martha. "Biting again?" She nodded. I turned scornful eyes on him. "What did I tell you about that, Hunter?" He threw his bottom lip out. "Hun uh. Don't even try that." I looked to the daycare worker again. "I'm sorry, Martha. We've really been working with him on that."

"No harm, dear. I just thought you should know."

"Thanks. See you Monday. Let's go, fella."

I got Hunter strapped into his car seat, pulled the Lincoln Navigator out of the parking lot and headed home. Tonight was my night to make dinner, since Dag was seeing patients until six. Tonight was also a special night for Hunter. Carrie and Paul were bringing their five-year-old, Brianne, and two-year-old, Jake, to our house. Once a month, they went out for a night on the town, just the two of them, and we watched the rugrats. They had very busy and stressful lives, Paul a professor at the University of Oregon, and Carrie a painter with her work in some of the best galleries in Oregon.

I pulled into the garage, turned off the engine, and opened the back to get my boy out.

"Come on, big guy." I unstrapped him and lifted him to rest on my hip as I went into the house. Our dog Gracie, a beautiful Husky fur ball, barked excitedly as I walked through the kitchen. "Hello, baby. How's my girl?" I knelt down, letting her greet me and Hunter with excited wags of her tail and licks to our faces. When I received a tongue in my mouth that wasn't Dag's, I knew greetings were over. Hunter followed me around as I put his diaper bag in the closet and went over to the answering machine. He rambled on and on about his day, and all the toys he played with at "dare". He hadn't quite figured out that there were two words to day care, and that dare wasn't one of them.

Hitting the play button on the answering machine, I gathered the ingredients for my specialty, homemade pizza. Hunter happily munched on a graham cracker and sipped at his little cup of juice as I kneaded the dough.

The first message was from Dagny's mom, telling us they'd be able to make it in two weeks. I smiled; Dag would be thrilled. The next message caught me unawares, and I stopped to listen.

I could not help the grin spreading across my face as I took the cordless from the breakfast bar and quickly dialed Dag's voicemail.

"Hey, beautiful. I just wanted to call and tell you I love you, and to hurry home. I am *not* handling these monsters all by myself. Oh, and Joie called. Seven pounds, nine ounces, twenty inches long. I love you."

I set the phone down and continued creating my pizza. My mind began to wander back to a time so long ago. Talking to Shanita had made me realize just what I had. Things were not absolutely perfect, of course. Life isn't perfect, nor are the people who comprise it. Even so, I had an incredible woman by my side and a son who was beautiful, smart — sometimes a little too much for his own good — and a wonderful career and home.

Taking my little journey back through my early life for that troubled girl had reminded me of so much. It had been such a hard time in some ways, but a valuable time, too. I had learned who I was and where I was going.

After graduation I went on for my masters while Dag finished up her doctorate. She got a job at the university until I finished, then we both found work in Portland, Oregon. We'd been there ever since. The climate was great, the landscape beautiful, and the people friendly and giving.

Five years ago we had started discussing children; Dag's clock was ticking so loudly it kept me awake at night. Finally I had agreed, and we had started to look into having a baby. Dagny got pregnant three years ago, and I have to admit, I was not so happy about it. I was scared that I would turn out to be the kind of parent mine were. Dagny assured me that would not be the case, but still I wondered. The day arrived, a rainy day in December, Hunter Marin-Robertson was born. He was so beautiful, just like his mother. His skin and hair fair, but his eyes blue like the father's. He was truly the greatest joy I could ever have imagined. He and Dagny made my life complete.

Carrie and Paul had followed us to Portland a year later, Dag getting Paul on with the local university where she still taught classes part time. He also still taught there, receiving his tenure four years ago. Natalie and I still spoke on occasion, I'd say about four or five times a year, either through email or phone calls. She, married to her career, was a geneticist in New Jersey, and had also decided to come for a visit in two weeks. Dagny was very excited about it.

Family. Ah, now there was an interesting subject. My father and I had made great strides toward reestablishing a relationship. He came by himself to both my graduations, which had meant a lot to me. My mother and I had not spoken in far too many years. Once Hunter was born, my father made her come to Oregon, and when she saw his little face, I swear I saw a light go on in there somewhere. She took him in her arms and began to cry. We were not close by any means, but she did call on occasion, and we see them for Christmas about every second year.

Carla and I have turned out to be surprisingly close. She and Todd had started their family practice in D. C. six years ago, thanks to donations from their fathers. They had yet to have children, so my dad was beside himself to have a grandson in Hunter. He was a wonderful grandfather, far better than I had ever imagined. But then, he was almost retired now, so he had the time.

I put the pizza in the oven, and just as I closed the door, the garage door opened.

"Hunter boy, mommy's home."

"Mommy?" He came tearing around the corner, toy car in his hand. "Mommy, mommy!" I grinned as I watched his face light up, blue eyes huge with excitement.

"Hunter!" could be heard from the other side of the door to the house from the garage.

"Mommy!"

"Hunter?"

This was a game they played nightly, until finally Dagny appeared, and our son squealed at the sight of her. Dag, looking gorgeous in her green suit, walked in, picking up the little guy as she did. "How are you, baby boy?" she asked, kissing his forehead.

"Good, mommy. Pizza!" he exclaimed, pointing to the oven.

"Pizza?" He nodded, a grin on his face. "Sounds yummy." Again he nodded. She kissed him again and walked over to me. "So? Is it Aaron or Erin?"

I smiled and kissed her soundly on the lips. "Hello to you, too."

"I'm sorry, baby," she said against my lips. "I just was so excited after getting your voicemail. I missed you today."

"I missed you, too. Are you ready for three monsters and homemade pizza?"

"Well, I'm ready for pizza." We kissed again. "Okay, so tell me."

"It's Erin."

"Yes! I just knew it would be a girl." She put Hunter down and grabbed the phone. "I'm so excited for them." As she dialed the number, she glanced over at me. "Don't you think it's time to get a permanent playmate for Hunter?" She wiggled her eyebrows. "And remember, you promised me you'd have the next one."

"Of course I promised you that. You were in the throes of labor; I would have promised you anything." I grinned when she snapped me with the kitchen towel. As she left her message of congratulations on Joie and Jenny's answering machine, I looked at my son and my partner, and I thought to myself, *How could life get any better?*

\* ~ \* ~ \* ~ \* ~ \* ~ \*

I re-read what I had just written, humming along with the notes. Yeah, this was good. I wanted to write a song to let Dagny know just exactly how I felt about her, our son, and our life together on such an important day.

This was her day, as she'd dreamed of a ceremony for our love for years. To me it had seemed moot. We were happier not married than my parents had ever been with thirty-odd years of marriage under their belts. But she had won me over, saying she wanted something special for us and for those who cared about us. She also wanted to set a good example for Hunter.

Sitting in the basement, where all my musical equipment was and where my band practiced, I picked Melo up and began to strum, the intro into the song soft and gentle, the words flowing from my heart.

*Precious*
>*The years have passed quickly*
>*Since that stormy night*
>*When my world spun off kilter*
>*With your love in sight.*
>*It always astounds me*
>*Each morning I wake*
>*The look in your eyes*
>*Says you're mine to take*
>>*Chorus: Your breath on my skin*
>>*Keeps my fears at bay*
>>*The look in your eyes*
>>*Gets me through each day*
>>*There is nowhere*
>>*I'd rather be*
>>*Than in your arms*
>>*Tucked ever gently*
>*Before you admitted*
>*To feeling the same*
>*I hoped beyond hope*
>*You'd one day whisper my name*
>*With love on your lips*
>*Matching that in your eyes*
>*I thought of you often*
>*With nothing but sighs*
>>*Chorus*
>*Now when you're not near*
>*I'm dying of thirst*

*With you by my side*
*My full heart will burst*
*For your hands give me strength*
*Your words, my power*
*There's nothing I can't do*
*With you I stand tall, never cower*
> *Chorus*
*With you in my life*
*My puzzle piece fits*
*There is no strife in my days*
*You inspire such bliss*
*And now there are three*
*In this family of ours*
*Each moment is precious*
*Ev'ry minute, every hour.*

\* ~ \* ~ \* ~ \* ~ \* ~ \*

The last chord faded, just as I had rehearsed that morning, and I stopped playing and looked up into Dagny's eyes. I smiled at the tears that had already begun, lazily falling down her cheeks. She sat next to me on the stage, looking achingly beautiful in her dress, ivory satin, but simple. She looked at me with such love in her eyes that it reached out and touched me until I was choked up too.

I leaned over and kissed her. "I love you, Dagny."

"I love you, too, Chase."

Wrapped up in each other and in our kiss, we didn't even hear the clapping of our guests. I felt someone tugging at the arm of my pants suit. I turned to see Hunter staring up at me, his blue eyes filled with worry 'cause both his mommies were crying.

"Hey, big guy." I pulled him onto my lap before my eyes returned to Dag's. Yeah, this was the way it should be. Life had so many lessons to teach, and boy did I still have a lot to learn! I relished the thought.

Kim Pritekel is a Colorado native, and has been writing since the age of 9. She is currently working on other books, as well as projects as co-owner of ASP Films, LLC. She can be reached at either XenaNut@hotmail.com or kpritekel@officialaspfilms.com